JOSEPH HAYES

D0885279

THE
WALL

Copyright © 2018 Joseph Hayes
All rights reserved
Shadowpoint Publishing

ISBN: 978-0-692-14793-1

For more information about Joseph Hayes and his books, see his website and his Amazon Author Page:

https://www.josephhayesbooks.com
https://www.amazon.com/author/josephhayes

OTHER BOOKS BY JOSEPH HAYES

When No One Is Watching

Consequential Damages

To the Dreamers

Chapter 1

THE BOY AWOKE and sprang to his feet, kicking the dusty blanket. No snakes came slithering out, nor were there any spiders, scorpions or other unwelcome nocturnal visitors. There rarely were, but their occasional visits made for restless sleep, as he felt the creeping and crawling under the blanket or across his skin, often imagined but sometimes frighteningly real. He always welcomed the daylight, even though it meant the beginning of another brutal and exhausting trek in the searing heat.

His stomach growled, but he ignored it. Two backpacks were on the ground nearby, where his father and their guide had been sleeping. The men were nowhere in sight. That made him nervous. He was 15 now and considered himself the equal of any grown man—strong, clever and resourceful. Still, he was out of his element, and he felt uneasy whenever his father disappeared without explanation.

He climbed out of the shallow ravine where they had camped for the night and scanned the horizon. People were easily spotted in this desolate place, but he saw no one. Fear evaporated as his mind switched into problem-solving mode. His father had scolded their guide last night, accusing him of straying off course. They must be trying to survey the area to get their bearings. The boy scoured the harsh landscape in front of him—nothing but dry sage, mesquite and cactus spread out over an endless vista of rugged hills and gulches. His eyes instinctively sought the highest spot around. On a rocky hill about a hundred yards away, he spotted two figures, peering northward while lying flat on their bellies. That was strange.

The boy hurried in their direction, doing his best to dodge the thorny mesquite bushes. Both men spun around at the sound of rocks giving way beneath the boy's boots as he climbed the steep hill. The father beckoned excitedly to the boy.

"Look, Sal! There it is—America!" Antonio Rios handed his son a pair of binoculars and pointed. "Stay close to the ground," he cautioned.

Sal scanned the horizon in the direction his father was pointing. "I don't see anything. What am I looking for?"

"Right there! See that dark line across the horizon? That's the border fence. If you look closely, you can see a gap dead ahead. That's where we're going."

Peering through the binoculars, Sal could see a dark fence extending west as far as the eye could see. Looking to the east, the fence also extended out of sight. However, directly in front of them was a gap where there was no fence at all. Although it was hard to gauge from that distance, the gap had to be a sizable one to be visible from this range.

"I don't see any guards there. Can we just walk right through that gap?" Sal asked.

"That's the plan," his father replied. "But the Americans have roving border patrols, so we'll need to be careful. That's where we'll really be counting on Juan," he said, looking at their guide. "And, once we get across the border, the terrain gets even rougher than this," he said, gesturing at their surroundings. "Then it's another three-day hike before we reach our destination."

Antonio Rios looked up at the heavens and made the sign of the cross. Then he put his hands on his son's shoulders and stared intently at him for a long moment. The look of grim determination that had defined the father's face for countless weeks was gone. His face beamed, his eyes were wide and bright. "This is the home stretch, Salvatore. You're about to begin the adventure we've talked about for so long. Your new life is just over there," he said, pointing north. "*Vamonos*! If we hurry we can make the border by nightfall."

They shook the dust from their blankets and stuffed them into their backpacks, then set out on the final leg of their journey. The exhaustion they had felt from weeks in the desert melted away. Their strides were now brisk and purposeful. Juan marched ahead, father and son trailing behind by nearly half a mile, all of them keeping a wary eye out for aircraft, jeeps and people.

"Why don't we all walk together?" Sal asked his father.

"What do you think?"

"Because you don't trust Juan?"

"I trust very few people, Sal. But there are other reasons as well. I'm sure you can figure them out."

They walked in silent contemplation for a few minutes. "If anyone is out there, they'll see Juan first," Sal observed. "So we'll have a better chance to escape."

Antonio nodded approvingly. "Better to sacrifice, Juan. If he gets caught, they'll probably just send him back. No big deal. But our mission is far too important. We can't take that risk."

"His name isn't even Juan, is it?"

"Of course not. And you needn't concern yourself about him. Think about what lies ahead, just beyond that fence there." They both stared at the fence, which was now clearly visible in the distance. "That's America. Right there! The wealth and the opportunities are beyond anything you can imagine, and they're ours for the taking."

"The Promised Land, eh Papá? And we will blend right in and be living as Americans. It sounds amazing!"

"It is amazing. The riches, the opportunities, the education—like no place else. El Jefe has trusted me to expand his businesses on that side of the border. And he has big plans for you, too. But we must never forget the real mission. We're part of a great battle. It's a just and righteous war and we will be fighting it from within. America is the enemy, and she is utterly clueless about what's happening. The war is mostly invisible now but that will change over time. We are soldiers in this fight and soldiers do what must be done to serve the Cause. Never lose sight of that, Sal. You will face temptations. It will be easy to be seduced by America's riches and get caught up in all the trappings of material wealth. Don't let that happen! Always remember that we serve a higher purpose."

"I will. And Mamá, and the girls? When will they be joining us?"

"It may be awhile—a year or so, maybe longer. I'm not happy to be apart from them, but it's not safe yet. Family is so important and being apart is a big sacrifice for all of us. But like I said, we do what we must."

Daylight was fading. They were barely half a mile from the border. Juan had vanished. Father and son settled in on the side of a hill covered with thick brush, shielding them from any eyes looking southward from the other side. They waited. Darkness came. Antonio's eyes darted from the gap in the wall to the surrounding brush to the rising moon, which was nearly full and becoming far too bright. It helped light their pathway but also acted as a massive searchlight, eliminating any possibility of crossing unseen in the darkness if anyone was watching. That meant they would have to hope no one was waiting on the other side. He didn't like the idea of just hoping for the best. They had come too far and had too much at stake to take foolish risks.

They were no more than 10 minutes' walk from the fence, less if they ran. The gap was about a quarter mile to the east. It was so close, beckoning them and taunting them at the same time. An hour passed, then another. Still no Juan.

"Should we make a run for it?" Sal whispered.

"Shhhh! We stay put. I don't know why Juan's not back yet, but he's not, and that means we have a problem."

Antonio opened his backpack and reached in. Sal saw the moonlight glinting off the shiny Smith & Wesson revolver. Antonio whirled at the sound of footsteps behind them and pointed the gun in that direction.

The footsteps stopped. "Pssst... *Señor* Antonio? It's me... Juan." The guide stepped out from behind a large cactus, hands raised as he stared down the muzzle of Antonio's 38 Special.

"Where the hell have you been?" Antonio demanded. He kept the gun trained on the guide and stared at him with unblinking eyes.

"Scouting, *Señor*. So sorry, I couldn't get back sooner. It's not safe."

Antonio slowly approached his guide, keeping the revolver levelled directly at Juan's forehead. "What do you mean it's not safe? Where were you exactly? Who were you talking to?"

"Please *Señor*, believe me." Juan's voice quaked as his arms remained raised in the air. "I talked to no one, but this place is crawling with people waiting to get across. I didn't see Border Patrol or anyone else on the other side, but it's hard to see. There's a gully just past the fence, so you can't see what's going on from this side, but the brush is full of people. I saw at least twenty. Maybe thirty. Maybe more. They're all over, taking cover, just this side of that no-man's land there." He gestured to a long strip of barren area that had been cleared of all vegetation, forming a buffer approximately a hundred yards in width between the brush and the fence.

Antonio lowered his gun but kept a tight grip on it. "So what do we do?"

"We wait and watch, *Señor*. Pretty soon they'll start running through that gap. If they get through, that means there's no Border Patrol here tonight, and we can watch and wait a bit longer. If the Border Patrol is nearby, the runners will flush them out. Either way, we're not going to follow them. There are too many. They're bound to attract attention. I know another way."

"Look!" Sal pointed, peering through the binoculars and then handing them to his father. In the bright moonlight, they could see two shadowy figures sprinting toward the gap. They crossed and then vanished from sight. About ten minutes later, another lone runner bolted through the gap, following the path of the two previous runners. After another few minutes, six figures could be seen following the same path. Then small groups began appearing from everywhere, all following the same route.

"Looks like it's safe!" said Sal, gripping his father's forearm. "Do we go now?"

Antonio looked at Juan, who shook his head. "No, we can't be sure. Sometimes the Americans wait until a large group has made it across before they round them up. That way they don't have to cross over onto this side. C'mon, we're going this way," he whispered, motioning westward, away from the gap.

Juan began running parallel to the fence line, father and son following closely behind, dodging rocks and brush. After several hundred yards, they stopped and looked back toward the gap, where runners were still visible in the bright moonlight. Following Juan's lead, they bolted across the no-man's land to the fence, then veered left, away from the gap, and continued running in the shadow along the fence line.

"Stop where you are!" It was an American voice booming over a loudspeaker. They looked back toward the breach in the fence and saw runners abruptly reversing course. Bright vehicle lights bounced behind them in the distance. Then they heard the unmistakable sound of automatic weapon fire. "Stop and turn yourselves in. You will not be harmed," blared the voice over the speaker.

"Let's go, keep moving!" Juan shouted as they continued their sprint along the fence line, in the opposite direction from the commotion.

"Should we turn back?" asked Antonio.

"No, this is good!" Juan said. "They're looking in the other direction. I know a way." They ran until they could run no more, then walked for a stretch, and ran some more. After about three miles, Juan stopped. "There!" He pointed to a ladder perched against the twelve-foot-high corrugated steel fence.

"What's with that?" demanded Antonio. "Is it a trap?"

"No, *Señor*. This is private ranchland. Sometimes the ranchers leave ladders out so their fences aren't knocked down. They don't want their livestock escaping. I'll check it out." He scurried up the ladder and disappeared over the fence. Ten minutes later, Juan called out from the other side. "C'mon. It's safe! No ladder on this side, though. You have to jump."

Antonio went first. He climbed the ladder, sat for a moment on top of the fence surveying the darkness beyond, then hung from the top of the fence and dropped to the ground. Sal followed right behind. He leapt off the wall and rolled in the dusty earth. As he stood up to dust himself off, his father embraced him. "Welcome to America, Salvatore Rios. This is the beginning of your new life!"

They set out in the darkness, stumbling on unseen rocks, but feeling energized and light on their feet. They hiked due north for several miles, then abruptly veered west, in the opposite direction from the activity at the border. As dawn broke, they stopped to rest and to get their bearings.

Juan pulled out a crude map. "This is where we are," he said, with the confidence of a man who was thoroughly familiar with his surroundings. "This is good. Most people do what the runners did last night. They cross through the gap in the fence. There's no border station there but there's a road less than a mile to the east. There's a border station on that road about twenty miles north, so they hike parallel to the road until they get past the border station. Then they find their way back to the road to meet their rides or they just keep walking near the road. Lots of them get caught. That's where the Americans will be looking after last night. Not many people come this way. If they do, they mostly don't make it. This is rough country—even rougher than where we've been."

They surveyed the surrounding area. The vista was the same in every direction. Rough, scrubby brushland with no water in sight and little shelter from the blazing sun.

"It's about sixty miles to our destination, but it's a lot safer," said Juan. "Not much living out here except snakes, bugs, and coyotes. Oh, and those nasty buzzards and the wild hogs. They'll devour any poor souls that come this way and don't make it."

As Juan and Antonio strolled to the top of the nearest hill, Sal sprawled out on the ground, resting his head on his backpack. Sleep overtook him immediately. Juan provided Antonio with a thorough briefing regarding the map, their route and landmarks they could expect to find along the way. Antonio insisted that Juan walk him through it a second time, and then he recited it back to him.

"Now you know the route as well as I do, *Señor* Antonio," said Juan, as he folded the map and handed it to his employer.

Antonio held out his hand. "I can't thank you enough, my friend," he said shaking the guide's hand warmly. "You've provided safe passage for my son and me. I will never forget it. On behalf of my entire family, please know that you have our eternal gratitude."

"It was my pleasure, *Señor*. I don't know your business but know that you are an important man with an important mission. It has been an honor serving you. In just a few more days, we will reach our destination."

Antonio reached behind his back and pulled the revolver from his belt. He held it up against Juan's forehead. The guide's eyes grew wide and his mouth opened, but no words came out.

Sal's peaceful slumber was shattered by the sound of the gunshot. He leapt to his feet and stared eastward toward the spot he had last seen his father and Juan. He shielded his eyes from the blinding morning sun and saw his father striding down the hill, the motionless body of the guide behind him. "Why?" he asked in a trembling voice as his father approached.

"We do what we must, Salvatore."

Chapter 2

MANY TEXANS WOULD have considered San Mateo to be a small, South Texas border town, if they considered it at all. It was situated 75 miles north of McAllen, 90 miles due east of Laredo, 80 miles southwest of Corpus Christi and 160 miles south of sprawling San Antonio. To an outsider, this was the middle of nowhere. The residents liked it that way. They were far from the dangers and unpleasantries of life on the border.

San Mateo was small, with a population of slightly less than 8,000, although the official census would show less than half that. Because of its small size and remote location, it was of little interest to drug dealers, human traffickers or immigration officers. For the most part, the outside world left them alone.

There were a few white folks in San Mateo, mostly descendants of the city's founding fathers, who owned vast ranchlands in the area and developed thriving cattle and dairy businesses. San Mateo's sweet cream butter was once known throughout Texas, but that was nearly a hundred years ago. Now, over 90% of the population was Latino, mostly of Mexican descent. Many of the younger generation were born here. That made them citizens. A significant portion of the adults who made their way to San Mateo came from south of the border, without papers and without permission. Some stayed for weeks or months, some for several years, and some never left. At any given time, a sizable portion of the town was in passing-through mode.

It was an ideal place for newcomers to get a foothold in America. It felt safe. They were isolated and free from nosy authorities. They could settle in, learn the culture and the language, and how to blend in. There was plenty of work for those who wished to stay off the grid and didn't mind long drives. The fertile Rio Grande Valley and surrounding areas supported a robust agricultural economy. Citrus, cotton, rice and other grains were grown throughout the area, providing plenty of seasonal work. The cattle ranches were another source of work. The big cities provided even more opportunities. There was a steady demand for unskilled labor in construction, landscaping, housekeeping and food service in Corpus Christi, San Antonio and Houston. Working in those cities required a long drive and time away from home, but small groups would drive together and find communal living arrangements near their place of work and then drive home at the end of the week or the end of a project. To them, it didn't feel like a hardship. It was an opportunity. They were accustomed to far greater hardships in their homeland. Many would eventually move to the cities to be near the work. Others would stay in San Mateo because they felt safe and anonymous. There was an unstated knowledge and acceptance among the residents that they all shared a common goal—making a good life in America—and that their immigration status and nationality should not be held against anyone pursuing that dream.

Bobby Rivera was one of the lucky residents of San Mateo—an American citizen. His parents had not been so lucky, having grown up in Juarez, just across the border from El Paso. They longed to escape the drug wars, kidnappings, corruption and utter poverty of their hometown, so they simply walked across the border crossing as tourists when Bobby's mother was newly pregnant and stayed with relatives until Bobby was born in El Paso General Hospital. They had the birth certificate to prove it.

Bobby's parents, Luis and Eva Rivera, were more fortunate than many residents of Juarez because they were educated, spoke fluent English and had marketable skills—Luis as a physician and Eva as a nurse. When they learned of the severe shortage of medical professionals in rural South Texas, they followed the appropriate procedures and were able to obtain temporary legal residency status to work in Carroll County Community Medical Center, 20 miles north of San Mateo. The hospital was desperate for qualified help and Eva had no problem securing gainful employment as a nurse. Although obtaining a full-fledged license to practice medicine in the State of Texas was a brutally long, arduous and uncertain process, Luis functioned as the qualified and experienced physician that he was even though his business card described him as a "Physician's Assistant." Outside of the hospital, as a result of his frequent house calls, Luis quickly became known as the town doctor in San Mateo. Their work visas were limited in duration, but thus far there had been no problem with renewals.

Like most 15-year-olds, Bobby was blissfully oblivious to the hardships his parents had endured, even though they frequently spoke of life on the other side of the border. His parents reminded him incessantly what a blessing his education was, and while he mostly took it for granted, he thoroughly enjoyed school because he was outgoing and loved being around people.

Bobby also relished the proximity to nature that San Mateo provided. It was remote, surrounded by The Brush, the vast wilderness that encircled their small community. Technically, almost all of The Brush was private ranchland and parts were fenced off, but most of it was easily accessible and utterly devoid of human activity. Most people would consider it harsh and desolate—endless miles of scrub, cactus, and mesquite spread out over dry, rock-hard, sand-colored dirt. To Bobby, it was a natural paradise. Wildlife was abundant for anyone who cared to look—jackrabbits, snakes, lizards, and occasionally bigger game, such as white-tailed deer or the foul-tempered feral hogs that weighed up to 400 pounds and sported sharp lethal-looking tusks that they wouldn't hesitate to use if they were disturbed by some unlucky hiker.

Today, as he had for much of the summer, Bobby was doing two things he loved to do—spending time with one of the newer kids in San Mateo and wandering off into The Brush. His companion was Miguel Sanchez, who had recently moved into one of the more dilapidated homes on the northern edge of town. They were the same age and would be starting high school together the following week. Judging by his first encounter with Miguel, Bobby felt that Miguel might really benefit from having a friend once school started. The first week of summer, Bobby had broken up a fight that Miguel had apparently started with two soon-to-be sophomores. Although he was loud, tough-talking and scrappy, Miguel was also scrawny and was being beaten to a pulp on the high school football field. Miguel's cockiness seemed to foretell future scrapes, particularly in a school where the level of machismo ran high. Classmates didn't mess with Bobby. For one thing, he was huge. At six-foot-two and 210 pounds as a fifteen-year-old, he had an imposing physical presence. Mostly however, he was able to avoid altercations because nearly everyone considered Bobby their friend.

It was scorching hot late in the afternoon as Bobby and Miguel strolled down Jefferson Avenue, the main drag through town. They ambled past the bustling little grocery store called *Supermercado Fernandez*, a diner that hadn't changed a lick since the 1950s, an abandoned movie theater, a dumpy little hardware store, a law office and a small handful of other commercial establishments that provided various essentials to the locals. Downtown San Mateo, such as it was, looked like many other small towns in rural South Texas—fifty years ago as well as present day. The commercial district was all of three blocks long and ended with Our Lady of Guadalupe Catholic Church, which had served as the town's central gathering place on Sunday mornings for the past 110 years. Its massive stone structure and towering steeple stood in sharp contrast to the row of modest homes that lined the rest of the street for another four blocks. The homes were mostly small, one-story stucco structures, painted in a variety of pastels, that might have been abandoned or considered tear-downs in other communities. However, in San Mateo, these houses represented property ownership and evidence of a good life in America and were mostly neat and well-maintained by their proud owners.

Jefferson Avenue ended at State Highway 281, and beyond that T intersection was a narrow dirt trail leading into an endless expanse of brush. At the corner of that intersection was a residence that differed from the others. It was modern, meaning less than twenty years old. It was two stories, with high, vaulted ceilings, and it was constructed of brick, painted white. It might have been considered ordinary in most big cities, but it bordered on opulent in San Mateo. It had been built and occupied by Jorge Fernandez, the owner of the local grocery store, but the house had been vacant since Mr. Fernandez sold his business and moved to Houston two years earlier.

"Hey, check that out," Miguel said, stopping and staring at the Fernandez house. "Looks like someone's moving in." A shiny black Ford pickup was parked in the driveway. A man and a boy about their age were moving furniture from the truck into the house.

"C'mon, let's give them a hand," suggested Bobby, marching eagerly across the street toward the driveway.

"How about let's not," replied Miguel, hanging back. "We've got better things to do."

Bobby didn't break stride. "Hi! I'm Bobby Rivera," he said to the man. "You moving in?"

"Antonio Rios," said the man. "This is my son, Sal. Yeah, we just got into town. We'll be renting this place for a while."

"Welcome to San Mateo!" said Bobby, smiling brightly and shaking hands with father and son. Sal nodded but said nothing. "This is my friend, Miguel," Bobby continued as Miguel moseyed up the driveway. "He's new here, too." Miguel stood back a few feet and gave a curt wave and a nod. "Can we help you unload?"

"Thanks, but we're about finished. Appreciate the offer, though," said Antonio, hoisting a television off the truck and heading into the house.

"So, Sal, we're going for a hike in The Brush here. Lots of cool stuff to see. Sometimes we run a bit too—training for football. Want to join us?"

"Nah, I better not. I've got work to do around here."

"We'll wait. And we can help," Bobby replied, sounding encouraging.

Sal turned and looked toward the front door his father had just entered. "Maybe another time," he said.

Miguel kicked a stone across the driveway. "C'mon, Bobby. Let's go."

Bobby glanced at Miguel and then turned back toward Sal. "OK, another time then. See you around, Sal." He offered his hand again and Sal shook it stiffly.

Before they were out of earshot, Miguel glanced over his shoulder and said in a loud voice, "Who needs him anyway. He looks like a prick!"

About 1000 yards into The Brush, they reached their favorite spot, which they had unimaginatively nicknamed "The Hill," because that is exactly what it was. It was one of the few hills in the area, with a steep incline about 50 yards long. The Hill was surrounded by a sprawling network of prickly pear cactus plants and dense brush, but over time, Bobby had cleared enough brush to form a clear path to the top. From that vantage point, they were able to take in the vastness of The Brush, spreading out as far as the eye could see in every direction.

All summer, the boys had used The Hill as their private training ground, running uphill wind sprints to get themselves in shape for high school football. Miguel was far more dedicated to the training regimen. After half a dozen sprints or so, Bobby would typically take a seat on the old log he had dragged to the top of The Hill, pull out his sketch book and draw pictures of the surrounding landscape. Today was no exception. Bobby ran the hill five times and then turned his attention to drawing. Miguel continued the uphill sprints for another twenty minutes, then set out looking for snakes, hoping to add to his growing collection of rattlesnake skins. The hunt was futile—it was too hot, even for reptiles. As the sun sank low in the western sky, they began the trek back toward town. In keep with their training routine, the last 100 yards of the dusty path was always a footrace.

Miguel assumed a sprinter's starting block position. "Ready, slowpoke? I'm gonna whip your ass even worse than usual. Bet I beat you by 20 yards!"

Bobby grinned. "You're on. Go!"

He took off. Miguel flew by him in no time and made good on his boast. As he bent over to catch his breath, he picked up a couple of rocks, and without a word strode purposely toward the Fernandez house. Bobby quickly caught up with him. "What are you doing?" he asked, looking concerned.

Miguel was shaking a golf ball-sized rock in his hand. "I don't like that new kid. Thinks he's hot shit—too good for us. Let's put a few rocks through their windows. Give his ass a real welcome!" Before Bobby could find words to respond, Miguel reared back like a pitcher, putting all his scrawny body into the motion as his arm shot forward.

"Hey, what the hell!" he shouted as Bobby caught his arm before he could release the projectile, causing the smaller boy to lose his balance and stumble awkwardly backwards. "What's wrong with you," Miguel snarled, as he regained his footing, approaching Bobby belligerently.

"We'll get caught. They might be looking out the window right now. Even if they're not, they'll know it's us. They just saw us, and no one else comes out this way."

Miguel shook his head, looking disappointed in his friend. "Man, you can't be such a puss," he said. "You gotta toughen up for football. It helps to be a little loco."

***

School was back in session the following week. San Mateo High School had about 400 students. Bobby expected to know most of them, but there were quite a few new faces, and plenty of pretty girls. He felt the sense of newness and excitement that always came with the beginning of a new school year, but it was more pronounced this time, as high school represented a new adventure.

He spent the first day catching up with old friends and making new ones. When the bell rang at three o'clock, he headed toward the gym where the coaches and athletes typically congregated after school. Coach Garza, the head football coach, had stopped him in the hallway that morning, obviously struck by size of the massive freshman, and asked him to drop by. Before reaching the gym, Bobby heard a familiar sound in the hallway behind him: the metallic bang of a slamming locker, loud, angry voices, the stampede of footsteps and yells of the spectators rushing to the scene. Fight!

Bobby joined the throng and began pushing his way to the front. He saw Hector Castillo leading the assault, flanked by his two sidekicks, Benny Cantu and Tommy Molina. All three of them seemed to be yelling at once, their hostility directed toward some unlucky victim who had been shoved up against a locker, whose face Bobby couldn't see through the crowd. Bobby knew Hector well, and they got along just fine, but Hector was a tough customer, volatile and violent. His favorite pastime was picking fights and he was good at it. He was a sophomore, but probably a couple of years older than most of his classmates. No one knew for sure. Benny and Tommy were cut from the same cloth, although Hector was clearly their leader. All three of them were on the football and wrestling teams, not that they were particularly good athletes, but more because it was a sanctioned form of violence.

"We don't want you around here, asshole!" Hector's voice rang out through the corridor. "Go back to whatever shithole you came from."

Tommy stepped forward so that he was shoulder-to-shoulder with his pal. "Let's kick his ass, Hector! Pretty boy here has been coming on to every chick in the school. I heard him say he wanted to get into Rachel's pants."

"Yeah, and when I told him Rachel was your chick, he called you a useless piece of shit," shouted Carlos, stepping forward and forming a line with his comrades. "We all heard it."

"That's bullshit," came the response in a strong and steady voice.

The voice sounded familiar to Bobby. He pushed his way to the front of the crowd, where he could see the recipient of the verbal assault. Sal Rios stood there with his back against the lockers, fists clenched, eyes blazing, silent but looking utterly unafraid.

"Is that so?" hissed Hector. "We'll see about that!" He moved forward menacingly until his face was within inches of Sal's. "C'mon, you prissy sonofabitch, give me your best shot!"

"Hey Hector! Why don't you just leave this guy alone?" Hector whirled to face Bobby Rivera.

"Back off, Bobby. This isn't your fight."

"C'mon, Hector. He's new around here and he's a friend of mine. Give him a break."

"I don't give a shit who he is. His ass is mine!"

"Hector, listen to me," Bobby raised his voice but there was no hostility in it, just an insistent tone that a parent might use with an unreasonable child. "I'm trying to help you out. You *should* care about who this guy is. His name is Sal *Rios*. His father is *Antonio Rios*. You know that name, right? MMA Fighter? Former middleweight champion of the world? If there's a fight here, it'll be a bloodbath, but it's not going to be his blood."

"Get lost, Bobby," said Sal, taking a step forward. "I've got this. I don't need your help."

"Don't be stupid, Sal. Remember what happened last time? They put you away for eighteen months after you killed those two guys."

"Only one died. The other's in a wheelchair. Don't worry, I'm not going to kill these idiots. I'll just break a few bones and put 'em in the hospital for a while."

"Sal—they'll send you back to Mexico! Besides, these guys are my friends, too. C'mon, everyone just back off. He says he didn't say anything about you, Hector. I know this guy and I believe him. You got bad information, that's all."

The three belligerents looked unsure of themselves, their eyes darting back and forth between Bobby and Sal. Hector took a step back and his cohorts did the same.

"Cool it! Everybody outside!" Coach Garza came bustling through the throng of onlookers and some of the crowd slowly dispersed. "I mean it! Now!"

The rest of the crowd moved out, leaving Bobby, Sal, Hector, Tommy and Carlos still there glaring at one other.

"What's going on here?" Garza demanded. "You and your boys causing trouble again, Hector?"

"Everything's OK, Coach," said Bobby. "Just a bit of a misunderstanding. It's all over. Everything's fine."

"Alright then. Get on out of here! Rivera, meet me in my office in five minutes."

Hector shot a menacing look at Bobby. "I let this asshole off the hook because of you, Bobby—because you're a friend." Then he turned and pointed a finger in Sal's face. "You better not be talking any shit about me. If you do, you'll be sorry!" He hurried away, his cronies at his heels.

Bobby looked at Sal. "You OK?"

Sal glared at him defiantly. "I didn't need your help. I can fight my own battles."

"I'm sure you can, but it wouldn't have been a fair fight. All three of them would have piled on. Even if my story was true and you really kicked their butts, you don't need to be making enemies of those guys. That could make your time here miserable."

Sal stared at Bobby momentarily and then stormed off. "Like I said, I don't need your help," he shouted over his shoulder.

Chapter 3

ANTONIO RIOS STRUGGLED to stay awake in the seedy hotel room, the local newspaper in his hands as he sat upright on the beat-up mattress, propped up against the headboard. It had been a long drive in the dark after a busy day and he was drifting in and out of sleep. The ringing of his cell phone jolted him into alertness.

"I heard you were in Brownsville. We need to meet." The voice was deep and gruff, the Mexican accent thick and unmistakable.

Rios paused before responding. "Who is this?"

"I work for the largest import business in town. We have a job for you, so we need to talk—now! Meet me in 30 minutes behind the grain silo on Old Calhoun Road, north of town."

Rios looked at his watch. It read 11:40. He didn't like being ordered around. That's not how he operated. And he didn't like this kind of client—probably some drug dealer. He hadn't survived as long as he had and achieved the professional status he enjoyed by meeting lowlife drug dealers in dark, deserted places. "If you want to meet with me, I'll be at the Waffle House at 8:00, in a booth near the back." He hung up.

Rios pulled into the Waffle House parking lot at 7:45. He pulled out the newspaper he had begun reading the night before and leisurely read it sitting in his car for the next 30 minutes. Then he sauntered into the restaurant and looked down the row of booths leading back toward the restrooms. His "clients" were easy to spot as he made his way toward the back. Facing him was a short pudgy man in his early forties with a goatee and dark sunglasses, sitting alongside a much younger man who was taller and rail thin, both of them wearing expensive suits and plenty of gold jewelry. He couldn't see the face of the third man, who sat opposite his colleagues in the booth.

"*Señor* Rios?" asked the smaller man, whose deep voice was clearly the one he had heard on the phone last night.

Rios nodded. "Good morning, gentlemen."

The man whose back was to him stood up and stepped out of the booth, offering Rios the interior seat near the window. He was dressed like his companions, although the bulky muscles of a serious bodybuilder gave shape to the tight suit. Rios stood where he was. "No, please, after you," he politely insisted. The bodybuilder hesitated a moment and then slid back into the seat by the window.

There were no introductions, so Rios got right down to business. "You said on the phone that you were a client. Obviously, we've never met. Who are you?"

The short man leaned across the table. "Like I said, we're in the import business. We're having problems with a competitor. We need you to handle it."

"You haven't answered my question," said Rios. "I don't even know who you are."

"With all due respect, sir, I think you do, or you wouldn't be here."

Rios had a pretty good idea about the identity of the alleged client. He was still in the process of arranging personal meetings with his boss's existing contacts in South Texas and looking for opportunities to expand those contacts. Their goal was to further develop their influence and seek out legitimate cross-border business opportunities. In the past, their business network had included periodic contacts with drug smugglers, human traffickers and weapons dealers, but only from the perspective of using influence to clear the way for certain transactions or assist those clients when problems with law enforcement or the legal system arose. They kept their distance from direct involvement in selling or moving contraband and carefully avoided taking sides when there were competing enterprises. Rios and his boss considered involvement in those businesses to be necessary but temporary evils because they were lucrative, and that enabled them to raise the capital needed to expand their other operations. They had been gradually phasing out their involvement with these distasteful businesses, and one of the sole remnants of that line of work was their connection in Brownsville with the Pizzaro organization, the biggest player in the drug business along the border areas between Brownsville and McAllen. Navigating the phase-out of these business relations was delicate by nature, since it was imperative to keep the clients from getting angry.

Rios looked around the table at each of his three breakfast companions. "Let's be frank, gentlemen. You work for—"

"Good morning, guys! Ready to order?" The perky young waitress smiled at them, holding her order pad and pencil at the ready.

They placed their orders and she hurried away. "This is a lousy place for this kind of meeting," the short man grumbled. "It's hard to speak freely here. That's why we wanted to meet last night."

"OK, here's my assessment," Rios said in a low voice, leaning across the table. "Without discussing the specifics of your business, I am assuming that you work for a man named Pizarro. If that's not correct, tell me and I'll shut up. I'll also walk out that door, because we don't have any other clients in your line of work here."

"There's no need for you to leave," said the short man, who was obviously their leader. "Let's continue the conversation. My name is Johnson. I'm part of the management team here in Brownsville. We have reason to believe that someone who used to work for us here in Brownsville has been recruited by a competitor and they're cutting into our business in a serious way. We need that situation taken care of."

"So why are you calling me, Mr. Johnson?" Rios asked. "I think there's been a misunderstanding here. I'm a businessman. I don't provide the kind of service you seem to be looking for. Sorry."

Four plates of waffles and bacon arrived. The men silently attacked their food while the waitress filled their coffee cups. Once she was out of earshot, Johnson put down his fork and stared hard at Rios. "I've been told by my colleagues that we pay your organization a hefty retainer to help us out when we're in a jam. You just confirmed that Mr. Pizarro is a client. We need you to earn your fee and take care of our problem. I'm sure Mr. Pizarro will be most unhappy if you don't do as we ask."

Rios leaned back in the booth and folded his arms. "Do you know anything about our organization?" he asked. "Do you know who my boss is? His name is Carlos Calderon. He's a businessman. He doesn't sell drugs. Or weapons. Or passage to America. Or any other commodity. He doesn't sell muscle. He's certainly not a hit man. He is revered and respected because of who he is and what he does. I suggest you do your homework."

"Then what the hell good is he, and why would Mr. Pizarro or anyone else pay him a retainer? What does he do, exactly?"

"Think of him as a very well-connected diplomat. He has respect and influence in many circles. Within the government, within the legal system, in the press, and with people like your boss. He can help him with legal and political matters, make the right connections. But he absolutely does not get involved in disputes between drug dealers. We can't help you."

"Then this will not turn out well for you, Rios. Or for this useless Calderon character. I'll give you twenty-four hours to tell me you're ready to earn your fee."

"Pizarro doesn't even know you're meeting with me, does he?" said Rios. "You're clearly just middle management. Probably never even met Pizarro. If I were you, I'd have a little chat with him before you do something you will certainly regret. I'm sure he'll tell you that threatening *Señor* Calderon is not good for business."

Rios stood up, threw a twenty-dollar bill on the table, and strolled toward the exit, smiling at the waitress on his way out.

"Should we check into this Calderon guy?" the thin man asked his two comrades.

The man who had called himself Johnson gave the speaker a scornful look. "Hell no!" he scoffed. "I don't know who he is or where he's from and I don't care. He may think he's a player in some little shithole in Mexico, but his name don't mean squat around here. This is our turf. We call the shots."

Chapter 4

BOBBY WALKED HOME from his second day of high school singing softly to himself. It had been a good couple of days. His teachers seemed OK. His classes didn't appear too daunting. It was great reconnecting with pals he hadn't seen over the summer. He had made some new friends and knew he would make more. Pretty girls were everywhere. And news of the previous day's altercation and Bobby's role in it had created quite a buzz around school. He was being treated like a celebrity.

He turned into his driveway and was surprised to see his parents' white Toyota parked there. It was 4:30 in the afternoon. They normally drove home together around 6:00. His jubilant mood vanished as he looked into their grim faces staring at him from the kitchen table.

"What's wrong?" he asked, as a host of scary possibilities raced through his mind.

"Mr. Martinez, your principal, called me a little while ago," his father replied. "At work." His voice and countenance were uncharacteristically somber.

Bobby stared at his father, blinking, uncomprehending, his mouth open but no words coming out.

"He told me there was a fight at school yesterday and that you were in the middle of it."

"What?" Bobby's voice sounded both confused and irritated.

"Is that true, Bobby?" his mother asked, looking as if she were near tears.

"Well, sort of… not exactly. Hector Castillo and his pals tried to pick a fight with a new kid. I just broke it up."

His parents stared at him silently, looking as if someone had died.

"I don't get it. What did Mr. Martinez tell you?"

His father rose from the table and began pacing. "Pretty much what you just said. In fact, he called me because he said the whole school was buzzing about it and he was proud of how you handled it. Proud enough that he felt compelled to call me at work to tell me about it."

"So… I don't get it. How come you look so upset? Am I in trouble?"

"Oh, Bobby!" His mother sprang up from her chair and embraced her son. Then she pulled back and grasped his hands in hers. "You're not in trouble. What you did was a good thing. You've got such a big heart. But you're in high school now. Teenagers find a lot more ways to get into trouble than little kids. You've really got to steer clear of it."

"But I thought that's what I was doing. I tried to stop trouble from happening. Isn't that a good thing? Isn't that what Father Paul would want me to do?"

Dr. Rivera stopped pacing and faced his son. "Under normal circumstances, what you did would be admirable. That's certainly how Mr. Martinez saw it. And your mother and I are really proud of you. But we don't live under normal circumstances. We love our jobs and we love our life here, but all that can be taken away in an instant. Mom and I have visas that allow us to live and work here, but they can be revoked at any time. We could be deported. We live in fear of that every day of our lives. So, we need to stay off the radar screen. If you get into trouble, that puts all of us at risk."

"I still don't get it. I didn't cause any trouble. And it sounds like Mr. Martinez is glad I did what I did."

"But that situation could have turned out very differently, Bobby," his father replied his voice getting louder and more harsh. "It could have turned into a brawl and you could have been drawn into it. Someone could have gotten hurt. Police could have been involved."

Bobby sat down at the kitchen table and put his head in his hands. His father sat down next to him, putting his arm around his son's broad shoulders. "All we're saying is be careful, son. Trouble has a way of finding teenage boys. You need to stay as far away from it as you can."

Mrs. Rivera sat on the other side of her son and put her slender hand on his giant forearm. "You're a great kid, Bobby, and you can have such a wonderful future here in this country. You just need to be really careful, OK?"

"I understand," Bobby said softly. "I'm sorry."

"No need to apologize, Bobby," his father said in a gentler tone. "You did a good thing. But we live in a crazy world. We just want you to learn from this and always remember that, for now, we are guests in this country. It's our home, but it can all be taken away in a heartbeat by one unfortunate situation. So it's important for us to keep a low profile. Anything that could draw attention to us in a negative way is dangerous. So if you see trouble coming, run the other way as fast as you can!"

Bobby nodded quietly. "I will," he said. He walked into his bedroom and picked up an old worn-out backpack that contained his sketch pads and drawing implements. "I'm heading out for a bit," he announced to his parents. "Just taking a little walk to clear my head. I'll be back before dinner."

He headed straight for The Brush and made his way up The Hill. He sat at the top on the old log, facing a giant Yuca plant. He began sketching, trying to catch every minute detail of the cactus. Then he drew a picture of himself striking a thoughtful pose standing next to the cactus. He had drawn so many self-portraits in the past that he needed no pictures or mirrors to guide his hand.

"That's pretty impressive!"

Bobby started at the voice directly behind him. He had heard no one approaching. He spun around and was temporarily blinded as he looked directly into the sun, seeing only the silhouette. He sprang to his feet and found himself face-to-face with Sal Rios.

"Is this your hangout?" asked Sal, nodding at The Hill.

"Just part of it." Bobby spread his arms and turned toward the vast expanse spreading out away from town. "*This* is my hangout."

"Nice! I saw you walk past my house heading this way. Hope you don't mind that I followed you out here."

"No problem. It's a free country."

"Look man, I acted like a jerk yesterday at school. You tried to help and I treated you like crap. You didn't deserve that. I came out here to say I'm sorry."

"Ah, that's OK. Forget about it."

An awkward silence hung in the air for a few moments. Sal broke it, with a quiet laugh. "You were really quick on your feet. You had *me* believing that my father was a professional fighter."

Bobby's face brightened. "You sure picked up on that and ran with it. I was hoping you would."

"Well, it worked. Thanks." Sal held out his hand and Bobby shook it. "And by the way, I didn't mean to give you the cold shoulder last week when you invited me out here. Guess I'm just feeling like an outsider and not quite sure how to fit in."

"Sal—everyone in San Mateo is an outsider, or they used to be not too long ago. Don't sweat that. And let me help. I was born here. I know pretty much everyone. I can introduce you, show you around, tell you who to avoid—which includes those three idiots you met at school yesterday."

"Thanks. My dad told me that a new kid in town should watch and listen and keep his mouth shut. I've been trying to do that at school and one thing I noticed is that people really respect you—even those three idiots."

Bobby smiled sheepishly and shrugged. "Ah, that's just because I'm big."

"No, it's more than that. You have a way with people, and that's really cool. They like being around you. They listen to you. I hope some-day people will treat me that way."

"Don't sweat it, man. You'll fit right in."

"Speaking of fitting in, can you help me with one other thing? I'm new to this country and I'm nervous about my English. Can you correct me whenever I make a mistake or if my accent sounds funny?"

Bobby looked surprised. "What are you talking about? Your English is perfect. You speak better than me!"

"Well, my father arranged for private tutors. He always wanted me to end up in America, so I've been taking English lessons almost since I could talk. The instructors were all Americans and tried to teach me to talk like American kids do, but I've never had to use it in a place where everyone speaks it. It's kind of scary."

"If I hear any mistakes, I'll tell you, but you really do sound like everyone else around here."

Sal looked over Bobby's shoulder toward town. "Someone's coming. Is that your friend?" He pointed to a small figure jogging toward them on the dusty trail.

"Yep. That's Miguel—the guy you met last week. We come up here a lot together. It's a good place to run. We've been training for football. Starts next week."

Miguel was moving at a brisk pace, and even the steep hill didn't slow him down. He reached the top and approached Bobby, spat, put his hands on his hips and glared at him. He ignored Sal. "Hey, what gives, man? You were supposed to call me. Decided to hang with this guy instead?" he asked in an accusatory tone, cocking his head toward Sal.

"Sorry about that. I got hung up at home. Had to deal with some issues with my parents. I got distracted and lost track of time. I figured you would have headed up here without me."

Miguel turned toward Sal. "So, you're a fighter?" His tone was defiant, with a trace of skepticism.

Bobby and Sal looked at each other and laughed. "I guess people really bought into that," Bobby said, looking both proud and amused. "I just made that up and Sal rolled with it."

Miguel looked from one to the other, a rueful smile crossing his lips. "That was good, I gotta admit it. You fooled me. You fooled everyone!" Then he looked at Sal. "I guess that means you're not a badass."

"Let's just keep that to ourselves, Miguel," said Bobby, grinning.

"OK. So, you ready to run?"

Bobby and Miguel began their routine of wind sprints up The Hill. Sal watched the first sprint and then joined in, handling the steep sprint effortlessly. Bobby gave up after five sprints and watched Miguel and Sal do five more. They headed home as the sun was starting to set and reached the starting point for their customary 100-yard dash.

"C'mon, new guy, let's see what you got," said Miguel. "Bobby, go to the finish line and tell us when."

Bobby welcomed the excuse to avoid losing another race to his speedy training partner. He trotted ahead and stopped at the large honey mesquite tree that marked their finish line. Miguel and Sal were poised in the starting position. Bobby raised his right arm and then let it drop. "Go!"

Miguel and Sal raced toward him. At fifty yards, they were neck-and-neck. Bobby could see their faces. Miguel's was strained and contorted by the effort. Sal's looked utterly calm, as if the effort required no exertion. At seventy-five yards, Sal appeared to kick into another gear that he had been holding back. He rocketed toward the finish line, pulling away and winning by a wide margin.

"Wow!" Bobby exclaimed. "And I thought Miguel was fast! We need to get you on the football team."

"American football? Never played it before."

"That doesn't matter," Bobby assured him. "If you can run like that, you can play football. And if you become a football star, you won't have any problems with people like Hector. And the girls will be all over you!"

Miguel was hunched over, hands on his knees, gulping in air. "You're lucky, man," he gasped. "I was running with a bad foot. I'll get you next time."

Chapter 5

"THIS IS VARGAS. Where can we meet?"

"I'll be in San Antonio the day after tomorrow. Let's meet at the Alamo at noon."

Vargas hung up. Antonio Rios didn't like these calls or the meetings. Prior to his recent relocation, he had always dealt directly with his boss, Carlos Calderon, and was one of the few people who enjoyed that privilege. He didn't like using a middleman because it required blind trust, and he couldn't control the message that made its way back to Calderon. But there was no other way, and he knew it. Calderon was far away. He would not come to the States and Rios himself needed to avoid border crossings. So, he had to deal with Francisco Vargas.

Rios arrived promptly at noon, paid the $15 admission fee like all the other tourists, then walked inside what remained of the old mission that was constructed in the 18th century and later converted into a fortress. It was a Wednesday afternoon in early September, so the summer throngs were gone but the oppressive heat still lingered. Rios relished the natural coolness inside the old stone structure as he meandered around the chapel, the only building to survive the battle against the Mexican army in 1836. He made his way to the barracks and around the shady interior courtyard, stopping nonchalantly along the way to take in the exhibits, artifacts and paintings.

From a distance, he could see Vargas's lanky frame looking at a collection of Bowie knives and reading the accompanying story of Jim Bowie, who perished along with Davy Crockett and over 200 others during the famous battle long ago. He sidled up next to Vargas and feigned interest in the knife collection.

"Did you know that Jim Bowie was a notorious knife fighter?" Vargas asked. "Legend has it that he got into a brawl on a sandbar in the Mississippi River. Took on a handful of enemies and wound up getting shot, stabbed, and beaten, but managed to win the fight using his trusty knife—probably one like that." He pointed to the largest knife in the glass case. As he pointed, Rios stared at the hand with two missing fingers, which he knew had been sacrificed in some showing of loyalty to his boss. Although grotesque, it somehow fit the rest of the physique to which it was attached: tall, lean but rugged looking, pock-marked face, slicked back dark hair, with intense eyes that were almost black, currently hidden behind stylish sunglasses. The sunglasses only partially concealed a prominent scar that extended from his right ear across his cheek and over the bridge of his nose.

"Interesting. I didn't know that," Rios replied, watching the elderly couple at the adjacent exhibit out of the corner of his eye.

The couple moved on, out of earshot. Vargas leaned over the exhibit case, examining the knives more closely. "You've been here for a month now," he said in a low voice without looking at Rios. "He wants to know how it's going."

Rios kept his eyes fixed on the storyboard in front of him. "You can tell him it's going very smoothly. I've met with almost all of our contacts here in San Antonio, and also in Corpus, Brownsville and McAllen. I plan on focusing on Austin and Houston over the next month or so. Then Laredo and El Paso after that."

"What kind of reception have you gotten?"

"Overall, it's been positive. I've been making contacts, introducing myself, assessing the level of loyalty and cooperation and very subtly feeling out opportunities to expand our network."

"And what are your impressions?"

"It's clear that our boss's name carries almost as much weight here as it does on the other side. There is definitely an eagerness to cooperate. So far, I've spent most of my time meeting the judges, politicians, lawyers and law enforcement. Met a few of our media contacts, too. Those meetings have been easy. I haven't met many of our... uh... pharmaceutical clients and... uh... defense suppliers, because we're going to be phasing out of that work. But I've met a few, and for the most part, those meetings have gone well."

"What do you mean, *for the most part?*"

"Just one small problem in Brownsville a few days ago. Some penny ante goon in Pizarro's organization doesn't understand the nature of what we do. Tried to push us around. Made some threats against me and bad-mouthed our leader."

"Have you taken care of it yet?"

"Not yet. It just happened. I'm on it."

"You better be. You know how the boss feels about that kind of thing."

"Like I said, I'm on it."

"Anything else the boss should know?"

"No. That covers it. Think I'll go learn a bit more about Davy Crockett." He meandered off to the next exhibit.

***

Three days later, as he was having breakfast, Antonio Rios unfolded *The Brownsville Tribune* and spread it across his kitchen table. The headline jumped off the page:

Grisly Find at Local Cemetery.

A decapitated human head was found mounted on the entrance gate to Restlawn Cemetery on Old Sawmill Road. Police say the victim was a Hispanic male, approximately forty years old. The victim's identity has not been determined and the rest of the body has not been found. Sources say police suspect gangland violence involving drug traffickers, but no suspects are in custody.

Chapter 6

FIVE MINUTES INTO the first algebra exam of the semester, Bobby felt a sharp poke in his back. "Rivera, slouch down a bit," Miguel whispered in an urgent tone.

Bobby nervously glanced up at the teacher, Mr. Mendoza, who was sitting at his desk in front of the classroom. His eyes were cast downward and he appeared to be occupied grading papers.

"C'mon, man. I can't see your paper! Move it over a little bit." Bobby squirmed and ignored the request.

The poking from behind continued and grew harder. "Rivera!"

Bobby kept his head down and continued working.

"Hey, don't be a prick, man. Help me out!"

Bobby glanced at the teacher, then slid down a little in his chair.

"A little more!"

Bobby slouched further and slid his paper to the side of his desk, trying to appear nonchalant and deep in thought, as he continued filling in the answers. He was sweating profusely. His right knee bounced up and down beneath his desk.

"Time's up!" Mr. Mendoza announced. "Drop off your test on the way out." Most of the class stood and began walking toward the door, handing their completed tests to Mr. Mendoza as they filed out. "Pencils down!" Mendoza barked at the few laggards who were still at their desks racing to finish.

Bobby stood in the middle of the line filing past the algebra teacher, still sweating and avoiding eye contact. He handed his test to Mr.

Mendoza and tried to hurry past. The teacher's arm shot out in front of him, blocking his path. "Not so fast, Rivera."

Bobby could feel his heart pounding in his chest. The voice seemed to come from far away. "Take your seat," the teacher commanded, handing Bobby's test back to him. Miguel followed behind Bobby and received the same treatment.

"I think we're screwed," Miguel muttered under his breath as he and Bobby shuffled back to their seats.

Bobby said nothing. His eyes seemed glued to the floor. He managed to look up for just an instant to see Mr. Mendoza approaching them. He quickly looked away. Mendoza grabbed Bobby's test paper off his desk and ripped it in half. Then he ripped it again and let it fall to the floor. He did the same with Miguel's paper. He stood over the two freshmen, glowering at them.

"I don't tolerate cheating in my class. That's an '*F*' for both of you."

Chapter 7

SAL AWOKE BEFORE daylight, as was now his habit. He'd joined the football team and liked to supplement the grueling afternoon workouts with a brisk 5-mile jog early in the morning to beat the late September heat. He walked downstairs and was surprised to see the light on in the kitchen. His father had been gone for days.

"Papá! Welcome home! When did you get back?"

Antonio Rios sprang up from his chair, his face beaming through the dark circles under his eyes as he embraced his son. "A couple of hours ago. Drove most of the night. It's good to be home."

"Where'd you go this time?" Sal asked.

"South—near the border. Sit down. I'll make you some breakfast."

Sal gladly complied as his father pulled bacon, eggs and cheese out of the refrigerator.

"How's school?"

"It's good. A lot different than back home. Way more kids, more teachers, more subjects. Sports teams, too."

"Tell me more."

"Well, I've made a few friends. Mostly I've been hanging with those two guys you met in our driveway when we were moving in—Bobby Rivera and Miguel Sanchez. Bobby's the big guy. He's really cool. Been here his whole life. Knows everybody, and they all like him. He's been showing me around. Teaching me about football, too."

"Excellent! How about Miguel? What's he like?"

"Hmmm…. He can be fun, but he can also be kind of a punk sometimes."

Rios laughed. "Sounds like a lot of people I know. Here you go," he said, serving up a massive omelet covered in salsa, along with four strips of bacon. "Better eat hearty if you're playing football."

Sal attacked the food with gusto as his father poured them each a cup of steaming hot coffee and sat down. "Are you going to be home for a while now?" Sal asked, sounding hopeful.

"Just a few days, then I've got another road trip. Might be kind of a long one."

Sal silently broke the bacon with his fork and began moving the pieces around without eating them.

"Look son, I'm truly sorry that I'm away so much and I'm really proud of how well you're getting by on your own. That gives me real peace of mind. The fact is that the work I'm doing takes me to a lot of places, all around South Texas. It'll probably expand to other places soon. It's not work I can do from here."

"I know," Sal replied with quiet resignation. "I just wish I knew more about what you're doing. Can you tell me where you're going on this next trip?"

Rios stared steadily at his son over the rim of his coffee cup. "I think you know the answer to that question."

Sal nodded. "The answer is no, you can't tell me."

"And why do you think that is?"

"Obviously, you think it's better that I don't know."

"Yes, but why?"

Sal continued staring at the pieces of bacon as he moved them around his plate. "Because it could be dangerous—for me and for you. If the wrong people wanted to know where you were or what you're doing, it's better if I can't tell them."

"Exactly! I can assure you that I'm doing important work for a great man. For now, that'll have to be enough."

Sal glanced at the clock on the wall then abruptly stood up without looking at his father, gathering the breakfast dishes and noisily tossing them into the sink. "Well, I better go. Gotta get in five miles before school—unless you want to tell me more about your business and the man you call *El Jefe*."

His father nodded slowly and smiled to himself. "Fair enough," he said, gesturing to the chair Sal had just vacated. "Have a seat. I suppose it's time I tell you more about him. What would you like to know?"

Sal hastily returned to the table, sitting on the edge of his seat and leaning forward. "Whatever you can tell me—his history, his business, his real name, where he lives, what he's like, how you got to know him."

"He lives in Mexico now, but I can't tell you exactly where—for the same reason I can't share my travel plans with you. But, since you and I are both here because of him, I guess you're entitled to know more than I've told you so far." He paused, staring at the ceiling fan, collecting his thoughts.

"He is the most brilliant person I know. He's a highly successful businessman, but he's also a scholar and a warrior. He understands politics and he understands people. Perhaps most importantly, he understands power. He is an absolute genius when it comes to developing power and influence and using it effectively.

"He's a lawyer by training. When you speak with him, you feel like you're speaking with a law professor. He doesn't say much. He listens and he asks questions. When someone asks him a question, he typically responds with a question and not an answer. They call it the Socratic Method and he's very good at it. It forces the person he's speaking with to think more deeply and it gives him an opportunity to evaluate their thought process and their intelligence."

Sal grinned. "Sounds like you. Now I know why I always get questions instead of answers when I talk to you. So, he's a lawyer?"

"No, he started out in that direction, where he grew up, in El Salvador, but then all hell broke loose in that country back in the 1980s. That's when he became a warrior."

"So you met in El Salvador?"

His father nodded. "We were comrades in arms, fighting against the corrupt government, which was backed by the Americans. His parents were professors who spoke out against the atrocities and the corrupt foreign influences. His family had their lands taken by the government and then his parents were assassinated. El Jefe was blinded by rage. He planned an attack against those who were responsible. It was a suicide mission. I was able to rescue El Jefe and his brother, but the rest of his party was slaughtered. Then I persuaded him to get his revenge another way, one that would have a lasting impact rather than settling for the immediate satisfaction of killing a small handful of scoundrels."

"How?"

"By being patient and changing the power structure from within. I had become a leader in my own small town back in El Salvador by developing influence and connections. It takes boldness and courage. It takes cleverness and diplomacy. It takes people skills and an understanding of human nature. It also takes ruthlessness sometimes, and to really grasp power you have to be willing to do what it takes. Like you've heard me say before, we do what we must."

"And what happened?"

"The student quickly surpassed the master. El Jefe is much better at this than I ever was, but we've worked closely together ever since. That's why we're here. It's all part of a grand plan that he's been developing for years. We've been extending his organization into America, and we're ramping up those efforts to a much greater degree now."

"You mentioned ruthlessness. Is that the kind of person El Jefe is?"

"No. He can take ruthless actions when necessary, but he's not a ruthless person. He cares about people. He genuinely wants to improve living conditions for the little people. But he is also a warrior and sometimes brutal tactics must be employed in warfare in the pursuit of a noble cause. There was a time when he was working with the leaders of the new government that came to power in El Salvador after the war. He disagreed with them on a number of important issues, but they were the people in power and he was content to work with them rather than against them. But, there was a group of former military officers that was actively trying to undermine the new regime. There were kidnappings, assaults and other terrorist tactics directed at the new leaders and their families. There was no doubt who the enemy was, but it seemed there was neither the willingness nor ability on the part of the authorities to stop the atrocities. Then something happened. One child of every opposition leader was blinded—eyes gouged out. So, they took great precautions to protect or conceal their families. It did no good. A few weeks later, ears of small children were cut off and mailed to the opposition leaders. After that it was hands. The opposition withered and went away."

"And that was El Jefe's doing? That's terrible!"

"Yes, it was. But it was also brilliant. And courageous."

"But they were just little kids! That's not courageous, that's just cruel! He sounds like a monster! Why didn't he just kill them rather them maiming them for life?"

"Why do you think?"

Sal thought in silence for a long moment. "Probably because if the kids were killed, the parents would eventually get over it, at least a little. But this way, they will be staring at a reminder for the rest of their lives."

"Correct. But a reminder of what?"

"What a monster El Jefe is!"

"I suppose they might think that. But what else would they be thinking about? Remember—these children were all under tight security. Guarded; protected; hidden."

"He was sending them a message, wasn't he? He was letting them know that he could get to their families, no matter where they were or what precautions they took. And they would realize that if they tried to retaliate or continued with their plans, that would bring more harm to their families."

Antonio smiled and his bloodshot eyes gleamed. "Correct. That's when word spread far and wide about El Cazador—The Hunter. No one knew who he was, but people knew that if you crossed El Jefe, then El Cazador would be unleashed. He would find you and brutal repercussions would follow. The reality is that El Jefe and El Cazador are one and the same."

"That's quite a story. But still, to do that to innocent children? He must have no heart at all."

"He has his own children and he loves them like any parent would. He understands how horrific it is to harm helpless children in such a way. On an emotional level, it would trouble his heart immensely. But that's where courage and conviction come into play. He had the courage to do something so horrific because he knew it was necessary to serve the greater good. We do what we must."

"And word gets around, right? People hear stories like that and don't mess with him. Does he still do things like that?"

Rios pushed the Brownsville newspaper across the table and pointed to the headline: *Grisly Find at Local Cemetery.* Sal's eyes grew wide as he scanned the article. "El Cazador?" he asked apprehensively.

"Maybe. This guy worked for one of the big drug rings that operates along the border. He insulted El Jefe and made threats. This is what happened to him. Who did it? Who knows? Maybe the drug lord found out and then took care of this guy himself rather than risk getting on the wrong side of El Jefe."

Sal eyed the clock and drummed his fingers on the kitchen table. He was eager to learn as much as possible while the opportunity presented itself. "So, you said he's a businessman. Is he in the drug business?"

"No, he owns several ranches and farms in Mexico but he's not in the drug business. He doesn't buy or sell anything illegal. That's beneath him. Mostly what he offers is influence and protection. He's got connections in law enforcement, politics, and the legal system. He acts as a facilitator. He helps people get things done. He doesn't take sides when he's dealing with competing businesses. His power and influence have gotten immense south of the border and he is very well paid for wielding that influence. He's been gradually expanding that influence into America. Until now, he's been doing that through various intermediaries, but he wants a single person he can really trust to pull it all together—to solidify the relationships we have and really focus on expanding our influence here. He has entrusted that task to me and I consider it a great honor. We are doing this partly for the business opportunities here, but also because we're on a mission to make life better for our people. There is so much opportunity here, Sal. Look around this town. Look all over Texas. People pour across the border from all over Latin America because there's a better life to be had here. Education, jobs, the opportunity to build a life for your family, the opportunity to get rich if you're smart and you work hard. This will be your home and you will become a wealthy and successful American. El Jefe is making that possible for you and we will help make it possible for countless others."

"So why doesn't El Jefe come here himself?"

"For a couple of reasons. First, he and I were both on the wrong side of the conflict in El Salvador as far as the Americans are concerned. That could present problems if we try to enter the country with a passport at the border crossings. Someday that may change, particularly as he becomes better known as a highly successful and legitimate businessman, but for now, it's still a concern.

"The other reason he won't come here is that he despises America. It has oppressed our people and looted our resources for 200 years. America supported the brutal military regime in El Salvador because it didn't agree with the political ideology of the opposition. It cared more about a philosophy than it cared about our people. As a result of America's involvement, countless good, simple people in El Salvador were slaughtered, including El Jefe's parents. America has helped oppressive regimes all over Latin America. It must be held accountable. It's a paradox, Sal. America provides great opportunities for our people, but it is also our greatest enemy. But El Jefe has plans. He will bring this country to its knees and we will help him."

"But how? We have no armies. We can't conquer this country."

"There are other ways to wage war, and you may play a part in this someday. Why do you think El Jefe let me bring you here?"

"But he doesn't even know me."

Antonio looked steadily at his son, nodding slowly. "I've been waiting for the right time to share this with you. I suppose now is a good time. The fact is, he knows much more than you think, and he has taken a special interest in you. He is your godfather, Salvatore, and that is an honor he has bestowed upon no one else. So he has been watching you. He has eyes and ears everywhere. He's gotten reports about how you excel in your studies, and how quickly and capably you've learned English. And he's heard about some of the stunts you've pulled off with your friends back home. He thinks you're bold and brash and he likes that. That boldness can serve you well, but it can also be a problem if you don't control it. You need to keep a low profile here. And remember, what I've just shared with you must go no further than this room."

"I understand. And I'm happy to know that I have a godfather who is such a great man, but just one more question. You've always referred to him as *El Jefe*. What's his real name?"

"His name will become widely known soon enough. He's becoming a great capitalist because accumulating wealth goes hand-in-hand with building influence and power, especially in this country. In addition to his enormous agricultural businesses, he's acquired an auto parts manufacturer as well as a clothing business. Other deals are in the works and they're all completely legitimate enterprises. His name is well known, and that name and reputation will grow even more rapidly as he expands those enterprises into the U.S. But that will be down the road a bit. Right now, our operations here involve cultivating relationships and influence, as well as phasing out some of the more unsavory lines of work that were necessary in the interest of building capital to fund the other enterprises. While we're still in this stage, my work must be very discreet and must not be linked to El Jefe. That's another reason we had to be very careful crossing the border. Even if I were allowed entry, it's likely the authorities would keep close tabs on me, and I am a known associate of his. If anything went wrong, it could be tied back to him. So, I'm afraid that his name is another detail you're better off not knowing—at least for now. Before long, I'm confident that he will be well known as a very successful international businessman, and my transition work here will be completed. At that point, there will be no need for secrecy regarding his identity."

Sal's shoulders drooped and he looked down at the table. "I get it," he said quietly. "It's just hard knowing that I have this connection with him but I don't even know him, not even his name."

Antonio Rios reached across the table and placed his hand on his son's forearm. "You will know him someday, Sal. I am completely confident of that. For now, you're in training as a soldier in his army. Someday you can be a general if you play your cards right. America will provide a wonderful home for you, and someday for your family. But America is the enemy and we will take her down from the inside, I promise you. Never forget that."

"I will make you proud, Papá."

"I know you will. Now go take your run."

Sal looked at the clock. "Yikes! It's 8:20. No run today. I'm almost late already. Gotta go!"

Chapter 8

BOBBY STOOD IN the hallway, feeling like he was awaiting the executioner. The sign on the door read "*Mr. David Martinez, Principal.*" Miguel was inside already. The loud voice was muffled by the thick wooden door, so Bobby couldn't make out the words, but it was obvious that a serious tongue-lashing was being administered.

Then the verbal assault halted. The door opened and Miguel emerged. He smirked at Bobby and rolled his eyes as he walked past. Bobby was ushered in by the stern-looking principal and sat down in the worn leather chair opposite a massive desk buried in papers and files. He felt a combination of shame, humiliation and dread.

"Do you care to explain yourself, Mr. Rivera?"

Bobby hung his head and tried to think of the right thing to say. Good answers eluded him. "I don't know what to say," he mumbled.

"I know you're just a freshman, but I shouldn't have to tell you how seriously we take cheating around here." Mr. Martinez was all business and his voice was harsh. "It is absolutely unacceptable," he said, raising his voice. "Under any circumstances. It violates our honor code. I will not have it! Do you understand?"

"Yes sir," Bobby replied. He hunched over in his chair, head down, avoiding eye contact.

Mr. Martinez continued. "Do you mind telling me why you did it?"

"I guess I just wasn't thinking," Bobby stammered. "Miguel kept poking me from behind and asking to see my answers. Maybe I was afraid the teacher was going to see that and we'd get in trouble, so I was just trying to shut him up. Or maybe I felt like I was helping out a friend. I don't know. I didn't really think about it. I guess I just kind of panicked."

"So you and Miguel didn't talk about this beforehand? You didn't plan ahead of time to help him out?"

"No. I was taken by surprise. I didn't know how to handle it."

"And now you do, right?"

There was a soft knock on the door and it was opened by the principal's secretary. "Mrs. Rivera is here."

"Show her in," the principal replied. Then turning to Bobby, he said. "You'll be at detention every Saturday morning for the rest of the month."

"Yes, sir," Bobby said quietly, relieved to hear that he wasn't being suspended or expelled but feeling an even greater sense of dread at the mention of his mother.

Bobby's eyes met his mother's for just an instant before he looked away. He saw no anger in them, just fear, which made him feel even worse.

"Thank you for coming in, Mrs. Rivera," the principal began in a tone much gentler than he had just used with his students. "I'm sorry we had to call you in, but we've got something serious to discuss. Bobby will be serving detention for the next month and I'd like to tell you why."

He proceeded to share with Mrs. Rivera exactly what had happened in algebra class the previous afternoon as well as a brief summary of the conversation he had just finished with her son. Her eyes shifted back and forth from the principal to her son as she listened. Had he dared look at his mother, Bobby would have seen her normally pleasant countenance transform into one of smoldering anger.

When he finished, Mr. Martinez asked Bobby to step outside. "Mrs. Rivera, I know this is upsetting and I can assure you that I made it perfectly clear to Bobby how serious this is. But I do want you to know that Bobby was not the instigator here. His teachers tell me that he has been a model student thus far. He's attentive in class, well-mannered and his grades are fine. My take on all this is that it happened because he was eager to please a friend. He knows that cheating is wrong and he didn't want to do it, but he did it anyway to avoid making waves with the other boy. His real crime here is not being strong enough to say no and being too eager to give in to pressure from a bad influence. But he's a good kid. I don't think we'll be having issues like this again."

"Thanks for saying that, Mr. Martinez. That's very kind of you. I can't tell you how embarrassed I feel right now." She wiped a tear with her finger and Mr. Martinez held out a box of tissue. She took a deep breath and composed herself for a few seconds. She stood up, shook the principal's hand and said, "I can assure you that his father and I will give this the attention it deserves."

Mrs. Rivera exited the principal's office and stormed past her son without looking at him. "Let's go, Bobby," she said in a clipped voice. Bobby followed behind, her stride and her body language leaving no doubt about the fury inside the petite figure in the white nursing uniform. He climbed into her old but pristine Toyota and slammed the door. As soon as his bottom hit the seat, the dread and emotion pent up within him came crashing through. A fit of quiet sobs overtook him.

"I'm sorry… I'm so sorry…"

"I hope so—you should be! We'll talk about this when your father gets home."

* * *

They sat around the kitchen table, just as they had a month before when they lectured him about staying off the radar screen on the second day of school, his father to his right and his mother to his left. He didn't mind so much being punished, but he hated getting lectures from his parents about how he had disappointed them. And this time he knew he truly had, perhaps more than ever before, which made him feel even worse.

"Do you have any idea how upset this makes us?" his father fumed. "Do you have any idea how concerned your mother was when she had to leave work to pick you up from school? And how humiliating it was—for both of us—once we learned the reason? Do you?"

Bobby started sniffling again and wiped the tears from his face with the back of his hand. "I know, I know… and I'm really sorry… I can't believe how stupid that was…"

"You're darn right it was stupid!" His father glared at him. "Didn't you hear anything we said after you got mixed up in that fight? This could have been really bad! Some other school might have expelled you. Your education might be finished. This kind of thing could really have an impact on your future!"

Bobby's sniffles grew louder. "Look at me, Bobby," his mother said. He looked up through watery eyes, struggling to get a grip on his emotions. Her face was no longer tight with anger, but there was a clear sense of intensity and urgency about her. "You've heard us talk before about the hardships of life on the other side of the border, but I really don't think you understand how good we have it here. How could you? This is all you've ever known. You take it all for granted—the safety of our little town here, the opportunity to go to a good school, the ability to go to college in a few years, the fact that you're playing football instead of being recruited by the gangs, and that you go to sleep to the sound of crickets rather than gunshots. When your father and I got married, we wanted nothing more than to find a way to live in this country and raise our child as an American."

"And you're putting all that at risk!" his father interjected. "If you get into trouble, we could all be deported. Our dream could be over. All this promise—gone!"

"But I was born here," Bobby said. "I'm a citizen. They can't deport us, can they?"

"Of course they can, Bobby! Your mother and I are not citizens. Our visas can be revoked at any time. We're working to become citizens but it's a long process and there are no guarantees. If there's any trouble associated with our family, all bets are off."

"And don't think that just because you're a citizen, you'll never be deported," said his mother. "What kind of chance do you think we'd have if we're up against the American government? They make the rules. They can do what they want. Who knows, your birth records might suddenly disappear. If they want us gone, they can make us leave."

His father nodded. "That's why we've been trying to tell you how important it is to stay out of trouble. Keep as far from it as you possibly can. Run the other way! I know that's hard sometimes. You found that out with that fight at school. You've got a big heart. You want everyone to like you. You always want to please your friends. Under normal circumstances, that's understandable, but we don't live here under normal circumstances. We are always at risk. Don't ever forget that!"

"That also means choose your friends wisely and stay away from the wrong kind of people," his mother added. "I know you try to be friends with everybody, but I don't know about this boy, Miguel. If he's bad news, you just need to steer clear of him."

"Miguel's OK, Mom. He's got a bit of an attitude—kind of cocky—but he's new here, and I think he's just trying to figure out how to fit in."

"Have you met his parents?" she asked.

"No. He doesn't want anyone coming around his house. Doesn't talk about his family at all. I think he's probably embarrassed because they don't have much."

"Well, be careful, Bobby. You're a good kid. Your father and I know that. But hanging around with the wrong kind can lead to trouble."

Bobby didn't argue when his father told him he was grounded for the next two weeks. He deserved it and he knew it. He realized that the consequences could have been far worse, both at school and at home. The first few days of his grounding didn't affect his routine much because he had football practice after school and he normally didn't go out in the evening anyway. Evenings were study time. When the weekend came around, he felt the sting of his punishment. He longed to be out in The Brush. Sometimes he'd go there by himself and enjoy the solitude with his drawing materials. More recently, it had become a regular pastime with his new pals, Sal and Miguel. They'd go hiking and exploring. Sometimes they'd go hunting with Miguel's bow, usually for jack rabbits, but occasionally they'd get a shot at a coyote or a wild hog.

It was Sunday afternoon and he imagined his friends out in The Brush without him. He sat in an old lawn chair in his small but tidy front yard, an easel and drawing paper in front of him. He amused himself by drawing anything he set his eyes upon, trying to draw as quickly as possible while still capturing enough detail to create a realistic and eye-catching depiction of the subject.

He drew the view of his front yard from the house. He drew the old pick-up truck across the street. He drew Mrs. Santiago, watering her flowers next door. A young girl on a bicycle pulled up in front of his house. He stared at her and flipped the page on his easel to begin a new drawing. He stared at her for a second as if she were an inanimate object and was jolted back to reality when she gave him a friendly wave and a smile.

"Hi there," she called out in a cheerful voice. "I'm Jenny. I'm looking for my brother. Have you seen him?"

Bobby put down his pencil. "Don't know. Who's your brother?"

"Miguel Sanchez. You're Bobby Rivera, aren't you?"

Bobby nodded, momentarily stupefied as he approached and looked at the girl more closely. She was striking. She had lustrous black hair, the front part of which was combed forward, creating perfectly straight bangs across her forehead. The rest of her shiny mane was parted down the middle and cascaded over her shoulders, seamlessly coming together and flowing halfway down her back. She had the same dark complexion as her brother, but her eyes were stunningly bright, the color of turquoise. Even the thick, dark-framed glasses that framed her face could not obscure the luminescent eyes. Her fine features were illuminated by the prettiest smile he had ever seen.

"Miguel talks about you all the time," she said. "He says he spends most of his time hanging out with you, so I thought he might be here."

"Sorry, he's not here. I haven't seen him today." His own voice sounded curt, maybe even harsh, like he didn't want to help. He hadn't meant to sound that way. He wanted to strike up a conversation, which was normally easy for him, but he felt awkward and words eluded him.

"OK, I'll keep looking." She started to peddle away.

"Wait! I think I know where he is."

The girl stopped and looked at him expectantly.

"He's probably out in The Brush. That's where we spend most of our time. It's just past the edge of town, across Highway 281, but he might be hard to find if you don't know where to look. I'd take you there, but I'm grounded." He shuffled his feet and looked down.

"So that's why you're sitting out here all by yourself?" She pointed toward the easel. "What's that?"

"I like to draw. Seemed like a good way to pass the time while I'm stuck at home."

"Can I see?"

Bobby hesitated. "OK, I guess so. I'm not very good, though, so don't laugh."

She dropped her bike and ran right past him toward the easel. She started flipping through the pages, eyes widening, gasping at what she saw. "These are incredible! I can't believe how good you are! How long have you been working on these?"

"Oh, I just threw those together in the last 30 minutes or so."

"That's amazing!"

"It's no big deal," Bobby stammered, shoving his hands in his pockets and watching the girl as she leaned in to examine his work more closely.

"Can you draw me?" she asked enthusiastically.

"What?"

"Draw me! Please…"

Bobby scratched the back of his neck. "OK, I'll try. Why don't you pose on your bike?"

She bounded toward the rusty blue Schwinn with the old whitewall tires, and straddled it, her feet touching the ground on either side as the bike was clearly too small for her. "How's this?" she asked, beaming at him as she removed her glasses.

"Perfect. Just hold that pose for a few minutes." He took his time, relishing the opportunity to have a good reason for staring directly into her face. He did his best to capture the bright spirit that accompanied the pretty face and the turquoise eyes.

He worked quickly, but with a laser-like focus. Then he stood back and surveyed his work, hoping he had done justice to such an intriguing subject. He set down his pencil, folded his arms across his chest and allowed a narrow smile to cross his lips, although he tried hard to suppress it. "OK. Done!" he announced.

His subject unceremoniously dropped her bicycle and raced around the easel. She let out a squeal of delight as she stared open-mouthed at the portrait. "Oh my gosh… that is *sooo* good! It looks just like me! Can I have it?"

"Uh… sure," Bobby replied, trying to hide his disappointment at having to give it away. He rolled it up carefully and secured it with a rubber band he took from a newspaper lying on his front porch.

"Bobby, aren't you going to invite your guest inside? It's hot out there." Bobby turned as his mother appeared in the front doorway.

He turned back to Jenny, feeling some mixture of embarrassment at his mother's sudden appearance and hopefulness at the prospect of prolonging the visit. "Uh… want to come inside?"

"Sure, just for a few minutes, then I've got to go find my brother." Then she approached Bobby's mother, extending her hand. "Hello, Mrs. Rivera. I'm Jenny."

Mrs. Rivera smiled at the friendly and confident greeting coming from the young teenager. She had grown accustomed to the inarticulate mumblings of teenage boys. "Come on in, Jenny. I'll pour some lemonade."

They sat at the kitchen table, Bobby feeling even more awkward now that he had to make conversation in the presence of his mother. "How come I've never seen you at school?" he asked.

"Because I don't go to your school. Not yet anyway. I'm still in eighth grade."

"Really?" Bobby replied, the surprise evident in his voice. "When you told me you were Miguel's sister, I assumed you were his older sister."

She laughed, a loud, confident laugh. "You're not supposed to comment about a girl's age, Bobby! Don't you know that?"

"Sorry," he stammered. "I just meant… you seem more mature… or more poised… than most girls your age. I didn't mean to—"

She laughed again, that big laugh. "I'm just teasing!" She poked him playfully in the forearm.

"It's just that Miguel never talks about his family," Bobby explained. "I think he mentioned once that he had a sister and a brother, but whenever the subject of family comes up, he cuts it off. He just says, 'Don't ask about my family and I won't ask about yours.' So I didn't want to pry."

"I'm not surprised," Jenny responded, turning more serious. "Our father left us a while ago. That was a good thing—he was terrible to my mom and he drank too much—but Miguel took it really hard." She glanced up at the clock on the wall above the sink. "I better go now. I'm supposed to be looking for Miguel. So you think I can find him out in The Bush?"

"The *Brush*," Bobby corrected her. "I'm sure that's where he is. Finding our entry point is easy—we call it the trailhead. But once you get there, he could be hard to find. There are certain places we usually go, but you could get lost if you don't know your way around. And it's pretty rugged out there—lots of snakes and scorpions and coyotes and other things you don't want to run into. You might want to just wait until he comes home."

"Don't you think you should lend a hand, Bobby?" his mother chimed in. "You know that area better than anyone."

"But I thought I was grounded."

"You are, but your friend needs help. Go help her!"

Bobby's face brightened. "I'll grab my bike. Let's go."

They arrived at the trailhead ten minutes later, left their bikes just off the road and began hiking.

"This is pretty desolate out here, isn't it?" Jenny said, surveying her surroundings.

"I suppose, but I think it's really cool. I've been coming here for years. It goes on forever, so there are always new places to explore. Sometimes I come out here with friends and we hike or explore or look for critters. Sometimes I like to come out here on my own. It's a good place to think and it's a *really* good place to draw. If you're interested, I'll show you around some time."

"I'd like that," Jenny replied.

"Look, over there!" Bobby pointed to two figures a few hundred yards away, making their way back toward the highway but avoiding the main trail. "That's them." He marched off in that direction, Jenny at his heels. He stopped about half way, gave a loud whistle and waved. They waved back and changed directions, heading toward Bobby and Jenny.

Miguel and Sal broke into a foot race and pulled up in front of them, dusty, sweating and panting.

Miguel shot a look of disgust at Jenny. "What the hell, Bobby! What are you doing hanging around with my skanky sister?"

Jenny jumped in before Bobby could respond. "Mom wants you home. She sent me to find you. Your principal called her today—again!"

"I don't give a shit. I'll be home when I feel like it. Now get your ugly ass outta here. Go bury your face in some books, like you always do." Then he turned to Bobby. "You blowing us off, man? You told us you were grounded but here you are with this bitch. What gives?"

"Hey, she needed help finding you, that's all," Bobby said.

Sal was grinning as he witnessed the verbal assault. "Hey Miguel, don't be so dense. Bobby's just trying to be Mr. Nice Guy so he can put the moves on her, that's all. Nothing wrong with that!"

"Well, you stay away from my sister!" Miguel hissed, glaring at Bobby. Then he pointed maliciously in his sister's face. "And you, keep away from *here!* This is our place. You don't belong out here."

Jenny returned her brother's glare, then looked at Bobby, who looked away and said nothing. She stormed off.

"I gotta go, too," Bobby said to his friends. "I *am* grounded. I gotta get back home."

He hurried after Jenny and felt heartsick when he saw tears streaming down her face. He fully expected to be chastised for not sticking up for her and he knew that he would be deserving of whatever reproachful words she might sling at him, but she said nothing.

"I'll ride you home," Bobby offered as they mounted their bikes. She was sniffling now and wiping her eyes.

"I know my way." She rode off.

Chapter 9

IT WAS EARLY October, Bobby's favorite time of year to be out in The Brush. It was still plenty warm during the daylight hours, but no longer blazing hot. Evenings were cool and dry, rain being a rare occurrence that time of year. Wildlife was more noticeable, since the desert creatures were no longer forced to hide out in cool, dark places seeking shelter from the sun.

Unfortunately for Bobby Rivera, spending time in The Brush during the week was getting increasingly difficult. Afternoons were consumed by football practice. Evenings were taken up with schoolwork. Even on the rare occasions when homework was light, the days were growing shorter, leaving little time for outdoor activity.

That didn't stop his friends. Miguel and Sal had started hanging with some of the older football players. Almost every night, they would meet at the church parking lot, or "The Lot" as it was commonly known among the teenage crowd. There were no church activities in the evenings and no neighbors nearby to complain. Father Paul and the local sheriff left them alone unless it got too rowdy or started attracting strangers from outside the area.

Bobby walked off the football field after practice with Miguel. "Hey, Bobby. We've got no tests this week. Come on down to The Lot and hang with us tonight."

It was a Tuesday night. Midterm exams had concluded the previous week, so most students were enjoying a bit of a respite from tests and homework. "I better not. I've got to study tonight," Bobby said.

"Aw, bullshit, man. We're taking the same classes. We don't have shit going on this week. Me and Sal go there almost every night. It's cool! C'mon!"

"Maybe another night, Miguel. Tonight's just not a good night." He walked away.

Bobby had had similar conversations with Sal and Miguel multiple times in recent weeks. He dreaded them. He felt torn and conflicted. He was a people person and he liked hanging with his pals and talking guy talk. He liked the idea of getting closer to the older boys, most of whom were his teammates. But he knew his parents wouldn't approve, and recent events and parental lectures were never far from his mind when he was at home. He couldn't risk upsetting them yet again, so he made excuses.

Later that evening, he sat in bed reading, after saying goodnight to his parents. He was starting to doze off when a sharp rap on the window jolted him into alertness. He listened closely. After a few seconds, he heard muffled voices just outside of his first story bedroom window, followed by soft knocking. He hurried to the window as quietly as he could, parted the curtains and pressed his face against the glass, shielding his eyes from his bedside lamp so that he could see into the darkness. Two faces popped up from just below the window—Miguel and Sal, laughing and sporting goofy grins. Sal held up a six-pack with two cans missing and Miguel pointed to it and then beckoned Bobby to join them.

Bobby opened the window slowly, putting a finger to his lips as he did so. "Shhh... Don't wake my parents!"

"Let's go, man," said Miguel in a stage whisper that was far too loud. "The moon's almost full. Great night to be out in The Brush with a few brewskies."

"Are you crazy? My parents are right upstairs. I'll be toast if they catch me. Besides, we've got school in the morning. It's after ten already."

Miguel's goofy grin transformed into a sneer. "Oh, stop being such a pussy, Bobby. We'll be out in The Brush. No one's going to see us."

Bobby looked over his shoulder at his bedroom door. "Sorry. Can't do it. You guys better scram." He shut the window and closed the curtains.

The words had stung. He wanted to be with his friends. He longed for the freedom they had. No one was busting their chops for staying out late or having a few beers. Then an idea came to him—an overnight camping excursion out in The Brush. Sal and Miguel would consider it an all-nighter. His parents had always encouraged Bobby's appreciation for nature and might consider time in the great outdoors preferable to hanging out at The Lot with a bunch of wild teenage football players. When he made the pitch for a Saturday night campout, his parents agreed.

They met in front of the old church late Saturday afternoon. Sal was sitting on the front steps as Bobby and Miguel approached, burdened down with camping supplies. "Jeez, I thought this was an overnight. Looks like you guys are planning on spending weeks out there! What's in those bags?"

Bobby reached over his shoulder and patted the oversized backpack he was wearing. "Got everything we need right here. Sleeping bag, tent, flashlights, and a boatload of food. We're going to eat like kings!"

Miguel set an old army duffle bag on the sidewalk, and rotated his shoulder several times, trying to alleviate the stiffness caused by the heavy load. He kicked the bag with his foot. "Sleeping bag, lantern, an extra jacket, and a little surprise I'll break out once we set up camp," he said, grinning mischievously. "So where's your shit?" He directed his question to Sal, who had neither bag nor backpack, just a thin rolled up blanket and a hoody folded in his lap.

"Amateurs! You guys look like a couple of weekend tourists," Sal replied, his voice thick with condescension. "Believe me, I've spent plenty of nights out under the stars. I've got everything I need. You don't need a tent if you know how to pick the right spot."

They walked the short distance to Highway 281, crossed the road to the trailhead and then trekked along their usual route, directly perpendicular to the highway, until they reached The Hill. They surveyed the vast expanse all around them. "Perfect place. Let's set up camp here," said Miguel.

"No. This is the perfect place to get a good look, but it's a terrible place to camp," said Sal. "Ground is way too rocky, it's not level and it's too exposed. The wind will pick up and you'll freeze your ass off. Follow me."

Sal marched down The Hill and veered to the northeast at about a 45-degree angle from the path. Miguel and Bobby scrambled to keep up.

At first, their feet felt light and their pace was brisk, despite their heavy loads. Two miles later, they found themselves beyond the limits of any of their prior visits.

"This is awesome!" Bobby exclaimed. "Never been out this far in this direction."

"Hey, let's pick a place and settle in," Miguel whined, after his third suggested stopping place had been summarily rejected by Sal.

"Over there," said Sal, pointing in the opposite direction from the setting sun. "See those big rocks? Looks like there's a little gully just to the right of that and then a good-sized hill. That's where we're going."

They walked another quarter of a mile. Sal surveyed the area with a sense of satisfaction. "Perfect!" he said. He walked in a circle, eyeing the ground, then stopped. "Here's my bed." He kicked a few rocks out of the way and laid out his blanket.

Bobby and Miguel chose a spot and clumsily began setting up Bobby's tent as Sal perched on a large boulder and watched with amusement. Eventually they succeeded and laid out their sleeping bags inside the tent. "There's plenty of room if you want to sleep in here, Sal," Bobby offered.

"Not a chance," Sal replied. "I like sleeping under the stars."

They spent the rest of the afternoon exploring the area, then gathered a supply of dry mesquite wood while there was still some daylight remaining. They dug a small pit and filled it with branches, which ignited easily using Miguel's butane lighter and some crumpled up newspapers Bobby had the foresight to bring along. As night fell, they sat around the campfire and attacked their dinner: ham and cheese sandwiches, beef jerky, potato chips and plenty of other junk food.

"Life is good boys! How cool is this?" Sal said, as he bit into one of the brownies Bobby's mother had made, a look of pure contentment spread across his face as he stared into the campfire. "The only thing that would make this better would be some ice-cold beer!"

"I can do better than that," said Miguel, sounding boastful and excited. "Time for my little surprise." He reached into his backpack and raised the trophy in the air. "Ta-da! Tequila!"

"Awesome!" said Sal. "How did you score that?"

"Let's just say it's a gift from my old man. He has this beat-up old trunk he kept locked all the time. I couldn't find the key, so I finally busted it open. Found this, too," he said, pulling a sheathed hunting knife from his backpack and holding it aloft. He slowly removed the knife from its brown leather sheath, revealing a polished walnut handle and a ten-inch stainless steel blade that gleamed in the firelight. He rotated the blade reverently, his eyes transfixed on his newfound treasure. "Look at this beauty!"

"Won't the old boy be pissed when he finds out?" Sal asked.

"Nah, he's gone and I don't think he's coming back. Let's get drunk!"

"You're the man, Miguel!" said Sal. "Toss me that bottle."

Miguel took a swig, closed his eyes and shook his head vigorously from side to side, then tossed the bottle over the fire to Sal who took a quick swallow and handed the bottle to Bobby, who quickly passed the bottle back to Miguel as if it were burning his hands.

"C'mon Bobby," urged Miguel. "Man up!"

"Aw, that's not really my thing."

"Bullshit! It's time you make it your thing," Miguel insisted. "What better time than right now, right here, with your best pals."

"Get off his case, man," Sal said, motioning for the bottle. "Bobby's got some issues at home. He doesn't want to get grounded again. Besides, that means more tequila for you and me."

Miguel gave Sal an irritated look, then quickly turned back toward Bobby. "Hey, you're not a little kid anymore. Shit, you look like you're twenty years old. You can't be scared of your parents. Tell them to get off your ass."

"It's not that simple," Bobby replied. "They live in fear every day of their lives. They're afraid something bad will happen and they'll be deported. I don't want to be the one to cause that."

"Your parents? Are you crazy?" Miguel asked, sounding incredulous. "This town needs them. From what I've been hearing, your mom and dad are the medical team for our entire town and half the county. If they left, there'd be no one to replace them, so stop worrying. It's not gonna happen."

"You never know," said Bobby. "I can't take that chance. Living in this country means everything to them. They love their lives here. They love the fact that I'm an American citizen because I was born here. I can't be the cause of them getting sent back to Mexico. And, besides, I agree with them. We've got it made in this country—you, me, Sal—all of us."

"I get it," Sal said, shrugging his shoulders. "My old man is always telling me the same thing. Don't attract attention. Stay out of trouble. People like us have to think that way."

Miguel shook his head and tossed a stick into the fire. "Look, Bobby—I get that you want to keep your parents happy. That's the kind of guy you are. But what about your friends? Every time me and Sal ask you to come out at night with us, you blow us off. How do you think that makes us feel? Don't you care about us? C'mon, have some tequila! There's no one out here but us. No way to get in trouble. Do it for your friends. We're your best pals, for Chrissakes!" He tossed the bottle back toward Bobby.

"Alright, you win." Bobby unscrewed the cap and cautiously put his lips to the bottle and took a small sip. It burned his throat going down and he struggled to keep from retching. "That's terrible!" he gasped, handing the bottle to Sal.

"You're not drinking tea, amigo." Sal laughed at the disgusted look on Bobby's face. "Don't sip it. Slam it straight back like this." He raised the bottle and tilted his head back in a single motion, letting the liquid fire shoot straight down his gullet. He belched, let out a satisfied sigh, and smiled through burning eyes.

Bobby followed Sal's instructions and was able to get a much bigger swig down. He let out a deep breath and pounded his chest with his fist. "Whoa! That still tastes like gasoline!"

Miguel threw more branches on the fire and it instantly blazed higher and brighter. "So, Sal," he said. "Tell us your story. You're the man of mystery. I never get a straight answer from you. You just told us your old man tells you to lay low. Why? What's that all about? Where you from anyway?"

"Like I've said before, I'm from down south. A little place you've never heard of," said Sal.

"See what I mean?" said Miguel. "That doesn't tell us shit! South of what? South of the border, right?"

Sal hesitated, staring into the fire. "Yeah, south of the border. A long way south."

"And what brings you here? What does your old man do?" Miguel asked.

Sal hesitated again and took a long pull from the bottle. "He's a businessman. He does business all around Texas and we came here because it's centrally located between the places he goes—Brownsville, McAllen, San Antonio, Laredo, Austin. But hey, who are you to be grilling me? You're worse than me whenever anyone asks about your family."

Miguel gestured for the tequila. "Give me another hit off that bottle and I'll tell you whatever you want to know. Give Bobby a hit first."

Bobby took another swallow and gritted his teeth, trying hard to avoid vomiting, and handed the bottle to Miguel, who did the same.

"Man, I'm getting a good buzz now!" said Miguel, standing up and staring up at the stars, swaying slightly. "This is so cool being here with you guys, getting smashed on a Saturday night. Life is good!" He paced for a few seconds, then his face turned serious. "The truth is, my old man is a lowlife piece of shit. He cheated on my mom all the time. He beat her up. He was gone a lot, and when he was around, he was a mean, nasty drunk, but she wouldn't throw him out because he paid the bills. He worked as an auto mechanic, but had a hard time keeping any job very long. Then he just vanished—left my mom and me and my brother and sister without a word and without a cent. We later heard he had another family in Houston. I hope he never comes back." He turned his back on his friends and wiped his eyes with the back of his hand. "That's why I don't like to talk about my family. It's painful." He sat back down, tears glistening on his cheeks in the firelight. "But I'm lucky I got you guys. You're like family to me now."

"That sounds rough, pal," Bobby said. "I can't imagine my dad walking out on us. I'm really sorry to hear that."

"Me too," Sal added. "But you've got us. We've got your back, no matter what."

"Thanks," said Miguel.

They passed the bottle around again. It was more than half gone now. Bobby was feeling flush and light-headed. He was also feeling mellow, relaxed and confident all at the same time. "You know, Miguel, that's a tough break, having your dad take off like that, but you've got a lot going for you, too. We're living in a pretty cool place, and you don't have to worry about being deported or having your mom deported. You're golden because your mother was born here. You don't have to be looking over your shoulder all the time or worry about attracting attention from the authorities. That's big!"

"Yeah, no shit," said Sal. "I've got family issues too—had to leave my mother and sisters behind. It might be years until we can bring them up here. And me and my dad—we *do* have to look over our shoulder. We want to stay here and we plan to, but Bobby's right. We could get sent back any time. You've got it made. Don't take that for granted."

Miguel nodded, staring at the fire. "You guys are right. Believe me, I know it. But don't feel sorry for me. I'm glad the bastard is out of our lives. We're better off without him. Plus, I can stay out all night. I can drink whenever I want and no one will hassle me." He took another long swallow from the bottle and handed it to Sal, who did likewise. "So, Sal, you've told us more in the last few minutes than you've told us since we've known you. You crossed the border with your old man; you left your mom and your sisters behind. Tell us the rest of the story. Where'd you come from? What's your old man doing here? Fill us in, man. I told you my story. It's your turn."

Sal stood up and walked around the fire, swaying gently but noticeably, staring up at the stars, gathering his thoughts. "Fair enough. You guys are my compadres. I've got no secrets from you. My family comes from El Salvador, but we moved to Mexico when I was little. Like I've told you before, my dad's a businessman. He works for a great man back in Mexico. A real leader—a visionary. You may have heard of him. He goes by several different names, but most people know him as El Cazador—The Hunter."

"Of course I've heard of El Cazador," Miguel said. "Everyone around here has. Some kind of spooky angel of death, right? But I've heard of Santa Clause and the Easter Bunny, too. That doesn't mean they're real."

"I can assure you, he's very real," replied Sal. "He's a businessman and my dad is his right-hand man. They're expanding their business on this side of the border, and my old man is the one that's making it happen. It's a big job—that's why he's traveling all the time."

"C'mon," said Miguel. "Don't bullshit us. Your old man's a drug dealer, right? Working for some Mexican drug lord?"

"He's not a drug dealer!" Sal shot back. "We're not into that stuff. That's way beneath El Cazador. He's a great man. He's going to change everything. He's going to change this country as you know it. People think America is such a wonderful place, but it's all screwed up. The U.S. exploits everything around it—Mexico, El Salvador, all of Latin America. It oppresses their people. And when our people come here, we're taken advantage of. And it's not just us. It's just about everyone else here, too. The ruling class controls everything and the little people barely get by. But we're going to change that. We're going to take them down."

"I think that tequila's gone to your head," said Bobby. "America is the most powerful nation on earth. No one's going to take it down."

Sal's face took on the look he wore when running with a football—intense and focused. "Hey, I may be a little drunk, but I'm not stupid," he said. "I'm not talking about a military invasion. You're right—that would never work. I'm talking about bringing about change from within. About using America's weaknesses against her. In fact, it's already happening. It's way below the radar right now but that'll change."

"This is crazy talk," Miguel scoffed, slurring badly, his voice louder than normal. "Someone's feeding you a load of shit. Don't be stupid, man. Your old boy wants you to think he's doing something respectable when the fact is, he's probably into drugs or guns or smuggling people across the border. Think about it—no law-abiding citizen has security cameras all around his house like you do. And have you ever seen this El Cazador guy? Does your father have an office somewhere? Or is he just gone all the time and real mysterious about it? Connect the dots, Sal! It's not hard."

Sal attempted to spring up from a sitting position but staggered backwards. He regained his balance and brought himself eyeball-to-eyeball with Miguel. "Hey, you don't know shit about my old man, so shut the fuck up," Sal hissed, poking Miguel in the shoulder.

Miguel swatted away Sal's hand and shoved him roughly in the chest. "You want to get tough with me?" Miguel taunted. "Just because you can knock people around on the football field doesn't mean you're a tough guy. You ain't shit out here, pal!"

Bobby quickly jumped between them. "Hey, knock it off! What's with you guys? We've been having a great time. Just cool it!"

"He's got no business talking trash about my old man," Sal shouted, still glaring at Miguel.

"Well, he's got a point there, Miguel. I know you didn't mean anything by it, but it's clearly a touchy subject so just let it go, OK?" Bobby looked from one to the other, his arms still outstretched between them like a referee. "Look, the tequila is going to our heads. We're all a little buzzed. Let's enjoy it, OK? Let's knock this stuff off."

Miguel looked down, shuffling his feet. "I guess I'm still really pissed at my old man and that made me lash out at yours," he mumbled at Sal. "You guys are like brothers to me. Sometimes brothers fight, right? Sorry, my bad. Let's get back to drinking."

The hard feelings evaporated as quickly as they had erupted, and the topics turned to football, girls and drinking. The laughter grew louder and their speech increasingly more slurred. It wasn't long before their laughter was interrupted, as Miguel staggered to some nearby bushes and threw up. Sal and Bobby laughed at the sight, but Sal soon joined him in a violent fit of vomiting. Bobby felt no such urge, partly because his size allowed him to tolerate more alcohol, but mostly because he had been far more careful about the quantity he was consuming. He watched his friends progress toward even greater levels of incoherence.

Miguel and Sal stood face-to-face, passing the bottle back and forth as they finished it off, both of them swaying like punch-drunk fighters still standing after too many rounds in the ring. "You're my brother, man!" Miguel stammered as he wrapped Sal in a rough bearhug. "You guys are my family. I'd do anything for you."

"Right back at you, dude," Sal said, returning the embrace.

"Hey, I've got an idea," Miguel said as he swayed from side to side. "We're like brothers. Let's take an oath that we'll always be brothers and always have each other's backs. Then we seal the deal by branding ourselves. My old man has a scar on his wrist that he got when he was part of a gang. Said it's an American Indian custom… or maybe it was Mexican… I don't remember—"

"Or maybe it was just a dumb-ass idea from some shit-for-brains moron!" Sal replied.

"Maybe. But we should still do it. What do you say?" He looked from Sal to Bobby through bleary eyes.

"You're crazy," said Bobby. "And you're drunk!"

"Stop being a pussy, Bobby. C'mon, Sal. I'll go first." He pulled out his hunting knife and set the blade in the fire. He squatted down and stared at the blade. "How about the back of our hands?" Sal and Bobby exchanged glances, Sal looking bemused and Bobby looking worried.

After several minutes, Miguel rose and staggered to the tent, emerging with a spare sweatshirt that he dragged along the ground behind him. He knelt by the fire and moved the knife away from the embers with a stick. Then he wrapped the sweatshirt around his right hand and in one quick motion picked up the knife with his wrapped hand and pressed the blade against the back of his left hand. He screamed as it seared his flesh. "Ahhhhhh! Son of a bitch!" he sprang up and began hopping up and down, yelling and swearing at the top of his lungs as he bent over and held his burned left hand under his right armpit.

Bobby's eyes grew wide as he watched Sal retrieve the knife and set it back in the fire. "Don't do it!" Bobby said. "Are you crazy?"

Miguel approached and handed Sal the sweatshirt. "Shiiiiittttt!!!" Sal screamed, flinging the knife into the ground after repeating the routine Miguel had just demonstrated. He held his hand stiffly away from his body, huffing and puffing to keep himself from further screaming. Miguel sidled up next to him and they both looked down at Bobby, who was staring back, mouth agape. "Your turn, amigo," Miguel said through clenched teeth.

"Hey, I never agreed to this," Bobby protested. "This is nuts! How would I explain this to my parents?"

"It's just a straight line down the back of your hand," said Sal, trying unsuccessfully to keep from wincing. "There's no design or shape to it so it won't look like some kind of gang thing. You can tell them you accidentally burned yourself tending the campfire. C'mon, we're counting on you, man!"

Bobby had watched each of his friends as they went through the ritual. They had held the blade to their flesh for what seemed like an awfully long time. He picked up the knife and thrust the blade back into the glowing embers of the campfire. He didn't wait long. He grabbed the dirty sweatshirt, wrapped his right hand to prevent burning it on the handle and made a slashing motion with the knife against the back of his left hand, intending to minimize the time of contact. Then he felt the most intense, searing pain he had ever felt. He dropped the knife and bellowed in pain. He ran in circles around the campfire, shaking his hand furiously. Out of the corner of his eye, he saw Miguel and Sal laughing and giving each other a high five.

Bobby pulled a small flashlight out of his pocket and directed the beam toward the back of his balled up left fist. Miguel and Sal thrust their fists under the light as well. Each fist showed a nearly identical angry red welt extending approximately two inches straight up the back of their hands toward their fingers.

"Brothers for life," said Sal. He stood between the other two and draped an arm around the shoulder of each friend.

"Amen," said Miguel. Then he turned and looked at Sal through half-closed eyes. "I didn't mean to dis your old man," he said. "I would never do that. I just want you to be careful and know what you're dealing with, that's all."

Sal pushed Miguel back, hands on his shoulders. "I get it man. We're cool," said Sal. "And you know what? I am going to check it out. We do what we must, my old man always says. And that's what I need to do. I'm going to figure out exactly where the old boy goes and what he does. I've got a plan."

"You do that," said Miguel. He flopped down and crawled on all fours into the tent.

Chapter 10

IT WAS DARKER than normal for mid-afternoon on a Saturday in Our Lady of Guadalupe Church, as storm clouds muted the light penetrating the stained-glass windows. Antonio Rios walked into the back pew, knelt down and bowed his head as he made the sign of the cross. From that position, he scanned the church and could see that he was alone.

Along the side wall of the church, between the murals depicting the Stations of the Cross, was the confessional: three large doors of dark stained wood, the middle intended for the priest, and the chambers on either side intended for parishioners coming to confess their sins. The red light above the priest's door was illuminated to indicate that the small chamber was occupied. The green lights above the other doors were dark, indicating those confessionals were empty, which was not surprising given that confessions were normally heard later in the afternoon.

Rios entered the chamber to the right of the priest's chamber. He knelt on the worn-out leather kneeler and waited for the opaque partition to slide open, permitting conversation but not sight between the two souls in the dimly lit and cramped quarters.

"Have you come to confess your sins?" Rios heard the voice whisper.

"I told you never to come to this town!" Rios hissed. "This is *not* OK. What's so urgent that we have to speak here and now?"

"I needed to meet with you before Friday," Francisco Vargas replied. "We are both busy men with demanding travel schedules between now and then, so it had to be here."

"Why not communicate by cell phone like everyone else?" Rios snapped, making no effort to conceal his irritation.

"You know how El Jefe feels about that. You never know if someone's listening. Anyway, he needs you to take care of some business next weekend."

"Where? I plan to be in McAllen on Friday for my son's football game. I've missed every game this season so far and I don't want to miss another."

"That should work out perfectly. The business happens to be in that neck of the woods."

"Tell me what I need to know."

"Mr. Arroyo is making preparations for a major transaction. He has a large supply of weapons that he needs to get across the border to his people in Mexico."

"How does that involve us? Arroyo knows how to get things across the border. He does it all the time. I'm sure he's got the right people on his payroll. Let them deal with it."

"El Jefe made certain assurances to Mr. Arroyo. He wants to be sure we live up to those assurances."

"C'mon, Vargas, you know how hot this issue is. Ever since that big cache of weapons made its way from the ATF to the drug cartels, this has been a dicey business—way too risky. Too high-profile."

"Believe me, El Jefe is well aware of that. He doesn't want us anywhere near the ground floor of this operation. We need to stay above the fray. No contact whatsoever with anyone on the front lines of The Border Patrol, ATF, Mexican customs, or the local authorities. He just wants you to go up the chain to our high-level contacts to make sure we can rely on our connections and that Arroyo's team won't have any trouble."

"Well, we can probably count on our friends at the Sheriff's office to look the other way. Mexican customs should be no trouble either. But ATF and the US Border Patrol are pretty tight, and they have some new players who might be the gung-ho type. And they're still livid about being embarrassed when the whole world found out about their weapons making their way to the Mexican gangsters."

"Yeah, but that was two years ago," said Vargas. "They've tightened up their procedures, so stealing weapons from them now would be like trying to get gold out of Fort Knox. At least that's what they think. What they don't know is that only half the weapons made it out of the country. Arroyo has the rest. It's a big shipment and he wants to get it across now while their guard is down. This would be very high-profile if it blows up. El Jefe doesn't want to see that happen. Arroyo is paying handsomely for us to grease the skids at the higher levels."

Rios was silent for a long time. From inside the tiny box, he could hear the rumble of thunder in the distance. "You tell El Jefe that I will follow orders, as I always do. But I want you to tell him that this is a bad idea—in my professional opinion—based on what I know about the climate here on that issue. I know Mr. Arroyo can be a useful ally in some ways, but this is not the right mission for us."

"I will convey that to El Jefe, word for word. Unless you hear otherwise, you will proceed to feel out our highest-level contacts in McAllen. It is imperative that these discussions happen no later than next weekend." The soft scratchy sound of wood sliding against wood could be heard as the partition abruptly shut.

The church was utterly silent except for the pattering of rain on the roof. Sal's legs were aching from crouching in the last row of pews in the balcony at the rear of the church. That spot offered a perfect vantage point. He watched his father exit the confessional and walk to the front of the church. He genuflected before the alter and made his way to the side exit, dipping his fingers in holy water and making the sign of the cross as he exited.

Sal remained motionless, his eyes transfixed on the confessional. Five minutes passed. Then ten. Then fifteen, and the door opened silently. A head peered out and surveyed the church quickly before the man emerged. It was not Father Paul. In fact, there was nothing about the man's attire to suggest he was a priest of any kind. The lanky figure moved quickly toward the rear exit, shooting a glance up at the balcony. Sal gasped audibly at the sight of the scary-looking face and quickly covered his mouth with his hands. The figure stopped in his tracks and looked hard at the balcony. He turned his head quickly and hastened out of the church as Father Paul walked through the side entrance.

Chapter 11

IT HAD BEEN two weeks since his chance meeting with Jenny Sanchez. Bobby found that no matter what he was doing, his thoughts kept drifting back to her. He was enthralled by everything about her: her sunny disposition, her confident demeanor, her big laugh, and that strikingly pretty face that was made even more alluring by the nerdy glasses and those turquoise-colored eyes. He had been captivated from the moment he saw her and had thoroughly enjoyed the brief time they had spent together—right up until he had failed to stand up to Miguel while he was slinging insults at her. He was angry with himself and fearful that Jenny might be angry and disappointed with him as well.

He desperately wanted to see her again, but just couldn't find a natural way to make it happen. He thought about walking past her school after dismissal time with the hope of running into her. He could play it cool and act like he just happened to be passing by. Maybe he could walk her home. The problem with that plan was that he had football practice every afternoon. He might be able to make up some excuse for missing practice, but that wouldn't sit well with the coach.

He thought about riding his bike past her home and hoping he would see her. He could act like he was looking for Miguel. That was problematic, too. Afternoons were taken up with football, and riding by in the evening after dark might seem creepy. More importantly, Miguel had made it abundantly clear that he did not want his friends coming around his house. It was a shabby old home in the poorest part of town and Miguel was clearly self-conscious about it, so Bobby needed to respect his wishes.

He could call, if he had her phone number. He got as far as calling directory assistance, but there was no listing. Anyway, there was always the risk that Miguel would answer the phone, which could make for an awkward conversation.

So he was stuck. He had no plan and that had him feeling discouraged and distracted.

"Did you hear what I just said, Bobby?" his mother asked as he was staring at his biology book at the kitchen table while she was putting away the dinner dishes.

"Sorry, Mom. Guess I was concentrating on my homework."

"I said, guess who I saw at Mass this morning?"

"No clue."

"Your little friend, Jenny. Miguel's sister."

"You did?" Bobby replied, dropping his highlighter and feeling a bit embarrassed because he knew he sounded much too interested.

"Yes, I did. She came right up and said hello to me afterwards. She told me she goes to Mass almost every day before school. She's such a nice girl."

"Uh… yeah… I guess so." He slammed his book shut. "I think I'll take a little walk to clear my ahead a bit. Be back soon."

He walked out the kitchen door, feeling a surge of hope. He walked quickly, staring straight ahead but focusing on nothing. He used to go to Mass every Sunday with his parents, but once they both started working the weekend shift a couple of years back, he just stopped going. It was Thursday. He couldn't go tomorrow morning. That would look too obvious. But he could go on Sunday.

He arrived at church early on Sunday morning to stake out just the right spot. He seated himself in the front row of the church's balcony, an ideal spot to watch all of the Sunday worshipers as they wandered in. By 9:55, a good-sized crowd had arrived there, filling most of the pews. From his perch, Bobby had a clear view of the entire congregation. The organ music began promptly at 10:00. His heart sank. She wasn't there.

The hymn concluded, and Father Paul welcomed his flock. Bobby's eyes were drawn away from the priest as he saw three people briskly walking across the back of the church, trying to remain inconspicuous as they slid into the last pew. It was Jenny, her mother, and her younger brother, Enrique, who was just a toddler.

Bobby spent the rest of the Mass oblivious to what was going on around him as he tried to gather his thoughts and decide how to approach her and what to say. As the recessional hymn began, Bobby watched Jenny and her family closely, trying to time his exit so that she would have to cross his path. He waited until he saw them move out of the pew, then he bolted down the stairs. He raced out of the church and then turned around on the front stairs facing the exiting throng, knowing she would have to walk past him.

"Hi Bobby!" She saw him before he saw her. He looked through the crowd and saw her waving at him, smiling brightly. The glasses were gone, and she looked even prettier than before.

"Uh... hi," he mumbled as she approached him.

"I was beginning to think I'd never see you again. You look really nice today."

She was standing right in front of him, looking radiant and happy.

Bobby's eyes met hers for an instant, then he cast them downward and cleared his throat. "Uh, thanks. You do, too."

She stood there for a few seconds as if waiting for him to say something more. Words eluded him.

"Well, maybe I'll see you next time. I better go," she said, nodding toward her mother and brother. "Bye," she called out over her shoulder as she hastened to catch up with them.

Bobby silently cursed at himself for an instant and then hurried after her. "Jenny! Wait!"

She stopped and turned. She looked at him with that same bright expression, her head cocked slightly, her eyes friendly but curious.

Bobby faced her and let out a deep breath. "Hey, do you still want to take a hike out in The Brush sometime? If you don't, it's no big deal, but you mentioned it before, so I thought I'd ask."

"That sounds great! I'd love to. When?"

"Well, my week is really full, with football practice and all, but we could do it on a weekend. I could even do it today if that works for you. If not—"

Her big eyes grew even wider. "That would be awesome! Just tell me when."

"How about if we meet at the trailhead at two o'clock?"

"Perfect! See you there!"

Bobby arrived at the trailhead early and watched as Jenny rode up on the rusty old Schwinn, wearing the thick glasses she had worn when they first met. He sensed that she was oblivious to whether the bike or the eyeglasses were unflattering. He also sensed that she was oblivious to how pretty she was—with or without the goofy glasses. Either she didn't know or just didn't care, or both.

They laid down their bicycles behind some bushes about 50 yards from the road. Bobby then led her down the main pathway toward The Hill, explaining the terrain, and the various points of interest in all directions.

"It's so barren, as far as the eye can see," she said as she surveyed the vast expanse from the top of The Hill.

"I don't think of it as barren," Bobby replied. "There's all kinds of life out here, if you look close enough. From a distance, all you see is sage brush and some gnarly mesquite trees and cactuses. But look at it up close. There are tons of different plants. And you should see it after it rains… especially in the spring. All kinds of colorful flowers just explode out of the ground. I love this place! I think it's beautiful."

"That's because you're an artist, Bobby. You see things that most people don't see."

Bobby shrugged his shoulders. "I don't know about that, but I love coming out here and being by myself. I can come here and think, or draw, and I never feel lonely."

She gave him a playful push in the shoulder. "So, do you want me to leave?"

"No, no, no. That's not what I meant. Sorry. I'm really glad you're here." He looked directly at her as he spoke, no longer feeling flustered. "I like the solitude here, but I also like showing it to others, especially people who haven't been out here before."

They veered off the main trail and headed southeast. "This terrain gets a little rougher, but I like it," Bobby explained. "I've never seen anyone else out this way. See these dried-up creek beds? You can hike along them for hours, except when it rains. Then they fill up in a hurry, and it's really something to see. If there's enough rain, there are some natural pools that form around here. They get deep enough for swimming. We'll have to come back here after a good rain."

"That would be great! I'd love to."

They hiked along the creek bed for a while, where the world seemed utterly silent except for the sound of their shoes crunching against the rocks and gravel beneath them. After a while, Jenny broke the silence. "I can see why you like this place," she said. "Thanks for bringing me out here."

"You're welcome. I'm glad you came. After your last trip out here, I wasn't sure you'd be interested."

She shot him a quizzical look. "What do you mean?"

"Well, after we found Miguel… and after what happened there… you seemed upset. I thought you might be mad at me."

"Why would I be mad at you? You were nice enough to help me find my brother. It wasn't your fault that he acted like a jerk when we found him. I was glad you didn't join in when he started mocking me, like most of his friends do."

Bobby stopped walking and stared at the horizon. "Does he always treat you that way?"

Jenny nodded quietly as a look of sadness darkened her countenance. "Pretty much. Miguel just seems angry all the time and he lashes out at people. Mostly me. He's always been that way, but it got worse after our father left."

"Sorry to hear that. Maybe I can talk to him," Bobby said.

"I'm not sure that would do any good. He'll probably just turn on you."

"I'm going to talk to him," Bobby said resolutely. "I'm a pretty good talker. I can handle it."

She gave his hand a quick squeeze. "Thanks, Bobby. That's sweet of you. But good luck! He can be a tough customer."

Bobby turned toward the west and nodded at the sun, which was getting low. "We'd better make tracks. Not much daylight left."

They walked back the way they had come and picked up their bicycles. Bobby rode her home, not caring if Miguel saw them together. Fortunately, he was nowhere in sight, so they were spared that encounter.

"Thanks, Bobby. That was fun," Jenny said outside the gate to her backyard, looking as if she really meant it.

Bobby hesitated, trying to summon up his courage. "How about same time next weekend?"

She smiled and nodded. "OK. See you then."

***

The next week seemed like an eternity. All of Bobby's waking moments were consumed with thoughts and visions of Jenny. He found himself daydreaming at school. He was distracted at football practice. At home, he spent most of his time in his bedroom, listening to music on his headphones, imagining what might come next with the pretty young thing with those hypnotizing eyes. When they were together, he was drawn to those eyes and longed to keep staring into them, but he could only do so for a few seconds at a time before self-consciousness forced him to look away. But the turquoise eyes surrounded by the long, thick eyelashes were etched in his memory and he held them in his mind's eye throughout the week. Visualizing her face and hearing her voice left him feeling hopeful and excited, but also unfulfilled.

They met at the same spot the following Sunday. This time, Jenny was waiting for him, even though he arrived fifteen minutes early.

"I brought us some lunch," Bobby announced, holding up a backpack. "We can have a picnic on The Hill before we start our hike."

When they reached the top of The Hill, Bobby unrolled the colorful Mexican blanket that was strapped to his backpack and spread it on the ground, next to the old mesquite log that served as their bench. Then he unzipped his pack and dumped out the contents: two ham and cheese sandwiches, potato chips, apples, water bottles and a bag of granola. They ate their lunch at a leisurely pace, then Bobby neatly stuffed the trash into his backpack and they set out in a northeasterly direction. The conversation came even easier than it had the week before. Bobby provided a running commentary on various sights they came across, but mostly their conversation was about other things. It meandered smoothly and effortlessly. They talked about their families, friends, school, football, drawing and a host of other topics. Bobby relished every moment of it. He didn't want the afternoon to end. Apparently, she didn't either. The sun hit the horizon, and they were still in The Brush, heading toward the trailhead but walking slowly. Jenny slid her delicate hand into Bobby's big paw and they walked hand-in-hand back to their bicycles.

Bobby rode her home. Again, they took their time, and again Miguel was nowhere in sight when they arrived. Jenny stuck her head inside the door. "Mom, I'm home," she called out. "I'll be there in just a few minutes."

"Hurry up, young lady. We already finished dinner and it's a school night!"

She returned to Bobby and they stood outside her back gate, which kept them mostly concealed from prying eyes inside the house, but not entirely. Bobby looked toward the kitchen door and could see Mrs. Sanchez peering at them through the curtain she had pulled aside. The curtain closed quickly.

Jenny faced Bobby and held both of his hands in hers. "I had a wonderful day, Bobby. Thanks. Can we do it again sometime soon?"

Bobby stared at her blankly. He had barely heard her. His mind was racing.

"Bobby? Come back—it looks like you spaced out on me. Can we do it again next week?"

"Uh… yeah… sure… sounds good."

He heard the door open and saw Mrs. Sanchez stick her head out. "Jenny! Time to come in."

"OK, Mom. Be right there." The door closed. Jenny didn't budge. "Well, I guess I better be going," she said. She was staring directly at Bobby and made no move to leave.

Bobby stared back at her, thinking she looked sweeter and prettier than ever. He looked away quickly. "Yeah, let's try next week. I'll take you out to the dried-up lake. I usually see more critters around there than anywhere else. I've seen elk there, javelina pigs, even saw a bobcat there once—"

The door opened again. "Jenny! Now!"

Jenny looked over her shoulder. "I better go." She looked down, gave Bobby's hands a firm squeeze and started to turn away.

Bobby felt panic setting in. He held onto her hands and pulled her toward him. "Wait! Jenny—I… uh… um… Will you be my girlfriend?" he blurted out. It sounded ridiculously awkward to his own ears.

She looked up at him, face beaming, her head nodding. Then she threw her arms around him and kissed him hard on the lips. He held her close. He heard the back door open and then close again, but no shout this time. He had no concept of time, but the kiss seemed to last a long time. He didn't want it to end.

The door opened again. "I gotta go," she whispered and turned away. "Coming, Mom!" she called out preemptively.

Bobby stood frozen in his tracks, gaping at her as she opened the gate and stepped inside. Then she abruptly turned around and ran back toward him. She flung her arms around his neck and kissed him again, quickly this time and then put her lips to his ear. "You're cool," she whispered. And then she was gone.

Chapter 12

LIKE MANY SMALL-TOWN schools, San Mateo High School faced a constant challenge when it came to fielding a decent football team. Simple math and probabilities were the problem. With a total student body of about 400, that meant approximately 200 boys. With such a small pool to draw from, the number of talented, or even capable, athletes tended to be small. In addition, given the significant drop-out rate among upperclassmen, freshmen made up over one-third of the male student body population. Most of those freshmen were undersized compared with upperclassmen and had never played a down of organized football, since there was no such thing for pre-high schoolers in San Mateo. It took them most of the season to learn the playbook and understand their position. Nevertheless, this was Texas, where even small towns were crazy about football, and San Mateo was no exception.

Bobby Rivera and Sal Rios had started every game of the season as freshmen. Bobby's size was an asset, even though his skill and speed were marginal. Coach Garza knew that he had to provide his younger players with experience that would enable them to be real contributors by the time they were juniors and seniors. Bobby fit into that category and played on the offensive line. Sal Rios was a rare treasure—a truly gifted athlete, blessed with blazing speed, remarkable agility and decent size for a freshman. Even more impressive was the smoldering intensity that he brought to the field with every game and every practice. He was a quick learner, who soon became the team's starting running back, and got better with every game. Bobby nicknamed him "Rocket" because of his speed, and the name caught on.

It was early November and the regular season had just concluded. Although the San Mateo Wildcats had gotten off to a slow start, they finished the season strong as their offense grew increasingly potent with each game. The speedy freshman running back had made their team a force to be reckoned with as the regional playoffs approached. The Wildcats would be traveling to McAllen Friday night to face Eastlake High in the first round.

Practices during the past week had been long and intense. It was Wednesday, just two days before the big game. Sal had begun playing linebacker at practices in addition to running back. The sound of him exploding into opposing runners with vicious tackles rang out across the practice field time after time, until the coach had to ask him to dial it back to avoid maiming his own teammates.

"Hey, Rivera! Rios! Over here!" Coach Garza barked as Bobby and Sal trudged off the field after the grueling workout.

Bobby and Sal trotted obediently over to the corpulent coach with the bellowing voice. Miguel followed at a distance. "Rios—I guess violence just comes naturally to you, doesn't it, son? You almost killed a couple of our guys out there today. You're playing both ways on Friday night—outside linebacker on defense."

"Yes, sir!"

"And Rivera—you, too. Both ways. Eastlake has a huge offensive line and I need our biggest and strongest up there against them. You up for that?"

"You bet, Coach. I can handle it."

The Coach took a step forward and grabbed a fistful of Bobby's jersey. He narrowed his eyes and pulled at Bobby's collar. "I don't need any gentle giants out there. I need brutes! Mean, tough, nasty brutes, like this guy here." He cocked his head toward Sal. "Got it, Seventy-Seven?" he asked, referring to the number on Bobby's jersey.

"Yes, sir!"

"Hey, what about me, Coach?" asked Miguel, stepping forward and joining the group. "Put me in there Friday night. I'm ready."

Garza shot Miguel an irritated look. "No you're not, Sanchez."

"Aw, c'mon, Coach. I've been on the bench all year. I can knock the crap out of those Eastlake guys. I deserve a shot."

"You don't deserve shit, Sanchez. You're a pain in the ass with our coaches. You pick fights with your own teammates. You need to take that giant chip on your shoulder and channel it into aggression on the field— aggression *plus* focus and discipline. You work on that, and you work on your attitude, and we'll see."

Miguel glared at the coach in silent defiance and then shuffled off toward the locker room.

***

Antonio Rios had arranged meetings in Brownsville and McAllen that were scheduled to consume most of the day on Friday. He met with his contacts at the Sheriff's Office in each city. He met with several local politicians and community leaders. He met with his INS contacts and he met separately with both Mexican and U.S. customs officials on the U.S. side of the border. The agenda and approach were the same. His spiel was essentially that he and his company were making plans to expand their business and establish new operations on the American side of the border. He told them he had convened these meetings because Mr. Carlos Calderon and his company greatly valued the longstanding relationships they had with these local officials and therefore wanted to keep them apprised of their expansion plans. He told them he was excited to report that these plans would likely result in the creation of numerous jobs in Brownsville and McAllen. There would be the usual trans-border types of issues that they would have to work through, including transporting inventory and materials across the border in both directions, as well as visa issues.

The storyline was mostly true. The burgeoning Calderon business organization included agriculture, auto parts, clothing and shoe man-ufacturing, and the Calderon brothers had a voracious appetite for acquiring other business enterprises. The State of Texas, with its massive population and relative affluence, was a natural market for competitively priced goods from south of the border. For those entrepreneurs with the capital, business savvy and the right contacts, there were real opportunities to establish business enterprises on the Texas side of the border, creating good American jobs. That was unquestionably a goal of the growing Calderon conglomerate. Just as importantly, these business activities would provide a respectable-looking cover for important people and plans.

Today's conversations were all about keeping the right relationships intact as well as nurturing and assessing those relationships. The talk about business expansion plans was primarily a vehicle for accomplishing those objectives and all the experienced players understood the code. As for the Arroyo operation, Rios knew that any necessary contacts would have been made by Arroyo's people, and that if there were any potential problems, Rios would learn about them during his meetings. Not a word or signal about that operation surfaced in any of his conversations.

Rios looked at his watch as he pulled into the parking lot of the U.S. Border Patrol in McAllen. It was 3:00, which would give him ample time to finish up and grab a quick dinner before heading to his son's football game at 7:00. So far, the day had gone smoothly, as he had expected. The only source of the knot in his stomach was this final meeting of the day with Brad Hanson, who had been Captain of the Border Patrol Station in McAllen for the past 12 years. Rios was not worried about Hanson himself, who was clearly a lazy bureaucrat focused on positioning himself for a comfortable retirement. The Calderon organization had worked with Hanson for over five years. They had an understanding and the relationship worked very nicely.

The source of concern was that Hanson had just informed Rios that his retirement was now imminent and wanted to take this opportunity to introduce Rios to his successor. Hanson had assured Rios that he would like his replacement, which Rios translated as a coded message confirming that it would be business as usual and that he would have no trouble working with the new guy. Still, it was a surprise, and it was an unknown, and the timing was bad, given the impending Arroyo transaction.

Hanson met Rios in the reception area with a hearty handshake and wide smile. The normally dour Border Patrol officer seemed uncharacteristically upbeat. "Nice to see you again, Mr. Rios. This may be our farewell meeting. As I mentioned on the phone, I'm retiring soon. Actually, sooner than I thought—it was supposed to be six months off, but they just told me yesterday I can pack it in after next week and still get paid for the next six months. So I'll be out of here next week. Moving to Florida."

"Congratulations. I'm happy for you," Rios said, trying to sound sincere.

"C'mon back to my office. We can talk there." Rios followed behind, noticing that even Hanson's gait seemed light-footed and carefree compared to the lumbering stroll Rios remembered. Hanson led them past the reception desk, swiped his ID against a magnetic card reader and walked through an opaque-glass door into the bowels of the old building.

Hanson's office door was open. Leaning against the wooden credenza behind the messy desk was a uniformed officer with the bulky physique of a former weightlifter who had clearly given up on the regular training and discipline that serious body-building required. His arms and legs bulged through his uniform, but so did a large belly. His sandy hair was cropped short, and he had the bearing of a military man but for the bloodshot eyes and a face that appeared splotchy and bloated for a man that couldn't have been more than forty. "Dan Lang," he said, standing erectly and reaching out his hand. "Brad has told me all about you."

Rios nodded and shook the beefy hand. "Antonio Rios," he said. On his first trip to McAllen to meet Hanson a couple of months ago, Rios had felt a bit of ironic pleasure from the warm hospitality and respect extended to him from the U.S. Border Patrol, given his absolute lack of any right or legitimate credentials justifying his presence on this side of the border. Now, he felt a twinge of nervousness in those surroundings. His bogus documents seemed foolproof, but they had never been put to the test.

Hanson closed the door and motioned to a small circular conference table. Rios sat between the two men and looked from one to the other. "As I mentioned to Brad previously, I really don't have any specific agenda," he said. "But now that we have a changing of the guard here with you, Mr. Lang, I'd like to tell you a little bit about who I am and why I'm here. My company is a conglomerate based in Mexico. We are in a number of businesses, including farming, ranching, manufacturing and several retail businesses. We've always made it a priority to maintain good relationships and good communication with important public officials in South Texas and to keep you apprised of anything significant going on in our company. Also, we want to be good corporate citizens, so if there are things we can do for the community, we want you to feel free to call on us. So I just wanted to check in with you to keep the communication lines open and tell you a bit about some expansion plans we have coming down the pike." Rios then went into his spiel about the new businesses they would be bringing into the area over the next few years.

Hanson stared down at the table, slouching in his chair while doodling absently on a yellow legal pad. His young replacement sat erect, staring intently at Rios, carefully absorbing every word.

"So that's what I wanted to share with you gentlemen," said Rios as he wrapped up his monologue. "Any questions? Or anything you think I should know as we make preparations to proceed with our plans?"

Hanson shoved his legal pad aside and straightened up in his chair. "Mr. Rios, I can assure you that I've shared with Dan here what a good relationship we've had with your organization over the years. I know I can speak for both of us when I say that we truly appreciate that relationship and we look forward to continuing it for many years to come."

"You can count on it, Mr. Rios," added the younger officer, still staring intently at Rios. "I hope the business start-ups you're planning are big successes. We sure could use more jobs around here." He paused and leaned forward toward Rios. "I understand that you also have some business that's much more imminent."

Rios glanced quickly at the senior officer, whose face clouded as he avoided eye contact. "I'm not sure I know what you mean," Rios said, giving Lang a puzzled look.

"I understand that there's an outfit run by a family named Arroyo, and that they're about to launch a new business venture. Imminently."

Rios paused and looked hard at Lang and then at Hanson. "I don't work for the Arroyo family. I couldn't tell you what plans they have." He had tried to sound nonchalant, but the sound of his own voice struck him as brusque and defensive.

"My bad," said Lang casually. "I must have gotten bad information."

"No sweat," said Rios. He stood up. "Thanks for your time, gentlemen. And Brad, I wish you all the best in your retirement."

Rios hurried out of the building, checking his watch. The meeting had lasted only 30 minutes, so he was not at risk of missing the big football game. That was not what was worrying him. He climbed into his pick-up, turned the ignition, then stared straight ahead without moving, both hands gripping the wheel tightly. The Calderon organization had always been able to count on Hanson, and his assurances should mean something. If he had just been dealing with Hanson, he would have concluded that everything was fine—with their relationship and with the Arroyo deal. But he couldn't read the new guy. Why would he bring up the Arroyo deal? Why would he do it in the confines of their office, where prying ears or recording devices could be all around them? Was this guy Lang naïve? Careless? Trying to show off by making it known that he had inside information about the weapons shipment that was about to occur? Was it a warning? Most importantly, was he trustworthy? He clearly did not have enough confidence to reach that conclusion, at least not yet. He would have to arrange another meeting before he left town, but for the next few hours, he would try to clear his head and proudly watch his son play American football for the very first time.

***

Sal and Bobby boarded the team bus immediately after school Friday afternoon and found a seat together. "Where's Miguel?" Bobby asked, glancing at his watch five minutes before their 3:30 departure time.

Sal scanned the faces approaching the bus and shrugged. "No idea. Something must have happened. He's been talking about this road trip all week."

The bus pulled away promptly at 3:30 and began the 90-minute trip to McAllen. Spirits were high, as was the adrenaline and noise level. Eastlake High was a heavy favorite, but San Mateo had been on a roll for the past three weeks and the team was brimming with confidence and bravado. After half an hour or so, Bobby pulled a sketch pad from his duffle bag, ready to tune out the boisterous chatter.

He noticed the bemused grin on Sal's face. "It helps me relax," Bobby explained, flipping to a blank page.

"Hey, we need your mind on the game," Sal chided him. "Draw something related to football."

Bobby pondered the request momentarily and then let his pencil take flight. Sal watched as the pencil moved in quick graceful strokes. Recognizable images soon took shape: three football players in full uniform, the numbers 19, 44 and 77 emblazoned across their jerseys, matching the numbers worn by Miguel, Sal and Bobby. Then the faces appeared, drawn entirely from memory, strikingly accurate and exuding a joyful confidence of young men ready to take on the world.

Sal looked on with admiration. "That's just amazing, man."

"Thanks," Bobby replied quietly, as he stared at his drawing for a long moment, nodding slowly in silent approval. He flipped the page and started another drawing, which he aborted almost immediately. He started another, then quickly gave up. "Enough of that. Time to start focusing on the game. I wonder where Miguel is."

The bus arrived at Eastlake Stadium and the team filed into the visitors' locker room to suit up and listen to the last-minute instructions from their coach. After Coach Garza's final speech had the team sufficiently amped up, he turned them loose and 42 boys raced from the locker room onto the field twenty minutes before game time. The stadium seemed twice the size of San Mateo's and it was packed. The visiting players tried to tune out the crowd and the noise, as well as the band and the cheerleaders, and focus on their warm-ups.

"Hey Seventy-Seven! You got the butterflies?" Sal hollered to Bobby over the din as they stretched.

"I'm scared shitless, Rocket! How about you?"

"I always get the butterflies before the game starts. As soon as I hit somebody, I get over it! Where the hell is Miguel?"

"No idea. I can't believe he missed the team bus."

Sal was scanning the crowd intently. "Don't see my old man, either. He promised he'd be here."

Bobby stopped and studied the crowd. "Look! Is that him?" He pointed to a man outside the fence just behind the visiting team's bench. Sal nodded and trotted off in that direction.

"Papá! Glad you made it!"

Antonio Rios beamed at the sight of his son in uniform. "How could I miss this? State playoffs—this is a big deal! And people tell me you're turning into a great player. I'm—"

The shrill ringing from the mobile phone in his jacket interrupted him. He glanced at the number. "This'll just take a second," he said to his son.

"I'm at my son's football game. I can't talk now,' he said curtly into the phone without any greeting.

"We need to meet." Rios had turned away from his son, but Sal could hear the equally curt voice on the other end of the line.

"I agree," Rios responded. "But I'm at Eastlake Stadium. I can't talk now."

"I'll meet you there later tonight. Two o'clock. Under the bleachers." Sal could hear the line click dead.

The first half was a war. The hitting was intense, and the trash-talking was nonstop. The defenses were dominating. The score was 0 – 0 when San Mateo's speedy freshman, Sal "Rocket" Rios, broke free for an 80-yard touchdown run just before halftime, sending the small but rabid group of San Mateo fans into a frenzy. The team poured into the locker room with a raucous enthusiasm, shouting, pumping their fists in the air, pounding each other on their shoulder pads. Miguel Sanchez was sitting quietly in the corner, pulling his jersey over his shoulder pads. Coach Garza walked down the line of players, shouting encouragement. He stopped briefly when he came to Miguel, lowered his hoarse voice and said gruffly, "Don't bother suiting up, Sanchez. You're on the bench." Then he gathered the team around him and rattled off a list of marching orders for the second half.

The rest of the game was all San Mateo. Rocket Rios had found his groove. He juked and muscled and simply outran everyone on the field as he racked up three more touchdowns. Antonio Rios cheered wildly with the rest of the San Mateo faithful, brimming with a father's pride at seeing his son excel on the football field. But he felt more than that. On and off the field, he watched his son cheered on and embraced by his teammates, coaches and classmates. Antonio Rios felt a profound sense of joy and satisfaction seeing his son fitting in so perfectly as a teenager in America.

After escaping the throngs that were mobbing him after the game, Sal raced toward the bleachers, scouring the faces. He saw his father approaching him, waving wildly. "Sal! Over here! You were amazing! What a game! Great job!" Rios embraced his sweaty son. "Can't wait for next week's game!" he shouted over the cheering crowd.

They sat down in the bleachers together and relived the game's highlights. After most of the crowd had filed out, Sal said, "I need to hit the showers and change. Any chance I could stay with you tonight instead of going to the hotel with the team?"

"Sal—after a game like tonight, you belong with your teammates. Besides, I have some business very early in the morning, so you better stay with the team and catch the bus back. I'll see you at home tomorrow."

The celebration parties would occur the next night, back in San Mateo. The post-game celebration Friday night would be tame and brief. It was being chaperoned by several coaches and parents, and a 12:00 curfew had been imposed. The team was scattered around the pool, the lobby and the breakfast area at their budget hotel. As the crowd began dispersing just before midnight, Sal approached Bobby and Miguel and silently motioned to the pool area with a sideways nod of his head. They pulled two chaise lounges together, Miguel and Bobby sitting side-by-side on one, Sal facing them on the other.

"You guys up for a little adventure later tonight?" Sal asked.

"Always!" Miguel replied.

"What kind of adventure?" Bobby asked, his expression quickly turning from cheerful to worried. He glanced at his watch. "We've got a 12:00 curfew. That's five minutes from now."

"My old man is in town," said Sal. "I just found out that he's got some business tonight at 2:00 a.m. I'm going to sneak out and see what that's all about."

"I'm in!" said Miguel without hesitation. "I've got a car too. Had to borrow one to get here for the game."

"I don't know about this," said Bobby. "If we get caught we're screwed. We'd probably be benched for the next game."

"They're not going to bench you two," said Miguel. "They need you. Don't be a wus, Bobby. Your parents are 80 miles away."

"Where'd you get a car?" Bobby asked. "Do you even have a license?"

"Hey, I just turned 16. I'm old enough to drive. If I get stopped, I'll have bigger problems than not having a license!"

"Yeah, like where the car came from for starters," Bobby shot back. He looked at Sal. "Your old man's not going to like it if he catches you spying on him. This sounds like a bad idea."

"Suit yourself," said Sal. "Who knows when I'll have another chance like this? You in, Miguel?"

"Definitely. What time?"

"They're meeting back at the football stadium. Let's leave here around 12:45. That'll give us plenty of time to scout it out and find the right spot."

Miguel pulled a set of car keys from his pocket and jingled them in Sal's face. "It's the black Camaro."

Sal nodded approvingly, then looked at Bobby. "Hey, good game tonight, Seventy-Seven. Get some rest. We'll see you in the morning."

Miguel and Sal slipped out the back door of the hotel promptly at 12:45, avoiding the lobby. All was quiet. They drove toward Eastlake High and parked on a residential street about three blocks from the school. They darted across the dark soccer field toward the football stadium, avoiding the stadium's parking lot. The lights around the periphery cast a dim glow over the lot, but the stadium itself was dark.

"This way," Sal whispered, pointing toward the visitors-side bleachers. There were three concrete structures supporting the bleachers—a wall at either end and a square building in the center housing the public restrooms, with doors facing the parking lot. Sal pulled at the men's room door.

"Locked," he said. "That's what I expected. Not a problem."

They made their way under the bleachers to an opaque window about four feet off the ground. It was open just a crack, imperceptible to anyone who was not closely examining it. Sal pulled upward, and the rusty window creaked against the frame as it slid open.

"I left it open just a crack before we left today," Sal explained.

Like experienced burglars, they silently and gracefully hoisted themselves up and through the opening and closed the window behind them, leaving just enough of a crack to see through without being conspicuous. Then they did the same with the window on the opposite wall. Sal checked the view from each window. From this vantage point, he could clearly see the entire span underneath the bleachers, which extended for fifty yards in each direction, parallel to the field. If a meeting occurred toward the far end of the bleachers, hearing could be a challenge, but the area was utterly silent, so sound might travel. In any case, he would have a perfect view.

Sal could not make out Miguel's face in the dark room, only his shadowy figure. "I'll take this side, you take the other window," he whispered. "Keep your eyes a few inches away from the crack so no one can see you from the outside."

Miguel shuffled toward the window on the opposite side, groping in the darkness. "Smells like piss in here, man. This is gross."

"Shhhh!" Sal hissed.

The handle of the door moved. They heard the metallic sound of the door handle jiggling and meeting the resistance of the lock. The door shook audibly with the force of someone trying to pull it open. Then they heard the sound of footsteps, hard soled shoes across pavement, walking away from the door and turning along the outside wall of the restroom, stopping just outside and to the right of the window. Sal crouched low. He could feel his heart pounding and he felt himself growing damp with sweat. The figure had emerged out of nowhere. There was not a car in sight. That was unnerving. Then he heard the flick of a cigarette lighter. A few seconds later, the smell of cigarette smoke reached his nostrils. It smelled familiar, even mixed with the overpowering stench of stale urine all around him.

Sal waited for what seemed many minutes. Fifteen perhaps. It could have been 20 or 30. Then he slowly raised his head until he was eye-level with the crack in the window, craning his neck backwards so that it was a good twelve inches from the window and beyond any light that might be streaming in from the outside. He couldn't see whoever was standing just a few feet away from him on the other side of the concrete wall, but he could hear the occasional repositioning of feet and audible exhale of cigarette smoke.

An SUV pulled into the parking lot, perhaps 100 yards away, turning off its lights as it did so. It drove directly toward the bleachers, slowly. As it approached, its lights flashed on, bathing the restroom building in bright light. Sal ducked instinctively. The lights went out after a few seconds, and Sal cautiously raised his head again and watched as another vehicle silently pulled up alongside the SUV. He could see writing in large letters on the door of the SUV. He couldn't make out the words in the darkness, but the emergency vehicle lights on top of the SUV were clearly visible.

Both doors opened and closed simultaneously, and two figures walked directly toward him. The man who emerged from the SUV was big and bulky. He was Anglo, with hair that was cropped short and appeared light in color under the glow of the parking lot lights. He was wearing dark clothes that did not appear to be a uniform of any kind. The other man looked Hispanic, of medium height and build, dark hair slicked back.

"What are we doing here, Lang? And who's he?" Sal froze at the sound of his father's unseen voice. The two strangers stood just ten feet away, directly in front of him, staring just to the right of the window. Miguel inched his way across the floor on all fours until he was side-by-side with Sal.

"You first, Rios," Lang said in a calm voice. "You told me you wanted to talk."

"Not until I know who I'm talking to. Who's he?" Rios demanded.

"This is Mr. Orozco. He's Arroyo's man. We're here to finalize arrangements for this weekend."

"And who the hell is he? And what's he doing here?" Orozco demanded, turning from Rios to Lang.

"This is Mr. Rios. He works for Calderon," said Lang. "So we're all friends here. We're all on the same side. Now what is it that you wanted to talk about, Rios?"

Rios paused and lit another cigarette. "I didn't like the way you spoke when we were with Hanson at your office this afternoon. You were careless. I don't trust careless people. But we can have that discussion another time. Why are we here?"

"As you undoubtedly know, Mr. Arroyo is engaging in a significant transaction," said Lang. "This weekend. I'm here to finalize the details with Mr. Orozco and I'd like a witness. That's why you're here."

"Whatever details you guys need to work out is between the two of you," said Rios sharply. "I don't need to be part of this. I'm out of here." He tossed his cigarette on the ground and started walking toward the parking lot.

"Not so fast, Rios!" Lang commanded. Rios heard the audible click of a firearm and stopped in his tracks. "I need you to stick around."

"What's going on here?" Orozco shouted at Lang.

"Relax, Orozco. This is all for your benefit. You need this thing to go smoothly, right? If not, it's your ass. I'm just trying to be sure I've got you covered. And I need him to be the witness to keep us all out of trouble in case anyone has any issues afterwards. So, with that in mind, tell me exactly when your shipment will reach the border and what kind of vehicle you'll be using."

Rios folded his arms and gave Lang a hostile stare. Orozco looked from one to the other, rubbing his chin.

"OK, we'll be crossing at 8:00 this morning. That's about six hours from now. All the wheels are in motion. We're using a big white produce truck. It says Buena Vista Farms all over it. It has pictures of fruits and vegetables on the sides. Your guys got paid half up front, the other half gets paid 48 hours after we make it across. That was the deal. So why do you need an extra hundred grand advanced from the final payment?"

"Is that a problem for Mr. Arroyo?" asked Lang.

"What do you think?" said Orozco. "He's not happy about it. He expects people to honor their word. But I'm prepared to make payment if you convince me there's a good reason."

"Oh, there's a very good reason," Lang replied. He turned quickly, raising his arm in one smooth motion, pointing his revolver directly at the forehead of Antonio Rios. The shot echoed across the parking lot as Rios hit the ground with a dull thud.

Sal reeled backwards and fell over, then he stumbled to get up, lunging for the door. Miguel tackled him, slapped his hand over Sal's mouth, and pressed his lips against Sal's ear. "Shhh…! Don't make a sound. He'll shoot us too!" Sal stopped squirming. He held his head with both hands. He was panting, gasping for breath, but struggling to stay quiet.

"What the fuck!" Orozco gasped.

"That was a loose end that needed tying up," Lang said coolly. "Too many people in the know. I couldn't trust him. Now I need a little help cleaning this up, which is why I need the extra cash right now. You got it with you?"

"Yeah, it's in the car, but are you out of your goddamn mind? That was Calderon's guy. Don't you know who Calderon is?"

"As far as I'm concerned, he's just one more Mexican thug who likes to keep his fingers in our pie. Well, I'm in charge around here now. I don't need him and this will send him a little message."

"You're crazy, man! You don't want to be messing with Calderon. He'll—"

Another shot rang out. The bullet caught Orozco square in the face. Lang stood over the prone body and fired two more shots into his chest.

A uniformed police officer sauntered up to the scene from somewhere outside of the line of sight provided by the bathroom window. "You'll take it from here," Lang said as the two men stared at the bodies and the spreading pools of blood. It was clearly an order and not a request.

"I'm on it, Danny. Just like we discussed. I'll put a few kilos in Orozco's trunk. We'll fill this guy's pockets with some cash. I'll call it in—drug deal gone bad. It'll be an open and shut case."

Lang pulled the car keys from the pocket of Orozco's jacket. He and the cop hurried to the dark sedan. Sal and Miguel could hear a beep as the trunk popped open before the men had reached the car. Lang reached in and pulled out a dark gym bag. Sal and Miguel could see him examining the contents. The cop walked out of their line of sight. A few minutes later, a squad car with its lights off pulled up silently next to Lang. The cop put a duffle bag in the sedan's trunk, then the two men returned to the corpses. Lang pulled several bundles of cash from the gym bag and stuffed them into Rios's pockets. He handed another stack to the cop, who walked back to his car.

Lang stood alone, looking from one corpse to the other. Then he looked up quickly and stared directly at the window. Sal and Miguel ducked their heads. A large shadow blocked most of the small sliver of light that had been making its way into the dark, smelly restroom. They held their breath. The shadow passed and they heard footsteps on the other side of the wall. The door handle jiggled back and forth. Then it was quiet, except for the faint sound of footsteps walking away. They watched Lang climb back into the SUV and drive away.

Chapter 13

BOBBY WAS EXHAUSTED from the exertion of playing every down in a fiercely contested football game. The emotional rollercoaster also had taken its toll—the fear and anxiety before the game and then the relief and jubilation that followed. He found himself pacing in his small hotel room, eyes fixated on the clock.

He had been assigned to room with Miguel. Coach Garza clearly hoped that Bobby would be a positive influence on his wild friend. Now it was nearly 3:00 a.m. and Miguel had not returned. Bobby knew that if Coach learned that Miguel had snuck out and violated curfew, Coach would hold him accountable too. If that happened, his status for the next playoff game could be jeopardized. And, he didn't even want to think about facing his parents.

He tried drawing. That normally relaxed him. After five minutes, he gave up and chucked his sketch pad back into his duffle bag. He couldn't focus. He turned off the light and sat upright in the cheap armchair near the window, feeling like a nervous parent waiting for his wayward teenager to come home.

Just as he began drifting into a fitful doze, the door burst open and his two friends rushed in. Their terror-stricken faces left no doubt that something had gone terribly wrong.

Bobby leapt out of his chair. "What happened?"

"He's dead!" Miguel cried out. "They killed him! Sal's dad—shot him right in the head!"

"What?" Bobby stared open-mouthed at his two friends.

"At the football stadium. We saw it all. Oh, shit, Bobby! Shit, shit, shit!" Miguel paced in a tight circle, gesturing wildly. He glanced toward the windows and seeing that the curtains were open just a crack, he hurried across the cramped room and pulled them tightly shut.

Sal was breathing hard and soaked with sweat. He was shaking all over. His face looked pale and completely blank except for the tears that were welling up in his eyes.

"We need to call the police," Bobby said. "Right now!"

"Hell no! Don't be an idiot, Bobby. We can't call the police," Miguel held his head with both hands as if trying to keep it from exploding.

"Calm down," Bobby urged. "Have a seat. Tell me exactly what happened."

Bobby and Miguel sat on one of the twin beds. Sal didn't budge. He stood transfixed in the middle of the room, staring straight ahead as if in a trance. "Looks like he's in shock," Bobby whispered to Miguel. Bobby stood up and gently put his hand on Sal's shoulder and guided him to a seat on the bed opposite him and Miguel.

Miguel launched into a frenetic description of the evening's events, speaking in rapid-fire fashion, eyes darting around the room, arms flailing. The story was disjointed and incomprehensible in parts, but there was no question about the conclusion: Antonio Rios had been murdered and Sal and Miguel had witnessed the entire horrifying event.

As Miguel concluded his narrative, Sal rolled over on the bed and buried his head face-down in a pillow. His shoulders began shaking as a fit of deep sobs overcame him. Bobby rose from the bed he was sitting on and sat down next to Sal, tears streaming down his own face at the sound of his friend's muffled sobs. "We're here for you, Sal. We'll always be here for you. I'm so sorry about what happened. But we'll help you through this." He put his big hand between Sal's shoulder blades, gently patted his back a few times and then left his hand there until the heaving subsided.

Sal sat up and took several deep, shaky breaths, trying to calm himself. Some semblance of alertness had returned to his tear-soaked face. "I need you to help me figure this out, Bobby. I can't seem to think straight."

"Like I was just telling Miguel, I think we need to call the police."

"No cops!" said Sal, his eyes focusing and his voice clear and firm. "If anyone finds out we were there, they may come after us. Even if the bad guys didn't find out, where would that leave me? An underage orphan with no legal status? They'd put me in a detention facility or send me back to Mexico. So no cops!"

"Maybe we should tell Coach," Bobby suggested. "He can help us figure this out."

"Bad idea," Miguel said." He's a goddamn moron."

"Miguel's right," added Sal quickly. "He'll just tell us we have to go right to the police. And on top of that, he'll probably kick us off the team for breaking curfew."

Miguel got up and resumed his pacing. Bobby and Sal sat opposite one another on the beds, staring at the floor, pondering their options.

After a few minutes of silence, Miguel stopped his pacing. "Hey, let's just get out of Dodge," he said. "We can head back home like nothing ever happened. There's nothing we can do for him here, Sal. That way, Coach doesn't know anything. You're not putting yourself at the mercy of the police or the INS or anybody else."

"Yeah, but then the police might come to San Mateo looking for you—not as a witness but just to inform you as next-of-kin," said Bobby. "Can you imagine all the fuss that would cause? Half the town would be looking over their shoulder."

Miguel shrugged. "Maybe not. Maybe they'll never connect the dots and come looking for Sal."

Sal sat upright on his bed and looked at his friends through clear and determined eyes. "I can't just walk away from this. I need to find out what they know and what they're going to do about this. So here's an idea: We all go to the police station today. We wait until late-morning, then we go there and tell them that we were supposed to have breakfast with my dad this morning and ride home to San Mateo with him, but we're concerned because he didn't show up. They'll break the bad news to me and I'll have to act shocked, but I can find out what they're planning to do."

"What about Coach?" Bobby asked. "What do we tell him? We're supposed to be on the bus at 9:00."

"We tell him the same thing," said Sal. "He saw my dad at the game last night. We'll just leave him a note saying we're meeting him for breakfast and driving home with him."

"Hmmm… I don't know about that," said Bobby, wringing his hands and tapping his foot. "He might get suspicious. I never mentioned this to him yesterday. He's expecting me on the bus. Maybe I should stay on the bus and I can tell him about your plans to spend time with your dad this morning."

"I'd sure like to have you with me when I go see the cops," Sal said.

"Miguel can go with you," Bobby replied. "There's not much I can add there anyway. At least if I'm on the bus, I can deal with Coach and prevent him from getting suspicious."

"Man, I really need you, Bobby! You're good at talking to people. You're quick on your feet. This is my whole world! Please!"

Bobby looked away. He could feel two sets of eyes staring hard at him. Both of his feet were tapping furiously now. He could probably handle Coach Garza, but what would he tell his parents if this spun out of control? What if it subjected his family to scrutiny from the authorities? But Sal was his friend, and his world had just been shattered. Sal *did* need him. The shock and grief from losing his father must be unfathomable. Any anger his parents or the Coach might feel would vanish once they found out about Sal's dad. It should. They *should* understand. He let out a deep breath and turned his eyes toward Sal. The anguish and the urgency in his friend's face put an end to his vacillation. "I'm here for you, Sal. I'll go with you."

"Thanks, pal. I'll never forget this."

***

At 10:00, the boys approached police headquarters in downtown McAllen. Miguel looked around nervously at the sea of police vehicles and uniformed officers in the immediate vicinity. "I'll drop you guys off and go park somewhere," he said.

"There's a parking lot right across the street," Sal pointed to a half-empty lot with a large, *Public Parking* sign in front.

"Too close to all these cops. I don't like driving around here. I don't need someone asking for my license or asking about this car."

"You didn't steal it, did you?" Sal asked.

"No. Like I said before, I borrowed it. I was desperate to get here when I missed the bus so I talked Louie Miranda into loaning me these wheels for the weekend. I'm going to owe him big time."

"Miranda? Isn't he the biggest drug dealer in school?" Bobby asked. "How do you know he didn't steal this car?"

"I don't. That's my point. Hop out. I'll go park somewhere else and catch up with you. Or maybe I'll wait outside."

Sal and Bobby approached the drab old concrete building and noticed several news vans parked in front, large antennas mounted on their roofs and their television station logos splashed across their sides.

"Do you think the press has found out about this?" Bobby asked under his breath.

"Looks like it," Sal replied. They walked up the steps and through the heavy wooden doors into a beehive of activity. Uniformed officers and plainclothes personnel were scurrying about or gathered in small groups, chattering excitedly.

They approached a plump, middle-aged woman in uniform sitting behind a counter. Her name plate read *Padilla*. "We need to report a problem," Bobby said, trying hard not to sound as nervous as he appeared.

"What kind of problem?" she asked, without looking up.

"Missing person," Bobby replied.

"Who's missing? And for how long?"

"It's my father," said Sal. "He was supposed to meet us for breakfast and drive us to San Mateo this morning. He didn't show up. That's not like him. Something's happened. I'm sure of it."

The officer looked up from her paperwork. "Look guys, we're real busy around here today," she said brusquely. "We've got reporters all over the place. We don't consider someone missing until they've been gone for at least 24 hours. I'm sure he'll turn up. If he doesn't, come back tomorrow."

"I'm telling you, something's wrong!" Sal insisted, raising his voice. "We need to talk to someone now!"

Bobby reached an arm across Sal's chest and gently held him back as he stepped forward and looked apologetically at the desk officer, who was about to snap at them. "I'm sorry, ma'am. He hasn't slept all night. Neither have I. I know you're busy, but the fact is, we've got nowhere to go. We were here playing in the football game last night at Eastlake. The team bus is gone already. My friend's dad hasn't shown up. I guess we can hitchhike home if we have to, but we'd sure like to talk to someone before we leave. We can wait."

"You boys play for San Mateo?"

"Yes, ma'am."

"I was there last night, at the game. You sure gave us a beating. What are your names?"

"I'm Bobby Rivera, and my friend here is Sal Rios."

"Rios? You're the kid that scored all those touchdowns against us?"

"Yes, ma'am. Sorry about that," said Sal, following Bobby's lead and trying to adopt a more amiable tone.

"Maybe you're right and there's nothing to worry about," Bobby continued. "We'd just like to talk to someone before we leave town to make sure that you don't have any accident reports or that he's not laid up in a hospital around here."

"OK guys, I'll try to find someone to talk with you. Have a seat over there and we'll get to you as soon as we can. It may be a while, though. Things are kind of crazy around here this morning."

They thanked the officer profusely and made their way toward the grimy old wooden benches in the waiting area. "Nice game last night, fellas," Officer Padilla called out after them. "Good luck next weekend!"

Half a dozen others were scattered around the waiting area, looking nervous, impatient or just plain bored. In stark contrast to those in the waiting area, there was an obvious sense of energy and excitement among the staff and whatever visitors happened to be there in a professional capacity. A group near the door was armed with notepads and small recording devices, looking eagerly at any face that came into view.

An hour passed. Then 90 minutes. Time dragged on as they watched the minutes tick away on the big clock over the reception desk. Just before noon, two men emerged from an interior hallway and began walking across the reception area. Sal sat bolt upright and grabbed Bobby's forearm, squeezing hard.

The throng of reporters swarmed the two men. One was trim, medium height, silver-haired, and dressed in what appeared to be a policeman's uniform bedecked with an array of colorful medals. The other was clad in a different uniform, olive-green shirt and matching cargo pants, sporting a shiny gold badge emblazoned with the words *US Border Patrol*. He was half a head taller, with short sandy hair and a big gut distorting what otherwise would be an impressively muscular frame.

"That's him!" Sal whispered to Bobby. "The guy from last night."

"Are you sure?" asked Bobby.

"Definitely."

The throng of reporters raced toward the two, recorders and notepads in hand.

"Chief Harper, how many men are in custody?" one of them shouted.

"Are they connected with the drug cartels?" yelled another.

"I'll be making a statement in the press room, then we'll take your questions," replied the man in the police uniform.

The Chief of Police led the way into a room behind the reception desk. There were rows of metal folding chairs facing an old wooden podium at the front of the room. A buzzing crowd followed behind him, including the small army of reporters as well as police officers and a handful of men and women wearing the same olive-green uniform the big man was wearing, the words *US Border Patrol* clearly visible on the badges above the breast pocket and on the patches on their left sleeve.

After all had filed in, Sal glanced around to see if anyone was paying attention to them. "Let's go," he said under his breath when it was clear that no one was watching them. With Bobby at his heels, he opened the door just a crack and peered into the packed room, then they silently slipped inside and made their way to the back row.

Chief Harper stood at the podium, with the big man standing just to his right. The chief raised his hand and the chatter in the room abruptly ceased. "I will be making a brief statement and then Deputy Chief Patrol Agent Lang and I will answer whatever questions you may have." He cleared his throat, put on his reading glasses and stared down at the paper he was holding against the podium. "At 8:00 this morning, just this side of the border crossing, The United States Border Patrol, working together with The McAllen Police Department, intercepted a significant shipment of stolen weapons about to be illegally driven into Mexico. We believe that this shipment was being organized by a large and well-known criminal enterprise and is the largest such shipment ever intercepted. This is an extremely important arrest, both because these weapons could have caused untold damage in the hands of the gangsters they were intended for, and because it may help us ferret out the corruption on both sides of the border that has facilitated such endeavors in the past. I would like to publicly recognize and thank Dan Lang of the Border Patrol for being primarily responsible for the intelligence gathering and planning that led to this morning's joint effort between Border Patrol and McAllen PD. Without his efforts, this arrest would not have occurred, and these weapons would have found their way into the wrong hands and caused significant loss of life. It would also have made organized crime south of the border even more powerful and dangerous. Thank you, Dan."

The room broke into applause and cameras clicked as the two men shook hands, then the media types launched a barrage of questions. Sal fumed silently as Lang soaked up the praise and admiration, looking immensely pleased with himself.

"He's working both sides," Sal whispered to Bobby. "One of the guys who showed up at the stadium last night was working with the smugglers. Lang acted like he was on their side, and took a duffle bag full of cash from that guy. Bet he didn't turn that over."

Bobby nodded his head and said nothing, his eyes fixed on the big man holding court from the front of the room. Sal leaned in closer to Bobby so that he wouldn't be overheard. "My dad wasn't part of this! When he realized what was going on, he tried to walk away. That's when this bastard shot him!"

"One last question," the Chief of Police announced.

"What happens next, Agent Lang?" a voice called out.

"What happens next is I'll be celebrating at Sammy's—Happy Hour's going to start a little early today," Lang said, breaking into a loud laugh. "Drinks are on me!"

The audience joined in the laughter and began filing out of the small room. Lang was swarmed by a host of officers offering congratulatory wishes and handshakes.

Sal and Bobby followed the crowd and slid back into their seats in the waiting area, where Desk Sergeant Padilla promptly found them. "Detective Lopez will see you now," she said, her voice sounding noticeably softer than it had earlier. She guided them to an open area filled with cubicles, most of which were occupied, and from which multiple telephone conversations could be heard simultaneously, creating a noisy and hectic atmosphere. Detective Lopez's cubicle was empty, but they found him ensconced in a small conference room at the far end of the work area. Sergeant Padilla introduced the boys to the serious-looking detective and then excused herself.

The detective peered over the wire rims of his glasses. "We don't normally consider someone to be a missing person until they've been missing for at least 24 hours. That is, unless we have evidence that some sort of foul play is involved. Sergeant Padilla gave me some background but I need to hear it first-hand. Why do you believe something's happened to your father?"

"I saw him last night at the game," said Sal. "We were supposed to meet for breakfast and then drive home to San Mateo together this morning. He didn't show up and he hasn't contacted me. That's just not like him. Something must have happened."

The detective slowly rubbed his thick mustache. "Can you give me a physical description?"

"He's about five-eleven, a hundred and eighty pounds, Hispanic, dark hair, dark eyes."

"Any tattoos?"

"Yes. A rattlesnake on his bicep. The left one."

Detective Lopez winced ever so slightly. He laid both palms flat on his desk and exhaled deeply. "Son, I'm afraid I've got some bad news. A man meeting that description was found last night. He'd been killed. It was a homicide. We can't be sure until you've had a look at the body. I really hope it's not him, but you should brace yourself."

Sal had trouble catching his breath. His stomach did a somersault.

His throat went dry. He had been worried about whether he would be able to act surprised, but the shock of last night's events came rushing back upon hearing those words and eliminated any need for acting. "When? Where? What happened?" he stammered.

"We're still investigating, so I'm afraid I don't have any answers for you yet, except that the victim was shot late last night or early this morning at the Eastlake football stadium. There was another victim, too. Any reason your dad might have been out there late last night? Was he with anyone, to your knowledge?"

Sal shook his head and put a hand over his eyes as he sucked in a couple of deep, shaky breaths. "No. It just doesn't make any sense. Is that all you know?"

"It's possible that some sort of drug deal went bad. It's also entirely possible that your father was an innocent victim who just happened to be in the wrong place at the wrong time. But let's not get too far ahead of ourselves. I'll need you to take a look at the body to confirm whether it's him. Are you up to that?"

Sal nodded. "Yes, sir."

The next few hours were a blur. As Detective Lopez escorted the boys out of the police station to go to the county morgue, Miguel ran to join them from across the street. After the short drive to the morgue, Sal made a positive identification of the deceased. The sight of his father under a sheet on a gurney, grey and lifeless, caused Sal to vomit, then he wept quietly for several minutes as his friends made awkward attempts to console him. After leaving the morgue, the detective gently continued his interrogation in the squad car, asking Sal about his father's business, his associates and his reasons for being in McAllen. Sal was unable to provide any useful information.

They drove back to the police station where they waited a long time before meeting with Detective Lopez and another officer, who asked the same questions all over again. When Detective Lopez asked Sal about his family, Sal explained that his mother and sisters were living in Mexico but that he had relatives near San Mateo who he could live with for the time being. All of the boys gave the detective their addresses and phone numbers. He promised Sal that he would be in touch as the investigation progressed. Bobby had called his mother while they were waiting to explain why he had not made it home yet. He shared the horrific news about Sal's father. His parents were shocked and concerned but hesitantly agreed that Bobby should be there for his friend.

It was nearly six o'clock when they left the station, and already dark. "Let's get the hell out of here before they change their minds and decide to keep us here," said Miguel.

"You OK to drive?" Bobby asked. You've been up all night. We all have."

"I'll load up on caffeine before we hit the road. I'll be fine."

"Wait!" Sal ordered. The tears and the shell-shocked look were gone. His face had the determined and intense look it took on during football games. "This is screwed up. I can't just walk away from this."

Miguel looked baffled. "What are you talking about, man? We need to get out of town. Now!"

"Not yet. I need to find this Lang guy."

"Find him? For what?" asked Miguel.

"Look, this guy killed my old man. We both saw it. I want to meet him. He said he'd be drinking at some place called Sammy's. I'm going to find out if he's there. If you don't want to come along, I'll get home on my own. You don't need to wait on me."

"Sal, we're not going to leave you here," said Bobby. "C'mon, Miguel, I guess we better go find Sammy's."

They asked several passers-by for directions to Sammy's until they found one who knew it. It was on the outskirts of downtown, just a few blocks from the Border Patrol Office. They parked directly across the street, which gave them a perfect vantage point. "Bobby, go on in and see if Lang is in there," said Sal. "You look 21."

"Why don't we wait a while," Bobby responded, looking nervous. "We can see if he comes or goes from right here."

"For Chrissakes, Bobby, I don't want to sit here all night if he's not in there," said Miguel. "Just walk around the joint for 30 seconds and see if he's there."

"I don't like this," Bobby muttered as he left the car and hurried across the street. He was back in a matter of minutes. "He's in there.

Drunk out of his mind, too. Practically falling off his barstool. The bartender was trying to get him to leave."

"Now what?" asked Miguel.

"Now we wait," said Sal.

In a matter of minutes, the bulky figure of the Border Patrol agent staggered out the front door, a companion trying to steady him as they walked toward the parking lot. They stood outside a Border Patrol SUV and appeared to be arguing, although they were out of earshot. Lang grabbed the keys the other man was holding, shoved the man away and stumbled into the driver's seat.

"Follow him," Sal ordered. "At a distance."

They drove about ten minutes into a residential area. The SUV turned abruptly into a driveway, knocking over several garbage cans. Lang emerged from the vehicle, picked up the garbage cans and staggered into the house.

"Hey Miguel, you still have that bottle of tequila with you?" Sal asked.

"Yeah. We didn't exactly have time to drink it last night, did we?"

"Give it to me," said Sal.

"It's under your seat. What do you need that for?"

Sal reached underneath the passenger's seat and pulled out a brown paper bag. "I'll be back in a few minutes," said Sal. "Wait here."

Sal proceeded to march up to the front door and rang the bell. No one answered. He pounded hard on the wooden door with his fist. "What d'ya want?" a voice bellowed from within as the door flung open.

Sal stood face to face with the big border patrol agent, who looked both angry and confused. "Who the fuck are you?" slurred Lang, glaring at the young stranger.

Sal hesitated for a moment, saying nothing as he looked directly into the bloodshot eyes. Then he went into linebacker mode and flung himself at Lang, knocking him off his feet with a vicious tackle, slamming the man's head into the wooden stairs as he fell backwards. Sal rose to his feet, quickly surveying his surroundings. He spotted Lang's holster, gun and badge on the small console table just inside the entryway and made a beeline for them as Lang struggled to a sitting position, cursing and howling in pain.

Sal grabbed the gun. "Upstairs!" he ordered.

"Fuck you! What do you want?"

"I just want to talk, that's all," Sal said, pointing the gun directly at Lang's head. "If you answer my questions, maybe I won't shoot you."

"Talk about what?" Even in his drunken state, Lang could see the malice and danger in the young man's eyes.

Sal backed up toward the front door, keeping the gun trained directly on the stunned agent as he reached outside and grabbed the brown paper bag. He slammed the door shut, pulled out the bottle and showed it to Lang. Then he put it on the ground and kicked it toward the big man, keeping his distance. "Have a drink, Lang. This conversation will go better if you're more relaxed."

Lang reached for the bottle from his sitting position on the steps, glanced matter-of-factly at the label, then took a big swallow. "Who the fuck are you? What do you want?"

"Drink some more," Sal instructed.

"Not until—"

"Drink!" Sal commanded, taking a step closer and cocking the pistol.

Lang took a long pull from the bottle, guzzling nearly half the pint.

"Upstairs. Now!" Sal motioned with the gun.

Lang arose unsteadily and clumsily made his way up the stairs, gripping the railing tightly to maintain his balance. He paused to catch his breath at the top of the stairs and stumbled into the master bedroom. Sal followed and ordered Lang into the connecting bathroom.

"Sit there while we talk." Sal pointed to the toilet seat with his pistol. "And fill the bathtub."

Lang did as instructed. His belligerence and hostile demeanor were fading as he swayed back and forth and struggled to keep from passing out.

"Who ordered you to kill those men last night?" Sal asked, his tone sharp, hoping to jolt his prisoner into alertness.

Lang blinked at him several times, trying to grasp the meaning of the question. "Huh? What... you talking 'bout... I don't know what you're talking about," he stammered in a low voice while rocking bath and forth on the toilet seat, staring at the floor.

"You shot two men last night outside the football stadium. Why? Whose idea was that? Who were you working with?"

"No one. Came up with the plan all by myself." He laughed quietly, between hiccups. "I figured I could get a big payment from Arroyo's guy... I could find out the exact plan from him so I could plan the arrest... Then I got rid of him so he couldn't tell no one... Then there was this other guy..." Lang started to nod off.

"What about the other guy?" Sal shouted, getting right in Lang's face.

Lang struggled to focus. "The other guy? Oh, yeah. He knew I was working with the gun runners, so I had to get rid of him, too... Then I could ... make the bust and get the credit. I'd have Arroyo's money and no one would be onto me, except maybe Brad. But he's retiring and he don't want no trouble."

"I'm going to help you sober up, now. Take your clothes off and get in the bathtub."

"What? You some kind of perv? You want to see me butt-ass naked, is that it?"

"Do it! Now!"

***

"He's been in there a long time," said Miguel, looking at his watch. "Maybe we should go check up on him. He could be in trouble."

Bobby looked worried. "Let's wait a little longer."

"I'm tired of waiting," said Miguel. "We need to hit the road. I'll go check it out."

Miguel climbed out of the car and looked around. Seeing no one, he trotted from the car to the house and crept around the first floor, looking through the windows. He was able to get a good look at the first floor and saw no one. He opened the door, cautiously looked around, and then stepped inside. He stood motionless for several moments, listening. There was a voice coming from the second floor. It sounded like Sal's. He tiptoed up the stairs.

"This is for my father," Sal said to the passed-out drunk in the bathtub. He pushed the man's head under the water. There was barely a struggle, as even the lack of air could not penetrate the consciousness of one this inebriated.

"What the fuck, Sal! What're doing?" Miguel looked on in wide-eyed horror at the sight of his friend on his knees in front of the bathtub, holding the naked border agent's head under water.

Sal's head whirled to face his friend, but the rest of his body didn't budge. "Get out of here, Miguel. I'll be right behind you. And don't say a word to Bobby—or anyone else! Understand?"

Miguel acted as if he hadn't heard. He slowly walked toward the bathtub and peered over Sal's shoulders at the familiar face of the border agent, who looked like he was sleeping peacefully except for the fact that his mouth was wide open and he was underwater.

"Jesus Christ! Serves him right, that sonofabitch."

"I mean it, Miguel. Scram! Go start the car. I'll be right out. And did you hear me? Not a word to Bobby!"

Miguel backed slowly out of the room, his eyes fixed on the bathtub. Then he bolted down the stairs and out the back door.

Sal grabbed a washcloth and wiped the gun vigorously as he walked down the stairs. He returned the gun to its holster on the entryway table. He pressed the lock button next to the inside doorknob, putting it in lock position, then he wiped it with the washcloth and pulled the door shut. He wiped the outside doorknob, looked up and down the street, and casually walked back to the car.

"What happened in there?" Bobby asked? "You were gone for a long time."

"I was just trying to get some answers from that piece of shit," Sal replied. "He was so drunk, I didn't get much. He was mostly incoherent."

Bobby looked incredulous. "I can't believe he was willing to talk to you."

"Oh, he wasn't willing at all, not at first. But he left his gun lying around and I was able to grab it and then persuade him to talk."

"What did he say?" Bobby asked.

He was rambling mostly. Drunk out of his skull. Best I could tell, my dad was just in the wrong place at the wrong time, just like the detective said."

They drove home in silence, arriving in San Mateo well past ten o'clock. Miguel pulled into Sal's driveway. The house was well lit as it always was, but they all knew it was empty inside.

"I'm not ready to go home yet," Sal said, staring absently at the house. "Drop me off at trailhead. I think I'll go hangout in The Brush for a while."

"We'll go with you if you want company," Bobby offered.

"Nah, I think I need a little time by myself. Thanks though."

They drove the short distance to the trailhead and all three exited the car.

"You OK, Rocket?" Bobby asked. Sal nodded, his eyes beginning to water.

"We're here for you, pal," Bobby said. "Tonight. Tomorrow. And every day after that. You need anything, you just let me know." Bobby wrapped his arms around his friend in a big bear hug. He could feel Sal's body begin shaking with silent sobs.

Miguel embraced him as well, quickly and awkwardly, unable to find any words.

Sal looked at his friends through watery eyes. "I was alone a lot while my dad was alive. He was gone more than he was around, but I never felt alone. I liked being on my own. But I always knew he was coming back. But now ..." He wiped his eyes with the back of his hand and let out a deep, shaky breath. "The rest of my family is so far away. I don't know if I'll ever see them again..." His voice cracked and he turned away so that his friends wouldn't see the tears rushing down his face. "Now I really am alone. I don't know what to do... or where to go."

Bobby put a hand on his shoulder. "You're not alone, Sal. You've got us. We'll help you figure it out."

"Yeah, man, we're brothers," added Miguel. "You know that."

Sal continued to look out into the vastness of The Brush, avoiding eye contact. "Thanks. You guys are the closest thing to family I have now. You've been great pals ever since I got here. I'd do anything for you. Whatever happens, I don't want to lose that."

Miguel held out his left hand, backside up. "Remember this?" he asked, flashing his scar. That means friends for life, right?"

The others held out their hands. Three red scars faced upwards. Sal smiled sadly through his tears. "Yep, friends for life, no matter what." Then his tear-covered face brightened. "Where I come from, you show that you're friends for life by taking a blood oath. Each person makes a small cut on his hand or finger and writes his name in blood. What do you say, guys?"

"I'm game," Miguel said quickly, looking enthused.

"OK. Me, too," said Bobby.

Miguel opened the passenger side door and pulled his hunting knife from beneath the seat.

"Anybody got any paper?" Sal asked.

"I do," said Bobby. He hoisted his duffle bag out of the trunk and rummaged through it, pulling out his sketch pad. He flipped it, looking for a blank page as his friends looked over his shoulder.

"Stop! That one there. That's perfect!" Sal said as they stared at the picture of the three of them in their football uniforms that Bobby had drawn on the bus ride to McAllen. "Turn it over. We'll all sign the back."

They walked around to the front of the car and Miguel flipped on the headlights. "Lead the way, brother," Miguel said, handing the knife to Sal.

Sal placed the tip of the hunting knife on the middle finger of his left hand and gave it a quick flick. A tiny pool of blood instantly emerged and began running down his finger. Sal dipped his right index finger in the blood. "Turn it over," he said, nodding at the picture. He then wrote *Sal* on the picture, stopping after each letter to replenish the crimson liquid, using the bleeding finger on his left hand as a pallet and his right index finger as a brush. Miguel and Bobby followed, completing the ritual with a silent reverence.

"Keep that forever, Bobby," Sal said solemnly. "If we run into each other in 30 years, we'll expect you to have this and show it to us."

"You can count on it," Bobby replied.

"It's late," Sal said. "You guys better shove off. I'm going to stay out here for a bit. I'm just not ready to face that empty house yet."

They shook hands and Miguel and Bobby drove off. "Drop me off here," Bobby said when they were within two blocks of his house. "I could use a little more fresh air before I pack it in."

"Suit yourself," said Miguel. "I'm exhausted. Later, man."

Bobby stood on the deserted street corner and watched Louie Miranda's car drive away. He continued staring in that direction for a long moment after the car had vanished from sight. Then he turned away from his house and headed back toward The Brush.

From a distance, he could make out the silhouette of Sal Rios, perched at the top of The Hill, sitting Indian style, the moon illuminating the vastness of The Brush. Bobby climbed The Hill and silently sat down next to his friend, noticing the traces of tears glistening on Sal's cheeks in the moonlight. "I thought you might want some company," Bobby said after a long silence. "If you'd rather be alone, just let me know."

Sal continued staring straight ahead, as did Bobby. Through his peripheral vision, Bobby could see the tears starting to flow more freely. "I'm glad you're here," Sal said.

Chapter 14

BY NOON ON Monday, San Mateo was buzzing. That was always the case when death came calling, and even more so when the circumstances were tragic and sudden. In this case, there was the added element of mystery surrounding both the life and death of Antonio Rios. The fact of the matter was that virtually no one in the town knew who he was, except that he had rented the old Fernandez house last summer. Few of the town's residents had ever laid eyes on him. Most had never heard of Sal until the last few weeks, when he came to prominence as an emerging football star.

The town had a history of taking care of its own when tragedy struck. Meals were delivered. Neighbors dropped by to offer their condolences. Some brought flowers. Some would stay and sit with the bereaved. Some offered to do yard work, or run errands, or care for young children. When money was an issue, funds were raised. In this instance, no one knew what to do because they simply had no connection with the deceased or his surviving son. However, the thought of a 15-year-old boy losing his father and being left all alone tugged at their collective heartstrings.

Bobby's mother stepped up to organize the meal effort, although for the most part, her role became telling people that they had enough meals arranged already and that she would let them know if any more were required. It didn't take much to feed a household of one, and delivering meals or anything else was a challenge because Sal was not spending much time at home. Even when he was home, he tried to make it appear that he wasn't and rarely answered the door. The kindness of his neighbors was touching, but their words and gestures invariably had the effect of rekindling his grief and that was just too painful to bear.

Seeing the state his friend was in, Bobby took charge. He was the one who asked his mother to manage the meal chain. He handled the questions at school and tried to squelch the unseemly rumors that immediately erupted. He accompanied Sal to the principal's office and to see Coach Garza, both of whom were profoundly concerned and sympathetic, and both encouraged Sal to take some time off. Sal told them he would think about it but told no one other than Bobby what his real reaction was whenever that subject came up: *I've got nowhere to go.* Bobby also took the lead role in following up with the Medical Examiner's office in McAllen to figure out the process and the timeline for releasing Mr. Rios's remains so that he could be properly buried. The bureaucrats generally started the conversation by insisting that they were not authorized to speak with anyone about such issues other than adult next-of-kin. Bobby found that he could almost always keep the person talking long enough that he could charm or cajole his way into getting the information he needed.

Sal agonized over his inability to contact his mother, but his father's instructions on that point had been clear and forceful—no contact under *any* circumstances. That meant he couldn't ship his father's remains back home, where they truly belonged. The guilt was overpowering, but his father's words kept coming back to him: *We are on a mission, and we do what we must.* He was determined to honor those words and thereby honor his father, no matter how difficult it may be.

The week passed in a blur. Sal continued to attend classes but spent most of the time looking lost and dazed. Bobby intervened with their teachers and got them to agree to give Sal a pass on homework assignments and to postpone the exams that were scheduled for that week. Sal continued attending football practice after school. The first few days, he appeared disinterested and just went through the motions. Before practice on Thursday, the coach again encouraged him to take some time off. "It's only a game, son," he had said. "You've got a lot going on right now. If you're not really focused, you might get hurt, and you might let your team down."

That sparked a fire, and Sal approached the afternoon practice with a renewed intensity; however, it wasn't his usual controlled intensity. It was wild, and violent. Less than halfway through practice, he had gotten into multiple scuffles with his own teammates, mostly generated by ferocious hits that the victims considered unnecessary and far too rough to be applied to one's own teammates on a practice field. The coach then excused him from practice, partly to allow Sal to get his head on straight, and partly to protect his other players from serious injury before Saturday night's big playoff game.

By Saturday, most of the town was no longer focused on the death of Antonio Rios. The fact that people just didn't know him made that easy. Besides, it was high school football season in Texas and the town was working itself into a frenzy over the big playoff game on Saturday night. If they won this week's game against Liberty High School, they would be regional champions, on their way to the state playoffs, a feat never before accomplished by the San Mateo Wildcats.

San Mateo had home field advantage and a standing-room-only crowd was packed into the hometown stadium. Sal "Rocket" Rios picked up where he had left off the previous week. He ran wild in the first half, racking up 140 yards and three touchdowns, leading his team to a 24-7 lead. Shortly after the start of the second half, Sal let his emotions get the better of him on defense. He leveled the opposing quarterback with a brutal hit well after the ball had been thrown. One of the Liberty players then shoved Sal from behind in retaliation, knocking him off his feet. Penalty flags flew as both benches raced onto the field, a handful of shoving matches breaking out before the officials could restore order. Both Sal and Coach Garza were given warnings and a penalty for unsportsmanlike conduct was assessed.

Taunting and trash-talk continued on both sides as the game resumed. Despite being double-teamed, Sal broke through and sacked the Liberty quarterback again, another vicious hit but this time perfectly clean and consistent with the rulebook—until he stood over the fallen quarterback and shouted down at him, "You're mine, you useless piece of shit! Better stay down, 'cause I'm gonna keep coming back until they carry your ass off on a stretcher!"

"You're outta here!" he heard a voice explode in his ear, turning to see a red-faced referee glaring at him and pointing to the sidelines.

The crowd erupted in boos and Coach Garza came storming across the field. "Aw, let 'em play, Ref! This is the playoffs. That was a clean hit!"

"This is getting out of control, Coach," the referee shouted. "And he's the instigator," he said, pointing an accusing finger at Sal. "Now get off the field or I'll toss you, too!"

Coach Garza lumbered off the field, Sal following behind, his head downcast. Upon reaching the sideline, the coach grabbed Sal by his face-mask. "What's wrong with you, Rios?" he screamed. "You're smarter than that! Use your head, goddammit! You might have just cost us the title!"

The Liberty fans cheered wildly at the sight of Rocket Rios trudging toward the locker room halfway into the third quarter. On the field, the momentum swung quickly and dramatically, with Liberty scoring on its next two possessions, narrowing San Mateo's lead to 24 – 21. With the hometown crowd roaring behind them, the Wildcat's defense managed to dig in and hold off the visitors down the stretch, earning them a spot in the state playoffs.

In the locker room, Coach Garza gave a rousing victory speech and then headed out of the raucous celebration, grabbing Bobby by the elbow as he walked past. "We need to talk."

Bobby followed the coach outside and watched his facial expression quickly transform from jubilant to serious. "We've got a problem, Bobby. I need your help."

"Absolutely. Whatever you need, Coach."

"It's about Sal. He's a tough kid, but he's a basket case right now. Hell, who wouldn't be? I'd love to have him on the field for the state playoffs, but I can't have him disrupting what we've got going. We can't have another repeat of what happened here tonight and what happened at practice this week."

"I can make him understand that, Coach. He's a smart guy."

"Of course he's a smart guy, but he's not himself. He's not thinking clearly. He's angry, he's emotional, he's grieving. And believe me, I'm not being critical. My point is, he really needs support right now, and I think this poor kid is all alone. You're his best friend—"

"I've been trying to help—every way I can think of. The fact is that between school and football, we don't have a lot of free time."

"That's what I'm getting at, Bobby. I'd like you and him to skip practice next week—all week. Spend time together, away from all this. And this isn't about football. It's about the fact that he's hurting with a pain that you and I can't imagine. He's lost, and he doesn't know where to turn or what to do next. I don't think there's anyone in this town that's in a position to really help him—except maybe you."

Bobby nodded silently. "You shouldn't even have to ask me this, Coach. I need to be a better friend. I wish I knew what more I could do."

"You are a great friend to him, Bobby, and I know he treasures your friendship, even if he doesn't say it. Spend some quality time with him next week. As for football, I hope that he's ready to play next week, with his head screwed on straight. If he is, he'll be in the lineup. But if he's not, that's OK. I don't want him to feel any pressure from football. I want to help him get through this tragedy and maybe the two of you stepping away for the next week will help."

***

Monday after school, Bobby and Sal took a long hike out in The Brush. On the way out, they made small talk off and on, about school and football, but spent most of the time in silence. They stopped at The Hill on the way back and sat down on the old log bench, watching ominous storm clouds block out the setting sun.

"Thanks for being here, Bobby. And thanks for everything you've been doing to help me out. I don't know what I'd do without you."

"I wish there was more I could do. If there is, just ask, OK?"

"I'm afraid there's not much anyone can do for me at this point. I've got big decisions to make and nobody can make them but me."

"Have you thought any more about a funeral?"

Sal stared at the ground and shook his head. "A funeral would mean lots of questions about my dad. There'd be questions about his place of birth, family members and all that. Same problem if I try to have him shipped back home. That would raise questions about his legal status, and that would lead to questions about me. I can't have that. If I got sent home, I might never make it back to this country. Even if I did, it would be impossible to pick up right here where I left off."

"But can you keep living where you are now? If word gets out that a 15-year-old is living on his own, that could be a problem. Child Protective Services may come calling. The INS might put you in one of those detention centers they have for undocumented kids without parents. They all get deported eventually."

"I know. I haven't figured it out yet. I told the school the same thing I told the cops in McAllen—that I've got relatives nearby I can stay with. So far, nobody's checked up on that. If they do, I guess I could tell them I'm just staying in San Mateo to finish out the semester and I'll be going to stay with my relatives after that—in Houston or San Antonio or wherever."

"That's definitely the word going around—that you've got relatives nearby. I asked my parents if you could come stay with us and my mom told me she heard you'd be staying with relatives. But I can bring it up again. Would you like to come stay with us while you figure this out? I'm sure my parents wouldn't mind."

Sal smiled sadly. "I'm not going to do that to you, Seventy-Seven. I know how paranoid your parents are about attracting attention from the authorities. And with what just happened, there'd be good reason for them to be concerned. Thanks, though. I'll figure something out."

"How about if I talk to Father Paul? The church sometimes takes care of kids who have nowhere to go."

"Nah. That would just be temporary. I'm fine staying on my own for now unless someone starts harassing me about it. I just need to figure out my long-term plan."

"What about money? Do you have anything to live on?"

"My dad had a safe with some cash in it and I have his ATM card. I've been taking out the limit every day so I'll have a stash in case the bank shuts down the account. I'm OK for now, but I'm not sure what I'll do when that cash runs out."

Bobby put a hand on his friend's shoulder. "That's a lot to be dealing with. I just wish I could do more."

"You're doing plenty, pal. Thanks for listening." The rumble of thunder grew nearer, and the wind picked up. "Right now, we better get our butts out of here before the storm hits. "Let's go."

They ran down the hill and kept running but the deluge caught them before they reached the highway. They continued running until Sal veered off into his driveway. "I'll stop by tomorrow after school," Bobby yelled, without breaking stride. "See ya!"

The rain continued most of Tuesday and Wednesday, so hikes into The Brush were out of the question. They spent those afternoons in Sal's living room, playing cards and leisurely watching TV. They accomplished nothing and discussed nothing meaningful, but enjoyed the rarity of a couple of free afternoons with no responsibilities.

By Thursday afternoon, the sun was shining brightly. Bobby and Sal met at the trailhead after school and jogged toward The Hill, enjoying the warm South Texas autumn and the fresh smell of The Brush after a heavy rain. "I'll show you the swimming hole today," Bobby called out as they sloshed through the muddy trail. "These are perfect swimming conditions."

"Hey, wait up!" a voice rang out from behind them. It was Miguel.

"Why aren't you at practice?" Sal asked.

"Because that shithead Garza suspended me for the rest of the season."

"I thought he'd only benched you for one game." Bobby said.

"So did I—that's what it was supposed to be. That prick is still mad that I showed up late in McAllen. I told him it was a family emergency and that my mother had me out looking for my little brother who had wandered off. The sonofabitch checked up with my old lady and she didn't know what he was talking about, so he found out I was lying to him."

"So he suspended you for the rest of the season?" Sal asked. "We could have three games left if we keep winning—big games! That's pretty harsh."

"It started out being a one-game suspension. Then I told him he was being an asshole and he really blew a gasket."

"Sorry to hear that," said Sal. "Maybe a dip in the swimming hole will make you feel better."

"Let's take a look around first," said Bobby gesturing to the top of The Hill. "Sometimes this place looks really different after a good rain.

They climbed The Hill and surveyed their surroundings. Small quick-running creeks and glistening pools of water dotted the normally parched landscape. Bobby pointed south. "Over there—about a mile-and a-half that way. That's the best place to swim. There's a pool that always forms there after a good rain. It's almost eight feet deep."

They marched in that direction, enjoying the soggy trek in their favorite place as well as the fact that they were missing a grueling football practice.

"So, Sal... I've barely seen you since it happened," said Miguel. "What's your plan? Are you staying here in San Mateo?"

"Still trying to figure it out," Sal replied.

"Thinking about heading back south of the border?"

"Not a chance. My life is here now. I can't let anything change that."

"You got that right. Gotta love the good ole U.S. of A," said Miguel.

"Bullshit!" Sal replied. "I *hate* this country. My father always said that America is the enemy and he was right. America killed him."

"What are you talking about?" asked Miguel. "America didn't kill your old man. Some lowlife piece-of-shit cop killed him. He was a bad guy, but you can't judge a whole country based on one bad guy."

"It's not just one bad guy," Sal shot back. "The whole system here is corrupt. The values are all screwed up. The ruling class calls all the shots and takes advantage of everyone else. This country is my enemy, and I plan to do everything I can to bring it down and tear it apart."

"Aw, that's crazy talk," said Miguel. "You've got a good life here. Hell, man, you're a football star. You're going to have all kinds of chicks chasing you around. You'll probably go to college, get a big job, drive a fancy car and make a shitload of money."

"You're damn right. I will do all those things. I'll take all the good America has to offer, but I'll never forget the mission. America must pay. The seeds of destruction must be planted. I will do what I must."

Bobby noticed that Sal was getting progressively angrier. "Hey, lighten up, you two," he said. "Look around us. It's a beautiful day. Perfect weather. No football practice. No one to hassle us. Let's enjoy the best of South Texas, right here and now. I'm going to run ahead and check out the water hole."

Bobby trotted off and Sal was about to run after him when Miguel grabbed his arm. "Hey, hold back a minute, amigo," he said. "I need to ask you a favor."

"What is it?" Sal asked, looking impatient as he stared after Bobby.

"Talk to Coach. Tell him to let me back on the team. You're his golden boy. He'll listen to you."

"He's not going to listen to me. I'm in the doghouse, remember? I got thrown out of the last game."

"That don't matter. He wants you back. You can make a deal with him—you play only if he lets me back on the team."

"For Chrissakes, Miguel, you called him an asshole—when you were already on his shitlist! There's no way he's going to change his mind. Just be a model citizen around him and maybe he'll give you a clean slate next year."

"C'mon, man. I'm begging you! Football is all I've got. If I can't play football, I've got no reason to be in school. Remember who your friends are. I've kept your secrets. I haven't told anyone about you know what. You owe me!"

Sal thrust his face to within inches of Miguel's. "Are you threatening me?" His voice was low and menacing.

"No. I'm just reminding you that I'm your friend. I've got your back, so you should have mine. That's all I'm saying. I'd like to see us stay friends."

"So you're saying you won't be my friend if I don't talk to Coach for you?"

"That's not what I said. It would just be better—for both of us—if you did."

"Fuck you!" Sal stormed off, following Bobby's footsteps.

"Check this out!" Bobby shouted when the others had caught up to him. They were looking down at what had been a dried-up basin between several hills where water from the previous days' rains had accumulated. The water was murky, the color of café au lait, but it covered nearly an acre and was deep enough for swimming, at least in parts. Bobby was already stripping down to his skivvies. "Yikes! It's cold!" he yelled as he waded in. "Be careful, you can't see the bottom."

Sal stripped down and gingerly waded in, walking toward Bobby. In an instant, he went from knee-deep water to suddenly disappearing beneath the surface. He emerged, sputtering and laughing at the same time. "Shit, the bottom just disappeared beneath my feet!"

"Like I said, be careful! The bottom is uneven and there are big rocks all over the place. Swim out to the middle and it's plenty deep."

Within minutes, the three of them were frolicking around like little kids, splashing, dunking each other, and hollering with a joie de vivre that had vanished in recent days. They raced. They challenged each other to an underwater breath-holding contest.

"Let's do cannonballs!" Bobby shouted, checking the depth around a protruding rock with his feet. He climbed the rock and launched himself into the water in cannonball mode. Sal and Miguel followed. Bobby was the clear winner, as he outweighed the others by a longshot.

Miguel swam to another big boulder on the opposite side of the pond. "Screw the cannonballs! Let's do flips. See if you can match this!"

"Not there! There are too many rocks!" Bobby shouted.

Miguel ignored him and hurled his body into a full aerial flip, spinning awkwardly out of control and hitting the water hard.

Bobby and Sal howled with laughter. "Ouch! That's gotta hurt!" Bobby shouted.

"That was ugly, man. No style points there!" yelled Sal.

Several seconds passed. Miguel did not surface. Bobby and Sal looked at each other nervously and then stared back at the spot where Miguel had hit the water. Still no Miguel.

"Oh, shit!" Sal shouted, and they both began swimming furiously across the murky pond.

"Got him!" Bobby cried out as he stood in chest-high water and felt around with his legs.

Both boys instantly submerged and grabbed hold of the limp body, dragging him to the shore. Miguel was unconscious, a large lump growing out of his forehead.

"Is he breathing?" Bobby asked.

"I can't tell," Sal replied, holding his ear on Miguel's chest. "His lungs must be full of water." Sal placed his hands together on Miguel's chest and began a series of rapid chest compressions. "Shit! Nothing's happening," he said, continuing the maneuver. "You better run for help. I'll keep at this."

Bobby quickly put on his pants and shoes and sped off, pulling his T-shirt over his head as he ran. He was barely 100 yards off when Miguel began coughing. Water spilled out of his mouth and his eyelids fluttered, then opened. The coughing stopped, and the dazed eyes focused after a few minutes. "I can't feel my legs," he moaned.

Sal stood up and peered off in the direction Bobby had taken. Bobby was out of sight. He looked down at Miguel, whose eyes followed him but whose body remained limp. He paced back and forth several times, then stopped, turning away from his injured companion.

"Where's Bobby?" Miguel asked, his voice barely audible.

"Gone for help," Sal replied, without turning around. He continued staring off into the distance for several minutes, then he abruptly turned around and walked briskly back toward Miguel. He bent over and grabbed Miguel by the ankles and began dragging him back into the water.

"Hey, what are you doing, man?" Miguel asked, his voice suddenly stronger but his body offering no resistance.

Sal kept pulling until he found himself in knee-deep water. He put both hands on Miguel's shoulders and pushed down, then knelt on Miguel's chest, using all his weight to hold Miguel against the rocky bottom of the pond, eighteen inches below the surface of the water. Miguel began shaking his head violently from side to side. His hands weakly grasped at Sal's wrists, but the rest of his body remained limp. Through the shallow, murky water, Sal could see Miguel's eyes, wide with panic and horror. It wasn't long before air bubbles made their way to the surface and the struggling ceased. Sal continued holding the lifeless body beneath the surface for several long minutes, then he dragged it back to where it had been when Bobby took off.

It was over an hour later and nearly dark before Bobby arrived in an ATV with two EMTs sent by Carroll County Hospital. They found Sal, sitting on the ground, next to Miguel. "I think he's dead," said Sal softly without looking up. "He never came to."

Chapter 15

"I'M REALLY SORRY about your friend, guys," Sheriff Ortiz said, looking genuinely sympathetic. "I know you've already spoken with the EMTs, but I need to go over this with you myself. It's routine procedure whenever there's been an accidental death."

Sal, Bobby and Bobby's parents were gathered in the small but tidy living room of the Rivera home. Bobby and Sal sat side-by-side on the couch, both staring at the floor looking shell-shocked. Sheriff Ortiz sat opposite them, leaning forward in an armchair as he pulled out a hand-held recording device. Bobby's father paced silently while his mother stood behind the couch, her eyes wide and a hand over her mouth.

Bobby spoke softly, pausing occasionally to take a deep breath to control his trembling voice. He recounted the afternoon's events in as much detail as he could remember, from the time they arrived at the swimming hole until the time he raced off to get help.

The Sheriff turned toward Sal. "Sal, can you tell me what happened after that? Also, if you remember anything differently or if you think Bobby left out anything, tell me what it is."

"The way Bobby just described it is exactly how I remember it," Sal said. "After he left, I kept trying to revive Miguel. I pumped his chest. I was screaming at him and slapped him across the face a couple of times to try to get him to come to. He just didn't. After a few minutes I could tell that he was gone. He wasn't breathing. I couldn't feel a heartbeat..." His voice trailed off and he covered his eyes.

Sheriff Ortiz clicked off the recorder. "Thanks, fellas. That's all I need."

"How's Mrs. Sanchez holding up?" Mrs. Rivera asked.

"Not good," Ortiz replied. "We couldn't reach her by phone, so I had to stop by her house to break the news to her. She was hysterical. Who wouldn't be? I stayed with her until Father Paul got there and then I came right over here."

"Poor thing." Mrs. Rivera wiped her eyes with a handkerchief. "We should go over there." She looked at her husband who nodded his head slowly.

"I suppose we should," Dr. Rivera replied. "I don't know if she has any family nearby or not."

"She doesn't," said Bobby. "I'll go with you."

"We'll drive you home first, Sal," said Mrs. Rivera.

"That's OK. I can walk."

"It's no trouble at all. We'll drive you," Dr. Rivera insisted.

They said goodnight to Sheriff Ortiz and then piled into the Rivera's white Toyota. It was barely a mile across town to Sal's house and they made the ride in silence. Bobby and Sal sat on opposite ends of the rear seat, each staring absently out the window. Sal's senses perked up when they drove past a dark sedan parked at the end of his block, which was normally deserted. He could see the silhouette of a man behind the wheel.

Dr. Rivera pulled into Sal's driveway. The sight of the dark, lonely house and the knowledge that Sal was living there all by himself jolted Mrs. Rivera. "Are you OK being here by yourself tonight, Sal? You're welcome to stay with us." Her tone was a blend of both kindness and sadness.

Her husband shot her a quick glance, the disapproving nature of which was not lost on Sal. "I'll be fine. Thanks for the offer, though." He climbed out of the car and made his way to the front door. He made a pretense of fumbling with his keys as the Rivera car pulled out of the driveway. Out of the corner of his eye, he could see the sedan still parked up the street.

He opened the door and felt something flutter to his feet. Flipping on the light, he noticed a folded-up piece of paper that had been wedged between the door and the doorjamb. He bent over to pick it up and then stepped outside, staring directly at the dark sedan as it slowly pulled away.

He stepped back inside and unfolded the paper. *Meet me tomorrow morning. Confessional at Our Lady of Guadalupe. 9:00.*

Chapter 16

SAL LAY IN bed, staring at the ceiling, his mind racing. Who was in that car? Who had left the note? Why did that person want to talk to him? Was there some suspicion about the day's events? How could there be? They had been in the middle of nowhere. No one could have seen, and there was no reason for anyone to suspect that anything happened differently than what he and Bobby had described. It was a perfectly plausible story. Hell, it almost *was* exactly what happened. It could have been.

The day's events brought renewed focus to the other questions that had been consuming him lately. How long could the status quo continue? How can a 15-year old be allowed to live on his own in this town and this country? Would the authorities disrupt his life and try to send him home or put him in an orphanage or some other undesirable place? And what about his family? He suddenly missed his mother and his sisters. Should he return home? Should he contact them? He told himself that was out of the question. His father wouldn't want that. His father had brought him here for a purpose. Besides, he liked living in America. He liked school and his friends and football. He liked the idea that he had a bright future in America. But how would he get from here to there? Where should he go and what should he do? What would happen when the money ran out?

He tossed and turned in bed as those questions raced through his mind. He tried calming himself by lying on his back, hands behind his head, eyes closed, trying to remain absolutely still and blocking all conscious thoughts from entering his mind in the hope that sleep would overtake him. It was a futile effort. He gave up trying shortly before dawn. He went downstairs and sat in the big leather armchair in his father's study, where his father had often sat quietly deep into the night. Sal had wondered what was going through his father's mind on those occasions and what his father was up to. That led him back to the note and the confessional. He remembered spying on his father when he went there. He remembered the tall, sinister looking individual who had emerged from the priest's chamber. Is that who wanted to meet with him? He hoped so, because that would mean there was some connection between this meeting and his father's business. He would demand answers. Perhaps this would help him figure out what must come next. He was energized by the prospect of having a purpose and a plan. The anger and grief at his father's loss were hard enough, but the uncertainty that accompanied that loss was almost too much to bear. He was determined to resolve that uncertainty, one way or another.

Sal arrived at the church a full hour early and went straight up to his previous hiding place so that he could get a clear look at whomever entered that confessional. He stopped in his tracks as soon as he reached the balcony. The confessional light was already illuminated. It couldn't be Father Paul, because confessions were scheduled only on Saturday afternoons. There were two other people kneeling in pews toward the front of the church. That was not unusual, and they seemed to be minding their own business, lost in prayer.

Sal thought about waiting until 9:00, the appointed time. Not a chance, he decided. He wanted to be in control. For all he knew, this person could have had something to do with putting his father in harm's way. He was not about to be intimidated. He was not about to let anyone control him. He marched into the confessional and pulled the door firmly shut, rattling the thin walls between the small chambers. The partition slid open with a scratchy sound of wood moving against wood, leaving the opaque fabric separator between the him and whomever was in the adjacent chamber. After a few moments of silence, Sal cleared his throat.

"In the name of the Father, and of the Son, and of the Holy Spirit," came a whispered voice from the other side. "Have you come to confess your sins and seek forgiveness from your Lord and Creator?"

"No. I have a 9:00 appointment. I'm early."

There was a hesitation. Then a voice continued. "That's good. I like punctuality. My boss always says, if you're not early, you're late. He would appreciate your eagerness."

"Why am I here? What do you want?" Sal asked, doing his best to sound forceful and impatient.

"I am here as a messenger from someone who was very close to your father. For now, I will refer to him as simply El Jefe. First and foremost, El Jefe extends his deepest sympathies. He and your father were very close. I don't think there was anyone El Jefe held in higher regard."

"Is it his fault my father is dead?"

"That's a fair question. The fact is that your father was engaged in a dangerous line of work. There were certain occupational hazards that were just unavoidable. Your father knew that as well as anyone. So, no, El Jefe was not at fault. Nevertheless, he has taken a special interest in you, partly out of loyalty to your father, but also because he believes you have special talents and that you could play an important role in his future plans here."

"He's never even met me. How could he possibly know whether I have what he's looking for?"

"El Jefe has eyes and ears everywhere. He knows a great deal about you, and has for a long time. Why do you think he encouraged your father to bring you here? He knows how you're doing in school. He knows who your friends are. He's been following your football exploits with great interest."

"Then if he knows so much, what is he doing about the situation in McAllen?"

"Believe me, he was all over that as soon as it happened. I have never seen him so upset. The fact is, the bad guys are dead already, so there isn't much to be done. The cop who called in the shooting was dirty. He was shot and killed three days later during a routine traffic stop. That Border Patrol agent who orchestrated the bust didn't even make it through the night. Went out celebrating and got so drunk that he passed out and drowned in his own bathtub. Pretty convenient, wouldn't you say?"

"I read about that. Serves him right. Are you saying that El Jefe had something to do with that? Or El Cazador?"

"Not at all. Quite to the contrary. El Jefe was alerted to the situation immediately and was prepared to take appropriate measures to address it, but it took care of itself. Know anything about that? As I recall, you stayed over in McAllen that night."

"All I know is what I read."

"Like I said before, El Jefe has eyes and ears everywhere. You can assume he knows a lot more than you think he does."

"So, back to my question. What do you want? What am I doing here?"

"As I said, El Jefe has big plans for you and those plans involve keeping you in America. But not here in San Mateo. You'll need to move elsewhere—someplace where no one knows your past. He'll make it worth your while. Right now, you just need to be patient while we find the right situation. Keep doing what you're doing. Stay where you are. You won't need to worry about money."

"What if I don't want to do that? I like my life here just fine."

"There's nothing for you here! If you stay, people will start asking questions. It'll be just a matter of time before INS catches up to you. Besides, San Mateo isn't even a speck on a roadmap. It's a gnat on an elephant's ass. You've got a very bright future and you need to be someplace that presents greater opportunities. You can play a significant role in a very important cause. I'm sure your father told you something about it?"

"Just a little."

"You'll learn a lot more about it once your new life begins. But that means getting away from here, and soon. So, what shall I tell El Jefe? Are you in?"

Sal hesitated for a long moment. "Anything else I should be aware of?" he asked.

"Yes—football. You can't be drawing attention to yourself. If San Mateo wins tonight, you'll be in the semi-finals in Austin. Based on your recent performances, you're bound to be attracting attention from the opposing coaches. They're always trying to find out if a school has brought in ringers from outside their district. They'll be looking for birth records, prior addresses, family history and all that. You don't want that,

I assure you. So, it would be good if you get sick, or get hurt or have a falling out with the coach. Maybe say you can't play because you're dealing with your father's death. Figure it out—you're a smart kid. So, are you in?"

The door to the priest's confessional was flung open. Sal stood in the doorway, staring at the scarred face of Francisco Vargas, the man he had seen leaving the confessional after meeting with his father. "I'm in." he said, looking defiant. "What happens now? How do I reach you?"

Vargas looked angry. "You wait," he snarled. "And you don't contact me. I'll contact you."

Chapter 17

SAN MATEO WAS a town in shock. It had lost two of its residents in a matter of weeks. Few knew Antonio Rios, but the thought of a fifteen-year-old high school freshman losing his father and being left entirely on his own had cast at least something of a pall over the town. That sense of loss was compounded immensely by the untimely death of Miguel Sanchez. His family had engaged with the community. Jenny was well-known and well-liked by her classmates at Cargill Elementary. Mrs. Sanchez was still new to the area, but in the five months since her arrival, the town had embraced her. She was active in the church and had begun working in the church's day care center, which enabled her to keep an eye on her own two-year-old toddler, Enrique. While they didn't know the story, the neighbors realized that there was no husband in the picture, which made life harder than normal for her, and that caused the towns-people to warm up to her more quickly than they otherwise might have.

Once again, Bobby's mother led the meal brigade, coordinating the effort to keep the meals coming to the Sanchez household. Bobby tried to lend a hand, but it was evident that his mother had that effort well under control. He wanted to do something, but he felt useless.

He walked slowly across town and approached the creaky old gate to the Sanchez property. He paused, remembering the special moments he had spent there with Jenny just a couple of weeks before. He had felt awkward then and felt even more awkward now. He knocked on the door. He could hear voices inside and could see people through the cracks in the curtains, but no one answered. He thought about leaving.

What could he do there after all? Miguel's mother had company around her. He had brought nothing. He took a deep breath and prepared to knock again. The door swung open. Jenny stared at him through weepy eyes. She flung her arms around his neck and wept quietly. He held her tight, his own eyes flooding with tears as he tried unsuccessfully to hold them back. "I'm so sorry," was all he could get out.

After several long minutes, Jenny composed herself and invited Bobby into the kitchen, where a handful of neighbors nibbled on food while they engaged in quiet conversation. Bobby scanned the faces, looking for Mrs. Sanchez. She wasn't there. The back door opened, and he could see a small group gathered outside around an old wooden picnic table, smoking. Miguel's mother was sitting at the end of the bench, staring downward with unfocused eyes, oblivious to the small talk going on around her.

"Mrs. Sanchez?" She looked up at him, her red-rimmed eyes coming into focus.

"I'm so sorry... Miguel was a great friend... So full of life... I'm really going to miss him."

She smiled sadly. "Thanks, Bobby. You were his best friend. You really took him under your wing when we got here. You meant a lot to him."

"Is there anything I can do?"

She shook her head and looked down, the daze overtaking her again. Bobby tried to make himself useful by taking out the trash and picking up the paper plates. He inconspicuously tidied the front yard and the back. He found a screwdriver and fixed the loose hinge on the front gate. After 30 minutes, he had run out of things to do. He tapped Jenny on the shoulder. "I should be going and let you visit with your guests."

"Can you stay a while longer?" she pleaded.

"Sure. I just didn't want to get in the way. If there's anything I can do to help out... running errands, cleaning up... whatever... now or anytime..."

"Thanks, Bobby. You don't need to do anything. Just having you here really helps." Her eyes shone with gratitude. She reached out and grabbed his hand. "How about a walk?"

They strolled through the dark and quiet neighborhood for a long time. It felt aimless, as there was no destination, but it also felt purposeful, because there was a goal, and that was to be close. Bobby held her hand the entire way. They said little. Beneath the profound sadness, they both felt other emotions—hope, and a trace of something resembling happiness—emanating from their togetherness. Even the tragedy couldn't completely squelch those feelings. They found themselves walking through Washington Park and sat down on the old wooden park bench adjacent to the makeshift soccer field.

Bobby tentatively put his arm around Jenny's shoulders and she snuggled into him. "I'm glad I know you, Bobby Rivera," she whispered as she rested her head against his chest.

"I'm here for you, Jenny. I'll always be here for you."

She pulled her head away from his chest and stared deeply at him. There was still an aura of sadness around her, but it was overpowered by the look of longing in her eyes. She leaned in and kissed him on the lips. It was tender and sensual at the same time. She kissed him again, harder and longer.

Bobby desperately wanted to throw caution to the wind. He wanted to kiss her long and passionately. There was nothing he wanted more. He had been dreaming and fantasizing about this moment incessantly, for weeks. But she was grieving. The timing was all wrong. He didn't want to take advantage of her, and he sure didn't want her to feel that way later. He pulled away and wrapped her in a tight bearhug. "It's late. I better get you home. Your mom might be worried."

Sleep would not come that night. Bobby tossed and turned in bed, endlessly replaying the scene in his mind, wondering whether he had blown his chances with Jenny. He couldn't be sure. The walk home with her had seemed awkward. Or was he just imagining that? He knew he should be thinking about how he could help Jenny and her family in the coming days. He had told Jenny he would be there for them but what could he do, really?

From his bed, he looked at the drawing across the room that he had just pinned to his bulletin board—the picture of him and Sal and Miguel in their football jerseys, looking carefree and full of life. How things had changed in that short time! Sal's world had been rocked by the loss of his father and Miguel was just plain gone. He was glad he had drawn that picture. It froze a moment in time that would always mean something to him. He walked across the room and looked more closely at the picture, admiring his work. It was a particularly good likeness of Miguel and a zest for life sprang off the paper.

He jumped out of bed and began rummaging through his closet. He emerged with several picture frames and held them up against the picture for size. He had been struggling with what he could do for the Sanchez family. Perhaps this was the answer. It was unique. It was personal. It was a wonderfully flattering picture of Miguel that they might cherish. Then he saw the bloody signatures scrawled on the back. He despaired momentarily at the realization that presenting Miguel's family with a picture doused with Miguel's blood might be the ultimate in poor taste.

Inspiration returned, and he set about creating a new picture, copying carefully the image of Miguel from the original and adding bold colors in place of the previous pencil sketch. He left Sal and himself out of the drawing. He framed the completed picture just as daylight was breaking.

Bobby delivered the picture along with freshly picked flowers to Mrs. Sanchez later that morning. She was genuinely touched and insisted that the picture be displayed next to the casket at the funeral service that afternoon. Jenny thanked him profusely. She hugged him, long and tight, rekindling hope that he hadn't offended her by rebuffing her advances the previous evening.

Our Lady of Guadalupe Catholic Church was jam-packed for the one o'clock funeral service and the reception that followed in the church hall. The football team and their coaches had to excuse themselves by mid-afternoon to prepare for the big game that evening. A week earlier, the prospect of making the state playoffs had the entire town buzzing. The untimely death of Miguel Sanchez had sucked all the excitement out of San Mateo and put football into its proper perspective.

That evening, the glorious football season enjoyed by the San Mateo Wildcats ended with a thud. The enthusiasm that had overtaken the town over the previous three weeks was tempered by recent events before the game even started. On the field, San Mateo quickly found itself on the wrong end of a good old-fashioned drubbing. Star running back Sal

Rios fumbled three times in the first half before limping off the field and being benched for the remainder of the game. The Wildcats lost 24 – 0.

The following afternoon, Bobby met Sal at the trailhead at Sal's request. Bobby had tried to beg off so he could spend time with Jenny, but Sal seemed agitated and insistent. They walked into The Brush, saying little. Bobby had seen his friend display a multitude of different moods: brash, feisty, passionate, gregarious, but never morose, which is how he appeared now.

"My world is totally and completely screwed up right now," Sal began. "I don't know where to go or what to do, but something's got to give."

"I get it," Bobby replied. "You lost your dad, you have no family here. I can't imagine how difficult that's got to be."

"No shit. It really is. You know, I try to act like a tough guy—and I am pretty tough—but I don't even know which way to turn. Maybe I need to go somewhere else. Maybe I need a fresh start."

"But where would you go? That's not going to bring your dad back. At least you have friends here."

Sal smiled ruefully. "Not sure I have many friends left after yesterday's game. I really stunk it up, didn't I?"

"Hey, we all have bad games. With everything that's happened around here—your dad, Miguel—it's not surprising you weren't at your best."

"Well, I could have played better. I feel responsible. I could have made a difference and I didn't. That's a shitty feeling. I don't ever want to be in that situation again."

"No one blames you, Sal. Don't take it personally."

"I blame me."

They walked up to the top of The Hill and sat on the old log bench, staring at the vast expanse of wilderness laid out in front of them. They were quiet for a long time. "Anything I can do?" Bobby asked.

"Nah, I don't think so. You've been a big help already. You were my first friend in this town. You showed me around. Brought me into the right circles. Got me on the football team. Everything good that's happened to me here has been because of you, Seventy-Seven. You're the best friend I've ever had."

"Aw, don't get sappy on me now."

"I just want you to know how grateful I am. Just having you to talk to, having you as a friend—that means a lot to me. I'll never forget it."

Sal leaned over and picked up a stick and began absently drawing on the ground with it. Bobby watched the stick as it made indiscernible patterns. "There's something else on your mind, isn't there?" he asked.

Sal nodded slowly and turned to Bobby. He appeared about to say something, then abruptly looked away.

"Never mind," he said. "It's not important. Let's go."

***

Over the next two weeks, Bobby made regular visits to the Sanchez house after school. Sometimes he would cut the grass or do other chores around the house. Sometimes he watched Enrique if Jenny and her mom needed to go out. Sometimes he would offer to help Jenny with her homework, which they both knew was a joke because she was by far the better student. Mostly, he just wanted to be there for Jenny, and he was happy that she seemed to appreciate his company.

On Thursday afternoon nearly three weeks after the funeral, he made plans to meet Jenny on Sunday for a hike in The Brush. He was determined to summon up all his courage and tell Jenny how he felt about her. He was both thrilled and terrified at the prospect of having that conversation with her and spent most of the next two days obsessing over his plans and trying to find exactly the right words. He stressed over that, but at the same time, he remembered their last kiss and he fantasized about picking up right where they had left off. Noon on Sunday couldn't come quickly enough.

When Sunday morning came, Bobby was waiting at the trailhead at 11:30. Their date was at noon, but on most prior occasions, she had arrived early. This was not one of those occasions. Noon came and she had not yet arrived. Bobby stared at his watch: 12:05, then 12:15, then 12:20. Something must have come up. Given what their family had just gone through, that would be understandable. At 12:30, he decided that he would head over to her house. Maybe they had gotten their signals crossed.

He rode his bike across town and turned right onto Caminito Silvela, Jenny's street. Something seemed amiss as soon as the Sanchez home came into view. As he approached, he could see that there was neither car nor bicycle in the driveway. Enrique's toys were not strewn around the front yard as they usually were. He knocked on the door. No answer. He looked through the crack in the curtains. The house was empty. No furniture. No people. They were gone.

Bobby spent the rest of the day moping around the house. He thought about hiking out into The Brush but decided he needed to stay home in case Jenny called or stopped by. He tried studying but was too distracted. He tried drawing. Same result.

Late in the afternoon, his mother stuck her head into his room and found Bobby lying on his bed staring at the ceiling. "Something wrong, Bobby?" she asked.

Bobby continued staring at the ceiling. "I think the Sanchez family has moved away," he said quietly.

Mrs. Rivera sat down on the bed, "You know how it is around here. A lot of people come and go. After what they've just been through, they must have decided they needed a fresh start somewhere else."

"But they didn't even say good-bye. Jenny was supposed to meet me today to go hiking. She never showed up. Didn't even call or stop by. I don't get it."

"Sometimes good-byes are painful. She might be traumatized by the thought of moving. I'm sure you'll hear from her eventually."

Bobby hoped he would find answers at school on Monday, but he was disappointed. No one knew anything. He asked around and discovered that no one even realized they were gone. When he told his classmates, no one was surprised. Many people who moved to San Mateo didn't stay long. He looked for Sal. He needed someone to commiserate with. And Sal was good at getting answers. Perhaps he knew the real story or could find out. But Sal wasn't in school that day.

Bobby rode his bike directly toward Sal's house after school. After their recent conversations, he knew that Sal was searching for answers and direction, so the fact that his attendance at school had become spotty was not surprising. As Bobby approached the big white-brick house, he had a feeling of déjà vu. From a block away, he could see a sign posted in Sal's front yard: *For Sale or Rent*. He pulled into the driveway and jumped off his bike, letting it crash to the ground unceremoniously as he raced up the front steps. He pounded on the door. No answer. He jogged around to the back of the house and looked through the windows. No sign of Sal. At least the furniture was still there. He turned the doorknob. It offered no resistance and he stepped inside.

"Hey, Sal! You in here? Sal! Anybody home?"

No answer.

He walked around the lower level of the house. Everything looked normal. He opened the refrigerator and saw milk, eggs, soda, condiments and leftover pizza. He walked upstairs and entered Sal's bedroom. His posters were on the wall. His game ball from the district championship was still mounted on the dresser. He looked in the closet. It was empty— not a stitch of clothing. He turned abruptly and began pulling at the dresser drawers. They were empty as well. He picked up the phone on the nightstand. The line was dead.

Sal was gone.

Chapter 18
Twenty Years Later

MICHAEL SANCHEZ JUMPED out of bed earlier than usual. The clock on the nightstand read 5:05. This was going to be an action-packed day and he was eager to get on with it.

A blast of humidity hit him as he exited the hotel. It was already warm at this hour, which portended a scorcher of a day in Washington, D.C. He briskly walked the few blocks to the National Mall and began jogging when he arrived at the Lincoln Memorial. His feet felt light and his pace was quick, to match his high spirits.

He relished the tranquility of the nation's capital at this early morning hour. It was late June, but aside from a small handful of early morning runners in the Mall, the city seemed quiet and peaceful. He ran the length of the Mall, along the Reflecting Pool, past the Washington Monument and the Smithsonian Castle, then veered right as he approached the Capitol Building. He circled its vast parklike grounds and soon found himself at the front steps of the Supreme Court. He stopped and gazed at the magnificent building. He had walked through those massive bronze doors for the first time eight months ago. He distinctly remembered feeling awestruck, both because of the physical beauty of the classical architecture with the gleaming white marble and also because of the history and power the structure represented.

Sanchez walked slowly around the building, observing it from all sides and appreciating the intricate design and artwork much more than he had during his previous visit. It was different then. He had walked the same grounds but saw very little because his mind was focused on something else—the abstract concepts of the oral argument he was preparing to make to the Supreme Court. At the age of 35, he had the opportunity many lawyers aspired to but few actually achieved—taking a case all the way to the nation's highest court and presenting it to the nine Supreme Court Justices.

That in itself was an accomplishment and reason for excitement. In this instance, it was far more than that, because the case he was arguing was one of the most closely followed cases in years. Immigration was a hot-button issue. It sparked heated debate and passionate feelings from all sides, with far-reaching ramifications from a legal, political and societal perspective. The case of *Munoz vs. The State of Arizona* would have a profound impact on the future of immigrant rights, as well as how much authority the states would have in dealing with these issues. And that decision would be handed down by the Supreme Court in a matter of hours.

Michael Sanchez had positioned himself perfectly to be the ideal advocate for this case. Following his graduation from Yale Law School, he had gone to work for a boutique law firm in South Texas, with offices in Austin, Houston and San Antonio. He started his career representing business enterprises with cross-border operations. Having been raised in South Texas, he had been able to develop a network of business and political contacts that enabled him to navigate the complex web of treaties, tax, and import/export issues that impacted the business transactions of his high-paying corporate clients, as well as the visa and immigration issues that such businesses had to deal with on a regular basis. While the large business transactions generated most of the revenue for his firm, he had become much more passionate about the immigration issues, largely because they felt personal to him. He had grown up surrounded by people who had no official status or right to be in this country. He had become a committed and effective advocate for that element of society and his reputation quickly spread. He was flashy and charismatic and had developed a talent for drawing media attention to his cases and causes. Although those immigration causes typically generated little revenue for his firm, the reputation he had built resulted in more business than the firm could handle. The firm's growth exploded because of Michael Sanchez, and his power and influence within the firm and outside of it grew rapidly. At first, the calls had come from various places around Texas, but soon clients were pouring in from the entire Southwest, and then from across the nation. When he was approached by an immigrants rights group from Phoenix about the *Munoz* case, he instantly saw the potential for huge publicity and even the possibility of a case he could take to the United States Supreme Court if he played his cards right.

He had orchestrated a brilliant legal strategy and an even more impressive PR effort and succeeded in bringing national attention to the case. At issue was a set of highly controversial laws enacted by the State of Arizona that many regarded as anti-immigrant and inconsistent with the constitutions of both the United States and the State of Arizona. The primary issue involved a challenge to the State of Arizona's legislative restriction on rights of "illegal" residents to health benefits, welfare payments, food stamps and access to education at the state's public colleges and universities on the same terms as legal residents. The legislation at issue also prohibited any municipality from acting as a sanctuary city by refusing to cooperate with federal immigration enforcement actions and gave the state's law enforcement agencies broad authority to question an individual's legal status, thereby touching off allegations of racism and profiling. There was speculation that the Supreme Court would go beyond addressing these specific issues and would take this opportunity to address complicated and controversial issues pertaining to states' rights and the federal government's power to preempt state legislation in this area.

To the media and the public, the legal nuances and technicalities of the constitutional arguments were of no concern. In the minds of the masses, this case had been reduced to simple sound bites. One side represented law and order and the need to protect our borders above all else, whereas the other side represented basic human rights and compassion for those who, by accident of birth, were not possessed of US citizenship.

The Justices would enter the courtroom at 9:00 sharp, although the doors would open at 8:00. Sanchez found himself back at the courthouse steps at 7:30, having showered and swapped out his jogging suit for a navy pinstripe. He had left his shoes with the bellhop last night to be shined for the occasion and he stared down at them admiringly. He was ready. He surveyed the plaza and the front steps to find the perfect background for the interviews that were sure to come after the ruling was announced. He decided to try to situate himself front and center, on the lowest step, since that provided just the right distance between him and the building to allow the cameras to capture the inscription above the doors that read "Equal Justice Under the Law." That would make for a great picture, worthy of cover pages on newspapers and magazines all across the land.

He was in a no-lose situation. If he won, he could speak out eloquently about this great victory for the cause of immigrants and natural law and America's commitment to passionate inclusion. He would be even more sought after for such causes than he was already. If he lost, he could speak with righteous indignation about the need to continue the battle on other fronts. He would still get plenty of face time with the news media, maybe even more than if he won because the supporters of the cause would be motivated to continue the fight and he would be seen as their crusader.

Sanchez made his way through the buzzing crowd shortly after 8:00. These Supreme Court announcements always attracted a throng of media types, but this crowd was larger than normal. Most of them were gathered outside the courtroom, since only 50 were lucky enough to be allowed access to the courtroom itself. No telephones, cameras or other electronic devices were allowed in the courtroom, which assured that those in attendance would hear the results before the rest of the world.

As he was escorted to a seat in the front row, his excitement turned to nervousness. He realized how badly he wanted to win. The tension escalated as the nine Justices walked in precisely at 9:00, black robes billowing, and took their assigned seats facing the spectators. Protocol dictated that the Justice who wrote the majority opinion in the case would read a summary of the Court's ruling. Simultaneously with that reading, copies of the complete written opinion would be circulated to the reporters. Until that moment, the results would be a mystery, one of the best kept secrets in the land.

Sanchez attempted to make eye contact with Justice Orlando when it was announced that she would be reading the Court's decision in the *Munoz* case. He took that as a good sign, since she appeared to be supportive of his case during oral argument. He briefly succeeded in making eye contact, but Justice Orlando quickly looked away. The court clerk opened a box and lifted a stack of papers—the opinion—and began circulating them, starting in the back row. A hush overtook the crowd as Chief Justice Conlon announced that Justice Orlando would begin reading a summary of the Court's opinion in *Munoz vs. State of Arizona*.

Some Justices liked to start by announcing who had prevailed and then explain their rationale. Others enjoyed the drama and suspense and would begin reading the opinion without revealing the ultimate ruling until the end. Much to Sanchez's dismay, it became quickly apparent that Justice Orlando fell into the latter category. She began by acknowledging the merit of various points made by the opposing side.

"*Shit!*" Sanchez thought to himself. It appeared that the Court was setting up a rationale for finding against his client.

He did not yet have a copy of the written opinion. He looked to his right, two rows behind him. John Lucas, a reporter friend of his from New York who was very much on his side, had promised to give him a thumbs-up sign as soon as he saw the opinion if it went their way. Lucas had his head buried in the opinion as he flipped through the pages, a confused look on his face.

Sanchez began feeling light-headed and a wave of nausea overtook him. He had awoken feeling that even a losing decision would generate huge publicity and be a big boost to his public profile and career. Now the thought of that prospect was making him physically ill. He stared down at his shiny shoes, unable to look at the Justice as she read the opinion.

She ought to be a suspense novelist, Sanchez thought to himself, squirming in his seat. Justice Orlando was five minutes into reading the summary of her opinion and he had no idea which way the opinion was going to go, but he was getting increasingly pessimistic. So far, other than acknowledging that there were complex issues with far-reaching implications and meritorious arguments on both sides, she had spent most of her time recognizing the merits of opposing counsel's case. The courtroom was utterly silent, all eyes transfixed on the slender brown-haired Justice with the dulcet voice.

"However," she said. Sanchez felt his heart leap and a sudden surge of optimism kick in. "I find the arguments of Appellant Oscar Munoz to be even more compelling from both a legal and a societal perspective." Sanchez balled his fists and pounded them silently on the table in front of him, exercising every ounce of restraint he could muster to avoid hoisting them into the air and shouting. He barely heard the remainder of her pronouncement. A copy of the written opinion was thrust over his shoulder by someone sitting behind him. He flipped to the final page of the Court's opinion and confirmed what he thought he had just heard. He had won!

Microphones were thrust into his face the moment he set foot out of the courtroom. He ignored the questions being shouted at him as he made his way through the marble passageway known as the Great Hall, lined with busts of the former Chief Justices. He exited through the brass doors and motioned to his preordained spot, front and center near the bottom of the stairs. Once he was situated exactly where he wanted to be, with the perfect angle of the Supreme Court Building as a backdrop, he raised his hand in a gesture for silence as he looked out over the sea of reporters.

"First of all, I would like to thank Mr. Oscar Munoz and the other members of this class, for having the courage, fortitude and patience to fight this fight all the way here to the Supreme Court. This is your case and your victory!" Shouts and applause arose from many of the onlookers. "I would also like to thank the Supreme Court for understanding the far-reaching ramifications of these issues and being willing to treat this matter with the gravity and careful consideration that it deserves. This decision paves the way for thousands—maybe millions—of immigrants in this country to lay claim to basic human rights that we as Americans enjoy.

"America is the land of opportunity. It is also a land of immigrants. This is still a young country, and we are all descendants of immigrants.

White, black, brown—they came from Europe, Africa, Asia, Latin America—all over—in search of a better life. Immigrants are the lifeblood of America and always have been. This diversity provides us with a cultural richness that is unique to this country and that makes us a great nation. In recent years, some of our people and institutions seem to have forgotten that. Too many are forced to live in the shadows, because immigrants are persecuted, demeaned and discriminated against—based on something they had no control over—where they were born. Yes, America is a nation that respects laws, but our laws must be grounded in compassion and fairness. I was fortunate enough to be born here, so by that accident of birth, I enjoy the rights of an American citizen. But my father was not. He was born in Mexico. He came here without papers and without legal status. He spent most of his life living in the shadows. Today's decision represents a big step in helping people like him come into the light and enjoy the rights and opportunities this great nation has to offer. Today is a great day and a real milestone in immigrant rights. I couldn't be more pleased with this result!"

"Mr. Sanchez, are you taking up other causes relating to immigration issues?" shouted a booming male voice from near the back of the crowd.

"Absolutely!" Sanchez responded. "We've won a major victory here today, but there are many other battles still to be fought. This is a cause I am passionate about. I will fight in the courthouse and I will fight in the legislature. That's where we can make the most difference—changing our laws—so educating and persuading lawmakers is of paramount importance."

"Sounds like you should run for office!" yelled a stylishly dressed young Hispanic woman holding a recording device. The crowd laughed and cheered. "Are you considering a political career?"

Sanchez laughed. "Never say never, but I'm way too busy for that right now and I love doing what I'm doing."

He answered a few more questions and then attempted to politely excuse himself. Several reporters asked if he would be willing to appear on camera later in the day in their studios. His highest priority now was generating as much PR for himself as possible while this was still news, so he happily agreed. His secretary, Lindsay, contacted him with a long list of television stations and newspapers that were requesting interviews. He gave her strict instructions about prioritizing those appointments. Those media outlets with the highest audience numbers were given top priority. He instructed her to try to schedule all of those within the next few days, starting with that evening's national news broadcasts and the early morning television talk shows the following day. He asked Lindsay to try to accommodate everyone else she could over the next few weeks.

After hanging up with Lindsay, he checked his cell phone. His voice-mail box showed a message indicating that it was full, and he had a long string of text messages. He scrolled through them quickly, intending to return calls and messages later in the day unless something really grabbed his attention. One text message did. *Professor Vega* was the name attached to it. *Congratulations, Counselor! I'm truly proud of you. I'll be back at Yale for Fall Semester. Let's get together then. Have things to discuss.*

Chapter 19

"AH, THAT FEELS good!" Sheriff Ray Reid stepped into the cool air conditioning of Lucia's Diner, breaking the silence with his exclamation and the tinkling of the little silver bell attached to the front door. It was the quiet time between lunch and dinner and the restaurant was technically closed, but this was small-town Texas and the door was unlocked. He knew that the staff was off duty, but Lucia would be there and she would be cheerful and welcoming, as always. She jumped up from the back booth where she was reading a fashion magazine.

"Well, hey there, Sheriff. Come on in," Lucia Rojas called out, flashing a bright smile. "Have a seat. I can't believe you wear that uniform in this heat. It must be 100 degrees today."

"One hundred and two, according to my dashboard thermometer," the sheriff replied. "Am I too late for lunch?"

"Of course not. We're never off the clock when Sheriff Reid stops in. What can I get you?"

"How about your famous Reuben sandwich and a tall glass of iced tea. I better skip the fries or I won't be able to wear this uniform much longer. And just leave the whole pitcher of tea here, will you? I've got to rehydrate. Been out in this blasted heat all day."

"You got it, Sheriff."

Ray Reid had been Sheriff of Carroll County for nearly ten years. He wore his uniform proudly and would never consider taking it off while on duty, no matter what the circumstances. He could have gotten away with khaki shorts that matched his official shirt, but he considered that undignified. He took his job seriously and had an image to uphold. There were not many professional opportunities for a young man in rural South Texas. The truly talented and highly motivated typically moved away in search of greater opportunity as soon as they were old enough. But Reid had found his calling. He had grown up in the area. He was likable, hard-working and serious, and jumped at the opportunity to join the Sheriff's Department as a junior officer when he was twenty-one. After seven years on the job, he was the natural choice to take over when his predecessor retired ten years ago. Now he was a big wheel in this little universe and was treated as such. People like Lucia Rojas, who also grew up in town, held him in the highest regard and treated him with the utmost respect.

He was famished, but Sheriff Reid munched on his sandwich slowly, relishing the cool and the quiet. His cell phone vibrated before he had consumed half his sandwich. He recognized the number on his caller ID and let out a heavy sigh.

"Hey, Tom. What's up?" He tried his best to sound positive and energetic, rather than cranky and tired, which is how he felt.

Tom Serbin was a Border Patrol agent. Their respective job duties brought them into frequent contact with one another. "Sorry to bother you again, Ray, but we just got word that more corpses have been found. Appears to be at least three—could be more. It's a good four miles south of the place where we found that body about two weeks ago. Rugged terrain out there."

"Damn! This is getting out of hand," Reid replied. "I'll take it from here, Tom. Looks like I better go round up Bobby Rivera."

"I'm told it's a pretty grisly scene. Worse than the others."

"Not sure how it could get any worse. Anyway, all the more reason for me to find Rivera ASAP. I'm on it."

"Thanks, pal. Fill me in once you've investigated."

"Will do."

Reid pushed his half-eaten sandwich across the table, his appetite gone.

Lucia watched him from behind the counter. "Something wrong with the sandwich?" she asked.

"The sandwich was great, Lucia. Duty calls, I'm afraid. Thanks. You're a gem."

"Everything OK, Sheriff?"

He looked at her, trying to find a suitable response, but words failed him. He just shook his head grimly and shuffled toward the door, pausing briefly to brace himself against the oven-like blast of heat that was about to assault him.

Chapter 20

ALEX ZAMORA HUNG up the phone and cursed under his breath. As a lifelong funeral director and the proprietor of Zamora Family Mortuary, he had learned to sense trouble even before it walked through his front door. This was one of those cases he wished he could simply decline. However, as San Mateo's only funeral home, that was not an option. Not only would it be insensitive, it would be bad for business. It might hurt his reputation, which was critically important in the highly sensitive funeral business. More importantly, it would create an opportunity for some competitor to open up against him. The town wasn't big enough to share funeral cases with another mortuary. He barely eked out a living as it was. So, he had always made it his policy to work with everyone in their time of need, regardless of financial means, immigration status, challenging personalities or difficult family circumstances.

He walked through the quiet funeral home in search of his younger colleague, and found him in his small but tidy office, proofreading an obituary. "Hey, Bobby, I need you to handle Dr. Duran's case. It might be a little touchy—right up your alley."

Bobby Rivera looked up and removed his reading glasses. "Sure thing, boss. What's the story?"

"You knew Dr. Duran, right? Big shot at Carroll County Hospital?"

"Of course I knew him. Used to be the head cardiologist there, and then he was put in charge of the entire hospital. My parents worked there, so I've known him personally for years. He was a great guy."

"Then you should know that he married a much younger woman a couple of years ago after his first wife passed away—a nurse, barely out of school. Quite a looker from what I've heard."

Bobby sat back in his chair, rocking slightly. "And why do you think this is going to be touchy?" he asked.

"The obvious reasons. First, Dr. Duran's two children may resent the fact that their father remarried so quickly after their mother died. Second, they may question the motives of their new stepmother, Judy, who's younger than they are. She can't be older than 30. Dr. Duran must have been nearly 80, and he was very well off."

"Anything else I should know?"

"Yes, Mrs. Duran is going to be in here to make arrangements this morning at ten o'clock. I just got off the phone with her and she was adamant that she didn't want her stepchildren to have anything to do with the funeral. Says she's hired a lawyer and she'll sue to keep them away if she has to."

"I get the picture. I'll handle it."

"Thanks, Bobby. This will be a high-profile funeral and I'm sorry to dump this on you, but I know you'll handle it beautifully, as you always do. I'll be available if you need me. Keep me posted."

Zamora walked back into his office and shut the door. He looked around at the numerous pictures of himself with local dignitaries and the various plaques and awards adorning the walls and bookshelves, expressing appreciation for his community service. It was his life's work and he was proud of it. A few years ago, he would not have dreamed of handing off a high-profile case like Dr. Duran, but he had total confidence in his young protégé. Bobby would handle the case better than he could. Probably better than anyone could. He was well-known and well-liked. He had a way with people. He had a big heart. He was compassionate and empathetic. He seemed to be able to make a personal connection with everyone he encountered, particularly when they were grieving. Zamora couldn't imagine anyone better suited to be a funeral director and he realized how lucky he was that Bobby Rivera worked for him and represented his firm, even if it meant that people now often asked for Bobby rather than him when death came calling. He and the business clearly benefited immensely from Bobby's involvement. And in a case like this, where all of his instincts told him there were going to be major headaches, he felt relieved that he could just hand the case off to Bobby and know that it would be handled masterfully.

Bobby spent the better part of the day acting as mediator. Dr. Duran's young widow refused to speak to the doctor's children and vice versa. Both sides were adamant about getting their way and quick to threaten legal action against the funeral home if it didn't take their side. It became clear to Bobby that the widow and her aggressive big city lawyer were posturing for leverage in the battle over the estate that was sure to follow and cared little about the details regarding Dr. Duran's funeral services. In fact, they said that they wanted no services at all—just a private burial in the county cemetery. The doctor's children were blinded by their hostility toward the young woman they believed had taken advantage of their aging father and couldn't even be in the same room as her.

Bobby carefully avoided taking sides and worked diligently to convince all parties of the merits of temporarily setting aside their differences and finding common ground for a dignified service that would be appropriate for a man of Dr. Duran's stature in the community. Eventually, after many hours of back-and-forth diplomacy, and realizing that Bobby was neither going to take sides nor be intimidated by threats of legal action, the family members agreed to a compromise. They would proceed with a visitation and a funeral service, at the expense of Dr. Duran's children, so that Dr. Duran's many friends and colleagues could pay their respects. Following the services, his remains would be cremated and the ashes would be divided equally between the widow and the children.

After all parties had agreed to those terms, Dr. Duran's widow Judy stopped by the funeral home to sign the standard cremation authorization forms. While Bobby was guiding her through the paperwork in his office, Mrs. Delgado, the silver-haired receptionist, gently knocked on his door and opened it just a crack.

"I'm sorry to interrupt you, Bobby," she said, "but Sheriff Reid is here to see you. He said it's urgent."

"Thank you, Mariana. Please tell him I'm busy with a family right now."

"I already told him that. He says it's urgent and that he'll wait." She closed the door softly, leaving Bobby alone with the young widow to complete the paperwork.

When they were finished, Bobby escorted Judy to her car, then briskly walked back into the funeral home. "He's in there," said Mrs. Delgado, nodding toward the arrangement room.

The feeling of relief and satisfaction at resolving the family dispute was fleeting, as Bobby paused momentarily in the lobby and stared at the closed arrangement room door. A sense of dread overcame him. "This can't be good," he muttered, as he tried to steel himself against what he knew was coming.

Chapter 21

A GRIM-FACED SHERIFF Reid was talking on his cell phone when Bobby entered the arrangement room.

"I'm not sure when I'll be home. Depends on what we find. Looks like there are three more bodies, but we won't really know until we get there," the Sheriff said into his phone, giving Bobby a slight nod as he entered. "I'm picking up Bobby Rivera right now. Don't wait up."

A concerned look crossed Bobby's face. "Can you come with me, Bobby?" Reid asked.

"More bodies?"

"Yep. Just got a report from a ranch hand down on the Jacobson Ranch, about 45 miles south of here. He saw buzzards flying over a remote part of the ranch and went to investigate. Found three bodies, or at least he thinks so. Couldn't be sure because it looks like the buzzards and coyotes got there first. Pretty gruesome site. And it's in the middle of nowhere—miles from the nearest road."

"Count me in, Sheriff. I know that area."

"I thought you would. Too bad those poor devils didn't. They must have been wandering through The Brush for a long time."

Bobby looked down and shook his head sadly. "Same old story. It tears me up every time."

"I know. Me too." The Sheriff glanced at his watch. "We've got about three hours of daylight left. Think we can get there and find them by then? If not, we better wait until the morning."

"It'll be cutting it close, but I think we should go for it. I hate to leave them at the mercy of the critters for another night. You've got the location?"

"Yeah, the rancher sent me the coordinates, so we know where they are. The challenge is getting there in our four-wheeler. It's rough terrain out there."

"No sweat. I can get us there. Are we stopping by the M.E.'s office to pick up Manny?" Bobby asked.

Sheriff Reid stood up and they walked out of the arrangement room. "No. I filled him in but he said he's really swamped and that if you were available, he didn't need to come along."

"OK. Daylight's wasting. Let's go. I'll grab some body bags and meet you in the parking lot."

The drill had become all too familiar to both Bobby Rivera and Sheriff Reid—responding to reports from the Border Patrol or local ranchers involving dead bodies discovered out in the remote brush areas of Carroll County. Invariably, they were the remains of those who had crossed the border from Mexico and perished after days or weeks of wandering through the scorching heat and the rugged desert terrain. That unforgiving land encompassed hundreds of square miles, much of which was private ranchland, but there were few signs of private ownership or human presence at all.

Illegal border crossings were a common occurrence in that part of South Texas. Some succeeded but many were apprehended. Some deliberately chose to avoid the higher risk of apprehension along the roadways and take their chances crossing the unpopulated desert. Others were given no choice in the matter. They were hustled across the border by human traffickers and guided into the remote desert areas where there was little risk of immediate capture by the Border Patrol. The smugglers preferred that approach because there was less risk for their business enterprise. Sometimes they would send a guide along to help the illegals find their way through the desert, but that was rare. Typically, they would be guided across the border and into the desert and then left to fend for themselves as they headed north. There was no food to be found unless they were skillful or lucky enough to capture some form of edible wildlife, and virtually no water during most of the year. They were forced to subsist on what they could carry. Far too often, their journey, which had begun far to the south with high hopes, came to a lonely and desperate end in the cruel South Texas desert.

The plight of those travelers and the families they left behind tugged at Bobby's heartstrings. His professional life was devoted to providing dignified and meaningful farewell tributes to the deceased and comfort to the bereaved family members that survived. When he was first contacted by Manny Quintana, the local Medical Examiner, to help retrieve remains found in the desert, he felt called to assist. Technically, the M.E. had jurisdiction over these cases because the deaths had occurred in Carroll County and there was no one else to take custody of the remains and handle their disposition. However, Manny packed nearly 300 pounds into his 5' 6" frame and was badly out of shape, so the concept of making strenuous treks into the desert was not the least bit appealing to him. Bobby was the perfect person to lend a hand. He knew the desert as well as anyone, having been raised nearby and having personally hiked and explored a significant portion of the vast desert expanse. In addition, good funeral and legal protocol dictated that a licensed funeral director oversee the removal of dead human remains, particularly in cases where the condition of the remains or the circumstances surrounding death required delicate handling.

There was not much to be done by the Medical Examiner's Office in most cases. The cause of death was obvious, so there was no need for an inquest or an autopsy. The most valuable service the M.E. could provide was locating the next-of-kin. Unfortunately, that was virtually impossible in most cases. A small percentage of the unfortunate travelers had enough foresight to bring some sort of identifying document or picture or letter, which might be found on their person, giving the M.E. at least something to go on when trying to identify and contact next-of-kin. That information often was not particularly helpful or it might have been lost or destroyed by the elements. The vast majority left absolutely no trace of their identity, which left the M.E. in a quandary about what to do with their remains. He was reluctant to cremate them because a family member might turn up asking about their lost loved one. That was unlikely—in fact it had never happened with any of these desert cases. But the cases had started piling up and taking up scarce space in his refrigeration unit, so he had sought advice from Bobby Rivera.

Bobby brought his boss, Alex Zamora, into the discussion and the three of them devised a plan. Living in South Texas, they were acutely aware of the plight of illegal immigrants, and profoundly sympathetic. They all agreed that finding a respectful way to handle these remains was the right thing to do and something that would be appreciated by the community as well as families of those who had perished on their journey to a new life they never found.

Cremation was not a good option because it precluded any possibility of later identifying remains—it completely destroyed all DNA. They decided that burial was a better option and were able to persuade Carroll County officials to donate a parcel of land in the county cemetery for the burial of these remains. The funeral home agreed to provide simple wooden caskets at no cost to the county, which were used when bodies were recovered reasonably intact. Where only body fragments were discovered, other containers were typically used, sometimes body bags and sometimes whatever smaller containers the M.E. happened to have on hand. Bobby took photographs and kept meticulous records of everything that was found, and those records were kept at the funeral home. There were no grave markers over individual graves because no one knew the identity of the person buried there. In some cases, only partial remains existed because the remains had been devoured and scattered by the desert beasts, so it was not even possible to determine whether a collection of bones and fragments found belonged to one individual or more than one. A single headstone was placed at the entrance to this section of the cemetery with an inscription that read: *"In honor of those who risked everything in search of a better life in America. May you rest in peace."*

It was a dignified final resting place and there was at least a chance that if someone showed up searching for a lost loved one, their remains might still be found based on matching the records to whatever information the surviving family members could provide.

The drive to the Jacobson Ranch took nearly two hours. An unpaved road marked the eastern property line and Sheriff Reid drove his Land Rover over the bumpy road until he reached a point that placed him about two miles due east of their destination. He and Bobby got out of the vehicle and surveyed the property on the west side of the road.

"You gotta be kidding me," Reid exclaimed, frustration in his voice. "This Land Rover is pretty rugged and can handle just about anything, but if we go down that ravine, we'll never get out!" They walked about thirty yards through thick brush and stared down a steep ravine that looked rocky and unstable.

"You're right, Ray" Bobby said. "We can't drive through this. But I know another way. We need to drive farther south about a mile or so. It levels out there."

Bobby directed Reid to the place to start their off-road trek. The Land Rover bounced over rocks, climbed and descended hills and gullies, all the while crashing through thick brush. The Sheriff was a confident driver, but experience had taught him not to underestimate The Brush. He drove slowly and cautiously, watching the terrain directly in front of them for holes, rocks and other obstacles, and at the same time regularly scanning the horizon to keep his bearings. He looked nervously at the sun as it sunk low in the western sky.

Just before sunset, they approached a line of large boulders that provided some shelter from the still blistering sun. They smelled it before they saw it. Sheriff Reid parked the Land Rover in a small clearing. Bobby was first out of the car and immediately made his way toward the rocks, holding a handkerchief over his nose and mouth. The rocks provided shade from the late afternoon sun, so it made sense that exhausted and overheated travelers would have sought refuge in the only shade they could find.

Then he saw them. Two bodies lying side-by-side and what was left of another about forty feet away. He tried to tune out the sound and the sight of the buzzing flies as he approached the two bodies that were together. They had clearly been there for quite a few days. The desert heat had accelerated the natural decomposition process to the point where the faces would have been unrecognizable even to those who knew them well. Judging by the size and the long hair, it seemed likely that one of the bodies was a young girl, probably no more than nine or ten years old. Her remains were significantly more decomposed than the adult body lying at her side. The child probably died first, and then the parent refused to leave her side, Bobby surmised.

Both bodies were clad in jeans and T-shirts. Their footwear was not made for desert hiking. They both wore cheap canvas athletic shoes with holes worn through their soles. Bobby noticed a dirty red backpack leaning against the rocks. He opened it and rummaged through the contents: two empty water bottles, plastic wrappers from candy bars and beef jerky, a baseball cap and some dirty socks and T-shirts—no pictures, papers or identification of any kind. As usual. He searched the pockets of the adult. They were empty. He searched the girl's pockets, then gently turned her over, to find her arm clutching a dirty, ragged stuffed animal. It may have once been a replica of the Snoopy dog from the Peanuts cartoon, but it was too battered to be certain.

Sheriff Reid stood by silently as Bobby examined the bodies. He noticed the tears streaming down Bobby's face as Bobby stood up and continued staring at the small figure laid out before him.

"I hate this," Bobby whispered, wiping his eyes with the back of his hand.

Chapter 22

IT WAS PAST midnight when Sheriff Reid's Land Rover swung into the driveway adjacent to the dark funeral home. He backed the vehicle up to the garage door, then Bobby climbed out and punched numbers into a keypad. The garage door creaked as it slowly rose. Bobby ducked his head and entered as soon as the door cleared his height and emerged with a gurney that he wheeled up next to the Land Rover.

They pulled the first body bag onto the gurney and wheeled it through the garage and into the back room, Bobby at the front end and Sheriff Reid pushing from the rear. They stopped at a large stainless steel door, where Bobby punched in a number on another keypad, then opened the funeral home's walk-in refrigeration unit and flipped on the light. Metal shelves lined both sides of the refrigerator, forming twelve spaces for storing human remains, two high and three across on each side of the unit, with a number stenciled on each individual shelf space. More often than not, the cooler was empty, but tonight there was one body covered by a white sheet in the middle space on the upper shelf. Bobby glanced at the clipboard resting on that shelf, confirming that it was Dr. Duran who was still in the custody of Zamora Family Mortuary. They put the body bag on the shelf opposite the doctor, then made two more trips to the vehicle to move the other body bags.

"Thanks, Bobby," Sheriff Reid said, yawning and rubbing his bleary eyes. "Don't know what we'd do without you around here. Get some rest."

"Goodnight, Sheriff," Bobby replied. "I'll meet you at the M.E.'s office in the morning."

These were technically Medical Examiner's cases and belonged in the custody of Manny Quintana, the M.E. However, Bobby didn't want to force Manny to wait up half the night, so he took temporary custody of the remains to spare Manny the inconvenience. Bobby grabbed three clipboards from outside the refrigeration unit, each of which had several sheets of paper clipped to it. The top sheet bore the heading "Decedent Information" and had multiple lines for the name of the deceased, date of death, names of the next-of-kin, place the body was retrieved, social security number and other identifying information. On that page, Bobby wrote the words *Doe 42, Doe 43 and Doe 44* and placed one such sheet on each of the three clipboards. He knew without checking his records that these were the forty-second, forty-third and forty-fourth bodies he had recovered from The Brush. There was no other identifying information he could add to the forms. The other pages on the clipboard would be left blank. One was an inventory sheet for personal effects, another was an embalming authorization, and a third was an application for a death certificate. There were also forms for the family to sign authorizing either burial or cremation and to capture the family's wishes regarding the funeral service. Bobby ignored those forms and simply attached the handwritten notes he had made at the recovery site about the condition of the remains, the clothing and personal effects found at the site. In the morning, he would transcribe his notes and print out pictures he had taken on his camera phone before delivering the remains and copies of those documents to the Medical Examiner.

He closed the refrigerator and walked wearily through the quiet funeral home to his office to check for messages before heading home. There was a newspaper article on his chair, with a pale yellow post-it note affixed to it stating *Bobby, we need to talk.* Bobby glanced at the article. It was an advertisement by a San Antonio Funeral Home marketing their expertise in shipping remains back and forth across the Mexican border.

***

Early the next morning, Alex Zamora pulled into the funeral home to find Bobby already there, loading the last of the three body bags into the funeral home van for the short trip to the M.E.'s office.

"Morning, boss," Bobby called out brightly as Mr. Zamora got out of his car and shuffled toward him. "Got your note about San Antonio. I'll stop by as soon as I've dropped these cases off with Manny."

Zamora shot him an irritated look and continued walking through the garage toward the funeral home's rear entrance. "How many?" he called over his shoulder.

"Three," Bobby replied, slamming the van's rear door and wheeling the gurney back into the garage.

"Jesus Christ," Zamora grumbled.

An hour later Bobby returned to the funeral home and stuck his head into Zamora's office, where he found his boss sipping coffee and punching numbers into an old-fashioned adding machine as he scrutinized some messy-looking spreadsheets. "Is now a good time?" Bobby asked.

"Good a time as any. C'mon in, Bobby." Zamora leaned back in his desk chair and exhaled loudly as he clasped his hands behind his head. "I need to make some changes around here. We're barely keeping our heads above water."

"What can I do, Mr. Zamora?" Bobby asked, trying to sound positive and eager to help out despite the feeling of dread that was settling over him.

Zamora gave him a long look. "You know how it is in this business. We're a small town in a sparsely populated county. We're the only game in town, but as you well know, there just aren't a lot of deaths happening around here. The population here is mostly younger people. Sometimes we go for weeks without handling a single service. And even when we get cases, most people don't have a lot of money."

"Isn't that why you bought the San Antonio business last year? That puts us in a market with an exploding population."

"That was the plan when I bought it but we're barely breaking even on that front."

Bobby looked down. "I understand. Are you letting me go?' he asked with quiet resignation.

"No. Hell no! That's not what this is about. I just need you to start doing things that will bring in money. This is a business, Bobby. You're a great funeral director—a wonderful and compassionate caregiver—but this is a business and we need to make money. It's great that you spend all that time helping out the Sheriff and the M.E. with cases like you picked up last night, but that doesn't bring in any revenue. I let you talk me into helping out with that as a community service. I wanted to charge the M.E. for the containers and your time and at least make a little something on that but, as you know, we decided not to."

"So you think we should start charging the county for those cases?"

"No, that's not what I'm saying. That would look awkward now, and Manny would throw a fit. What I am saying is that I need to use you differently. Look, most of the revenue we bring in from San Antonio is the cross-border stuff. You're the one that has the connections and knows how to make that happen. But now the big funeral home company is aggressively going after that business." He waved the newspaper advertisement in front of him. "Anyway, that shouldn't be our bread and butter. We should be competing for the local funerals there. We've got a great location, but we just have Alberto manning it part-time and he's already in retirement mode. He'll be retiring completely by year-end. We need a presence in that community. I need *you* up there, doing what it takes to grow that business, getting involved in the community, meeting the local clergy, being the face of our business there."

"But what about our business here?"

"What business? There's not much happening here and there's nothing we can do to grow our business here in Carroll County. We already get all of it, what little there is. When we have funerals here, I can handle them, or you can come down and handle it if it's someone you know and there's nothing going on in San Antonio. It's less than three hours away, so you can shuttle back and forth as needed. I'll make it worth your while."

Bobby scratched the back of his head and stared at the pictures on the wall behind Zamora's desk. "So you're asking me to split my time between here and San Antonio?"

"What I'm really asking is for you to move up to San Antonio and drive that business. I may need you here on occasion but I need San Antonio to be your focus. You can't get immersed in that community unless you're living there. What do you say?"

Bobby nodded slowly, a smile taking shape on his lips. "Seems like everyone I grew up with around here was looking for a way out—a path to a good job in a big city. I've never felt the need to move on. This is my home and I love it here. But... I suppose I can serve a lot more people up there than I can here."

"That's absolutely right, Bobby. You've touched a lot of lives around here. People know that when the need arises, Bobby Rivera is the person to call. You can become that person in San Antonio, and touch so many more lives than you ever could around here. And, you'd be doing me a favor I will never forget."

Bobby stood up and held out his hand. "I appreciate the opportunity, Mr. Zamora. Five minutes ago, I thought you were going to fire me! When do I start?"

"Dr. Duran's funeral is tomorrow. As soon as we wrap that up, I'd like you to head up to San Antonio and start looking for a place to live. And Bobby—I know you're going to want to spend time on all kinds of civic and charitable activities—which is good. But remember what I said. I need you to really focus on things that will bring in business and make us some money."

Chapter 23

MICHAEL SANCHEZ MILKED the publicity boon for all it was worth. During the weeks following his Supreme Court victory, his schedule was jam-packed with television appearances. He wanted his face in the public eye—and it was. He first appeared on the major network and cable news shows to discuss the results of the *Munoz* case and the other battles remaining to be fought in the name of immigrant rights. He was a natural on camera: good looking, passionate, eloquent, and capable of verbal jousting with anyone in a manner that came across as witty, charming and persuasive, without ever being negative or mean. That led to countless invitations from local news programs across the country. He accepted many of the invitations from television outlets in the major markets, particularly where the immigrant populations were known to be the highest—Los Angeles, San Diego, Phoenix, Las Vegas, New York and Chicago, among others. His long-term plan dictated that he pay particular attention to his home state, so he sought out appearances in Houston, San Antonio, El Paso, Dallas and Austin. He worked in interviews with the print media between his television appearances.

The results were immediate and powerful. His law firm was receiving far more business than it could handle, and embarked on an aggressive recruiting effort to hire talented lawyers to help perform the work that Michael was bringing in. Many of the requests were routine immigration issues, such as visa and green card matters that paid little or nothing. His firm did its best to keep up with that, handling much of it on a pro bono basis. That work was supplemented by a flood of engagements from companies of all sizes whose businesses involved imports, exports and cross-border transactions. Those clients were willing to pay top dollar, knowing that having Michael Sanchez's name behind them meant influence as well as aggressive and effective representation. The firm's profits were exploding, and no one profited more than Michael Sanchez.

As summer turned into fall, the interest in the *Munoz* case had run its course and the news cycle had turned to politics, as the following year was a presidential election year. It would be a free-for-all, as President Halphen's second term was expiring and there was not yet a clear-cut frontrunner for either party. It was clear that one of the hot-button issues would be whether to embark on a significant reform of federal immigration laws and policies. The news networks fanned the flames as the prospective candidates staked out positions they hoped would motivate and inspire their constituencies. Given his expertise, high profile and lively television persona, Michael Sanchez had become a regular television commentator and analyst on immigration issues for the major networks. Several of them attempted to lure him with a big contract to become an exclusive contributor for their station, but he politely refused all such offers. He wanted the face time and the public stage far more than he needed the money, and being a freelancer served that purpose well.

Just after Thanksgiving, Michael attended a fundraiser for Melissa Masterson, a long-time Democratic Congresswoman from Texas's 21st congressional district, which included some of the wealthier areas of Austin and San Antonio. His growing celebrity made him a sought-after guest at such functions, as did his increasing wealth and obvious interest in legislative matters. The event was held at the LBJ Presidential Library on the campus of The University of Texas in Austin, in the hopes of inspiring donors by immersing them in memorabilia involving the legendary Democratic politician. After chatting with the Congresswoman and pledging his support, Michael attempted to make a discreet exit but was collared by David Mullins, Chairman of the Texas Democratic Party.

"Can I get a few minutes of your time, Michael? In private?" Mullins asked.

"Sure thing, David." Michael replied amiably. "What's up?"

Mullins guided him into the Oval Office exhibit, which was a replica of the famous room from the White House as it appeared during LBJ's tenure. Congresswoman Masterson followed and closed the door behind them. "David and I have been talking, Michael, and we'd like to share some exciting news. Our illustrious Senator, Mickey McDaniel, is about to drop a political bombshell on Monday. He's going to announce that he is not running for reelection next year. He's retiring from the Senate."

Michael's eyes grew wide. "Are you kidding me? He's been there for three terms now. He's a Texas institution. No one had a shot at beating him. What's the story?"

"His wife Kayla has stage four breast cancer," the Congresswoman replied.

"And regardless of what anyone might say about McDaniel's politics, he's a class act," said Mullins. "He wants to be there for his wife, and he can't do that from Washington."

Mullins paused and stared at Sanchez, looking for a reaction. Michael's eyes swept the room, but they were unfocused. "I can see the wheels turning in your head, Michael, and I can guess what you're thinking—same thing we all are. This is a golden opportunity for Texas to finally send a Democrat to the Senate. It's been over 25 years since we've held that office, but the timing is perfect. The Republicans have assumed McDaniel would be there forever. They're scrambling. They don't have a Plan B yet."

"And the demographics are with us." Michael replied excitedly. "Texas has been a red state for way too long, but it's been gradually turning blue. Hispanics now make up over 50% of the population. That's our constituency. We just need to make sure they're energized and engaged so we get the vote out. You've got to find a candidate who can do that. Who are you thinking of running, and how can I help? Fundraisers, working the media… just let me know what I can do and I'll get all over it!"

The congresswoman and the party leader looked at each other in silence. Then Mullins said, "I don't think you understand, Mike. We don't want you helping from the sidelines. We want you to run! We want *you* to be the next Senator from the great State of Texas! What do you say?"

Michael's jaw dropped, and he looked from one to the other, words failing him.

"What about it, Michael? I can't think of anybody better suited," said Masterson. "You're already a known commodity. You're high profile. Charismatic. Accomplished. And you're on the right side of the immigration issue. You're exactly the right person to energize our base."

"I'm stunned… I've always had politics in the back of my mind, but I've considered that something I'd explore way down the road. I need to think about this."

"Of course you do," Mullins replied. "But don't think too long. Others are sure to jump into the race pretty damn fast. They'll start raising money and ginning up supporters and it will be harder to deal with them once they get some momentum. If you act quickly, that'll keep a lot of others out of the race. I wouldn't be telling you this if I didn't believe it, but I think this nomination is yours for the taking. Think about it, but time's a-wasting, so do it fast and let me know."

Michael thanked Mullins and Masterson for their votes of confidence, then quietly slipped out of the building and found himself wandering the dark University of Texas campus. He walked quickly and purposefully, but without any destination. There was a fall chill in the air, but he wore no overcoat. He was oblivious to the cold. The campus was known as "The 40 Acres" by the faithful and he was pretty sure he had roamed all 40 before he set his sights for home. The shock was wearing off, replaced with a feeling of exhilaration as he contemplated the opportunity. It fit in perfectly with his long-term plan, only it was happening unexpectedly, and far sooner than he had ever imagined. But he knew that David Mullins and Melissa Masterson were exactly right—there was no one better suited than him to win this election.

The following Monday morning, Michael Sanchez found himself in David Mullins's office across the street from the State Capitol in Austin. He stared out the window at the massive Texas State Capitol building with its soaring rotunda and imagined another gleaming marble hall of power about 1300 miles to the east. At noon, they watched Mickey McDaniel tearfully announce that he would be giving up his Senate seat the following year.

Sanchez had made his decision and was ready to devote all of his considerable energy to the new challenge in front of him. He spent all of Monday afternoon with Mullins, talking about the team he needed to build. He had never given any thought to it, but quickly realized that he needed to build an entire enterprise, which meant hiring a campaign manager, a PR expert, a pollster, a social media guru and countless other administrative support types. Mullins would be an invaluable resource in helping him identify the right candidates for those roles. Mullins advised him to announce his candidacy within a week of Senator McDaniel's resignation to keep potential competitors on the sidelines. That had them scrambling to find the key players for the campaign team. At a minimum, he needed to have his PR manager and his campaign manager on board immediately because it was critical that his own announcement be handled strategically and adeptly for maximum impact.

Michael scheduled a lunch meeting on Thursday at noon with Russ Miller, an experienced Austin-based political operative, who was being considered for the role of campaign manager. He arrived a few minutes early and was seated in a quiet booth toward the back of the restaurant. The hostess knew Miller well and promised Michael that she would escort him to the table as soon as he arrived. At 12:15, Michael glanced at his watch, irritation growing. He looked up expectantly each time the door opened, only to be disappointed.

"Mr. Sanchez?" Michael turned around to face a fresh-faced college girl. "A gentleman outside asked me to give this to you." She handed him an envelope and hurried away.

Michael opened the envelope and an index card fell out. *Meet me in the black Cadillac in the parking lot* was scrawled across it. He looked around and saw nothing unusual. No one appeared to be watching him. "I'll be right back," he said to the hostess as he stepped outside and around the corner into the parking lot. He immediately saw the shiny Cadillac at the far end of the lot and approached. He leaned over and attempted to peer in through the drivers-side window, but the dark tinting made it impossible to see the driver. He knocked on the window and it slowly and silently slid down.

Michael started at the sight of the familiar face. "Vargas! What the hell? What are you doing here?"

"Get in," Vargas replied.

Michael stood perfectly still, staring uncomprehendingly at the unexpected visitor. The window began rising silently. Mike quickly surveyed the parking lot, then he hurried around to the other side of the vehicle and climbed in.

"Don't worry about missing Miller. He won't be coming. He was notified that you had to cancel your meeting."

It had been 15 years, but Vargas looked the same. The oily black hair was still thick and slicked back, without a trace of gray. It was difficult to tell whether his skin had aged, since the pock marks and scars were still prominent and drew attention away from the rest of his facial features. The years had added some bulk to his previously lanky frame, which had the effect of making him even more imposing. His right hand held the steering wheel, tapping it with the two fingers still attached to the hand.

He gave Michael a sideways glance. "Nice to see you again, *Miguel*. Or should I be calling you Michael now. Or is it Mike? I like that better—more American."

Michael stared in stunned silence. Vargas wasn't smiling. It wasn't exactly a smirk either, but there was something smug or self-satisfied about his demeanor. Vargas was enjoying this little surprise. Michael was not. His encounters with the man had been few and far between but there was always something threatening and intimidating about those visits, and he associated them with bad news and bad times.

"What are you doing here, Vargas? And what do you think you're doing cancelling my lunch appointment? That was an important meeting." Michael made no attempt to hide his irritation, nor did he have any interest in exchanging pleasantries or catching up. All his instincts told him that Vargas's sudden appearance was not a good thing.

Vargas stared straight ahead through the front windshield. "He doesn't want you to run for Senate."

"Who told you I'm running for Senate? I haven't announced that, and neither has anyone else."

"C'mon, Mike. Don't insult me. I told you the first time we met that the big guy has eyes and ears everywhere. That's more true today than it's ever been. Anyway, that's the message, directly from him: Do not run for Senate. Period. Under any circumstances." He turned and stared at Michael with cold black eyes. "Are we clear on that?"

Michael returned the stare, his jaw tight. "Just who the hell do you think you are, showing up here out of the blue and telling me what to do with my life? I've done just fine without you—or him. Fuck off!" He pulled the latch on the door handle. It was locked.

Vargas shifted in the driver's seat, turning his sizable frame toward the passenger seat and grinning slightly as he watched Michael fumble with the door lock. "I'm just the messenger, as you well know. You also know that our leader has had a vested interest in you for a very long time. You wouldn't be where you are today without his support. I suggest you remember that. It would not be in your best interest to become uncooperative after all he's done for you."

Michael glared silently. The sound of the door lock popping open broke the silence and he opened the door and quickly climbed out. He bent over and leaned back into the car. "Go fuck yourself, Vargas! Stay out of my life." He slammed the door and stormed across the parking lot back into the restaurant.

Chapter 24

TERESA CRUZ GLANCED up as her replacement, Pam, walked through the sliding glass doors, shaking the water from her umbrella.

"Brrr… It's freezing out there!" Pam announced cheerfully, as she peeled off her raincoat. "Maybe we'll get a white Christmas. Hi Teresa!"

Teresa greeted her colleague with a subdued smile. Pam immediately understood. She and Teresa were very much alike—positive, happy, talkative. They were naturally wired that way, but in their line of work, those traits were essential defenses against the sadness and despair that could otherwise overwhelm most people. They must have lost someone during Teresa's shift.

"Let's go into the office. I'll fill you in," Teresa said.

They walked out of the lobby area and down the bright hospital-like corridor, turning into the small private office they shared. That was where they made the handoff on most days, Teresa briefing Pam on what happened during the day shift so that Pam would be adequately prepared for night duty.

"We lost Mrs. Vasquez today," Teresa said. "Her whole family was around her. The two grandkids made it in from Dallas this morning. They got here just in time." She smiled sadly.

"Aw, poor thing," Pam said. "I'm glad the grandkids made it. I didn't think she'd last this long. What a sweet lady. Wonderful family, too. What's going on out here?" Pam nodded toward a lounge area just across the hall, where there was a spacious seating area that resembled a living room and kitchen, with couches and comfortable chairs spread around, some facing a large screen TV and others off to the side, conducive to more private conversations. There was also a counter with bar stools and a small kitchenette, complete with a refrigerator, microwave and coffeemaker, as well as an oven and a large table covered with trays of food and beverages. Approximately a dozen people were gathered there, visiting casually, speaking in quiet voices.

"That's Mr. Hoffman's family and some of their friends," said Teresa. "His vitals all look good. He was awake most of the afternoon but the pain got pretty bad again so he asked for morphine a couple of hours ago." She glanced at his chart. "At 3:15 to be precise. He's been sleeping peacefully since then."

Teresa proceeded to brief Pam on the status of each of the other residents of Stoney Creek Hospice Care. There were 18 patient rooms, although only 14 were presently occupied. That was unusual, as it generally operated at full capacity. Given the nature of the business, the residents were temporary. Most stays could be counted in weeks, although the occasional patient would linger for months and some lasted only days. They would be brought in from a hospital or from their homes and they would leave in a funeral van.

When she finished with her briefing, Pam put an arm around Teresa's shoulder and gave her a gentle squeeze. "Well, you've had a rough few days, sister," she said. "Mrs. Vasquez today, Mrs. Campos yesterday, and two more the day before that. Sometimes I think you get too close to your patients, but I know that's who you are and that's why you're so good at what you do. You make a real difference to them. Just remember that you've got to leave it behind sometimes. I hope you're going out tonight to have a little fun. You're off tomorrow, right?"

Teresa took a deep breath and looked warmly at her friend. "I'm OK, Pam, really I am. I love what we do here. There's nothing else I'd rather be doing. And yes, I am off tomorrow. Tonight I'm meeting some old high school girlfriends down at the River Walk. I haven't seen them in ages. It'll be a great way to clear my head."

Mrs. Villareal, the night manager, abruptly opened the door and stuck her head in, smiling but harried looking. "Sorry to break this up girls, but Mrs. Gomez needs you right away in Room 3, Pam. And Mrs. Bonner is on the phone—Line 2. She's the new patient who was supposed to be checking in today."

"You go take care of Mrs. Gomez," Teresa said, looking at Pam. "I'll take the call."

"Thanks!" Pam called over her shoulder as she hurried away. "I owe you! Have fun tonight!"

Mrs. Emily Bonner had been scheduled to check in earlier that afternoon, but she had not yet arrived. Teresa recalled meeting her some months before when Mrs. Bonner was trying to decide where to spend her remaining time on this earth. She was in her mid-eighties, and fighting a losing battle with liver cancer. After their meeting, Teresa learned that Mrs. Bonner had decided to live out her time in the comfort of her own home. The trouble was, she hadn't expected to survive this long, and she was at risk of running out of money. Having around-the-clock care as well as constant medical attention at her home had turned out to be costlier than she'd anticipated, so she had made the decision to leave her home and move into Stoney Creek Hospice Care.

In recent weeks, Mrs. Bonner had been mostly bed-ridden and was often mentally foggy, but she had occasional bursts of energy and clarity. Today was one of those days. She had tidied her house and packed her belongings. Everything she cared to take with her was packed into one small rolling suitcase. She was dressed neatly and had done her hair and applied make-up for the first time in months. She wanted to look good for her final journey. The only problem was that her escort had not shown up and was not going to, at least not until sometime the following day.

"Is it OK if I still move in today?" Teresa heard the small shaky voice asking over the telephone. "My niece was supposed to come here from Atlanta to help me move in, but her flight was cancelled because of the bad weather there. But I'm ready. If you can give me the address, I'll call a cab."

"Well hello, Mrs. Bonner. This is Teresa. We met a few months ago. Of course you can move in tonight. We're all ready for you. You just wait right there. I'm hopping in my car and I'll pick you up myself. Just give me your address and tell me when to be there."

"I'm ready now. 6520 Maplewood Drive."

"Then I'm on my way. I'll see you in 10 minutes."

Teresa drove slowly down Maplewood squinting to read the addresses on the homes. The rain had stopped and the sky was now clear and cold. The tiny houses along the street looked warm and inviting. Christmas lights were draped along trees, shrubs and houses, giving the entire street a cheerful holiday feel. Toward the end of the block, she saw a small one-story house with no Christmas decorations. A single porchlight shone on a frail woman, tiny but erect, standing on the doorstep with a small suitcase at her side. Teresa parked on the street directly in front of the walkway.

She waved brightly as she climbed out of her car and marched up the sidewalk. "So nice to see you again, Mrs. Bonner! My, you look lovely tonight!"

"Thank you, dear. What's your name again?"

"It's Teresa."

"That's a lovely name. You can call me Emily."

"Do you have everything you need, Emily? Shall we walk through the house once more to be sure?"

The older woman shook her head. "I don't want to look back. I'm ready." Teresa could see the tears welling up in the older woman's eyes. Fear and apprehension were unmistakable in the quavering voice, but Teresa sensed that Emily was attempting to will those feelings aside with courage and resolve.

Teresa held out her elbow and Emily grasped it tightly as they walked slowly toward the car. After helping Mrs. Bonner into her seat and putting the luggage in the trunk, Teresa looked closely at her passenger, who was in a trance-like state, staring straight ahead. Her cheeks were moist now, glistening in the glow of the Christmas lights, but her eyes seemed unnaturally large and bright amidst a sea of ancient, wrinkled skin.

"Tell me when you're ready, Emily. I'm in no hurry.

The woman turned her head slowly, her eyes becoming alert and focused. "Thank you, dear. We can go now, but would you drive slowly, please? This street always looks so beautiful to me this time of year, all lit up like this. This will be a good way to remember it."

They drove slowly down the length of Maplewood Street. "Our neighborhood really goes all out around the holidays," Emily said. "You should see some of the other streets around here."

Teresa gave her passenger a playful look. "Well, what do you say, Emily? How about a little Christmas ride through the neighborhood?"

"Oh, could we?" the old woman replied, her face brightening. "I'd really enjoy that."

They drove around the neighborhood, up and back through the grid-like streets. Emily pointed out the houses where friends and neighbors had lived years before. They were gone now, but the ride was stirring happy memories. They stopped in front of an old movie theater on First Avenue, the main commercial street running through the neighborhood, which had the look and feel of a small town Main Street from a bygone era. "That's where Jerry and I had our first date," Emily said. "I remember sneaking a look at his handsome face in that dark theater and thinking to myself 'This is the man I'm going to marry.' And I did. We got married when we were nineteen and were married for 55 years. Then God called him away. Heart attack. But we had a great life together. He was my one true love."

They drove a bit further down First Avenue and passed an old courthouse. "That's where Jerry worked. Spent his whole career as a bailiff in the courthouse. All the judges loved him. Everybody loved Jerry…" Her voice trailed off momentarily, and then her face brightened. "Would you like to see where I worked?"

"Absolutely," Teresa replied. For a fleeting instant it crossed her mind that her friends might be missing her and wondering where she was, but she quickly banished those thoughts. She was thoroughly enjoying the company of a dying 84-year-old woman.

Emily guided her to the local public school and explained that she had taught first grade there for eight years and then became principal for the next thirty. She became more animated and chatted happily about how fulfilling she had found that job. Getting to know the neighborhood families and watching the children grow into adults created a close and lasting bond with the community. All her former students remembered her name and everyone knew who she was. Her own two children had attended school there as well.

Hours passed as they continued their leisurely drive through the neighborhood. Prolonged periods of lucidity had become increasingly rare and Emily was relishing both the time away from a hospital bed and the period of mental clarity that enabled her to bask in the fond memories. She chattered incessantly. Teresa listened. Then abruptly, Emily's face darkened as the reason for the ride came back to her. "I am so sorry, Teresa. You've been such a dear, listening to me blather all evening. You must have places to go. You don't need to entertain me."

Teresa pulled the car over in front of a public park. It was dark except for a lighted Christmas wreath hanging on the backstop behind the baseball diamond. She turned and faced her passenger, taking hold of her hands. "I have all the time in the world, Emily. I am having a delightful evening. There is nothing in the world I would rather be doing right now. I mean it."

"You're so sweet. You almost made me forget why I called you and how this evening is going to end. Can we make one more stop?"

"Absolutely. Just tell me where."

Emily stared out the window without responding. She pointed at the baseball field. "See those bleachers there? I spent some of the happiest moments of my life right there. My son Jimmy played Little League at this park. It was so much fun watching him. He was such a good little player. And it was such a wonderful bonding experience for the parents. We met people in those bleachers who became friends for life. Having children is a great way to make friends. Such a blessing, in so many ways. Do you have children, dear?"

"Not yet. I hope to someday. I have to find the right guy first."

"Well, I'm sure you will. Take a left at the stoplight. Just one more stop if you don't mind."

Fifteen minutes later, Teresa approached the gates of Mount Carmel Cemetery. "Is this where you wanted to stop?" she asked.

Emily nodded her head slowly. "That's where my entire family is now. I buried my husband Jerry almost 10 years ago. My boy Jimmy and my little girl Megan are there too. Jimmy was just 13 when he passed. Megan was killed in a car wreck driving home from college."

"Would you like to get out and pay them a visit?" Teresa asked.

Emily pulled a handkerchief out of her purse and dabbed her eyes. "No," she said in a faraway voice. "I'll be seeing them soon enough. I want my next vision of them to be their smiling faces when we're all together again in heaven. I don't want to look at gravestones. Let's go now. I'm ready. And Teresa?"

"Yes?"

"I just want to tell you how much this evening has meant to me. I thought I was ready to check myself into the hospice, but I'm much more ready now. The time you've spent with me tonight is one of the greatest gifts anyone has ever given me."

"It's been a special night for me, too, Emily. I will never forget it. But hey, I'm at the hospice five days a week, so you'll see plenty of me there. I know we'll be great friends."

Emily looked at Teresa, fear and sadness returning to her big eyes. "I just wanted to thank you tonight because I probably won't remember this tomorrow. I may not even remember you. Please don't be angry with me."

It was nearly midnight before they arrived at Stoney Creek Hospice Care to begin the check-in process. Teresa introduced Emily to Pam, who greeted their new guest warmly and ushered her off to her room. Teresa lingered long enough to give Pam time to get their new patient comfortably situated, then she peeked in to find Emily sitting upright in bed and Pam softly explaining to her what their morning routine would be. Emily looked dazed. Dressed in a simple nightgown, without her makeup, she looked even older and more frail.

Teresa walked in and held her hand. "Goodnight, Emily. Thanks for a delightful evening."

Emily looked confused. "Have we met?" she asked.

Pam and Teresa exchanged a knowing look. "This is Teresa," said Pam. "She works here too."

"Oh, I see," the elderly woman said. "Well, nice meeting you, young lady."

"It's my pleasure, Emily," said Teresa. "I look forward to getting to know you better. Good-night."

Chapter 25

BENEATH A BRILLIANT blue sky, the Yale campus was blanketed with new-fallen snow. In a day or two, the roads would be a muddy mess, but last night's heavy snowfall was still pristine and undisturbed at this early morning hour as Michael Sanchez walked through the quiet campus. He had taken the first train out from Grand Central in Manhattan that morning after appearances as a guest lecturer at Columbia and NYU the previous day. Michael wore neither hat nor gloves but the biting cold and wind did not diminish the feeling of euphoria he was experiencing. His rubber-soled boots squeaked against the virgin snow as thoughts about his future raced through his mind, jumbled with the fond memories of his past life in New Haven that were conjured up by the familiar surroundings.

He had spent seven years of his life here, four as an undergraduate student and then three in law school. His high school grades certainly would not have earned him a spot at this elite institution; however, his test scores had been stellar and Yale's football program really wanted him. He was certain there were other forces at work behind the scene, although exactly what they were remained a mystery. What was not a mystery was the financing of his education. It was the generosity of the man who had long ago promised to look out for him. During the fall of his senior year in high school, he had received word that his benefactor was prepared to finance his education if he could gain admittance to a prestigious American university. They did not get any more prestigious than Yale, and within a week of his admission, a generous deposit was made into his bank account. He was overjoyed, both at the prospect of having a way out of South Texas, and at the opportunities that were sure to come his way as a Yale graduate. There was no mention of any strings being attached to this magnanimous gesture, but he was not naïve enough to believe he was being given something for nothing. That didn't bother him. His loyalty was steadfast even before he learned that his education was being paid for.

He had almost blown it during his second year. As with many college sophomores, drinking had become his favorite pastime. Foolish antics often followed. Yale did not condone unruly behavior, particularly when coupled with insolence and defiance. His attempt to justify stealing a policeman's Segue, recklessly riding it around campus and then scuffling with three campus police officers, fell upon deaf ears. The Dean of Disciplinary Affairs had summed it up accurately at his hearing: "Mr. Sanchez, I believe you have an allergy to alcohol. When you drink, you break out in stupid!"

Michael was confident that, without the intervention of Professor Vega, his career at Yale would have been over at that point. Somehow, Vega was able to convince the administration that the wild young man was ready to turn over a new leaf and would someday make them all proud. Total abstention from alcohol for the remainder of his time at Yale was part of the bargain. He had honored that bargain, and had imbibed only rarely since then, realizing that booze in fact did cause him to lose his filter, say foolish things and become careless. He possessed too much self-discipline to subject himself to those risks.

Professor Juan Carlos Vega was an integral part of his Yale experience. Michael had been instructed to seek out Professor Vega and do his best to cultivate a relationship with him. Vega was on the faculty of The National Autonomous University of Mexico, commonly known as UNAM, in Mexico City, but occasionally taught at Yale as a visiting scholar. His specialty was Latin American Studies, which focused on the history and politics of Central and South America. Michael had enrolled in his class first semester of freshman year and was utterly captivated by the man's brilliance. As instructed, he sought out the Professor outside of the classroom and the two struck up a close relationship. Michael's questions and interests went far deeper than the classroom discussion. He thirsted for practical lessons and insights that could be applied to the present and the future. The Professor was more than happy to assume the role of mentor and they became fast friends. They spent many an evening talking deep into the night, strolling the campus when weather permitted or ensconced in the Professor's cozy faculty office when it didn't.

Michael remembered their first such conversation vividly. They had made small talk over dinner at a noisy pizza joint near campus, and then the Professor had invited Michael to join him on his nightly exercise walk around campus. He was a pleasant-looking man in his early forties, Hispanic, with a fair complexion, dark curly hair and warm but penetrating brown eyes. He was trim and fit, which he attributed to his vigorous walking routine. The small talk stopped and the conversation had taken a very different direction once they were alone on their stroll.

"You are clearly a young man with ambition and talent, and a Yale pedigree will be a big asset, Michael. So tell me about your plans. What happens after you leave Yale?"

"I guess like most people around here, I want to change the world," Michael had responded with a laugh.

"I know you're being flippant when you say that, but I sense that unlike most people, you really mean it. What do you think needs changing?"

Michael had instantly warmed up to the idea of a serious conversation with a man of the Professor's experience and intellect. He thought carefully before responding. "I want to make life better for our people. I grew up in South Texas, where I was surrounded by people who came to this country without complying with our immigration laws. I saw them being oppressed and forced to live in the shadows. And through them, I learned about life in countries south of the border. It could be harsh. People were poor—they lived in a type of poverty unknown in this country. Safety, education, medical care, job opportunities—things we take for granted—were denied them. If you weren't among the wealthy or the governing class, you didn't matter. Life was cheap. And America perpetuates that."

"Interesting. You think America does that? How so?"

"It wants cheap labor and cheap products, so it has every incentive to keep the masses there living in poverty. Then they'll work for slave wages. Whether it's cars, gym shoes or the food on our tables, America gets it for cheap as long as the status quo stays the same. So America uses its wealth to bully or bribe its neighbors. The rich and ruling classes in the neighboring countries are kept happy and they kowtow to America's interests. This country supports corrupt leaders all over Latin America. It always has. We need to put an end to that and we should hold America accountable for its past sins."

"What do you mean by accountable? Vengeance?"

"Absolutely."

"How?"

"First and foremost, we seize power from the ruling elite. That would be the strongest punishment we can inflict on the existing power structure. Then, once we have control, we can take measures that will undermine America's economic strength. Then it won't be in a position to bully the rest of the world. But vengeance is a secondary objective. It's more about providing opportunity for our people."

Professor Vega nodded slowly and tried, not quite successfully, to suppress a smile. "You speak with great confidence, Michael. I admire that. The passion and brashness of youth is something to be envied, even where the wisdom that comes from hard-earned experience is lacking."

"You think I'm naïve, don't you?" Michael had responded. "And I may be—I realize that. But I'm not just spouting off without thinking. I've spent my entire life believing in that cause—making the good things about life in America accessible to immigrants, whether they have the right documents or not, and also to the children of immigrants who remain second-class citizens, as well as future immigrants who have not even crossed our borders yet. I've believed in that cause since I was a kid and I intend to act upon that belief and make a difference—in this country and south of the border. And if you don't mind, I'd sure appreciate the opportunity to pick your brain. I can't imagine anyone who is in a better position to help me understand these issues better."

"Have a seat," the Professor said as they approached an old stone bench outside of Harkness Tower, a 200-foot-tall masonry structure that formed part of the Memorial Quadrangle. It was late and the campus was eerily quiet under the light of a full moon. Vega pulled an ornate Mediterranean Briar wood pipe out of the inner pocket of his jacket. He poured tobacco from a leather pouch and struck a stick match against the arm of the stone bench.

"One of the few bad habits I allow myself," Vega had said, pulling the pipe away from his face and nodding at it. "I justify it by telling myself that it helps me think, and nothing is more important or relaxing than deep thought." He took another pull on the pipe, leaned his head back, exhaling a plume of fragrant smoke in the direction of the bright autumn moon. "Nothing would give me greater pleasure than acting as a mentor to you, Michael," he said, looking at the trail of smoke as it vanished into the night sky. "Our mutual acquaintance thinks you are a young man with immense talent and drive—someone who can make a real difference. I have made it my business to look into your background, and I must say that I share that assessment. And, the way you just described your cause is remarkably consistent with our friend's highest priority."

"That would be fantastic, Professor. I don't know how I can begin to thank you. I really—"

Vega held up his hand. "No need to thank me. We want the same things and it would be tremendously gratifying to me if I could play some small role in shaping your future. Central America has been like a giant Petri Dish—an ongoing experiment in the politics of power, with valuable lessons for those who are close enough—and insightful enough—to understand what has happened there. Understanding that, as well as understanding how those same principles apply here, in the context of democracy in this country, has been my life's work. It would mean a great deal to me to be able to share those lessons and concepts with someone who will really take them to heart." He stood up. "Well, young man, thank you for joining me on my evening stroll. I'm sure you have class in the morning and I should not have kept you out this late."

"I don't mind at all! There's nothing I'd rather be doing. I could stay up all night! There's so much I'd like to ask you."

The Professor looked at the eager young man and raised an eyebrow. "Really? Then let's keep walking. Ask away!"

They resumed their walk around campus. Michael bombarded

the Professor with questions. At first, they were questions about the Professor's background and experiences, which were met with straightforward answers. As the evening wore on, Michael's questions became more philosophical and focused on politics and government. He rarely got a direct answer. After he posed a question, the Professor would respond with a question of his own and sometimes a series of questions, forcing Michael to think out loud, and leading him to his own conclusions. Michael appreciated the intellectual sparring, although he thirsted for concrete answers that would reveal the Professor's own insights and deeply held beliefs. He felt a sense of impatience and frustration when the Professor announced that he would answer just one more question before calling it a night.

They walked in silence toward the Professor's home. Michael rubbed his chin. He brought his fist up to his lips and held it there, staring straight ahead, his eyes intense but focused on nothing. Then he abruptly stopped and stared at the Professor. "You know what my goals are. Pretend that after tonight, you would never see me again. What is the one thing you can tell me right now that I really need to understand in order to position myself to make a difference?"

"That's easy, Michael—you need to understand that power is not just a means to accomplishing your goals. Power itself is the goal. Power is more important than principle. Political leaders, political systems and governmental policies are all imperfect and they all create winners and losers. If you change a policy to help certain people, you will likely harm others in the process. People have competing interests and you can't make everyone happy. No matter how noble and just you think your mission is, there will be those who consider your agenda harmful. So when it comes to politics, you can't be married to any specific principle, because if that principle becomes unpopular, you will go down with that ship. Focus on doing what it takes to assume control and keep control. Then you can do what you want. Then you can pick the winners and losers and you can control your destiny. Look at Congress in this country. They get it. Their primary motivation is to keep themselves in office, and they've become very good at it. So the country suffers because the will of the people is subservient to the self-interest of those in power, and they get away with it because America is mired in complacency. Watch that and learn from it. Power is the goal that matters most—the one ultimate truth."

That was sixteen years ago. The mentor and his eager student went on to form a deep bond during the course of Michael's time at Yale. Professor Vega served as a visiting professor for four semesters scattered over Michael's seven-year stint there and made several other short visits for a day or two here and there as a guest lecturer. Although football, studies and an active social life kept Michael insanely busy, he relished the time he was able to spend with his mentor and made it a priority. Looking back, he felt that the opportunity to engage in deep, intellectual discussions with the Professor was by far the most rewarding part of his education. Their interactions had been few and far between after law school, so he was delighted by the Professor's recent invitation and the timing could not have been better. He needed an understanding ally and was confident that Professor Juan Carlos Vega was ideally suited for that role.

"Knock, knock!" Michael called out, as he stuck his head through the half-open door to Professor Vega's office. The familiar scent of pipe tobacco and the soft glow from the desk lamp gave the room a warm and comfortable feeling.

Professor Vega peered up from behind a tidy mahogany desk. "Michael! What a treat!" He broke into a broad grin, springing up from his chair and warmly shaking Michael's hand.

Michael was surprised by his mentor's appearance, not because it had changed dramatically over the years, but because it hadn't. Although some gray was sprinkled around the temples, his hair remained mostly dark and thick and his face showed barely a wrinkle. He exuded energy and good health.

After exchanging pleasantries, Vega said, "My apologies, my friend, but I need to rush off to a lecture in about 15 minutes. Your message made it sound like you have something important to discuss. How about over dinner tonight?"

"Sorry, Professor, my schedule is crazy and I've got a three o'clock flight this afternoon, so let me get right to the point. You and I have often talked about my desire to enter the political arena in some fashion. You have always told me that I need to be able to see the right opportunities when they come along and to be ready to pounce on those opportunities."

"Indeed I have. Go on."

"That opportunity is staring me in the face right now. Mickey McDaniel is relinquishing his Senate seat. The Texas Democratic Party wants me to run and the timing couldn't be better. After the Supreme Court decision last summer, I've become the most well-known immigration rights advocate around. I'm all over the airwaves. People know my face and my name. I'm well-known and respected in legal and political circles. And, immigration is likely to be the hottest issue in this upcoming election cycle, so I could motivate the electorate like no one else could."

"I agree. So what's the problem?"

"I've been told that our mutual friend south of the border doesn't want me to run. I don't get it! It's a perfect opportunity. I may never get a chance like this again. I was hoping you could contact him and explain how things are here so that I can get his support."

"Are you saying you won't run for Senate if he disapproves? What do you care whether he approves or not?"

Michael looked down and slowly shook his head. "No," he said quietly. "If he objects, I won't run. Call it loyalty. Call it deference to someone who's made a big difference in my life. I have my reasons. It just wouldn't be wise—or right." He stood up and walked over to the globe mounted on the Professor's desk, spinning it idly. "I really think that he must not understand the situation here, or he *would* be supportive. That's why I was hoping you would talk to him." He turned and faced the Professor. "Would you be willing to do that?"

Vega folded his arms across his chest and leaned back in his chair. "No," Vega said, calmly but firmly, looking Michael directly in the eyes.

"But—"

Vega held up his hand. "Listen to me, Michael," he interrupted, ignoring the hostile glare his response had evoked. "I already have spoken with him, and as usual, I agree with him."

"I don't get it. Surely you can see the opportunity."

"Of course I see *an* opportunity, but it's not the right opportunity."

Michael closed his eyes, bit his lip and shook his head. He reopened his eyes. "What are you talking about?" he asked, exasperation projecting from every pore.

"OK, let me walk you through this. What have you always talked about as your political goal?"

"Well, I've always said that I would like to become a force on the national political scene. Local politics would be the logical stepping stone to national politics—being mayor of a big city or a governor—but if an opportunity came along to be a Congressman or Senator, then I could skip the local politics and get to Washington a whole lot faster. I'm looking that opportunity in the face right now!"

"Is being a United States Senator the highest level of political power you would seek?"

"You're making it sound like it's no big deal. It would be huge! Obviously, I'd love to end up in the White House someday. Who wouldn't? But I have to be realistic. That's a pipedream—it would be the longest of long-shots and a long way off, but being Senator would be a big step in that direction and it would be an accomplishment in itself even if I went no further."

"Connect the dots, Michael! You're right—you *could* motivate the electorate like nobody else. Immigration *will* be the most emotional issue of the campaign. Your popularity and name recognition—not to mention your very name and ethnic background—are tailor-made for this. You're young, at a time when people are sick and tired of the old dogs. So why limit yourself to Texas? You could attract nationwide enthusiasm and support."

"You've lost me. Both parties have already identified their leading presidential candidates. The primaries are still a long way off, but it's becoming pretty clear who the frontrunners are. So what are you saying?"

Professor Vega stared at him, saying nothing, a slight smile creeping across his face. He looked expectantly at Michael.

Michael's expression turned from bewilderment to wide-eyed understanding. "You're saying I should run as a third party? An independent?"

Vega stared back, arching his eyebrows, silently urging Michael to continue the thought process. "So, I run as a third party, get even more name recognition, eventually get clobbered in the election like all third parties do, but earn the right to be considered for national office in future elections."

Vega shook his head. "Close, but not quite."

Michael paused and then clapped his hands together. "So you're suggesting that I run as an independent and that maybe the timing is finally right for a third party and I could catch on and actually win!"

Vega's eyes gleamed and he flashed a satisfied smile. "Exactly! And, if it looks like you're getting a lot of support but not going to win, one of the other candidates will beg you to join his ticket as VP candidate. That would virtually assure him of the White House and you would be vice president at the age of 35—one heartbeat away from the Presidency. And who knows what might happen then? Presidents have been known to die in office, haven't they?"

Chapter 26

BOBBY RIVERA PULLED into the parking lot of Stoney Creek Hospice Care. He turned off the ignition and sat in the funeral home's shiny black Buick for several minutes. He'd been in San Antonio for three months now and had been diligent about following Mr. Zamora's instructions to develop the right contacts. He'd never had to worry about developing business in Carroll County. Everyone knew him, and Zamora Family Mortuary was the only game in town. But now he was starting from scratch, and he set about introducing himself to people who were in a position to send funeral cases to their fledging business—clergy, the local cemetery operators, and the county medical examiner. He also joined a multitude of local civic and charitable organizations. Those business development efforts had now brought him here, to Stoney Creek Hospice Care.

Mr. Zamora had been insistent about tapping into as many of the local hospices as possible. Bobby knew it made sense from a business perspective, as virtually every patient checking into hospice would soon be in need of funeral services, but he had been slow getting around to it.

Teresa Cruz greeted him pleasantly and ushered him into the office she used for meeting with potential patients and their families. They sat opposite each other across a round glass conference table.

Bobby cleared his throat and sat upright on the edge of his chair. "Thank you for seeing me, Ms. Cruz. I really appreciate your time."

"Please—call me Teresa," she said, sensing his nervousness and smiling encouragingly.

"OK. Thanks. I will." He cleared his throat again. "The reason I'm here is that I think we may have occasion to work together in the future, so I thought I should introduce myself. I imagine that many of your clients ask you for guidance or recommendations regarding funeral homes from time-to-time. I wanted to tell you a bit about our firm so that you will be at least somewhat familiar with us in case any of the families you serve want to know what their options are regarding local funeral homes."

"Well, I know a little about you and your firm already," Teresa said. "I've done some homework. A nurse friend of mine at San Antonio General Hospital comes from San Mateo and used to work at Carroll County Hospital. You may know her—Laura Aguillar? She knew both of your parents and said they were absolutely beloved by everyone there. Said she met you at several funerals and told me that everyone throughout Carroll County knows that if you're in need of a funeral director, Bobby Rivera is the man to call. She said that from everything she's heard, you're just like your parents—a talented and truly compassionate caregiver. That's high praise from someone whose opinion I really respect. Laura wasn't sure you'd remember her but told me to say hello."

Bobby's face brightened. "Of course I remember Laura. I didn't know she was here in San Antonio. Please tell her hello for me."

"I will. So, I know that you're an experienced funeral director with a fine reputation. I also know that Zamora Funeral Home is trying to expand its business into San Antonio and you're the man in charge. What else should I know?"

Bobby sat back in his chair and took a closer look at the young woman seated across from him. She was petite, with lively dark eyes and a quick smile befitting her perky personality. She was undeniably cute, but wore no make-up and her long lustrous hair was tucked into a messy bun on top of her head. She had made a point of trying to put him at ease and he appreciated that.

"Like I said, my main reason for dropping by was just to introduce myself and our funeral home. To tell you the truth, I feel a bit awkward approaching a hospice business—no reflection on you or Stoney Creek. I'd feel that way with any hospice. My boss really wanted me to make this a priority, but I've been dragging my heels."

"Why's that?"

"I just don't want anyone to misconstrue my motives. If someone were to think I was twisting your arm to send business our way, that would look bad—for both of us. Or, if someone thought there was some kind of quid pro quo—like we were paying you for referrals or agreeing that we'd send you business if you'd send us business, that would look bad, too. It would look like the hospice is taking advantage of the family's trust and acting out of its own self-interest instead of the family's. So those possible misperceptions make me a little nervous—even though I would never participate in any kind of arrangement like that."

"I understand and that's a legitimate point," said Teresa. "I'm sure my bosses would share the same concern. But you're here, so you must have gotten comfortable with the idea of us working together in some fashion."

Bobby leaned forward, folding his hands and placing them on the table in front of him. "I've thought long and hard about this, and here's where I come out. For me, it's all about serving a family in their time of need. My job is all about helping people through the most difficult time in their life and doing whatever I can to make that time just a little bit easier and a little bit better. I will always put the best interest of the family first. I think I'm good at that. It seems to me that a hospice has a very similar mission. You handle the end-of-life situation and then the funeral home steps in once your patient has passed on. The funeral is the final part of that end-of-life event. A hospice would be serving its clients well if it could help them prepare for that eventuality by making sure they have thought about those arrangements and being in a position to advise them of their options and perhaps even make a recommendation that it truly believes would be in the family's best interest. So, I think the interests of our professions are closely aligned. You will be asked about funeral homes on occasion and I will be asked about hospices. We're in a better position to help our client families if we are well informed about each other's business. So, to be perfectly clear, I am not asking you to send business to Zamora Family Mortuary. I will never ask that of you. I just hope that you're open to learning more about us. I think you'll be favorably impressed. Whether you choose to mention us to any of your patients is entirely up to you. I hope you don't think there's anything inappropriate about what I'm suggesting."

Teresa leaned forward, her face bright and sincere. "Not at all. In fact, the way you described your commitment to your client families is exactly how I feel about what I do."

"I'd like to show you around our facility sometime and explain our processes and procedures and approach. I think you'll be impressed by our commitment to treating the deceased and their families with the utmost dignity and respect and also finding creative and fitting ways to celebrate someone's life."

"I'd like that. I often attend the funeral services of patients I've gotten to know. I tend to get pretty close to them. That's one of the toughest parts of my job, but also one of its greatest blessings."

Bobby pulled a glossy brochure out of his briefcase and slid it across the table. "This will provide a bit more detail about our business and our facilities. If you'd like more copies to share with colleagues or patients, let me know. I only brought one copy—didn't want to appear pushy or presumptuous." He stood up and offered his hand. "Thanks again for your time, Teresa. Don't hesitate to call me if I can ever be of service."

"I'm glad you came by, Bobby. I'm sure our paths will cross again, and I look forward to it." They exited the office and walked toward the lobby. "How are you liking San Antonio so far?" she asked as they stood at the doorway.

"Still trying to find my way around and get settled in. I've been staying in a small room above the funeral home, but I really need to focus on finding an apartment. It's kind of daunting—the city is so big compared to what I'm used to and I don't even know where to begin looking."

"Why don't you let me show you around? I've lived here most of my life. I can show you what areas to avoid and what parts of town might suit you, depending on what you're looking for."

"Oh, I really don't want to impose. I'm sure you're plenty busy—"

"It's no trouble at all—really. I'd enjoy it. This is a big city and you'd be wandering around aimlessly on your own. We'll make it fun. I'll show you the sights at the same time."

The positive energy radiating from the energetic young hospice worker was unmistakable and contagious. Her enthusiasm seemed sincere. "That would be great," he said. "I'd really appreciate it. Just tell me when."

"I'm off tomorrow. How about early afternoon, say one o'clock? I can stop by the funeral home and pick you up."

"Awesome! See you then."

Chapter 27

MICHAEL SANCHEZ WALKED into his quiet San Antonio campaign office before daylight, a large cup of Starbucks in one hand and a stack of newspapers in the other. He savored the silence. In a couple of hours, phones would be ringing and a small army of eager young staffers would be buzzing about the office. This was the time of day he could play offense. The solitude enabled him to think and strategize and carefully digest the previous day's developments rather than just reacting to the never-ending onslaught of issues that would occupy him throughout the remainder of the day.

He sat behind the cheap metal desk in his office, which was the only space that provided some semblance of privacy amidst a sea of cubicles commonly referred to as the "war room." Even that privacy was limited by the thin walls and the glass windows that enabled anyone in the war room to see him at all times, but he liked it that way. A general needed to be seen by the troops and easily accessible to keep morale high.

He scanned the front pages of the five newspapers he had brought with him: *The New York Times, USA Today, The Washington Post, The Houston Chronicle* and *The Wall Street Journal.* "Dammit!" he whispered to himself. Not a single front-page mention of him or his campaign. He would have to speak with his PR Director about that. He shoved the papers aside and reached for the stack of newspapers piled neatly on the corner of his desk. It was a stack of the same publications four weeks earlier, the day after he publicly announced his third-party candidacy. That announcement was the headline article, splashed across the front page of each of those publications. He kept those papers handy and glanced at them often, deriving a sense of satisfaction and motivation every time he did so.

The past four weeks had been a whirlwind. He'd been through something similar last summer after his Supreme Court victory, only there the interest had waned at least somewhat after a few weeks. Now, it was rapidly increasing with no end in sight. He had purposely created some drama around the announcement of his candidacy. A press conference had been called in front of the Capitol Building in Austin within days of Senator McDaniel's stunning announcement that he would not be seeking a fourth term. Michael's campaign manager saw to it that word was leaked that the purpose of his press conference was to announce his candidacy for the soon-to-be-vacated Senate seat. He began his speech by commending McDaniel on his years of public service and pointing out how important it would be to fill those legendary shoes with just the right candidate. He spoke of the issues that the Senate and the nation were facing, with particular emphasis on the need for immigration reform. He mentioned that he had been urged to throw his hat in the ring. Then he discussed what an honor that would be and that it would provide a great forum for pursuing the agenda that was so important to him and the American people. Then just when everyone thought he was going to say that he was indeed running for Senate, he had said just the opposite. He told the world that after much soul-searching and deliberation, he had decided not to run for Senate. After a dramatic pause, he announced that the reason he had decided not to run was that he felt that he could better serve the American people and the causes he felt so strongly about through a different channel—as president of the United States.

It was great theater and the media loved it. It created the tremendous media splash he had hoped for, and he spent most of the next three weeks in front of television cameras, getting his face and his voice and his message to the American people. Part of every speech was a call to action—a plea to those who shared his vision to climb on board and be part of the effort. He got the word out that in order for a third-party candidacy like his to succeed, he would have to organize a massive, powerful and effective grass-roots campaign, the like of which had never before been seen in American politics. The results had been nothing short of overwhelming.

Michael had been able to persuade Russ Miller to act as his campaign manager. Miller was a loyal Democrat, but like many political operatives, he was more concerned with his own brand and personal opportunities than anything else. It didn't take much to persuade him that the exposure and experience he would gain by being part of a Sanchez campaign was a unique and potentially life-changing opportunity that he could not pass up.

Miller bustled in as Michael was finishing his coffee. Miller was not an early bird, but today's meeting was important and he needed Michael's full attention, so he had agreed to meet at the office at 7:00 a.m., when they could be assured of privacy and a distraction-free environment.

"Morning, Mike!" he called out as he marched directly across the war room to the two large whiteboards hung on the painted cinderblock wall. The board on the left was a calendar, showing meetings, deadlines, goals and significant campaign events for the next 90 days. It looked busy and full. The adjacent board showed the latest poll numbers from Gallup, Rasmussen, CNN and Fox News, reflecting the percentage of likely voters who would cast their vote for Sanchez if the election were held today. Miller grabbed the eraser and wiped the board clean, adding the most recent figures. While there was some discrepancy in the numbers, they were generally hovering around 20%. Neither Hugh Connett, the Republican candidate, nor Thomas Nelson, the Democrat, exceeded 35%.

"What do you think, boss? Looking pretty good, eh?"

Michael wandered into the war room and leaned against the wall, looking at the new numbers with satisfaction. "Not where we need to be, but I like the trend," he said.

"Hey, it's a horserace. You're a longshot, but we're closing the gap. What really matters is how we do down the homestretch. So, let's get after it. We've got work to do!"

They entered Michael's office and he waved the morning newspapers. "No front-page coverage today. I feel neglected," Michael said with a grin.

"That's OK, we can use a little time out of the limelight so we can prepare for the next phase of this campaign. Phase One was a smashing success. You rocked the political world and got incredible media coverage. We've used that to generate interest and excitement and a good-sized army of supporters. Now we need to focus on filling out the campaign team and then really doing a deep dive and developing talking points and position papers on all the major issues."

"I thought we'd already filled all the key jobs."

"I've given that a bit more thought and I'd like your approval to add two more people. We need a real expert in fundraising to keep the cash flowing and we need our own internal pollster. The polls we're tracking on our whiteboard are helpful, but we need to be digging deeper. We can get great information about the minds of the voters if we have the right person developing the right questions and contacting the right people."

"Do it! I trust you to find the right people. I'd prefer to focus on developing our positions."

"Perfect. You've already done a pretty good job outlining your thoughts about immigration reform: making the path to citizenship faster and more inclusive, expanding the number and duration of visas; amnesty for many of those already here; eligibility for various social and financial benefits, all that stuff. You can handle those issues in your sleep, but we need to think about how to better package your ideas and come up with some catchy slogans. Most people don't think deeper than sound bites, so we need to have some good ones. We also need to focus on all the other major issues, like taxes, entitlements, gun control, minimum wage laws, organized labor issues, government spending, foreign affairs—all that stuff. We can have staffers prepare the detailed position statements, but I'd like you to think hard about this so you can really own this and speak with real conviction on all these points. So try to find some quiet time over the next few weeks because the next phase will involve getting your positions out there in a way that's attention-getting and inspiring, and you've got to be thoroughly prepared to defend those positions."

"I'm on it, Russ."

Miller stood up and closed the door, even though no staffers had yet arrived. "There's one other issue we really need to discuss, Mike. You need to be prepared to defend the nastiness that's sure to come now that your rivals know you're a real threat. In fact, it's already starting." Miller reached across the desk and grabbed the *USA Today*. "You obviously didn't get past the front page. Check this out." He opened the newspaper to Page 4 and read the headline aloud: *"Sanchez Nearly Expelled from Yale.* It's just a few sentences but it basically says that unnamed sources have reported that you were involved in brawls and public drunkenness during your time at Yale and were almost expelled."

He slid the newspaper across the desk and Michael quickly perused it. "Shit," he muttered, shoving the paper back across the desk.

"Any truth to that?"

"Yeah, some I guess. I punched out a belligerent fan who was heckling me after the Harvard-Yale game. And I did have to appear before the Disciplinary Committee after I had a few beers and borrowed a cop's Segue. Do you think Yale released that information?"

"Nah, schools are pretty sensitive to privacy issues, but there are probably plenty of your former classmates who remember these incidents, and now that you're a presidential candidate, it's newsworthy. Get used to it."

Michael glared at the stack of newspapers in front of him. "Shit!" he muttered again.

Miller sat up on the edge of his chair and leaned in. "Listen to me, Mike. So far, this has been easy. It's been fun. It's been exciting. You've been a media darling. The entire country has been enthralled to see this impressive young man with a ton of charisma and no political experience explode onto the political scene and become a real contender. If you were polling at one or two percent, or even if you were a VP candidate, no one would waste much time trying to dig up dirt on you. But now that you're a real contender, there will be a world of enemies out there determined to destroy you. Politics is ugly and dirty. You know that because you've witnessed it your whole life. But there's a big difference between witnessing it and being the victim of it. The truth will be distorted. Lies will be told about you. It's infuriating and it hurts, so you've got to steel yourself against it. And, we've got to be prepared for it, because this is just the beginning," he said, pointing at the *USA Today* article in front of him. "The slightest vulnerability will be exploited. Your Yale pedigree should be a big asset, but someone is trying to make it a liability by putting this garbage out there. So I need you to think hard and tell me about any vulnerabilities, so we can prepare. Remember, I'm on your team and I'm your biggest supporter, but I'm not going to be able to help you unless you tell me everything—and I do mean everything. Tell me about anything the other side might try to portray as a skeleton in your closet, no matter how long ago it happened and no matter how trivial it may seem. Tell me what I should know."

Michael folded his arms and stared out the window. "I can't think of a thing, Russ. Yeah, there were a few incidents when I was in college, but it was just the harmless, stupid kind of things nineteen-year-olds do when they're drunk. I'll give you all the details, but beyond that, there just isn't anything. I've never been arrested. Never had any run-ins with the law, I don't cheat on my taxes…"

"I'm glad to hear that, Mike, but keep thinking about it over the next few days. I guarantee you that the opposition and the press are going to be all over this. I'm sure they're already talking to your former classmates at Yale. They'll go back to every school you ever attended and every neighborhood you ever lived in to try to find people who remember you and hope that they remember something juicy. So think hard. No one knows your history like you do. If you can think of anything that would be potentially embarrassing or problematic, tell me about it. And, by the way, if they can't find any dirt on you, they'll go after your family, so think about any potential trouble there."

Michael leaned back in his chair and let out a deep sigh. "I should have known this was coming, but I got so wrapped up in getting myself into this position that I never focused on it. Would people really sink so low as to bring my family into this, and start pestering my friends and my former neighbors?"

"I think you know the answer to that. C'mon, don't look so glum. As long as there's no dirt out there, we've got nothing to worry about. Besides, I think your family and your background will be a big part of your appeal. You and your siblings are first generation Americans, children of a father who was here illegally. People will relate to that. Your mother raised the three of you on her own. Now you're a Yale-educated lawyer and your sister is a Ph.D. and a professor—what a great American success story! I think we should really develop that angle and play up your early years, your humble beginnings. It's the perfect backstory for the immigration reform challenges you're about to take on. I'm getting excited just thinking about bringing that story to life!"

Michael listened with his elbows on the desk, rubbing his temples. He began slowly shaking his head. "I don't like it."

"What's not to like, Mike? For Chrissakes! This is a great angle and you're sitting there looking like I'm giving you a migraine. Are there family issues I should know about? Come on—out with it!"

Michael hesitated for a long moment. "No scandals. Nothing like that. It's just that my mom is in poor health. She's also got some emotional issues and gets stressed very easily. And my younger brother is just kind of a dipshit. Lazy, not very bright, usually unemployed. He would not make a good impression."

Miller stared hard at his somber-looking boss. "OK, I can see that you've got some concerns. If there's anything beyond what you just told me, you need to fill me in—soon. If there's not, then I urge you to give serious consideration to building a narrative around your childhood and your upbringing and making that a major part of the campaign. Hell, maybe we should go to the town where you grew up. We could have a town hall meeting, get footage of you rubbing elbows with the people from your old neighborhood, reuniting with old friends. The press would eat that up!"

"I'm not sure that's a good idea, but I'll think about it, Russ," Michael said in a voice completely devoid of enthusiasm. "But two things you can be sure of. First, there are no skeletons in my closet. Second, I want to keep my family out of this to the greatest extent possible. If I think of anything that could be damaging, I'll let you know. But right now I think I better go hole up in a quiet place to start working on my position statements. Can you look after things around here today?"

"You got it, boss. Why don't you take a few days? You look like shit all of a sudden. The holidays are over and we need you sharp and full of positive energy as we start the New Year and really ramp up our campaign. It's been a crazy pace so far, but you ain't seen nothin' yet!"

Miller stood up and reached for the doorknob. "Oh, and one more thing. We should really be playing up your Latino roots, so let's start transitioning to *Miguel* rather than *Michael*. That's your formal name and it will appeal to your base."

Chapter 28

WITH TERESA AS his guide, Bobby spent the afternoon apartment hunting, focusing mostly on neighborhoods rather than specific apartments, although they did one or two quick walk-throughs in each area they visited to get a feel for what was available as well as rental rates in the various parts of town.

"So did you see anything you liked, or should we continue looking over the weekend?" Teresa asked as she turned into the parking lot behind Marino's, a local Italian restaurant.

"It's so different than what I'm used to," Bobby said. "And there are so many options. My head is spinning!" He gave the hostess his name and they sat on a nearby bench waiting for a table. The restaurant was packed, mostly with college students, which was not surprising given the proximity to the university.

"Any particular area you want to focus on?"

"Well, I need to be reasonably close to the funeral home, because I'm sure I'll be getting calls in the middle of the night. Anything within 20 minutes should be close enough. I'd also like to find an area that's conducive to making new friends—someplace where there are plenty of young, single people—because right now I don't know a soul around here."

"You know me!" Teresa said. "Anything I can do to help as you're trying to settle in, just let me know."

After they were seated, Bobby ordered lasagna, Teresa ordered a Caesar salad with grilled chicken, and they ordered a bottle of Chianti to share. "So what made you decide to become a funeral director?" Teresa asked as Bobby poured the wine.

"My parents were in medicine. My dad was a doctor and my mother was a nurse. They were real caregivers—full of compassion and committed to serving people who really needed help. I saw what a difference they made, and wanted to follow their example, but I was never much of a student, so medical school was out. Then, in high school, I was close to some families who lost loved ones and I saw that I could really make a difference by helping them through those tough times. Then my parents were killed in a plane crash when I was 18 and I was really impressed by how the local funeral director took care of them and took care of me. That inspired me to ask him for part-time work at the funeral home, and here I am. I love what I do. It's like a ministry. I feel like I make a difference by helping people through the most difficult time in their lives. I can't think of any higher calling."

Teresa had stopped eating and was staring at him admiringly. "I can't either. You know, I'm really glad I met you, Bobby." She raised her wine glass. "Here's to you. Welcome to San Antonio! I wish you great success in your business here, and I look forward to working closely together and getting better acquainted. Cheers!" Her eyes shone warmly as they clicked glasses.

"What about you?" Bobby asked. "Your job's probably even tougher than mine. Spending time with sick people who are on the brink of death—the fear, the sadness, not to mention the pain and suffering—it must take a really special person to do that kind of work. I'm sure that you handle it as well as anyone could."

"The way you described your job is exactly how I feel about what I do," Teresa said. It's a calling. It's tough, but it's important, and it's rewarding. Just like you, I feel that I make a difference."

Bobby drained his wine glass and poured another. "What do you do to take your mind off work?"

"I like to run and workout. The physical exertion clears my head. I have a precious little dog—CT—he's a Cairn Terrier. I like to take long walks with him. I'm also a bit of a political junkie. I've worked on a few campaigns, volunteering to help candidates I find inspiring. I got my feet wet working on a mayoral race a few years ago and since then I've gotten involved in a few campaigns for city council members and state legislators. I seem to have a knack for picking the losers, but I love the process. My mother brought me here from Panama, where she lived under the oppressive military dictatorship, so for me it's really exciting to see democracy at work up close and personal. I get a kick out of being part of the process. I'm thinking about getting involved with the Sanchez campaign?"

"Who?"

"Miguel Sanchez—the guy running for president as an independent. Surely you've heard of him?"

"Yeah, it just clicked. I don't follow politics at all, but I remember him because he's got the same name as one of my old friends. Common name, I suppose."

"You should pay attention to this guy, even if politics isn't normally your thing. He's special. He's like us—first generation American—and he's really tuned into immigration reform. He wants to make life better for all the immigrants still living in the shadows and people who are still trying to find their way here. It's exciting!"

"Personally, I think figuring out how to change the world is way beyond my small mind. I'm content if I can make the world a better place by helping one family at a time." Bobby moved a piece of lasagna around his plate with his fork, absently moving it in circles. "Hey, mind if I change the subject and ask your advice on something?"

"Sure, fire away."

"These big city rents are expensive, so I'm thinking it might make sense to find a roommate to share the cost."

"That shouldn't be a problem. There are plenty of places to advertise—online, in the newspapers, with the housing departments at the local schools. I'll bet there are plenty of guys out there looking to share a place."

Bobby put down his fork and drummed his fingers silently on the table. "Actually, I had something else in mind. What if I advertised for a female roommate? I'm kind of intimidated by the whole dating scene—always have been, but it was at least it was easier back home because

I knew everybody. I never found anyone there I wanted to get serious with because the girls who were interesting or motivated mostly moved away to the big cities as soon as they were old enough. Anyway, if I had a female roommate, I certainly wouldn't get involved with her— that could be awkward and I would definitely make that off-limits. But I was thinking that she could introduce me to her friends and bring them around sometimes and it would be a natural way to get to know some young ladies without any pressure." He looked up hesitantly. "What do you think? Does that sound weird or creepy?"

Teresa was about to crack a joke when she saw the nervous look on Bobby's face as he continued playing with his food. "Hmmm... That's an interesting thought," she said, taking on a serious tone. "Some women might be uncomfortable about moving in with a guy, particularly when they find out you're a funeral director. No offense, but some people probably think that your profession attracts strange people. That said, the world is becoming more open-minded about living arrangements, so I imagine at least some girls would be open to it. I think you'd have better luck in a neighborhood like this, around the university, where people tend to be less judgmental and willing to try new things."

"Well, I kind of like this neighborhood anyway. It's pretty lively. It's only fifteen minutes from the funeral home and it's close to the freeway, which will come in handy when I need to hurry back to Carroll County. I'll still be doing some work down there."

"This is one of my favorite parts of town. I used to live around here. I loved it and I think you would, too. If you want, we can come back here next week and check out some of the options."

"I hate to impose again, but if you wouldn't mind, I'd really appreciate it."

"No trouble at all. I'd enjoy it, Bobby."

***

The next weekend, Bobby found a place in a massive modern apartment complex several blocks from the campus. A high percentage of the residents were students, but there was a healthy presence of young professionals living there as well. As the weeks passed, he found himself spending considerable time with Teresa Cruz. Some of it was business-related, as she enthusiastically took him around town and introduced him to people and organizations that made for good professional contacts. But it wasn't all business. He found her to be delightful company and he looked forward to their time together. He got into a routine of joining her several times a week for her dog walks. At times, he was tempted to ask her out on a date. He liked her—a lot—and she was definitely attractive. Even though she was nearly always dressed in sweats or her nurse's uniform when they were together and rarely took the time for hair or make-up, she didn't need to as far as he was concerned. She was cute by any standards and her lively personality made her even cuter. But that was a line he dared not cross, partly out of fear of rejection, but also because, if it didn't work out or she wasn't receptive to the idea, it could introduce an element of awkwardness into what was becoming a very close friendship. So he told himself he had to keep the relationship strictly professional and friendly, and banish any notions of romantic involvement. The only problem was, that notion just wouldn't go away. The better he got to know her, the more alluring she became.

Chapter 29

"THANKS FOR MAKING time for me, Professor. I can't imagine anyone better suited to help me flesh out my position statements." Michael Sanchez sat opposite his mentor on the worn leather sofa in the familiar confines of Professor Vega's faculty office at Yale.

"I can't imagine anything I'd rather be doing," Vega responded. "We both hoped this day would come and now it's upon us—much sooner than either of us anticipated. We've spoken about all these issues dozens of times over the years, so this should be easy! Let's jump into it." He pulled out his pipe and poured tobacco from his leather pouch, quickly scenting the room with a sweet and familiar aroma.

"Immigration reform has become my marquee issue, so let's start with that. There are several key planks to this platform—"

"Wait! Slow down! Before we begin discussing specific positions, let's take a big step back and talk about your goals. What are you hoping to accomplish by making whatever legislative changes you want to make?"

"Like you said, Professor, we've discussed this many times. My mission has been the same since I was a teenager. It was my father's mission. It was his boss's mission: I want to change the priorities and policies of this country's ruling class so that it will no longer be able to take advantage of our people—those living throughout Latin America and those who've made their way here. And others too—any cultures that have been oppressed and shut out from the opportunities that this country provides to members of the existing establishment. I want to lead a revolution, but one that happens quietly, and changes America from the inside out."

Vega rose from his chair and began pacing back and forth behind his desk like a caged animal, one hand behind his back, the other holding the pipe, his dark eyes staring intensely at the floor. "Go on," he urged. "What needs to happen in order to effectuate that kind of change?"

"Over the long term, we need more people here with those backgrounds so that we have critical mass in terms of voting power. It won't take long before the numbers translate to a clear majority. The challenge is that many of those people don't vote, either because they're not eligible or because they're disinterested or afraid. Many of them were raised to be fearful and suspicious about government—any government. So lots of them won't bother to vote or even register to vote. We need to be able to convince them that they have real power. We need to show them the vision of what can be accomplished if they choose to engage and wield that power."

"OK, so if those are the goals, what's the strategy?"

"I've got to inspire them and show them the path that will lead to real change. I've got to get them behind the policies that will facilitate that change and support our long-term goals. The various planks of my immigration reform platform will do exactly that. We grant amnesty and an easy path to citizenship for those who were brought here illegally as children and have grown up here, without any connection to the country of their birth. That should be an easy sell—the polls show that most Americans fully support this. We also push for broader amnesty and a path to citizenship for the undocumented adults that have been living here in the shadows. Those people will be our voters for life, as will their extended families. We also need to open up the floodgates by greatly expanding immigration quotas and work visas, especially for Latin Americans."

"You'll get strong pushback there. You know the arguments: foreigners taking jobs away from hard-working Americans."

"That's bullshit! You know it and I know it. I need to be able to make the case to the average voter. The American economy needs workers, especially for the millions of jobs that require unskilled labor. The economy is being held back right now because there simply aren't enough American citizens filling those jobs. Crops are rotting on the trees and in the ground because there aren't enough people willing to do that work. Many in the established middle classes consider those jobs beneath them. Also, there's a huge element of this society that would prefer to milk the entitlement system rather than do the hard work these jobs require. That's just a fact and we need to get farmers and business owners to speak up and make that point. And, the population here is aging and the birth rate is declining. There will be a huge shortage of workers across the entire spectrum—that will hold the economy back unless we open the immigration floodgates."

The Professor stopped pacing and emptied the contents of his pipe in an ashtray. He sat down again, leaned back in his swivel chair and put both hands behind his head. "Clearly, you've given a great deal of thought to these issues. Immigration reform is your wheelhouse. Your positions are well developed—we just need to strategize about the key messages and how to package them. Let's come back to that. I suggest we focus first on issues outside of that arena, starting with tax reform, minimum wage laws, and entitlement spending. Those issues are always controversial and divisive. How do you plan on dealing with them?"

"This is where I could really use your help, Professor. My base is clearly going to be the working class, middle and lower-income, and those who feel passionate about immigration reform. These are largely people who would vote Democrat if I weren't in the race. The Democratic Party line on those issues is raising taxes by vilifying those who are financially successful, increasing the mandatory minimum wage, and making all kinds of promises that cause entitlements to balloon out of control and be widely abused. From both an intellectual and a common-sense perspective, I'm having a hard time getting my head around those positions."

"Of course you are, because they are mostly foolish. Raising minimum wages won't help the working man. It's the last thing we should be doing because it will simply eliminate low-paying jobs and raise unemployment. The American tax code is oppressive and punitive already. Taking more money away from successful people to feed the bureaucratic beast is pure folly. And undisciplined entitlement programs sap the economy and create a dependent and unmotivated class that will never rise out of their sad predicament. Now I'm not an economist and I could be dead wrong, but whether I'm right or wrong on this doesn't matter. That's not the point! Your goal isn't to do what's best for the people anyway, is it?"

Michael cocked his head and looked confused. "Of course I want to make life better for the people. For some people anyway, but not necessarily those that have been riding the gravy train."

"No, you don't! It's not about that. Your goal isn't to promote the policies that are best for the country. Your goal is to assume power. In this country, that means you must get votes. So you tell people what they want to hear. You can motivate the electorate by being divisive. You appeal to their anger and resentment by making villains out of corporate America, and the wealthy and successful. Promise to make them pay their fair share! Promise the masses all kinds of goodies, like higher minimum wages and free healthcare, maybe even free college tuition. Promise to make welfare programs broader and more generous. Same with social security and Medicare. All those things are foolish and utterly unworkable, but remember, people are stupid! Their analysis on any of these issues doesn't go any deeper than the catchy sound bites they hear and mindlessly start parroting. So you should make whatever promises will get you their votes."

Vega rose and placed his palms on the desk and leaned across toward his young protégé. "And remember Michael, if these policies cause long-term harm to the economy and the country, that's a good thing—it serves the Cause. You want the working class to be restless. If they're satisfied, they become complacent. We need to keep them angry. That's what keeps them motivated. We feed on their anger and frustration. It gives us something to rail against, and they will believe we are waging the war for them. Just remember, it's not about winning that war. It's all about power—nothing else! Immigration reform is a noble goal in itself and definitely something we feel passionately about, but above everything else, it is a pathway to power for us. Do you understand that?"

Michael nodded and broke into a wide smile. "I've never seen this side of you before. You look so intense. It almost scares me!"

"We've had these types of discussions before, Michael, but they were hypothetical and theoretical. We both dreamed of an opportunity like this, but it was a far-out possibility as well as far off. But now it's here, and it's very real. And I can assure you that I will do everything within my power to help make this dream a reality. So let's start by doing a deep dive on every one of the core issues."

They spent the next several hours formulating Michael's positions on all the major campaign issues. Michael staked out his positions, waxing eloquently as if he were giving a stump speech, while the Professor shredded him like a trial lawyer attacking a hostile witness, exposing the areas that needed further work. They strategized about what the key messages should be and how to package those messages to make them simple and appealing. Michael took copious notes. When they had exhausted their list of issues, the Professor stood up and put his hands in his pockets.

"This brings me to one final point, Michael," he said. "Your opposition craves power. They want this thing just as badly as you do, and they will be prepared to do whatever it takes to stop you. They will be looking for every possible vulnerability."

"It's starting already," Michael acknowledged, looking serious. "Did you see the *USA Today* article about my disciplinary issues here at Yale?"

"Of course I saw it. That doesn't concern me. You did some goofy things as a college sophomore. Big deal! That may even score you some points because it paints the picture of a normal college kid rather than one of the elite. It makes you relatable. But they will be seriously digging into your background—your entire background—looking for something to tarnish your reputation or embarrass you. If you were polling a couple of percentage points, they wouldn't be wasting much time or resources on that. But you've got traction. You've got momentum. They now perceive you as a serious threat, so they're going to come after you."

"I understand. Any advice?"

Vega came around to the front of his desk and leaned up against it, folding his arms as he looked down on the young man who could be the next president of the United States. "We both know what your vulnerabilities are, Michael. Is there any indication that anyone is digging into that?"

"Not that I know of. So far, the biography being put out there has focused on my professional life and my Yale education. I've seen a few very cursory references to my graduation from College Park High School, but nothing going any further back than that."

"What about your family? Any worries there?"

Michael hesitated and shifted in his chair. "I don't think so. I really haven't had much to do with them in a long time. I went home for the holidays a few times while I was at Yale, mostly just to keep up appearances, but I've had almost nothing to do with them in years."

"That's not good," said the Professor. "If people realize that, they may ask about it. Even if you have a good answer, we don't know what your family members will say. We've got to be sure we have that under control."

"I don't think it's a problem, Professor. I'm highly confident that they've kept my secret. As far as the rest of the world knows, I am Miguel Sanchez, son of Anita Sanchez, who was born in El Paso and married Filipe Sanchez, an illegal immigrant who moved her to various small towns around South Texas. My father left us when I was a teenager and was later killed in a car wreck. My family was scared shitless when El Cazador came into their lives. I'm sure they're still terrified, so we shouldn't have to worry about any undesirable stories surfacing from that direction. Besides, I think they'll be excited about the possibility of being related to the next president of the United States. Who wouldn't?"

"Listen to me, Michael. We can't just assume that everything will be just fine. We need to be absolutely certain! You need to meet with your family and feel this out. If we have any doubts whatsoever, we will need to deal with them decisively."

"I'm not sure I like the sound of that. What do you mean?"

"If you take care of this and make sure they understand the importance of honoring the commitment that was made to El Cazador many years ago, then you won't have anything to worry about. If you feel that there is risk there, then we will do what we must."

Chapter 30

"HOW'S THE ROOMMATE search going?" Teresa asked, as they walked her little dog around Kennedy Park early one evening. It was early February, almost four weeks after Bobby had begun his search.

"Lousy," Bobby replied. "I'm striking out. I've had a pretty steady stream of girls come by but none I felt comfortable with. Some had bad credit, some seemed to be on drugs, a couple had boyfriends and told me they wanted to have their boyfriends staying over a lot. I don't need a package deal—my place is small enough as it is."

Teresa stopped to let the dog sniff around a light pole. She stared at the ground with unfocused eyes. "Well… let me throw out an idea," she said with some hesitation. "And if you think this is a bad idea, just tell me. I don't want you to feel any pressure at all."

Bobby looked at her quizzically. Teresa gave the dog's leash a quick tug and resumed walking. "My lease expires at the end of the month," she said. "What would you think of having me as a roommate?"

Bobby stopped and stared at her. "Really? Are you serious?"

"Just a thought. Again, please don't feel any pressure. I need to find a new place. You're looking for a roommate. We get along great. And it seems like you're never going to ask me out, so we wouldn't have that issue, which I know you were concerned about in a roommate. And CT loves you, right boy?" The little dog looked from one to the other, tail wagging furiously.

Bobby's mind raced. He tried to act nonchalant, leaning over and petting the frisky little Cairn Terrier. Had he blown it? Had she wanted him to ask her out all this time? All the reasons he had used to justify not doing so raced through his mind. He knew they were all valid reasons, but logical deliberation was rendered impossible by a feeling of sheer excitement at the prospect of spending a whole lot more time with Teresa Cruz.

"Wow," he said. "I never thought about that. Are you sure you wouldn't get sick of me if we're spending that much time together?" He stroked CT's head and avoided looking at her.

"I've given it a lot of thought. We're really compatible. I think we both enjoy our time together. You work a lot of evenings and weekends, so we won't be tripping over each other. But, again, if you have any hesitation at all, just tell me. It won't hurt my feelings."

Bobby looked directly into Teresa's eyes and noticed a sense of nervousness about her that he had never seen before. "I think it's a great idea!" he said, smiling brightly.

"Me too!" she said, her expression instantly transforming from nervousness to elation. "I wouldn't have suggested it if I had any reservations." She gave him a quick, affectionate hug. "Thanks, Bobby!" She picked up the little dog and nuzzled the furry face. "Yippee, CT! You're going to have a new home!"

Teresa moved in the following weekend. Over the next several weeks, they settled into something resembling a routine. As a result of Bobby's determined efforts to develop professional connections, and the favorable impression he invariably made, the funeral business had been growing quickly. Funerals were typically scheduled in the morning and visitations often occupied his afternoons and evenings. Saturday services and visitations were not unusual, so his schedule was erratic. When he did have evenings off, he and Teresa would take the dog on long, leisurely walks and they would use that time to catch up. When they were free on weekends, Teresa continued her role as tour guide, taking him around town and familiarizing him with the sights and amenities the thriving city had to offer.

Bobby looked forward to their time together. Teresa was easy to talk to—always full of positive energy, smart, witty, fun, and she had a special way with people. She connected with them effortlessly and had kind and encouraging things to say to just about anyone she encountered. She was inquisitive and thoughtful, taking a keen interest in the funeral profession and seemed genuinely eager to hear about Bobby's dealings with grieving families, a subject most people typically preferred to avoid. He felt a special bond with her because they shared a calling that they were both passionately committed to—helping people through the most difficult times of their lives. He had never met anyone whose level of commitment on that front rivaled or maybe even exceeded his own, but Teresa Cruz was such a person. He felt a profound sense of admiration—even awe—when she spoke about her interactions with her dying patients. She spoke about them as if they were her dear friends, not just passing acquaintances spending their final days in hospice care.

Bobby's original motivation for finding a female roommate was not panning out. Teresa did not bring a steady stream of girlfriends by the apartment. In fact, she had yet to bring by a single one, but he was fine with that. He had a new best friend—someone he could talk to and confide in—unlike anyone who had ever crossed his path before. He couldn't imagine a better roommate or companion. He just had to keep reminding himself of his vow not to mess everything up by trying to turn a roommate situation into something more than that.

Teresa found their living arrangement to be very much to her liking as well. Her initial instincts about Bobby were proving to be spot-on. He was not sophisticated or highly educated, but he possessed a simple and quiet wisdom about people and about life. He was not ambitious or motivated by money. He didn't care about fine clothing or expensive cars or other material possessions, nor was he concerned about politics or current events happening outside his little world. But he had a caring heart, full of compassion, as well as a true passion for his ministry in the death care profession, as he called it. They were very much alike in that respect, and his profession involved many of the same issues and challenges as hers. In fact, he seemed to be able to relate to her and her calling better than anyone she had met outside of a few other hospice professionals. She found herself looking forward to their walks together. It had become the highlight of her day and she sorely missed them when duty called and Bobby had to attend to a grieving family, which she learned could happen at any hour of the day or night, and often without any advance warning at all.

Teresa also appreciated how thoughtful Bobby always was toward her. He had demonstrated that many times, in many ways, and tonight was another example. It was Saturday evening and it was her 28th birthday. Bobby insisted on taking her out to celebrate in style, at one of the city's finest restaurants, along the River Walk, after which they would check out some music at the local watering holes.

She looked at the clock on the nightstand next to her bed and realized she was at risk of making them late. After carefully applying makeup and spending far too much time blow-drying and brushing her long dark hair, she tried on four different dresses and felt utterly indecisive as she scrutinized each one in front of the stand-up mirror in her bedroom. She was not accustomed to primping, and it made her feel a bit like a teenager. She finally settled on the shimmering black off-the-shoulder cocktail dress she had worn on New Year's Eve a few years back. It still looked chic and stylish and accentuated her petite but shapely figure. She gave herself a final look in the mirror, touched up her lipstick and turned toward the door. Just as she reached for the doorknob, she abruptly scurried back to her dresser and applied a few quick squirts of her favorite perfume to her wrists and neck.

"Wow!" Said Bobby as she emerged from her bedroom. "You look stunning!"

She gave him a fetching smile and then let out a short, nervous giggle. "Thanks," she said. "You look nice, too." Bobby wore a navy sports coat, an open-collared dress shirt and khaki pants. It was the first time she had seen him dressed up in anything other than a dark suit suitable for funeral home work.

They took an Uber to the River Walk and strolled along the water to Boudro's, a lively dining spot that had been an institution in San Antonio for years. They were both uncharacteristically quiet as they made their way to the restaurant, the silence only occasionally interrupted by stilted small talk.

The waiter handed Bobby a wine list as they were seated in a quiet booth near the back. He ordered a bottle of champagne and they watched in silence as the waiter popped the cork and poured two glasses of the sparkling gold liquid.

Bobby raised his glass and looked across the table at his roommate. "Here's to you, Teresa. Happy 28th! I hope this is a truly wonderful year for you."

She looked back at him, her eyes shining, her face seeming to flush in the flickering glow of the candlelight. "There's no one I'd rather be celebrating with, Bobby," she said, her voice now firm, the awkward nervousness gone. "I'm so glad you came into my life."

They clinked glasses and sipped the champagne. "So am I. And I'm sorry for repeating myself, but you look absolutely gorgeous tonight," Bobby said, fixing his eyes upon hers and then gazing around the room. "I think everyone in here is staring at you—as they should!"

She laughed. "Oh, please! You really know how to make a girl feel special!"

He smiled and leaned across the table. "You are special." They looked at each other in silence for a long moment, until the moment was broken by the vibration of Bobby's cell phone in his pants pocket. Bobby started and looked down, instantly becoming distracted. He pulled out the phone and looked at the caller ID. He didn't recognize the number. "Rats! I'm really sorry, Teresa, but I better grab this. Do you mind?"

"Not at all," she said, gesturing at the phone and doing her best to hide her disappointment that a special moment had just ended abruptly.

Bobby put the phone to his ear and leaned back, "Hello?" he answered in a hushed voice. As the waiter arrived with their salads, Teresa engaged him in small talk to avoid listening in on Bobby's call. She couldn't help but overhear the sound of the voice on the other end of the phone. She couldn't make out the words, but it was a male voice, loud and frantic. The words turned into unmistakable wailing.

"Have you called the police? A doctor or an ambulance?" Bobby said into the phone. The concern was evident on his face. "Listen, Julio. I'm coming. I'll be there myself, but I'm in San Antonio right now so it'll take me a while to get there. I'll make the phone calls. You just sit tight. I'm on my way."

Bobby pressed the end-call button and slid the phone back into his pocket. "I am so sorry, Teresa. There's been a terrible tragedy back home. A one-year-old little girl. That was her father. I need to be there. I can't tell you how sorry I am. I'll make it up to you, I promise."

"Duty calls, I get it. No need to apologize. Do what you need to do."

"Are you sure you don't mind? I feel terrible."

"Of course I don't mind. It's not like you have a choice, right? Do we have time to finish our dinner?" She stared at her champagne glass, which she was slowly swirling.

Bobby hesitated, looking at his watch and then looking at Teresa, who was avoiding his gaze. "I'm afraid not. I better run. I'll pay the bill on my way out. Sorry!" He jumped up from the table and hurried away.

Teresa nibbled at her salad for a few minutes and then left the restaurant. She walked along the River Walk, aimlessly, until she passed a bar playing Jimmy Buffet music to a noisy and appreciative crowd. She was dressed to kill and wasn't looking forward to going home at 7:30, so she stopped in and ordered a beer at the bar. Before she had finished half the bottle, several men had approached her, like moths to a flame. She was in no mood for it. She threw back her head and chugged the beer, then quickly walked out the door and hailed a cab.

She saw Bobby's car pulling out of the underground parking lot as she exited the cab. He must have hurried home to change his clothes and pack a few things before hitting the road. She was sniffling as she inserted the key into the door of their apartment. She closed the door behind her and leaned against it. Her sniffling became louder and she could see her reflection in the mirror across the room, mascara mixed with tears running down her cheeks.

"Crap!" she cried out, as she flung her small purse across the room, aiming for the couch but missing badly and nearly knocking over a table lamp. She trudged into her bedroom and flung herself across the bed, pulling a pillow over her head.

Chapter 31

"I DON'T GET it, Mike! We've got to come up with a narrative about your early days," said Russ Miller, frustration evident in his voice. "If we don't shape the story, the media and your opponents will. We need to take control and get out in front of this!"

Michael looked across the desk, past Russ through the glass windows forming the inner wall of his tiny office. He had set it up this way because he wanted the legions of volunteers to feel close to him. It was becoming a source of aggravation now, not just because of the constant interruptions, but also because the glass and the thin walls were not soundproof and not conducive to private conversations. At first, he had made a point of having confidential conversations out in the open air—on the streets, in the city parks, or along the River Walk—where there was no risk of eavesdropping. Those days were gone. He was a public figure now, attracting constant attention everywhere he went, so he felt forced into holding important meetings in the cramped little fishbowl of an office.

It was nearly 8:00 p.m., but campaign headquarters was swarming with volunteers, many of whom worked during the day and spent their early evening hours manning the phone lines, making cold calls to drum up support for the Sanchez candidacy. Michael had been making a concerted effort to be charming, enthusiastic and appreciative in all of his dealings with the volunteers, but that was becoming increasingly difficult as he craved private time for uninterrupted thought and serious conversations.

"I've told you before, I don't want to go there," Michael snapped. His voice was hushed, but urgent. "I have my reasons."

"Well, you need to reconsider those reasons," Miller insisted. "Whatever the facts are, they can't be as bad as what the other side is going to make up if we don't get the truth out there."

"We've been through this, Russ. I did not have an ideal upbringing. We moved around a lot because my father was a lowlife and a drunk. That's why we can't do the whole hometown reunion thing you keep pushing on me. I didn't have a real hometown. I don't have any real roots. We were always moving!"

"That's nothing to be ashamed of. Lots of former presidents had fathers who were scoundrels or just completely uninvolved. It'll make you seem more human. Yours is a story many people can relate to. The voters will eat it up—it will make you look like one of them."

"No! We'll deal with it as it comes up, but I don't want to push that story."

Miller leaned forward and silently pounded his fist on the desk. "Goddammit, Mike. You hired me to be your campaign manager. I know how to win elections. You're paying me to give you my best advice and that's what I'm doing! I need you to trust me on this. Think about it some more!" He stood up, flung the door open and stormed out.

An hour later, Michael found himself walking through Travis Park, about half a mile from the campaign office. It was dark, so he was not likely to be spotted and recognized. He pulled the prepaid cell phone out of his pocket and stared at it. Professor Vega had his own prepaid cell phone. He had admonished Michael to minimize any phone conversations between them. When it was truly urgent, he was to call from outdoors to avoid prying ears and listening devices and to use these phones, which were at least somewhat off the grid.

"Professor? I'm sorry to bother you but I thought I'd better check in. Russ is all over my ass to get the story out about my early years. I've been pushing back, but I'm afraid he has a point. If we don't get a story out there, somebody else will, and they'll be motivated to dig deep if we don't preempt that and get something out there that steers this in the right direction."

There was a long silence. Michael wondered whether the connection had been broken until he heard the familiar flick of a butane lighter. He had seen the Professor fire up his pipe many times just before he engaged in serious thought or discussion. "He's right, Michael. You've been able to dodge that issue up until now, but that time is coming to an end. You need to get in front of this."

"That's exactly what Russ said. But how?"

"Russ can advise you on the how. You need to focus on the 'what.' In other words, what is the story you're going to put out there. It's a good story for the most part. In fact, it's just about airtight. You were born in El Paso and have the birth certificate to prove that. Your father was here illegally but is now deceased. Again, there are records to confirm that. You attended College Park High School from sophomore year to graduation. Everyone knows all this and it's well documented, as is your time at Yale. As for your earlier years, there's little risk in putting your story out there in a general way. You lived in nearly a dozen small towns throughout South Texas between the time you were born and the time you wound up at College Park. Sanchez is a common name, you grew up in a transient part of the country, and many people there try hard to stay anonymous. People aren't likely to remember your family because you never stayed anywhere very long and you kept to yourselves, like many people in that part of the world. You can mention some of the cities and towns from your earlier years if you're pressed for details. Again, the risk of anyone remembering the family is low, but even if they did, they won't be able to determine how closely the Miguel Sanchez of 30 years ago resembles you today. And besides, those people will be on your side. They will be thrilled that one of their own could be president. They won't be trying to undermine you. So, I think it's fine to go ahead and get that story out. Obviously, the one landmine to avoid is the town where you started high school. Keep that out of the story."

"Anything else?"

"Yes. We need to be able to count on your family's complete cooperation. We can't have them saying anything that contradicts your narrative. That is absolutely imperative!"

Chapter 32

TERESA LOOKED UP from the pasta salad she was eating as she heard the sound of the key turning in the front door lock. Bobby looked exhausted as he walked in, bleary-eyed, his dark funeral director's suit uncharacteristically rumpled to match his mussed-up hair. It was early Tuesday evening, and she hadn't heard a word from him since he bolted from the restaurant on Saturday night. All she knew was that he was needed in connection with a funeral in San Mateo.

What she didn't know was that Bobby had been called by Julio Garcia, the brother of Sheriff Reid's wife. Julio had followed his sister to San Mateo from Reynosa about a year ago with his wife and infant daughter. His sister had convinced him that life was far better in this South Texas town than anything they had known on the other side of the border, and that Reynosa with its drugs and gangland violence was no place to be raising a child. Julio had found steady employment waiting tables at Rosa's, a busy restaurant not far from the funeral home. Bobby dined there often and had taken a liking to the shy young man, who lacked the polish and outgoing nature one normally associated with good waiters but made up for it with his hustle and sincerity. Julio's wife worked the night shift at Carroll County Hospital on the housekeeping staff so that she and Julio could alternate parenting duties for Elena, their daughter. Julio beamed whenever he spoke about his precious little girl, who was battling a congenital heart defect, so Bobby had always made a point of asking about her.

Tragedy had struck the Garcia household Saturday evening when baby Elena's heart gave out. Sheriff Reid and his wife were out of town for a long weekend in New Orleans and Julio could think of no one to call other than Bobby. Three hours after his dinner with Teresa had been interrupted, Bobby found himself in the Garcia's small apartment. Julio was holding the limp child on his lap, wrapped in a blanket, intermittently weeping and talking to her in an anguished voice. Bobby sat with them all night. No one else had come by to offer help or consolation because the family had no one else to call.

Toward dawn, Bobby broached the subject of funeral arrangements. The Garcias explained that they were not interested in having a visitation at the funeral home. Like many newcomers from south of the border, they had kept to themselves since moving to San Mateo. Even at work, they were guarded about their interactions with others. The thought of sitting in an empty visitation room staring at a casket was more than they could bear. Bobby explained that a visitation was not required and that they could gather at the funeral home about an hour before the burial to say their final goodbyes.

"Are you going to take her away now? On one of those stretchers in the funeral car?" Julio had asked, wide eyes filling with tears.

"There's no need for that," Bobby had said, putting a hand on Julio's shoulder. "Would you like to carry Elena out to my car? She can ride in the front seat, right next to me."

Julio had nodded, unable to speak, but clearly grateful for the opportunity to take that final walk with his little girl. He cradled her in his arms, wrapped in her pink blanket, and slowly followed Bobby out the door. The despondent father talked to the unresponsive child all the way to the car. After years of dealing with grief-stricken families, Bobby had trained himself to hold back the tears and avoid becoming emotional at times like this. It was contrary to his nature, but he understood that it was helpful to the families to have someone at their side who was compassionate but also thoroughly in control. As he walked out the front door and down the walkway toward his car, he had fought hard to hold back the tears as he listened to the one-way conversation between father and daughter. Bobby felt the floodgates open and the tears washing down his own cheeks as he listened to Julio's final words to little Elena: "There's so much I wanted us to do together... I'll never get to walk you down the aisle on your wedding day... I'll never get to see you graduate from high school and become a young lady... So many things a daddy should do with his little girl... I'll never get to take you for a ride in a little red wagon... I always wanted to do that with you..." The words faded into deep, heavy sobs as Julio kissed his daughter and handed her to Bobby. Bobby tenderly laid the child in the front seat of his car, embraced Julio, and drove away, leaving Julio standing in the street staring after them.

Bobby had slept for just a couple of hours on a couch in the empty funeral home. He had then set about making phone calls. After multiple attempts, he was able to reach Sheriff Reid on his cell phone to break the news and assure him that he was on the case. He could hear the normally stoic sheriff sniffling as he said "Those poor kids. They've got no one here except Natalia and me and we weren't even there for them. We're on our way, Bobby."

Bobby then called Rosa's and Carroll County Hospital and explained the situation to both employers. He also asked them to pass the word among the Garcias' co-workers and pointed out that it sure would be a wonderful gesture of support if people could show up at the funeral home Tuesday morning to pay their respects before the burial service. He made similar calls to friends and acquaintances who were customers of Rosa's and who might know Julio from their visits there.

He spent the remainder of the day driving to neighboring towns visiting toy stores, bicycle shops and sporting goods stores. He couldn't find what he was looking for. The next day, he made the three-hour trip to San Antonio and visited the same kinds of retail establishments until he finally found what he was after—a little red wagon. Then he hurried back to San Mateo to make final preparations for the funeral service.

At first, the pre-burial gathering was exactly what the Garcias had feared—just the two of them, Sheriff Reid and his wife Lucia, all by themselves in a room with a tiny casket. However, within a few minutes, visitors started trickling in, and the trickle quickly turned into a flood. Before long, the room was jammed packed and the crowd had overflowed into the adjacent hallway and the funeral home lobby. A sea of familiar faces, and even unfamiliar ones, offered handshakes, hugs and words of comfort.

Ten minutes before the burial procession was to begin, Bobby had asked Julio for a moment in private. As they made their way through the crowd toward Bobby's office, Bobby put his arm around Julio's shoulder and asked, "How would you like to take Elena for a wagon ride?" Julio's expression turned from puzzled to one of delight as Bobby opened the door, revealing a shiny red wagon. Julio's eyes turned to faucets but his face lit up.

The wagon was the perfect size for an infant casket. Bobby and Mr. Zamora solemnly hoisted the casket into the wagon, and Julio led the procession out of the funeral home. It would have been a strange sight to anyone happening by—a procession of nearly one hundred people walking down the middle of the street, led by a man pulling a little red wagon. The Sheriff's Department deputies halted traffic as they moved from the funeral home to the cemetery two blocks away. Julio chattered away to his daughter the entire way, his face streaked with tears but a spring in his step. His wife and sister walked behind him, followed by Bobby and Sheriff Reid and then the crowd of mourners.

"I owe you, Bobby," the Sheriff said wiping his eyes and staring straight ahead. "Thanks for being here for my family. I'll never forget this." Neither would anyone else in attendance.

Teresa knew none of that as Bobby flopped down on the couch. All she knew was that Bobby had walked out on their dinner three days earlier and she hadn't heard from him since.

"I'm taking the dog for a walk," she announced curtly.

"Mind if I come along?" Bobby asked.

"If you want but don't feel like you have to."

"Just let me change quickly," he said rising slowly from the couch and heading toward his bedroom, staring at Teresa, who was obviously avoiding eye contact.

"Better be fast. CT really has to go," she said.

Bobby changed quickly, throwing his suit on the bed and putting on jeans, a sweatshirt and walking shoes.

Sensing that something was amiss, Bobby spoke up as soon as they reached the sidewalk in front of their apartment. "Teresa, I am really sorry for the way I ran out on you Saturday night. I just felt like I didn't have much choice. You know how it is in our business."

"I get it. Duty calls and you need to answer. But it would have been nice if you had called me to let me know what was going on. You didn't give me any details. You never checked in. I had no idea when you'd be home." She yanked the dog's leash impatiently as he tried to sniff a fire hydrant.

Bobby gave her a sideways glance as they walked side-by-side. Still no eye contact. "I'm really sorry, Teresa. I just got busy and never stopped to think about it. It's not like we're dating. It just didn't occur to me to check in."

"Well, it seems to me that it's just common courtesy to keep your roommate informed about your travel plans when you're away."

Bobby hesitated. He was tired and was starting to get irritated by the conversation, but he held his tongue and thought carefully before speaking. "You're right. And I'm sorry. I should have called you. I guess I'm still trying to figure out this roommate thing. Anyway, let me tell you what I've been up to the past few days."

He proceeded to tell her about everything that had happened since he left Saturday night. She listened attentively as they walked the perimeter of the sprawling city park. They approached their favorite park bench as he was finishing the story and took a seat as they normally did. She finally looked at him, all traces of frostiness gone. "After all that, you come home and have to deal with a bitchy roommate. I'm sorry, Bobby. And I'm glad you're home."

"Me, too. I hope you'll let me have a do-over on your birthday dinner. I've got to get back to San Mateo this weekend, but any time after that is fine with me."

"I'd really like that. Maybe the weekend after next. What's going on in San Mateo this weekend?"

"I'm not sure exactly. Mr. Zamora said he needs my help with a few sticky situations, which sounds a little alarming. I'm heading down there Friday and should be back before Monday."

The stroll home was leisurely and comfortable, in contrast to the tension-filled start to their walk. Teresa flipped on the TV as Bobby sorted through mail that had piled up in his absence. "Hey, take a look at this, Bobby! That's my new crush—Miguel Sanchez, the guy I've been telling you about. He's from right here in San Antonio. He's been surprising everyone with his poll numbers. It's really exciting! He might actually win. I think I'm going to volunteer with the campaign. Isn't he handsome?"

"Looks like just another slick politician to me," Bobby said from across the room, casually glancing up at the television screen. The camera zoomed in for a close-up of the candidate. Bobby dropped the mail and walked briskly toward the TV. "Holy cow! That's Miguel Sanchez? He looks just like someone I used to know." He walked closer to the television, studying the face more carefully, but the picture vanished and the news anchor moved on to the next story.

Bobby grabbed the remote control and started flipping channels furiously, searching unsuccessfully for more footage of the candidate.

"What's up, Bobby? Interested in politics all of a sudden?"

"It's just uncanny. I feel like I know that guy!"

Chapter 33

BOBBY MADE THE weekend trip to San Mateo and arrived home early enough on Sunday afternoon to propose a do-over birthday dinner with Teresa. She gladly accepted, and they returned to Boudro's on the River Walk, the site of their previously aborted dinner. In keeping with the spirit of a do-ever, they ordered the same champagne as well as the same salads and entrees they had ordered the previous week. Teresa had dressed down, however, claiming that the shimmering black dress she had worn the previous week must have jinxed them. Still, she looked fetching in a bright yellow sundress that was perfect for springtime in San Antonio.

"So what was the big emergency in San Mateo?" she asked.

Bobby's face darkened. "I hate to say it, but I think the problem is Mr. Zamora himself. He's getting up there in years, and he's relied on me for so long that I think he's forgotten some of the basics of funeral directing. That's causing some real problems."

Teresa sipped her champagne as the waiter served their salads. "Does he need more help?" she asked.

"He hired a part-timer, a young kid named Eddie right out of high school. Eddie's not a funeral director, but he runs the crematory, picks up the bodies sometimes, and helps with the dressing and casketing and whatever else Mr. Zamora needs help with. But they've both been making mistakes, so Mr. Zamora asked me to do some basic training on policies and procedures and how to avoid mistakes. That's what I did all day yesterday and I really hope it sinks in. They've made some pretty serious mistakes and then they made it worse by not handling the mistakes properly."

Bobby looked pensively at his champagne glass. "That's always been a challenge with Mr. Zamora," he said. "When something goes wrong, I've always believed the best approach is to make full disclosure to the family and try to make it right. But, I'm not the boss, and Mr. Zamora sometimes sees it differently."

"I'm not sure I'm tracking," said Teresa. "What kinds of problems are you talking about?"

"For one thing, identification procedures are important, because we don't know everyone coming into our care. Our policy is to put an identification tag on every body as soon as we take custody of it. And then once a body arrives at the funeral home, it may be moved any number of times—when it's embalmed, or when we dress the body or place it in the casket, or move it into a visitation room. We're supposed to check the ID on the body every time we handle it and document that we've confirmed the ID. This is critical when we have multiple bodies in our care. It's also critical because cremation is becoming more common and once a body is cremated, there's no way to tell one person from another, so you have to have foolproof chain-of-custody procedures. Anyway, that's just one example. There are lots of other procedures that need to be followed meticulously to avoid mistakes." Bobby looked apologetically at Teresa across the table. "Sorry, I must be boring you with this shop talk."

"Not at all. I enjoy it. But tell me more. I can tell by the look on your face that this is bothering you. You're not just speaking hypothetically, are you?"

Bobby shook his head. "I'm afraid not. We've had some real screw-ups over the past few weeks, which I didn't know about until yesterday. The worst one happened early last week. There were two cremation cases in the house at the same time. One body was supposed to be cremated and returned to the family. The other body was supposed to be cremated and then scattered out in the desert. They failed to follow the ID procedures and got them mixed up. They cremated one body first and proceeded with the scattering, thinking it was the scattering case. When they went to pull the other body out of the cooler, they realized *that* was the body that was supposed to be scattered. So it turns out that they scattered the remains of the person that were supposed to go back to the family."

"So what did they do?"

"My advice was to tell both families exactly what happened and apologize profusely and figure out what we can do to make it up to them. It's bad enough to make a mistake like that, but it was an accident. Careless for sure, but an accident. If we don't tell them, now it looks like a deliberate cover-up, which just compounds the mistake."

"So did they tell the families?"

Bobby looked away and let out a deep breath. "No. Mr. Zamora decided to give the remains of the person who should have been scattered to the family who was expecting their loved one's remains—without telling them. So they now have an urn containing a stranger's ashes. Mr. Zamora said that both families were grieving over their losses and telling them the full story would serve no purpose other than compounding their grief. Cremated remains all look the same and DNA is destroyed by cremation, so there's no way they could ever prove that they got the wrong person. Besides, he said if they sued him, it could put him out of business, which would be a disservice to the entire town, because there's no other funeral home within 60 miles."

Teresa slammed her fork down on the table. "But that's so wrong! What if this guy Eddie tells them what really happened at some point? And even if he doesn't tell them, doesn't that family have the right to know what happened to their loved one's remains and that their urn has a stranger in it? Did you try to talk him out of it?"

Bobby shrugged sheepishly. "I gave him my opinion. I guess I really didn't argue with him. It's his business and ultimately he has to make the decisions and live with the consequences. I wasn't involved in the service and didn't know these families."

Teresa looked incredulous. "Has he ever behaved that way before?"

"A few times. Maybe more than a few, now that I think of it. But none of them involve mistakes I made. I'm meticulous when it comes to details. But there was a case a year or so ago where the family had a church service scheduled and wanted the body to be present for the final prayers and good-byes. I had let Mr. Zamora know the day before that the body needed to be embalmed but he got busy or just forgot and didn't get around to it. So rather than send the unembalmed body to the church, he sent an empty casket—without telling the family. He did the embalming later, put the body in an identical casket, and made the switch before the casket was sent to the cemetery. He never told the family that they were saying their final prayers and final good-byes to an empty casket at the church.

Teresa had stopped eating and was staring at him wide-eyed, with her mouth open.

Bobby leaned back and scratched his head. "Then there was the time that the family gave us a rosary and some jewelry, along with some pictures that they wanted to be placed in the casket before burial. Same thing. He just forgot and then we found the items back at the funeral home after the burial. He never told the family. He just got rid of those things."

"And you didn't call him on it? That doesn't compute. You're so focused on your clients, I can't believe you would let him deceive grieving families like that."

"Believe me, I don't feel good about it. But on some level, I understand his point—why add further stress to a grieving family? What does that accomplish?"

"Oh come on, Bobby, that's nonsense! You don't believe that! I know you! That's not how you're wired."

"Well, it is his business. I make my case and then let him make the decision. I'm just not sure what else I can do."

"Do you push him hard? Do you come on really strong and insist that he do the right thing?"

Bobby squirmed in his seat. "Probably not. He's the boss. I know that's not a good answer. I suppose it gets back to my upbringing to some extent. My parents trained me from an early age to steer far away from trouble and I guess I took that to heart."

"But sometimes trouble finds you and doing the right thing means you confront it head-on. Didn't they teach you that?"

"They were guests in this country. They were here on work visas. They lived in fear of being sent back if any sort of trouble found its way to our doorstep. They instilled that fear in me, and I guess they did a pretty good job. Over time, it just became second nature for me to steer clear of trouble."

"I get that, believe me. My mother came here as a single mom from Panama and had the same kind of fears. But she's gone now and so are your parents, God rest their souls. There's no reason for you to be afraid of them being deported. And you certainly have no risk of that. You were born here. I wasn't—I had to apply for citizenship and go through that drill—but I did it. You and I are both American citizens. This is our home and no one is going to try to send us away. So why keep living with that fear? It's just not rational!"

Bobby hung his head and stared at his untouched steak. "You're right," he said in a quiet voice. "Like I said, I'm not proud to have any association with those kinds of actions. I've tried to justify it by telling myself they weren't my decisions. But I guess I shouldn't be proud of being connected with a business that behaves that way." He paused and swirled the champagne in his glass. "But I need my job. Working for Zamora enables me to do what I do. Like I said before, it's my calling, my ministry. I love what I do. It puts me in a position to help others when they really need it. And I'm good at it. At least I thought I was until just now…" His voice trailed off.

Chapter 34

"BOBBY, WE GOT the McDaniel case!" Mr. Zamora was not prone to excitement, but the sound of his voice left no doubt that this was a big deal in his world.

"Senator McDaniel's wife?" Bobby asked. "That's been all over the news. Breast cancer, right? Poor woman. I thought for sure that funeral would be in Washington or maybe Austin."

"Nope. Turns out the Senator's wife was a San Antonio native. She grew up just a few blocks from our funeral home and went to a lot of services there when it was owned by Mr. Klein. Anyway, she never liked the political scene, so one of her last requests was to have the funeral and burial in her old neighborhood. I just got the call from the Senator's personal secretary."

The wheels were already turning in Bobby's head as he contemplated the various logistical challenges. It would likely be a huge service, with political types, celebrities, relatives and friends traveling from all over to pay their respects. He was still a one-man operation.

"I'll be heading up there this afternoon and I'll bring Eddie with me. Have you found any part-time help yet?"

"A few good candidates, but I haven't hired anyone yet. I could bring a couple of them in on a contract basis just for this service. I'm sure they'd jump at the opportunity to be part of this."

"This will be great exposure for our firm, Bobby. There's no better form of advertisement in our business than having hundreds of people streaming through our facility and seeing us put on a first-rate service.

Let's be sure that we really roll out the red carpet for this family and make the right impression. See you in a few hours."

With the assistance of Mr. Zamora, Eddie and two additional funeral directors hired for the occasion, Bobby spent the next 48 hours in heavy-duty preparation mode. An hour before the visitation, everything was ready.

Zamora Family Mortuary was an expansive facility that still looked very much like it did when it was built in the early 1970s. It had three large visitation rooms, and since there were no other cases being handled that week, Bobby had opened all three rooms for the McDaniel service. Mrs. McDaniel was lying in repose in the center room. A catering service occupied the room to the left of the visitation room. Finger sandwiches, cheese trays, fruit and desserts lined tables along the wall. Coffee, tea and soft drink stations were set up around the room as well. In the room to the right, a video tribute to Mrs. McDaniel was playing on an endless loop. Pictures of the Senator's wife from various stages of her life were scattered around the room, and her favorite songs played softly in the background. In keeping with the family's desire to make the event a celebration of life rather than a sad farewell, the room was full of memorabilia designed to remind visitors of the life of Kayla McDaniel—her causes, accomplishments and things she held dear. There were photographs of her beauty pageant days as well as trophies she had won in those competitions, including her Ms. Texas crown. There were posters for various movies she had starred in early in her life when she gave acting a go, movies that never caught on and were long forgotten, but that were part of her glamorous past before she became a politician's wife. There were pictures of her with her family members and pictures of her posing with countless animals, after she had taken up her lifelong cause of protecting animal rights. And there was a table covered with miniature bottles of what appeared to be *Jack Daniels*, except that the label read *McDaniel's* rather than *Jack Daniels*. Anyone who knew Senator and Mrs. McDaniel immediately appreciated the significance, as the McDaniels were known for hosting fabulous cocktail parties where their drink of choice was the famous Kentucky sour mash whiskey. The little bottles were intended as mementoes to be taken home by the guests rather than consumed on the premises, since the funeral home was not licensed to serve liquor and Bobby knew from past experience that drinking and funerals could be a volatile mix.

The visitation was scheduled to begin at 3:00. At 2:30, Bobby led Senator McDaniel and his two adult daughters into the visitation room for some private time with the deceased before opening the room to the public. It was the first time they had seen her body since she had passed away and all three broke into tears. To Bobby, they seemed just like the hundreds of other families he had accompanied in this situation.

"She looks beautiful, Bobby" said Melanie, the older daughter, wiping her eyes.

Bobby offered her a tissue. "Take as much time as you'd like. I'll be right here, and I'll be here for the duration. Anything you need, just ask." He stepped off to the side and stood erect with his head bowed in respect.

The room was silent except for the sniffles. One-by-one, the family members knelt in front of the casket, tenderly touching Mrs. McDaniel's stiff hands and whispering their farewells. Senator McDaniel and his daughters engaged in a long embrace, and then the Senator announced in a quiet but steady voice, "I think we're ready, Bobby."

Bobby gave them another couple of minutes to wipe their eyes and compose themselves, and then opened the large double doors to the visitation room. A good-sized crowd had arrived already and began streaming into the room to greet the family. Mr. Zamora stood quietly outside the entrance, looking every bit the lifelong funeral director that he was. Bobby's goal was to remain keenly attentive to the needs of the family, while otherwise remaining inconspicuous, and quietly ensuring that everything was running smoothly with the catering, the video and musical tributes, the parking, and the security.

By early evening, the funeral home was jam-packed. All three visitation rooms were overflowing. The normally spacious lobby and corridors seemed cramped and crowded. A receiving line extended all the way along the 90-foot wall of the visitation room into the hallway, as mourners lined up to share words of comfort and condolences with the family. Many of the faces looked familiar to Bobby, although he could not identify them.

There was an abundance of well-dressed, distinguished looking, silver and white-haired gentlemen who had the look of career politicians.

Late in the evening, Bobby noticed that one of the visitors seemed to be attracting an inordinate amount of attention. He sidled closer to the source of that commotion and started when he saw the young, handsome face he had seen on television just days before. It was Miguel Sanchez, candidate for president of the United States. The obvious presence of Secret Service agents hovering nearby left no doubt about that. Bobby stared hard, while trying to be subtle about it. He knew that face. It had to be him. He was even more sure about it now than when he had first studied that face on television a few days earlier. It just didn't make any sense.

Over the next thirty minutes, Bobby kept a close eye on Sanchez from a distance. He saw his opportunity as the candidate made his way into the catering area and moved toward the food tables. Bobby approached from behind, acutely aware that the Secret Service agents were watching him. "Hey Rocket! Is that you?" he called out, unable to conceal the excitement in his voice.

Sanchez whirled around and stared at the massive young funeral director standing directly in front of him. The candidate's eyes widened, and his face brightened. His open mouth started forming a smile, before he quickly suppressed it and his expression changed instantaneously to one of confusion. "Are you talking to me?" he asked, sounding stiff and formal.

"I'm Bobby Rivera," Bobby said, looking expectantly for a reaction. His eyes darted toward the candidate's left hand. It was gripping a paper plate holding crackers and cheese, palm side up.

The candidate glanced at the bronze nameplate on Bobby's jacket and paused, seemingly flustered and at a loss for words. It lasted just an instant and then he quickly composed himself, extending his right hand, saying, "Nice to meet you, Bobby. I'm Miguel Sanchez." He hurried away.

The visitation was scheduled to conclude at 9:00, but it was nearly 10:00 by the time the last visitors left with the family. Mr. Zamora left at the same time, being unaccustomed to being on his feet that long, and left the cleaning and closing up for Bobby and the part-time help. After the left-over food had been put away, Bobby dismissed the part-timers and asked them to return in the morning to help with a more complete clean-up. He then ensconced himself in his office and fired up his computer. He stared at the scar on the back of his left hand, still prominent after 20 years. He began searching for images of Miguel Sanchez and trying to find one that presented a clear picture of the candidate's left hand. After 15 minutes of futile searching, his concentration was interrupted by the harsh buzzing of the rear doorbell, which normally meant a flower or casket delivery, but it was way too late for that now. He hurried to the back room of the funeral home, pushed open the steel door, and found himself face-to-face with candidate Miguel Sanchez.

A familiar grin spread over the candidate's face. "Seventy-Seven! I can't believe it's you!"

"Rocket!" Bobby held out his left fist and tapped the scar. "It's me!"

Sanchez raised his left fist, pulled down his sleeve and displayed the back of his hand, revealing an identical scar. Then he wrapped Bobby in a rough bearhug. "Sonofabitch! I can't believe this!"

They walked through the quiet funeral home and pulled up a couple of chairs in the spacious room that had served as the catering room earlier in the evening. "Funeral director, huh?" the candidate said, looking directly at his old friend and nodding approvingly. "I guess I shouldn't be surprised. It suits you."

"And look at you!" Bobby replied, unable to conceal his excitement. "One of the most famous people in the country right now. Running for president. Holy cow! That's unbelievable! As soon as I saw your picture, I thought it was you. You look exactly the same and you sound exactly the same. Even when you didn't recognize me tonight, I knew it was you!"

"Sorry about that, pal. I was just so stunned. Everything about this whole campaigning business is so carefully scripted and orchestrated, I just had to think before I reacted. You threw me for a loop and I've been thinking about it ever since. I just felt like I had to come by—I couldn't leave you hanging like that!"

"I'm really glad you did," Bobby said. "It felt like you just dropped off the face of the earth. I figured you went back to Mexico and I'd never see you again. I'm glad to see you're alive and well and becoming a great American success story. Fill me in! You're still Sal Rios in my eyes but now you've got a whole new identity. What's the story?"

"Well, it's been quite a journey since I saw you last. Let's see, where to begin?" His eyes wandered around the room and then stopped on the tray covered with the souvenir whiskey bottles. "This may call for a belt or two." He got up and retrieved a handful of the tiny bottles. "May I?"

"Help yourself."

"I almost never do this, but this is a special occasion." Sal unscrewed the cap and raised a bottle. "For old times' sake," he said, then drained the bottle. "Care to join me?" he asked offering one of the miniature bottles to Bobby.

"I don't like hard liquor any more than I did on our camping trip! But, you're right—it's a special occasion." He unscrewed the top and swallowed the two ounces of amber liquid, wincing as it went down. "So, start with the name thing. How did Sal Rios become Miguel Sanchez? When I first heard that name, I thought our old pal had risen from the dead!"

"What a tragedy," Sal said, casting his eyes downward and shaking his head. "His time on this earth was cut way too short. Here's to Miguel." He downed another bottle, and Bobby did likewise. "So here's the story. I left San Mateo because I was adopted by another family. It all happened pretty fast. My father's former boss had taken an interest in me and helped arrange it. The family was moving to San Antonio shortly after my dad was killed and it just made sense to do it then, since I was completely on my own at that point. And after what happened with my dad, I didn't want people coming to look for me, so I started using my middle name, which is Miguel, and my new family's name, which is Sanchez. It was a little creepy at first, having the same name as our old pal, so I started going by Michael. It sounded more American anyway. Now that I'm campaigning, I'm transitioning back to Miguel—more appealing to the Latino voters. My friends still call me Michael or just Mike."

Sal got up and walked over to the drink table and grabbed another handful of the tiny whiskey bottles. He tossed one to Bobby then unscrewed the cap on another and chugged it down. "Feels like we're back in high school," he said wiping his mouth and grinning.

"So you've been in San Antonio ever since?" Bobby asked.

"Mostly. I was here through high school—graduated from College Park High. Played football there and did well enough that Yale recruited me. Stayed there all the way through law school and then I moved back after I graduated. Got my citizenship along the way, too."

"And now you're running for president. That's unbelievable! Did you get into politics right out of law school?"

"Hell no! I joined a law firm and I've spent the last 10 years building my legal practice. I've done pretty well there—making more money than I ever dreamed of. Made something of a name for myself as an immigration rights advocate and that led me to the political arena just this past year. Never expected to find myself running for president at the age of 35. I still can't believe it's happening!"

"I believe it! I remember how passionate you were when we were kids—always talking about changing America. I thought you'd be leading a revolution rather than becoming part of the establishment and running for president." Bobby laughed.

"It *is* a revolution, Bobby! That's always been the goal." Sal swayed slightly as he made his way back to his chair. "It's all about taking the reins of power away from the elite and the establishment and using that power to take care of our people."

"What do you mean by *our* people? The American people?"

"No, I mean *our* people—outsiders like you and me. People of color. Immigrants. Future generations of immigrants. People all across Latin America who've been oppressed by America. That's going to change. This country needs to make amends and make that right."

"Now you sound like the Sal I remember! Only thing is, you're on the inside now. So am I. We've prospered here. You just told me you're making more money than you ever imagined. You've got a great job and an Ivy League education. I'm sure you'll have a family someday and they'll have a comfortable life and a great future. Seems like the system is working pretty well for you."

Sal leaned toward Bobby and looked at him, intensity emanating from his bleary eyes. "We've been lucky, Bobby. Not everyone is so lucky. But we can't let ourselves get complacent. We can't become insiders. And I'll let you in on something, just between us. We've got some very powerful and influential outsiders working with us. And, there are insiders in the halls of power who are really outsiders. We're taking over! Do you understand what I'm saying?"

"I have no idea what you're saying," Bobby laughed. "But, that's not surprising. I never understood what you were talking about when you went on your political rants back in The Brush. Anyway, I'll leave politics to you. It sure is good to see you!"

"It's great to see you, too," Sal said, slurring slightly. "We knew each other for such a short time, but you were one of the best friends I've ever had. You were good to me during a very tough time in my life and I've never forgotten it. And I really want to keep in touch now that we've reconnected."

"That would be great, Rocket. But I suspect where you're going, you won't have much time for me."

"Bullshit! I'll make time, Seventy-Seven!" Sal's face suddenly clouded over with a look of concern. "You know, something just occurred to me. I need to ask you a favor." His eyes flitted around the room and he rubbed an eyebrow. Bobby looked at him expectantly, waiting for him to continue. "Let's keep this little reunion quiet, OK? I really want to keep my time in San Mateo out of the public eye."

Bobby looked hurt. "Why? Are you embarrassed of us?"

"No, no, nothing like that. It's just that everything I say and do now is going to be blown up by the media. That was a terrible time for me. Witnessing my father's murder. Then the grief and the shock and the pain that followed, not to mention the fear of being on my own at 15. I really don't want to relive all that, especially in a very public way. And it's not just about me. It would be hurtful for my adoptive family to focus on my previous life like that. We're very close and I don't want to put them through that. So, can we keep this between us? It would mean a lot to me. If you were to tell anyone that we're friends, word would travel fast and the press would be all over both of us in no time. And they'd be swarming San Mateo. It would be a mess!"

Bobby nodded and stuck out his hand. "You're my friend, Sal, and I want what's best for you. I can't pretend to understand what living in the media fishbowl must be like, so of course I'll do as you ask. Maybe a day will come when you're not so much in the public eye and we can reconnect again. Right now, I'm just glad that we've found each other, and I'm really thrilled for you!"

"Thanks, Bobby." They shook hands warmly and stood up. Sal listed badly and looked as if he might fall over. He steadied himself and gave Bobby a quick embrace. "I'll always be here for you, Seventy-Seven. If you ever need anything, just let me know."

Chapter 35

"BOBBY, ARE YOU at home? Turn on CNN right now!" The tone in Mr. Zamora's voice was urgent.

Bobby grabbed the remote control and pointed it at the television. A familiar image materialized on the screen: Carroll County Cemetery back home in San Mateo. A reporter was speaking with a man wearing jeans and a khaki work shirt identified on the screen as Rick Chamberlain, an anthropology professor at Northeast Texas State University. Bobby stood transfixed, his mouth open, watching in disbelief as the professor spoke of the mass graves he and his team had uncovered at the cemetery containing dozens or perhaps hundreds of unidentified human remains they were in the process of digging up. They were on a mission to identify the remains of migrants who had perished in the harsh South Texas desert, so that those remains could be shipped back to their grieving families south of the border.

"They're making this sound like Auschwitz!" Mr. Zamora sputtered. "It's all over the newspapers, too. It started with some hack reporter with one of those alternative newspapers in Austin, but now it's gone national. There are stories popping up in major newspapers all across the country, complete with gruesome pictures of dug-up caskets and skulls and bones."

"Do you want me to come down?" Bobby asked.

"I don't know yet. Sit tight for now, but I may need you here on short notice. Better read all the coverage you can find so we know what's going on."

It was past midnight when Teresa walked in after an overtime shift at the hospice. She was surprised to find Bobby at the kitchen table, glued to his laptop. He was not the night-owl type, nor did he spend much time on his computer. "Hi Bobby. What are you doing up so late?"

"Trouble back home," Bobby said, without looking up.

Teresa approached and walked around behind him, looking over his shoulder at the computer screen. *Migrants Found in Mass Graves in South Texas* screamed the headline of The *Los Angeles Times*. She noticed the byline: *San Mateo, Texas*. "What's that all about?" she asked.

"This story popped up earlier today and it's being picked up all across the country," Bobby said, his eyes fixated on the computer screen as he rapidly scrolled through the article. "They've got it all wrong! What they're saying just isn't true! And they're all just repeating the original story and it's spreading like crazy!"

"What are they saying?"

"It's about migrants who crossed the border and then died trying to get through the deserts in South Texas. Apparently, a couple of professors and their students have collaborated with a reporter out of Austin to investigate the burial of these bodies. They're making it sound like there was some big conspiracy among the Medical Examiner, the Sheriff's Office, the local ranchers and our funeral home to cover this up and hide the bodies. They're telling all kinds of horror stories about how disrespectfully these remains have been treated. They claim it's their mission to identify these bodies and get them back to their families in Mexico or wherever they came from."

Teresa's eyes grew wide. "Your funeral home was involved?"

"Absolutely. And I was personally involved—probably more than anyone. I made it a mission of mine to try to do everything we could to treat these poor souls respectfully and do whatever we could to find their families. It just wasn't possible in most cases. I got involved because I knew The Brush better than anyone else, so I could be helpful in finding the bodies and getting them out of the desert. And, as a licensed funeral director, it made sense for someone like me to oversee the handling of the remains. I worked closely with the M.E.'s office, the Sheriff and the county, which owns the cemetery. It was all done above-board and with the utmost care and compassion. I can't believe this crap!" He shoved the laptop across the table.

"Mind if I take a look?" Teresa asked, taking a seat and pulling Bobby's laptop toward her.

"Help yourself."

Teresa followed a series of links and scrolled through numerous articles while Bobby paced behind her. "The anthropologists and the reporters are sure trying to make themselves look like heroes, aren't they?" she said. "They make it sound like they're pursuing a noble cause while everyone else had devious motives."

"It's ironic," Bobby said. "As far as I know, they haven't even spoken to anyone involved. We could have told them exactly what was going on so they wouldn't have had to speculate and make all these erroneous assumptions. My guess is that they didn't even go through the proper channels to open these graves and exhume these bodies. A court order would have been required and the county would have been involved in those proceedings. It looks like they were oblivious to those requirements and probably violated all kinds of laws by digging up these graves."

Bobby proceeded to tell Teresa what he knew about these burials. The county was ultimately responsible for trying to identify next-of-kin and for disposing of the remains when relatives could not be located. The county worked with the Sheriff's Office in recovering the remains. The M.E. had serious budgetary challenges and a staff of exactly one, Manny Quintana, who was getting up there in years and seriously out of shape. Therefore, both the Sheriff and the M.E. were only too happy to have qualified help in the form of Bobby Rivera, who insisted on doing the work as a community service, without any compensation.

Bobby meticulously documented the condition of the remains and the recovery site with photographs as well as detailed notes. Occasionally, letters, pictures or other clues as to identity were found with the remains, in which case the ME would do his best to identify the remains and con-tact next-of-kin; however, a successful ID was a rarity. As the unidentified remains piled up in the county morgue, Bobby and the Medical Examiner persuaded the county to provide space for burial in the county cemetery, to preserve the possibility of identification at a later date, just in case.

Zamora Family Mortuary provided caskets and body bags to the county at cost and the M.E. would send the remains to the county cemetery, where they were buried in an area set aside for that purpose. There were no grave markers, since the names were unknown, but Bobby ensured that meticulous records were maintained at the funeral home, matching the case number to the plot in the cemetery where it was buried. In some cases, remains of multiple bodies were found commingled at the recovery site. Sometimes the remains had been scattered over a wide area by the desert wildlife. In those cases, it was impossible to determine which body parts belonged together or even how many bodies were recovered, so the remains were left together just as they had been found, and buried that way, with documentation explaining what was found.

No one profited from this process. All involved thought they were part of a noble and worthwhile effort, particularly when the alternative, and to some degree the past history, was to let the remains rot in the desert or to simply cremate them.

The story that spread across the nation bore little resemblance to that scenario. It was a timely story, with issues of immigrant rights so prominent in the national news. It made for great headlines—the desperate people who were deprived of a dignified life in their homeland now suffered the ultimate indignity in this country following their death. Newspapers demanded justice. Congresswoman Maria Pena railed about corruption in local government and the need to reform the shady funeral profession. The Texas Funeral Service Commission promised a thorough review of state funeral laws and regulations as well as tough sanctions against any licensed funeral director or funeral establishment that had violated its laws. Most ominously, the Texas Rangers were put in charge of conducting a thorough investigation with a goal of criminal prosecution in the event that it uncovered unlawful activity on the part of anyone involved.

By the next day the national media had set up shop near the small county cemetery. A steady stream of television broadcasts and newspaper stories detailed the alleged atrocities, the tone invariably one of righteous outrage. Pictures of the small cemetery showed the dug-up graves, making it look like an army of grave robbers had just conducted a raid.

Other pictures showed open caskets containing multiple skulls and a tangled mess of bones. In some cases, the name *Zamora Family Mortuary* could be plainly seen on the container. The professor and the reporter who broke the story were all over the airways denouncing the deplorable burial practices.

Bobby spent the next week in San Mateo. His name had not yet surfaced, as most of the allegations were levied against the funeral home itself as well as the M.E., the Sheriff's Department and the county cemetery. Mr. Zamora had refused all requests for interviews and had instructed Bobby to do the same, but he wanted Bobby to be available on-site in case the Funeral Service Commission or the Texas Rangers showed up in pursuit of their investigations. By week's end, the investigation was in full swing. Mr. Zamora was quick to send the investigators to Bobby when they came calling. Bobby approached those meetings with an eagerness to tell his story and set the record straight. The investigators were professional and seemed understanding, but they were clearly keeping their cards close to their vests and he could not read their reactions.

After several days of telling the same story focused on the discovery of the "mass graves," and the gruesome images that accompanied those stories, the attention shifted to the investigation. The press needed to put faces on their villains. Pictures of Sheriff Reid and Manny Quintana began making their way into the news stories. However, the greatest focus became the industry practices and laws pertaining to the handling of human remains, which shifted the focus to Zamora Family Mortuary. Alex Zamora's name and photo were everywhere, along with pictures of his funeral home.

After a week-long onslaught of media attention, Zamora summoned Bobby to his office late Friday afternoon. Bobby could see stress all over the older man's face. "Bobby, this has been a rough week, as we both know. In fact, this has been the toughest week of my professional career." He paused, looking down at the newspaper spread out on his desk. "This funeral home was started by my grandfather over 70 years ago. He passed it on to my father when I was a boy. For the last 30 years, I've carried on the family tradition." He paused again. His eyes met Bobby's for just an instant, then he cast them downward again. "I've got to do whatever it takes to make sure our business survives this mess. You and I know we did nothing wrong, but that doesn't matter. All that matters is what our community thinks, and I'm afraid that right now some of them are starting to think that we've been up to something sinister."

"I hear you, Mr. Zamora. It's so frustrating! We haven't gotten our side of the story out there. Maybe you should let me talk to the media. Or maybe we can hold some meetings around town and tell people what really happened. I know this community has trusted Zamora Family Mortuary for a long time, and believe me, nothing is more important to me than getting us through this."

"I appreciate that, Bobby. I really do. But the media is going to say what they're going to say. They're invested in their own narrative and we're not going to be able to change that. I'm in survival mode here, and right now the connection between this story and our funeral home is you. I'm afraid I've got to put the business first and do something that's absolutely tearing me up. I've got to let you go, Bobby. I'm really sorry."

Chapter 36

"THANKS FOR SPEAKING to my class, Michael. That was a real treat, for them and for me." Professor Juan Carlos Vega opened the door to his faculty office, which had the unmistakable look of a move in progress, a tell-tale box holding the Professor's personal effects serving as the centerpiece on an otherwise uncluttered desk in a barren office.

"I had an ulterior motive, as I'm sure you can imagine," Michael replied. "Looks like I got here just in time. You're leaving?"

"Semester's over. That was my last class. I'm teaching summer school in Mexico City starting in a couple of weeks. I'm not sure when I'll be back here at Yale. It may be a while."

Michael looked troubled. "The Democratic Convention is less than a month away. It's getting toward crunch time, and I'd sure like to have your counsel during the home stretch. Guess we'll just have to talk by phone."

"I don't think that will be necessary—or advisable. You never know who's listening. I'm here now and we definitely need to talk, but after today, I'll be checking out for a while. If you need to reach me, communicate through Vargas."

"Vargas? I don't like that idea. He gives me the creeps. Always has. Besides, I have no idea how to find him."

"Don't worry, he'll find you—soon. The two of you can devise a means of getting in touch."

"But I really need you right now. It feels like I've stalled in the polls. We got off to a great start, but our numbers have flattened out. I'm at about 23 percent and I'm just stuck there. Tom Nelson is at around 38%

and Hugh Connett's around 35%. Conventions are coming up and that might give each of them a bounce. I don't have a convention, so I'm at a disadvantage."

"What does your campaign manager say?"

"He says not to worry—they've had years to develop their constituency and I've had only a few months. We just have to get better about raising money so we can fund a more aggressive advertising blitz."

"Don't sweat it, Michael. There's been a development and I think you'll appreciate it."

"What kind of development?"

"As you know, Connett has settled on Anthony Rinaldi as his running mate. That's expected to be formalized at the convention, but it's not going to happen. It's going to blow up."

"Blow up? How? What are you talking about?"

"Mr. Rinaldi had no history of misconduct of any kind. That's what makes him so appealing to Connett, who really likes to flaunt his Mr. Clean image. Well, Rinaldi screwed up. He recently had a little dalliance with a 21-year-old intern. She's about to drop a bombshell and go public with sexual harassment allegations any day now. She's going to claim Rinaldi promised her a plum job in the new administration in return for sexual favors."

"Is she credible?"

"Absolutely. She's got video of them doing the deed and also recorded him insisting on her silence and making inappropriate promises. And threats. There's the little question of whether she set him up, but that won't matter. He did what he did, so he's finished."

"And how do you know this?"

"I have good sources in Washington. This isn't rumor or speculation. It's a certainty. Trust me on this."

Michael stood up and began pacing in front of the desk. He scratched the back of his head. "Wow! So you think this will help me because it will turn people away from the Republican ticket? Is that where you're going with this?"

"No."

"Then what?"

"This changes everything, Michael! Connett will be scrambling to find a new running mate. He's already trailing Nelson in the polls, and he's about to take a big hit. He needs to name a new running mate that can bring him votes. That person could be you."

"Me? Why would I do that? I've worked so hard to build support and develop a strong campaign organization. That was all based on me running for president."

"This is better, Michael. You've run a great campaign. You've generated higher poll numbers than any third-party candidate in history. But it's not enough. The likelihood of you closing the gap and overtaking the frontrunners by November is low. It's just not going to happen. This is a sure ticket to the White House! Combining forces with Connett will guarantee a Republican victory in November. It won't even be close."

"But I've always been aligned with the Democrats. My supporters have too."

"Your supporters are Republicans at heart—they just don't know it yet! Most of the pro-immigration supporters only vote Democratic because they've been brainwashed by the media and the Democrats into believing that Republicans are anti-immigration. The Republicans are too disorganized and inept to change that perception. But look at the profile of this voting group—they're religious; the majority are anti-abortion; they mostly come from traditional nuclear families and support traditional family values; they're hard-working and just want an opportunity to find decent work; they don't sympathize with those who want a free ride on the welfare state; their biggest issue is jobs, so the whole notion of stimulating the economy through lower taxes and less regulation is right up their alley. They're often fearful and resentful of government based on experiences in their home country so they should be in favor of a smaller federal government here. They *should* be Republicans and you're the one who can open their eyes to that."

"So I should be content with being a figurehead rather than a real leader?"

"Not at all. Think about it. First, Connett will see what you bring to the table—an energized and passionate base of support and certain victory if you combine forces. So you're in the driver's seat and you can condition your acceptance of the VP nomination on his commitment to give you real responsibilities. And he'd be crazy not to use you in that way, given the passion your followers have for you. Second, if you ride out Connett's term with him, you'd be the most logical candidate to succeed him down the road. And third, and most importantly, you'll be just one heartbeat from the presidency starting seven months from now. It's entirely possible that something could happen to Connett while he's in office and then you're in."

"But playing second fiddle? I'm struggling to get my head around that."

"Well, you'll need to act fast. Connett will be scrambling to fill that slot to stabilize his campaign quickly. You'll need to cut a deal before he publicly commits to someone else. And there's one other thing to consider."

"What's that?"

"We've both been concerned about the possibility of your early years coming under intense scrutiny, and for good reason. Under this scenario, that becomes less of a concern. The digging into ancient history will focus much more on Connett. That said, if it starts looking like you're going to be part of the winning ticket, your family will be under a brighter spotlight, so we need to be sure they're on board and under control."

"I'm managing that. It won't be a problem."

"By the way, you should know that our mutual friend is onboard with this approach. In fact, he's the one that asked me to recommend this to you."

"Recommend or insist?"

"Is there a difference?"

"I suppose not." Michael rubbed his chin and stared out the window. The room was utterly silent but for the ticking of the old wall clock as the candidate pondered his choices. "OK," he said at last. "You can tell him I'm all in. I'll visit with Russ Miller about how to approach Connett. Russ will be really pissed."

"And your family? Our friend is quite concerned on that front."

"You can tell him that I'm on it and he's got nothing to worry about."

"Sometimes being worried is a healthy thing, Michael. It keeps your guard up and protects against complacency. Remember that."

***

Two days later, Russ Miller burst into the campaign office, waiving the morning edition of *The New York Times*. "Check this out, Mike!"

Michael could read the headline from across the room: *Sexual Harassment Allegations Filed Against VP Hopeful.*

Chapter 37

BOBBY AND TERESA sat on the sofa watching the evening news on television. Congresswoman Maria Pena was on a roll, playing to the cameras. She denounced the unlawful and insensitive actions of everyone involved in the handling of the unidentified human remains that found their way to Carroll County Cemetery. She demanded accountability. She called the Sheriff's Office and County Coroner corrupt and the funeral profession careless and unregulated. She promised to reform that renegade profession and bring it under control through legislative hearings and a thorough overhaul of the existing regulatory framework. She begged for compassion for the immigrants, both those who had perished on their journey to America and those who had made it but were forced to live in the shadows. She vowed her support for comprehensive immigration reform. But mostly she wanted scalps.

It had been four weeks since the story broke. Bobby had devoted himself to correcting the misperceptions about the story and educating anyone who would listen about what really happened. In addition to multiple meetings with the Texas Rangers' investigators, he had spoken with the Texas Funeral Service Commission's investigators and had met with his local state senator and representative and a handful of other politicians who had taken an interest in the matter. For the most part, they seemed receptive to what he had to say and were quick to acknowledge that the press often got things wrong or were motivated by their own agenda. Congresswoman Pena had eagerly accepted his invitation to meet, but quickly became hostile when she realized that her narrative was entirely inconsistent with the facts as Bobby described them. He also met with the reporter who first broke the story in an attempt to correct some obvious misunderstandings.

"How did your meeting with the reporter go?" Teresa asked.

"Badly," Bobby responded. "She was just looking for confirmation of what she already wrote or something scandalous that would give her story new life. She was more interested in lecturing me and making accusations than actually listening. Seemed like an angry and frustrated person. I got the impression that she's been writing stories about the immigration situation in South Texas for years and couldn't get any of the major newspapers interested in her stories. Looks like she finally found an angle that worked."

"I don't know why you're wasting your time on this, Bobby. You're out of it now. They're focused on the M.E. and Zamora—serves him right after he threw you under the bus like that. You've done what you could, now you should just move on. You've got a new job here in San Antonio and you can put that Carroll County mess behind you."

It's just not right. The story they're telling just isn't true—not even close. That's causing real problems for people who are good friends of mine—Manny the M.E., Sheriff Reid, and even Mr. Zamora. I was upset when he fired me but I understand why he did it. Besides all that, it's created anger and angst that's completely unwarranted—among the immigrants' rights crowd and among families whose loved ones may be missing."

"Have you talked to that anthropology professor who started all this? Getting him on your side could really help."

"Professor Chamberlain? I called him but he never called me back. I haven't made it a high priority because he's probably another zealot who can't be reasoned with, but I'll try again."

"I met someone who might be able to help you with that," said Teresa. "She's a professor at the university. Her mother checked into our hospice a few days ago. Maybe she knows Chamberlain and could arrange a meeting. Would you like me to feel that out?"

"Sure. Couldn't hurt."

Two days later, Bobby pulled into the parking lot of Stoney Creek
Hospice Care late in the afternoon. Teresa had told him that her new
professor friend had agreed to meet him, and actually seemed excited
about it. Teresa met Bobby at the door and guided him into the patient's
room. An elderly woman was sleeping in an upright position. Aside from
the hospital bed and the IV bag with its tubes leading into the patient's
arm, the room looked more like someone's bedroom than a hospital. A
table lamp near the bed and an upright lamp in the corner of the room
provided a soft glow. A dresser, a small love seat and several upholstered
chairs filled the room tastefully without overcrowding it.

A younger woman was sitting in a chair next to the bed, talking on
her cell phone in hushed tones, her back to Bobby and Teresa as they
appeared in the doorway. Teresa knocked softly. The woman glanced
over her shoulder, gave them a welcoming smile and beckoned them
to come in. They silently made their way across the room to the love
seat. The woman concluded her call, then turned around and stood to
greet her guests. She was tall and slender, with shoulder-length dark hair
and glasses that gave her a stylish yet professorial look. She was casually
dressed in jeans and a white blouse, but had an air of elegance about her.

Teresa sprang up, looking from one to the other. "Bobby, I'd like you
to meet Professor Sanchez. She teaches History at the University—"

"Bobby? I thought it must be you!" the professor gushed. "I've been
following the news about Carroll County and saw your picture. I recognized you right away. It's great to see you!"

Bobby froze, staring at the striking face and the turquoise-green eyes
behind the glasses. "Jenny?"

She nodded excitedly, then rushed around the bed and wrapped him
in a long hug. His shock turned into elation, as she took his hands and
stepped back to look at him. He stared back, smiling like a child who had
just unwrapped a spectacular Christmas present.

Teresa stared from one to the other. "You know each other?" she asked.

"Bobby was my first boyfriend," Jenny said, her eyes sparkling. "Back in San Mateo when I was 13. I just adored you!" she said, not taking her eyes off him.

"Wow! I can't believe this!" Bobby replied, still gripping her hands. He shifted his gaze to the bed. "And that's your mother?"

Jenny nodded. "We brought her in last week. Lung cancer. She hasn't got much time left, I'm afraid. She's mostly conscious and lucid still but sometimes the pain is bad enough that they give her morphine. That really knocks her out, but then she can rest comfortably. They just gave her a dose about an hour ago so she'll be out for quite a while, but I know she'd be thrilled to see you. Can you come back for a visit sometime?"

"Absolutely. I'm so sorry about her condition, but I would love to drop by for a visit."

Teresa looked at her cell phone, which was vibrating. "I've gotta run. I'll leave you two to catch up." She scurried out of the room.

"Why don't we make our way to the lounge area? It's a little roomier and we can let Mom rest quietly. They've got plenty of snacks lying around in case you're hungry."

Bobby looked at his watch. "I've got a better idea. How about if we take a little drive and grab some dinner?"

They found a Mexican restaurant nearby and continued getting reacquainted over fajitas and beer. Time flew by. Just like twenty years before, Bobby found himself entranced by the pretty face and the fetching smile, but mostly by those stunning eyes. It was as if they had picked up exactly where they had left off. Talking to Jenny was like talking to no one else, except maybe Teresa. It was easy and natural. It was fun and enjoyable. She made him feel like there was nowhere else he'd rather be and nothing else he'd rather be doing.

He learned that she had moved to San Antonio after leaving San Mateo and wound up going to Stanford, where she received both an undergraduate degree and a Ph.D. She taught at UCLA for several years but told him that California had never quite felt like home, and she felt the need to be near her ailing mother, so she had made her way back to Texas three years ago, taking a teaching position at the University of Texas at San Antonio.

They lingered over coffee and dessert and lost all track of time until they noticed that the dinner crowd was mostly gone and the busboys were noisily clearing the tables around them. Bobby drove Jenny back to the hospice so that she could look in on her mother again before heading home. Twenty minutes later he entered his apartment, singing softly to himself.

"Hi Bobby," Teresa called out brightly. "How did it go with Jenny? I can't believe you know each other. Small world!"

"It went great!" Bobby gushed. "It's really strange to run into your old girlfriend after 20 years. Never thought I'd see her again."

"Was it awkward?" Teresa asked as they simultaneously pulled up chairs and sat down at the kitchen table.

"Not at all. It was like picking up right where we left off."

"Sometimes it's like that with old friends," said Teresa. "Is she going to introduce you to the anthropology professor?"

"Gosh, we barely talked about that. I asked her early on in our conversation and she said she would, but we never got around to when or where. We just sort of mentioned it in passing, then we both forgot about it, because we were so caught up with other things."

"But wasn't that the whole point of meeting with Professor Sanchez?"

"Yeah, I guess it was—until I realized that the professor was Jenny. We had such a great evening! I was absolutely smitten with her when we were teenagers and then she just vanished and I thought I'd never see her again. Now she's suddenly back in my life. It's so cool!"

Teresa abruptly rose from the table and began emptying the dishwasher. "You just met for the first time in 20 years and spent a few hours with her," she said. "Does that qualify as having her back in your life?"

"I sure hope so. I don't see why not. She lives right here in San Antonio."

Teresa moved briskly around the kitchen, opening and closing cabinet drawers loudly as she put away silverware and dishes, pots and pans clanging as she tossed them into the drawer under the stove. "Is she married?" she asked.

"She's been married twice but got divorced both times," Bobby replied, his voice slightly less chipper. "But she's single now," he said, his face brightening again.

"Sounds like she's got some issues—probably not very stable. I'd be careful there, Bobby." She slammed the dishwasher door, walked into her room without looking at him and pulled the door shut.

Bobby wandered into the living room, turned off the lights and put on his headphones. He found the music he was looking for—a compilation of love songs sung by John Denver and Placido Domingo. He had listened to that that music endlessly as a teenager after Jenny had disappeared. He had no desire to sleep. He stayed up long into the night, listening to that music as he contemplated a life that once again included Jenny Sanchez.

Chapter 38

"I NEED YOUR help, Francisco."

Vargas looked at the distinguished looking gentleman sitting in the driver's seat. They were in a dark parking lot adjacent to a forest preserve on the outskirts of the city. "That's what I'm here for. Just tell me what you need."

"There's about to be a major shake-up in the presidential race. I'm sure you've seen the papers—our little girl came through. Rinaldi's dropped out. Our boy will be approaching Connett and is almost certainly going to join his ticket as the VP nominee."

"So what's the problem?"

Professor Juan Carlos Vega kept both hands on the steering wheel and stared straight ahead. "The scrutiny on Michael's family is going to get a lot more intense. Michael assures me that he is dealing with them and that we have nothing to worry about, but I'm afraid that he might be overly optimistic, or naïve."

"So you want me to make sure that his family members keep our little secret?"

"Exactly! There's way too much at stake here to be taking unnecessary chances. This whole situation with Michael has played out better than any of us ever could have imagined. I always envisioned developing major influence in Washington, but never dreamed it would happen this soon and at this level. This is the opportunity of a lifetime. We can't leave anything to chance. We need to manage this risk and eliminate any uncertainty. Am I making myself clear?"

"Crystal."

"But we've got to proceed with the utmost care. If tragic accidents should befall his family members one after another, it could arouse suspicions. It's far better if the family sees fit to cooperate, so let's see what Michael is able to do on that front. But—we can't make assumptions and we can't trust that Michael will be sufficiently forceful. We can't just *hope* they won't divulge things they shouldn't. We must *ensure* that. And we don't have much time. I need you on this immediately. Consider it your highest priority."

Vargas rubbed the stubs of his missing fingers. His eyes gleamed in the dark car. "I understand. The situation will be handled—one way or another."

Chapter 39

"I BROUGHT SOMETHING for you, Mrs. Sanchez," Bobby said as he pulled up a chair next to the emaciated woman in the hospital bed. She was in her mid-fifties, but the cancer had ravaged her body, making her appear twenty years older. When she was sleeping, which was most of the time now, she looked gray and lifeless. During her waking periods, however, she was still mostly lucid and clearly appreciated his visits, so he came as often as he could. He did his best to visit around lunch time, partly because it was easier to get away from his new job then, but also because Jenny was often there at that time.

Jenny had reintroduced Bobby to her mother a week earlier. Mrs. Sanchez remembered him instantly. Jenny had told him that his visits had made her mother more animated than she had been in months. The dullness in her tired eyes had lifted and the dying woman actually engaged in lively conversations, remembering the good times when Bobby had taken Miguel under his wing in San Mateo.

Mrs. Sanchez looked up from the uneaten tray of food in front of her. "Hello, Bobby Rivera." Her smile was weak but her eyes lit up at the sight of her visitor. "Is that the surprise you promised me?" She looked at the package under Bobby's right arm. The giftwrapping looked like the work of a well-meaning but sloppy young child.

"Yes, ma'am. I hope you like it!"

Jenny walked in as her mother was struggling with the giftwrap. She watched silently from the doorway, smiling through misty eyes at the sight of her mother's beaming face. The wrapper came off, revealing a cardboard shoe box. Mrs. Sanchez lifted the box with her frail hands and attempted to shake it. "Hmmm... I wonder what could be in here."

She lifted the lid and pulled out a small stack of letters, held together by a bright green ribbon. "Those are letters I sent after you left San Mateo. Some were to you and some were to Jenny. I sent them to your old house and thought they might be forwarded to you but the Post Office just sent them back. Better late than never, right? There are a few pictures in there, too."

Mrs. Sanchez set the letters aside and pulled a handful of faded photographs from the box. Jenny approached the bed so she could see the pictures. "Here are your reading glasses, Mom," she said, handing her mother the glasses that were resting on the nightstand.

Mrs. Sanchez slowly examined the pictures, one-by-one, Jenny looking over her shoulder. There were two photos of Miguel, Sal and Bobby posing in their football uniforms. In one, they were smiling happily. In the other, they were wearing the most ferocious looks their 15-year-old faces could muster. There was a photograph of the three boys in The Brush, at the top of The Hill. "I remember that one," Jenny said. "I took it, didn't I?" There was a picture of the entire family taken after one of their high school football games—Miguel on one side of his mother with his arm around her shoulder and Jenny and little Enrique on the other side of her. The dates were scrawled on the back of each photograph.

Mrs. Sanchez reached into the box and pulled out two more pictures. They were sketches rather than photographs. The first showed Miguel racing through The Brush with a look of pure exhilaration on his face. At the bottom was a caption reading: *Miguel Sanchez in The Brush.* Underneath the caption were Bobby's signature and the date. The other picture was a recent rendition that Bobby had drawn from an older picture that he kept—the picture of the three boys in their football uniforms that the boys had all signed on the back, signifying their status as blood brothers and friends for life. Mrs. Sanchez studied each drawing carefully and handed them to Jenny, who did the same. "You are so talented, Bobby. You should be making your living as an artist."

Bobby smiled and shrugged modestly. "Thanks," he muttered.

"Read me the letters, dear," Mrs. Sanchez said, handing the stack of letters to her daughter. Jenny flipped through the faded envelopes. Two were addressed to Mrs. Sanchez and three were addressed to her. She opened one of the letters and read it aloud.

> *Dear Jenny,*
>
> *I don't know if you are getting these letters or not. If you are, please write back.*
>
> *I miss you. I think about you all the time, especially on my walks out in The Brush.*
>
> *It's beautiful out there this time of year, but it would be so much better if you were out there with me. I hope you and your mom are doing OK. I pray for you every night and I pray for Miguel.*
>
> *I hope you like your new home, wherever it is. Please write me sometime.*
>
> *I miss you, Jenny.*
>
> *All my love,*
>
> *Bobby*

Bobby looked down as Jenny read the letter. Had he been looking at her, he would have noticed a tear falling onto the old piece of paper.

Jenny looked up at Bobby through watery eyes. She smiled and gave a short, embarrassed laugh. "You were such a sweet guy, Bobby." She sniffled a bit and wiped her eyes and nose with a tissue. "You still are."

"This one is addressed to you, Mom," Jenny said, opening another envelope.

> *Dear Mrs. Sanchez,*
>
> *I hope you are doing well. I'm not sure where you are but I hope this letter finds its way to you. All of us here in San Mateo miss you. And Jenny and Enrique, too. Please tell Jenny hi for me.*
>
> *I wanted to let you know that I am looking after Miguel's grave. I put fresh flowers on it twice a week. I have enclosed a picture so you can see for yourself.*

I pray for Miguel every night. I pray for you too. And your family. I can't imagine how difficult this must be for you. I hope that wherever you are you will be able to find happiness again someday.

If you can, please let me know where you are and if you're doing OK. My parents said to let you know they think of you often and are keeping you and your family in their prayers.

Bobby Rivera.

Jenny peered into the envelope and pulled out a photograph, showing a neatly kept grave with a large bouquet of bright wildflowers at the base of the grave marker, which bore the inscription *Miguel Sanchez*. She handed the picture to her mother who stared at it in silence for several moments. "You were so kind to me after we lost Miguel," Mrs. Sanchez said in a quiet voice that was thick with emotion. "And you were so good to Jenny, too." She paused and took a deep breath, then playfully poked her daughter. "You should have married him, Jenny! What's wrong with you?"

"You're probably right, Mom." Jenny laughed and wiped her eyes again. She proceeded to read the remaining letters, which were similar in content. Bobby listened quietly, embarrassed but enjoying the fact that Mrs. Sanchez seemed genuinely grateful and more animated than he had ever seen her since he began his hospice visits. Jenny glanced at her watch. "Oh gosh, I've got to run!" she said. "I've got class in 30 minutes."

"I better move along, too," said Bobby. "Have a great day, Mrs. Sanchez! I'll stop by again soon."

"Thank you, Bobby. And thank you for this," the old woman said, motioning to the letters and pictures spread out across the bed in front of her. "I can't begin to tell you how much this means to me. You've brought some real joy to me today—something I haven't felt for a long time. I'm so glad we found each other after all these years."

"Me too, Mrs. Sanchez." He gripped her frail hand. "I'll see you soon."

Bobby and Jenny walked to the parking lot together. "I hate to run like this, especially when Mother is in such rare form." She stood outside her car rummaging through her purse trying to locate her car keys. She looked up at Bobby as she found the keys and pressed the automatic door opener. Her eyes were still watery. "You're a special person, Bobby Rivera. I knew that when we were teenagers and it's even more obvious now." She stood up on tip-toes, kissed him tenderly on the cheek, and threw her arms around his neck. "I'll see you soon," she whispered. Then she turned away and climbed into her Audi.

Bobby stood transfixed, giving her an awkward wave as she started the ignition and gripped the steering wheel. Her window glided down noiselessly and she looked up at him. "I can't begin to repay you for being so good to my mother, but can I at least buy you dinner tonight?" she asked.

"I've got to work a visitation at my new funeral home tonight and tomorrow night. How about Wednesday?"

"Perfect. I'll meet you at *Luigi's* at 7:00."

***

Two days later, Bobby looked across the table at the young woman he had wondered about for 20 years. She was even more striking in real life than he had dared to imagine in his fantasies. The setting was exquisite: upscale Italian food, dark wooden furniture covered by white linen table-cloths, bathed in soft candlelight. Jenny raised her wine glass.

"Here's to you, Bobby," she said, her voice warm and sensual and her eyes shining. "I'm so glad to have you back in our lives, and I can't thank you enough for everything you're doing for my mother. There's a sym-metry to all this that feels so right. You were there to comfort us during that awful time after we lost Miguel, and here you are again as Mom is preparing for her final journey. It means the world to me."

"I'm just glad that we've reconnected. These visits with you and your mom do my soul a lot of good, too. I hope it wasn't embarrassing for you to read those letters. It felt a little funny listening to my fifteen-year-old self."

"It wasn't embarrassing at all. It was touching, and beautiful."

Bobby averted his eyes and stared at the flickering candle. "I was really crazy about you back then. I guess that was pretty obvious in those letters."

Jenny laughed. "Maybe Mom was right. My life would have turned out a lot better if I had wound up with you!"

Bobby absently reached for the salt shaker and started moving it in a tight circle in front of him. He looked Jenny in the eyes momentarily and then shifted his gaze back to the candle, "Hey, Jenny... I've been thinking..." he stammered. "I know we were just kids back then when we started dating but I always felt a special connection with you... Do you think there's any chance we could... uh... you know... maybe pick up where we left off... see each other again?" He looked at her tentatively, trying to gauge her reaction.

"What do you mean? We are seeing each other. Do you mean dating?" She looked surprised.

Bobby could feel his heart pounding and sweat forming on his forehead. "Yeah, I guess that's what I mean. I don't want to seem too forward, so just cut me off if you think it's a dumb idea. I just feel like we know each other so well, and we really hit it off when we were together before..."

Jenny reached across the table and put her hand on his. "I'm flattered, Bobby. And I couldn't imagine finding a better person than you—you're kind, compassionate, easy to talk to, and just an all-around great guy. But my life is an absolute mess! I've had two failed marriages, my mother is dying, and my brother is a real problem. This would be a horrible time for anyone to get involved with me."

Bobby continued staring at the flickering candle, moving the salt shaker in widening circles. "It's never too late, Jenny," he said softly. "We all make mistakes and we all have challenges in our lives. Sometimes a fresh start is absolutely the right thing..."

"You're so sweet, Bobby. Under other circumstances... at another time... I could really fall for you. In fact, I did, way back when. Let's just be friends for now. We can still see each other. In fact, I'd be crushed if we didn't. And who knows what might come out of that?"

Bobby snapped out of his trance and sat upright, looking Jenny directly in the eyes, his demeanor returning to his normal positive and upbeat self. "I'm sorry Jenny. I shouldn't have gone there. That was stupid of me. I was completely insensitive to what you're going through right now. Let's enjoy the evening!"

The awkwardness passed quickly, and they spent most of the evening talking about their careers and what they had been doing over the past 20 years. Bobby steered the conversation toward her younger brother. "So, Enrique's having problems? I remember him as such a sweet little guy."

Jenny's shoulders slouched, and she stared down at her hands. "He goes by Ricky now. I'm afraid he's a lot like Miguel. He was a wild teenager, with no father figure around. We had lots of issues with fighting, drinking, and drugs. He seems to have settled down a bit, but he hasn't figured out the whole working thing. His options are limited, since he never even finished high school. He just doesn't seem to be motivated to find work of any kind. He's 23 now, and he's never held a job for more than a few months."

"Maybe I can help. Like I told you, I'm working at Norwood & Gonzalez Funeral Home now. I could probably get Ricky a part-time job. He'd be picking up bodies, driving the hearse or limousine during funerals and helping with the back-room stuff. It doesn't really require any particular skills or experience. Just a good attitude, good people skills and a willingness to work. That's how I got my start in the business."

Jenny's face brightened. "You're like a guardian angel for my entire family, Bobby! I'd be so grateful. Mom would too. I'll talk to Ricky and ask him to give you a call. But I have to warn you, you shouldn't expect too much. I hate to say it since he's my brother, but there's a pretty good chance he would wind up disappointing both of us, so you need to know that going in."

"I understand. You've made full disclosure, and I appreciate that. But I'd like to give him a chance. Maybe I can make a difference."

They lingered over dinner and dessert until closing time, neither one of them in any hurry to bring the evening to an end. As they walked slowly to their cars, Bobby did his best to fend off the awkward feelings that had tainted the first part of their dinner.

"Thanks for a wonderful evening, Bobby. I'll be in touch after I speak with Ricky."

"Sounds good," Bobby replied. He leaned over and gave her a stiff hug. "Goodnight, Jenny. I'll see you soon, probably at the hospice."

She pulled back from his embrace and reached up to kiss him on the cheek just as she had in the hospice parking lot. "Goodnight, Bobby." She turned away and walked a few steps toward her car. Then she abruptly stopped and ran back to him. She threw her arms around his neck and kissed him squarely on the lips. It was soft and sensual. It lasted just an instant, then she ran back to her car, hopped in and drove off, giving the horn a quick toot as she drove away.

Bobby stood motionless, staring after the Audi as it turned out of the parking lot and sped off into the night. His heart raced and his head was spinning. Utter confusion set in, but it wasn't a disturbing sensation, because the confusion was mixed with more powerful emotions—hopefulness, coupled with a strange and wonderful sense of elation.

***

Teresa looked up from her book as the apartment door burst open. Bobby entered, looking jubilant and triumphant, his arms thrust high in the air like a victorious athlete. "Congratulate me! I think I'm in love!" he bellowed.

"Must have been a good evening," Teresa said, remaining cross-legged on the couch and turning her eyes back toward her book.

"Let's take a walk! I'll tell you all about it."

"You go ahead without me. I'm pretty tired. I walked the dog earlier."

"Aw, c'mon, T! I've got to talk to someone or I'm going to burst. CT would love another walk, wouldn't you boy?" Bobby said, turning to the dog's plastic kennel in the kitchen. CT scampered over to him, his tail wagging excitedly.

Teresa closed her book. "Alright, let's keep it short, though. I'm tired and I have to get up early."

They took their usual walk, around Kennedy Park three blocks away. Bobby jabbered happily the entire time, telling Teresa about his youthful romance with Jenny long ago, and how excited he was about the prospect of rekindling that romance. She listened quietly and politely. When they were nearly home, Bobby glanced at his vibrating cell phone. It was a text from Jenny. *Thanks for a wonderful evening, Bobby. Are you free Saturday night?* "Yes!" Bobby cried out exuberantly, throwing his fist up into the air once again. He showed the text to Teresa.

"I've never seen you this animated—about anything," Teresa said, looking at the little dog walking in front of them. She had avoided eye contact throughout their stroll. "I'm happy for you and really hope things work out for the best." She finally looked him in the eyes. "But be careful, Bobby. You might be rushing into this a little too fast. When someone's been divorced twice, that usually means there are some issues there. And let's face it—a lot of time has passed. You're both very different people than you were 20 years ago."

Bobby stopped in his tracks. "I'm sorry, T. I've been rambling on like an idiot. I probably sound ridiculous. Thanks for listening. I'm lucky to have someone like you that I can talk to about anything."

"I feel the same way about you, Bobby. I just don't want to see you get hurt."

Chapter 40

MICHAEL SANCHEZ PICKED up *The Wall Street Journal* from his front doorstep. He pulled back the plastic wrapping and unfolded the paper, his eyes immediately drawn to the headline blaring across the front page:

SANCHEZ JOINS CONNETT TICKET AS VP CANDIDATE

In a shocking move late yesterday afternoon that stunned the political world, independent presidential candidate Miguel Sanchez and Republican presidential candidate Hugh Connett jointly announced that Sanchez was terminating his candidacy and joining forces with Connett as Connett's running mate. Although the move has devastated many of the Sanchez faithful, early reports from pundits describe it as a bold and brilliant strategy. Sanchez trailed Connett and Nelson by a significant margin, and despite an impressive showing for an independent, most experts considered the deficit to be insurmountable. Should his supporters now throw their weight behind Connett, it is likely that the Connett-Sanchez ticket would win by a wide margin in November. If that were to happen, Sanchez would be the youngest vice president ever and a strong bet for the White House down the road.

It had been a difficult week. He had poured his heart and his soul into his campaign and had set his sights on the presidency. Changing that plan did not come easily. His campaign staff and many loyal supporters were devastated and breaking the news to them had made him sick at heart. He felt like he was letting them down.

As he ruminated over the matter, however, he knew that Professor Vega was right. He was not going to win in November. He had known that would be the likely outcome when he entered the race, but he had relished the role of underdog and was energized and inspired by the fight. He was not a quitter and it was not in his nature to surrender. He just had to convince himself that this was really a victory and not a defeat. And it was. He had been playing the long game, knowing that this campaign would make him a national figure and position him well for high office in the future. Maybe even the highest office. The new strategy just made that much more likely. He would be part of a winning team rather than a noble loser. He would become a household name and his face would be in the public eye constantly, in a manner that associated him with the White House. He would be more than a figurehead—he would have real power and influence. Connett had assured him of that. And he was just one heartbeat away from the presidency.

He nodded his head slowly, a satisfied smile crossing his face as he folded up the newspaper and went back inside. It was his time now. The pieces were coming together.

Chapter 41

GLENN FOX OF the Texas Rangers looked at the three somber men sitting across the table from him in the small, sparsely furnished arrangement room at Zamora Family Mortuary in San Mateo. Manny Quintana, the Carroll County Medical Examiner, fidgeted while Alex Zamora poured coffee for the four of them. Sheriff Ray Reid noticed Zamora's trembling hand as he watched the old funeral director pour the steaming beverage into his cup.

Fox cleared his throat. "Gentlemen, we've finished our investigation. I wanted the three of you to hear this before we announce it to the press." A smile crossed the face of the normally stern investigator. "Relax, fellas—it's good news!"

Manny Quintana closed his eyes and clenched his fists. "Thank God!" he said. Sheriff Reid and Alex Zamora both sighed in relief.

"As you know, the Texas Rangers have been thoroughly investigating this matter for over a month now," Fox continued. "We have found no legal violations so we'll be closing the case."

"Thank you so much, Mr. Fox," Zamora said. "We've said all along that the way the media was portraying this just wasn't right. I'm really glad you were able to see through all that noise and not give in to the pressure and the politics."

"Ironically, we concluded that the only laws that were broken were broken by the people from the university who dug up these graves. They were oblivious to the legalities around burials and exhuming human remains. Well intentioned I suppose, but misguided. Not sure I can say the same thing about the media's motives. Another shoot-first-and-ask-questions-later story. Lots of inaccurate and irresponsible reporting in their efforts to sensationalize this."

Fox looked from one to the other, his face serious again. "I will say this: You all should be thanking your lucky stars for Bobby Rivera. His meticulous records and pictures really helped us understand how carefully these cases were handled. His sincerity and good intentions were obvious. He was convincing when he was interviewed by our investigators, and he also took the initiative to speak with some of the politicians and regulators. They all got the same impression. He saved your ass."

***

Bobby glanced at his cell phone as he climbed into his car following the Rotary Club breakfast. He recognized the number. "Hi Sheriff! What's up?"

"It's over, Bobby—the investigation. The Texas Rangers found no legal violations. They're holding a press conference in about an hour. We're in the clear."

"That's awesome! Fantastic! Too bad we can't make the press pay for making us all look like a bunch of scoundrels, but I'm sure glad it's over."

"I owe you, Bobby. Big time. We all do. I'm sure Manny and Zamora will be calling shortly."

"No one owes me anything, Sheriff. We all did the right thing in the first place. That's all there is to it."

"You're being too modest. We all know you went the extra mile to educate these people who wanted our scalps. It's because of you that they were able to see through all the hype. So thanks again. By the way, I think Zamora's going to offer you your old job back. Sure hope you'll take it."

"That's nice to hear, but I've got a new job here in San Antonio and it really suits me. It's with a big corporation that owns funeral homes and cemeteries all across the country, including the one right down the street from Zamora's place in San Antonio. They're really focused on ethics and compliance, so that's right up my alley. Also, I may have the opportunity to go work in other parts of the country and maybe move into management. It's a good career move for me."

"Sounds like a great opportunity, Bobby. We'll sure miss you down here, though. Zamora will be crushed, but it serves him right for treating you the way he did."

"I'm not going to hold grudges, Ray. Mr. Zamora was in a tight spot. I get it. I feel a little bad already because now we're competitors and I'll be taking a lot of business away from him here in San Antonio."

"I wouldn't feel bad about it. Anyway, the Texas Ranger guy just left and I wanted you to be the first to know. Call me next time you're in town. I'll buy you lunch."

"I'm heading down Sunday to clear out my place. Maybe I'll see you then. Thanks for the call."

Bobby pressed the end-call button and stared at his cell phone. He had to share the good news. He hit his speed dial and Teresa answered on the first ring. "I'm so happy for you, Bobby!" she said after he told her about his call from Sheriff Reid. "You showed real compassion when you stepped in to help those poor souls who died out in the desert and you showed real courage when you fought this battle to get the truth out and help your friends. I'm proud of you. Let's celebrate sometime soon!"

"Sounds good, T." Bobby replied. "Can't do it tomorrow night because I'm seeing Jenny. Then Sunday I'm driving down to San Mateo for the day to finish clearing out my place. Maybe next week sometime."

Chapter 42

THE DRIVE BETWEEN San Antonio and San Mateo was a straight shot south, through vast ranchlands with sparse vegetation. To most who made the 3-hour drive, it was frightfully boring, but not to Bobby Rivera. To him, this landscape had always held a certain allure, a rugged beauty that was an extension of his home. He was making the trek to clear out his apartment and move the rest of his things to his new place in San Antonio. Since his dismissal from Zamora Family Mortuary, there was no longer any need for him to keep living quarters in San Mateo.

He was in no hurry this Sunday afternoon. He equated drive time with think time, and he had plenty to think about. He had seen Jenny at the hospice Friday afternoon, two days after their dinner at *Luigi's*. As on his previous visits to the hospice, Jenny had seemed genuinely happy to see him. She had thanked him profusely for being so kind and thoughtful to her mother and for getting Ricky a part-time job at the funeral home. Then she delivered the news that she wouldn't be able to keep their date on Saturday evening. She hadn't explained why. "Something came up," was all she had said.

Bobby had returned to the hospice the next day but never made it inside. As he was pulling into the parking lot, he saw Jenny walking to her car, arm-in-arm with a well-dressed middle-aged man. When they reached her car, they kissed—a casual, comfortable kiss on the lips—before they went their separate ways. His stomach had done a somersault at the sight. He parked his car, waited until Jenny pulled away, then drove off, feeling too distracted to visit with Mrs. Sanchez.

He had dumped on Teresa that evening, sharing what little he knew and seeking her help in trying to interpret the recent events involving Jenny. He knew he must have sounded like a confused and heartsick teenager, but Teresa was a good sounding board. He smiled to himself as he thought about Teresa. He could tell her anything. He was grateful to have a person like her in his life, someone who was always kind and generous, as well as supportive and truly interested in his wellbeing. She had listened quietly and patiently. She didn't say much, but what she did say made perfect sense. She had pointed out that Jenny's mother was dying, so he needed to cut her some slack for breaking their date. She had also pointed out that Jenny was an attractive and accomplished young woman who had her own life before Bobby had stumbled into it a few weeks ago. Childhood bonds are strong, but people grow and change. Jenny was a scholar—a Ph.D. from Stanford—what did she and Bobby have in common anyway other than a brief period of shared history?

Bobby realized the truth in what Teresa had said, but he didn't want to accept it. He was good at reading people and he was confident that Jenny had feelings for him. As he drove, he pondered the fact that he had felt acutely alive over the past few weeks. He was naturally upbeat and positive, but this was different. He felt elated, every waking moment. He felt hopeful at the possibility of something wonderful happening in his life, a possibility that hadn't existed before he walked into Stoney Creek Hospice a few weeks back and came face-to-face with Jenny Sanchez. But then an element of pain and doubt had entered the picture when he witnessed her kissing that stranger in the hospice parking lot.

He spent the entire drive sorting through his feelings, trying to interpret Jenny's actions, fantasizing about how good it could be and yet dreading the possibility that things just wouldn't pan out. He tried to formulate a plan. Take the direct approach, Teresa had advised. Put your cards on the table. Tell her how you feel and what you want. That made sense, but it seemed risky. He had done that once and been spurned.

Bobby was jolted out of his ruminations by the harsh ringing of his cell phone. His heart leapt as he recognized the number that flashed up on his caller ID.

"Bobby? It's Jenny." Her voice was shaking. "Where are you? Can you come right away?"

"Jenny, what's wrong?"

"It's Mother. I think it's time. I think she's slipping away." Her voice broke and Bobby could hear her sniffling coming through the receiver.

"I'm so sorry, Jenny. I'm just a few miles outside of San Mateo. I can turn right around if you want me there. Some people think it's bad form for a funeral director to be lingering around before someone passes, but—"

"I don't care about that. Mother's been in and out of consciousness, but she keeps asking for you. No one else, just you. Please, Bobby, can you come right away?"

"Of course I can. I'm turning around right now. I'll get there as fast as I can."

"Thanks, Bobby. Please hurry. She doesn't have much time."

Chapter 43

MICHAEL SET OUT for his campaign office knowing it would be empty because it was Sunday afternoon. By later in the summer, the local campaign office would be buzzing seven days a week, but it was still June, so he still had the luxury of being able to give his staff Sundays off.

The signs in the window had changed. Instead of *Sanchez for President*, they now read *Connett/Sanchez*. Most of the volunteers had remained onboard and were now campaigning for the Republican ticket headed by Hugh Connett, although some had given up the effort, the feelings of betrayal and disappointment having sucked all the enthusiasm out of them.

He saw a lone vehicle in the small parking lot sandwiched between the campaign office and the dry cleaner—a shiny black Cadillac. A feeling of dread mixed with annoyance crept over him as he approached the vehicle. He heard the sound of the automatic locks popping open as he tried to peer through the dark tinted glass. He walked around to the passenger's side and climbed in.

"Just once I'd like to feel that we were meeting because you had good news to share," Michael said, trying hard to force a smile.

"I'd say your life is full of good news—you're rich, you're famous and you're on the road to becoming vice president of the United States. Seems to me that things are really going your way. I'm just here to help—to make sure it stays that way. Isn't that good news?" It was hard to tell whether Vargas was grinning or sneering.

"And why would I need your help?"

"I hope you won't. But I'm here in case you do."

"And I suppose you're going to tell me what I might need your help with?"

"I think you know, but let me spell it out for you," said Vargas. "This campaign is playing out very nicely. You and Connett are virtually certain to win in November. It's shaping up to be a landslide. Right now, there's almost nothing that can stand in your way. Except for one thing—your family. Outside of our own tight little circle, they are the only ones in the know. So that makes them a ticking time bomb that needs to be defused."

"I'm handling that," Michael said through clenched teeth.

Vargas pushed in the lighter, waited a few seconds and lit up a cigarette. "Our leader has great confidence in you, but we can't just hope for the best. We can't act on blind faith. We need certainty. So tell me— exactly how do you intend to handle it?" Vargas's stare became hard and his voice had an ominous edge to it.

Michael had been leaning against the door, as far away from Vargas as it was possible to get in the front seat of the Cadillac, avoiding Vargas's stare and looking out the window as they spoke. He shifted in his seat, deliberately turning to face Vargas. He leaned in and scowled. "This is my family we're talking about, Vargas. I know them better than anyone. I will speak to them. I will insist on their continued cooperation and I will use whatever persuasive tools I need to use to satisfy myself that they pose no threat."

Vargas returned the harsh glare, then responded coolly. "You do that. Then you report back. But you should know that I will be monitoring this situation myself—very closely. If I'm not convinced that the threat has been effectively neutralized, I will handle it myself."

"I'm telling you, Vargas, I've got this," Michael growled, raising his voice. "You can tell our friend that I expect some latitude and I expect some trust. I'm not a kid anymore. I don't need you or him or anyone else hovering over me. I'm about to become vice president of the United States, and I don't intend to stop there. So back off! You got that? Am I making myself clear?"

Vargas narrowed his eyes. "Yes, you are. Just let me be clear as well. You *are* trusted. That's precisely why it's being left up to you to control the situation, using whatever methods you think will be effective. Just make sure they are effective, because if you don't adequately control the risk, I will intervene. And I will do what I must."

Chapter 44

BOBBY WAS NOT accustomed to speeding but he knew time was short. He also knew that most of Highway 281 between San Mateo and San Antonio was lightly traveled and the likelihood of getting stopped by the police was low. Even if he were stopped, he had a good explanation, so he pushed his pick-up as fast as it would go without straining its capabilities. He could not afford to have the old Ford die on him now.

He gripped the steering wheel tightly with both hands, leaning forward and focusing on the road ahead, while constantly checking both the clock on his dashboard and his gas gauge. He made the trip in record time, careening into the hospice parking lot, leaping out of the truck and jogging up the walkway and through the front doors. "Am I too late?" he asked Janice, the receptionist, as he strode past.

"Her children are in there with her, Bobby. They're waiting for you," said Janice.

Jenny and Ricky peered out the door of their mother's room, the urgent sound of Bobby's footsteps alerting them to his arrival. They stepped out into the hall looking red-eyed and subdued. "Thanks for getting here so fast, Bobby," Jenny said. "It's been touch and go all afternoon. I thought we'd lost her a couple of times but she's still with us."

"She's been asking for you all day," Ricky added. "Hasn't taken her pain meds because she's trying to stay awake."

Jenny grabbed Bobby's hand. "Come on, I'll take you in there."

She leaned over and stroked her mother's hair as she leaned close to her ear. "Mom? Can you hear me? Bobby's here. He drove all the way from San Mateo to see you. Mom?"

The eyelids fluttered and slowly opened. Her emaciated body ravaged by cancer, Mrs. Sanchez did not have the strength to sit up in bed or even turn her head, but her eyes came into focus. "Bobby's here? Good. I'm so glad. Give me a few minutes alone with him."

"Sure, Mom," Jenny said. "We'll be right outside if you need us." She and Ricky stepped outside and quietly pulled the door shut behind them.

Bobby stepped to the bedside and grasped the cool, frail hands. The hands clenched, the eyes closed tight, and a grimace came over the face of the dying woman, but it lasted only a few seconds. She took a couple of deep breaths as if bracing herself for an effort that would require great strength. Then she opened her eyes. They were red and tired, but came into clear focus as she looked at him. "I'm so glad you made it here, Bobby. I know I don't have much time left." Her voice was barely above a whisper, but it was steady and clear. She appeared completely in control of her mind and her tongue.

"I'm glad I could be here," Bobby said warmly, caressing her hands.

"I've forced myself to hang on because there's something I need to tell you. It's about Miguel."

"I know losing him must have been the most difficult part of your life, Mrs. Sanchez, but you'll be with him again soon."

The old woman grimaced and shook her head. "Listen to me, Bobby. I'll be leaving this world soon, and I'll be leaving my children behind. I want them to be safe!" She closed her eyes as her body was racked by a short but violent coughing fit. "Miguel is evil. I hate to say that but it's true. Don't let him harm my children! You're his friend. He might listen to you."

Bobby cocked his head. "I'm not tracking, Mrs. Sanchez. Miguel's not evil. He was a bit wild, but so were lots of other boys that age. He was my friend and your son, and he's passed on. He's not here to hurt Jenny or Ricky."

"I'm not talking about my son, I'm talking about Miguel! He's not my son! I tried to be a good mother to him, but he never wanted anything to do with me. I made poor decisions as a mother—I put my kids at risk and subjected my family to bad influences. I can't do anything about that now, but I want my children to be safe and free from those bad influences. Miguel's dangerous, Bobby. I need you to know that. I'm afraid for my children. If anything bad happens to them, Miguel's behind it, you can be sure of that!" She winced again, closing her eyes and squirming in her bed. "The pain is so bad, Bobby. I've been fighting it off as long as I could so I could talk to you, but I need my medicine now. But please keep an eye on my children. You are such a wonderful man and I'm so glad you're back in our lives. Please stay close to Jenny and Ricky... please, Bobby... watch out for them... please."

She closed her eyes and continued squirming, her face contorting in pain. Bobby leaned over and whispered in her ear. "Good-bye, Mrs. Sanchez. I'll be praying for you. And don't worry about Jenny and Ricky. I'll keep an eye on them." She gave his hand a quick, firm squeeze and then released it.

Bobby opened the door and Jenny hurried to her mother's side, confirming that she was still breathing. "She asked for her medicine," Bobby said.

"Poor thing. She should have taken it hours ago but she was fighting to stay alert. She really wanted to see you." Jenny pushed the call button to summon the nurse. "What was it she wanted to talk with you about?"

Bobby hesitated as he stared at his shoes and shook his head sadly. "I'm afraid it was just gibberish. She wasn't coherent. She mentioned Miguel's name a few times but she just wasn't making any sense."

The nurse came and administered morphine through an IV. She proceeded to check Mrs. Sanchez's vital signs. "I think you'd better stay close by," she said looking at Jenny and Ricky. "It won't be long now."

Chapter 45

BOBBY SAT ACROSS the table from Jenny in one of the funeral home's arrangement rooms. Laminated pictures of caskets and flowers were spread out on the table, along with price lists and a catalogue of grave markers. "Here's how this works, Jenny. Under Texas law, any adult child of the deceased has the authority to make funeral arrangements. That means you have the legal right to make those arrangements, but so does your brother Ricky. As long as you and Ricky are on the same page, then we can proceed to finalize the contracts and the arrangements. If Ricky wanted to proceed differently, then he has legal rights, just as you do. So, our funeral home's policy is that we need all family members to consent before proceeding."

Jenny rubbed her temples. "What if the family members don't agree? Does that ever happen?"

"You'd be surprised—it happens a lot. One child may want cremation and another child may want burial. The funeral home often gets stuck in the middle, with one child threatening to sue us if we don't cremate and the other child threatening to sue us if we do. So, we don't take sides. We insist that the family work it out among themselves. If they can't, Texas law provides a process for having the dispute resolved in court." Bobby paused and pushed the catalogues aside. "Why do you ask? Are you and Ricky not on the same page regarding the funeral?"

"No, there's no problem with Ricky. He really doesn't care what we do. That's why he's not even here today. He told me to do whatever I want."

"Then there should be no problem. That is, unless your mother had other children that I don't know about. I guess I've been assuming it's just you and Ricky, but if you have other siblings, or half-siblings or adopted siblings, that would change things. Are there other family members in the picture?"

Jenny was silent for a long moment, staring absently at the laminated pictures of flower arrangements. She nodded her head slowly. "I have an adopted brother," she said in a quiet voice. "He's been estranged from the family for years, but he contacted me last night and told me he wanted to be sure Mother was being cremated. He told me that's what Mother wanted and that she was very clear with him about that. I don't believe that for a second. He hasn't seen or spoken with her in at least ten years, maybe more. She didn't want cremation, Bobby. She wanted to be buried in Sacred Heart Cemetery. She even bought two spaces there so we could move Miguel up here from San Mateo and bury him beside her at some point. So what do we do? I think I just heard you say you can't proceed if there's a family dispute, right?"

"I'm afraid that's right. Have you tried to reason with him? Is there any chance you and he can come to an arrangement that you both can live with?"

"I don't see how. He's adamant about cremation and I'm adamantly against it. I'm afraid this will turn into a big deal if he doesn't get his way."

"Would it help if I spoke with him? I've got a lot of experience with these issues. Sometimes it helps to have an intermediary involved."

"I hate to impose on you, Bobby, but you might be the perfect person to try to work this out. Would you mind?"

"Not at all. Like I said, I do this a lot. You'd be surprised how often someone's death brings out family conflicts. So, is there anything I should know about your brother before I meet him?"

"I'd love to be able to tell you the whole story, but I just can't do that right now. But you'd better brace yourself for this because once you meet him, you'll understand exactly what I'm dealing with."

Bobby smiled reassuringly. "Don't worry, Jenny. I've seen a lot in this business and I've heard that before. I can handle it. Obviously, I can't guarantee that I can bring him around, but maybe I can. Sometimes when you figure out what someone's motivations and concerns are, you can find a resolution. Why don't you get in touch with him and see if he can stop by this afternoon? The sooner we deal with this the better."

***

Bobby was finishing a sandwich at his desk around noon when his phone rang. It was Cheri, the receptionist. "There's someone here to see you, about Mrs. Sanchez's service."

Bobby finished the sandwich in two bites, wiped his mouth and put on his suit jacket. He checked his hair in the mirror and then walked briskly toward the lobby.

He stopped in his tracks when he saw his visitor, sitting forward on a couch in the reception area perusing one of the funeral home's brochures about grief counseling. The visitor looked up and smiled. "Hello, Bobby."

"Rocket! What are you doing here?"

Michael Sanchez smiled as if enjoying an inside joke. "You haven't connected the dots, have you?"

Bobby looked puzzled. "What dots? What are you talking about?"

"I'm your 12:00 appointment. Miguel Sanchez? Adopted son of Anita Sanchez? Brother of Jenny and Ricky? You were expecting me, right?"

Bobby stared with his mouth hanging open. "Well, yes... no... I mean sort of...," he stammered. "Holy Cow! I thought the name was a coincidence when I first heard it, but you didn't say anything about this when we met, so I never gave it another thought. Wow! Well, come on in. Let's go back to the arrangement room where we'll have some privacy."

They sat in the same room where Bobby and Jenny had met earlier that morning. Cheri brought in a tray of soda and snacks. Michael looked around the room at the casket segments and urns mounted on the walls and nodded approvingly. "Like I said last time we met, this really suits you, Seventy-Seven. You're perfect for this kind of work. You've changed shops though, haven't you?"

"Yep. I was with Mr. Zamora's business for over fifteen years and came here just a few months ago. But back to you—my head is spinning! I can't wait to hear the story. But first, I'd like to pass along my condolences. I'm really sorry for your loss, Sal. I'm glad I reconnected with Mrs. Sanchez and got to spend some time with her near the end."

"Thanks, Bobby. She was quite a woman. Taking me in like she did after I lost my dad and then treating me like one of her own—that takes a special person."

"Yes it does. So tell me how it happened. You all disappeared around the same time, but I never thought there was a connection. Frankly, I thought Mrs. Sanchez didn't care much for you—I seem to recall that you and Miguel got into plenty of trouble together and she was always trying to get Miguel to steer clear of you—no offense."

"None taken. You're exactly right, which makes it even more remarkable that she took me in. I guess she thought she could help a newly orphaned, trouble-prone kid and maybe fill part of the hole in her own life caused by Miguel's passing. So she adopted me and decided to cut all ties with San Mateo—too many tragedies and painful memories. She thought it was best to make a fresh start, so we pulled up stakes and moved here."

"I'm surprised Jenny never mentioned this. I've been seeing a lot of her lately."

Michael grinned. "Still have a crush on her, Bobby? I wouldn't blame you. She's grown into quite an impressive young lady. And she's hot, too! Anyway, I'm sure Jenny kept quiet about this because of me and this whole politics thing. We're all still trying to figure it out. My advisors are suggesting I keep my brief time in San Mateo a secret—because of what happened with my dad and the whole Miguel tragedy. It would be a huge distraction and the opposition would somehow try to use it to embarrass me. If it were just me, I'd say bring it on, but I don't want to put my family through that."

Bobby nodded. "I understand. At least I think I do. So, speaking of Jenny, we need to take care of a little business. She tells me that she wants to have her mother buried and that you would prefer cremation. Is that correct?"

Michael relaxed in his chair and rested his folded hands in his lap. "I'm really not sure what I want. I don't have any personal objections to burial, but it seems to me that when someone dies, their wishes should be respected. And Mom told me more than once that she wanted to be cremated. I'm not entirely sure I like the idea of cremation, personally. How does a family really know that the ashes they are getting are those of their loved one and not some stranger?"

"That's a fair question. We call them cremated remains because they're not really ashes—they're bone fragments—but in any event, you're right. They all look alike. So it's incumbent on the funeral home to have very detailed identification and chain-of-custody procedures so that it knows with one hundred percent certainty who's who. I can walk you through our procedures if you like."

"What about DNA? Can you identify cremated remains through DNA if there's any question?"

"I'm afraid not. DNA is completely destroyed by the cremation process, so the ID and chain-of-custody processes are critical. One little paperwork mistake, and the wrong person could be cremated or the wrong cremated remains could be given to a family."

A loud knock interrupted them and the door flung open. "I heard you were here!" said Ricky Sanchez staring at Michael, his face beaming. "You probably don't even recognize me, it's been so long. I'm your brother Ricky! I work here now. Bobby got me the job."

Michael jumped up and gave Ricky a warm embrace. "Hey there, little brother! It's been way too long. We have some catching up to do!"

"This is so cool, Mike! Running for vice president! I can't believe it! That means you'll probably be president someday!"

"Thanks, pal. I can't believe it either! Hey, why don't you join us for a few minutes? We're discussing Mom's funeral and I'd like to get your thoughts. It seems that Jenny and I have a little disagreement over what Mom would have wanted. I'd like to know where you stand."

"Hell, Mike, I don't really care. The way I look at it, she's dead. That body in the back room isn't really her. She's gone. If it were up to me, I wouldn't even have a funeral. I'd just have her cremated and then scatter the ashes somewhere."

"But you don't feel strongly about it, is that correct?" Bobby asked. "Jenny was heading down the path toward burial and she told me you were OK with that."

"Yeah, that's what I told her. Like I said, it doesn't make much difference to me." Ricky turned and looked at Michael. "What do you want, Mike? I'm flexible. Hell, if the next vice president of our country tells me he'd prefer cremation, I'm going to salute and say 'yes, sir!'"

"Thanks, Rick. I really appreciate that," said Michael. "I'm just trying to do what's right. I want to be sensitive to Jenny's wishes but I know what Mom told me, and I feel compelled to honor her wishes, so I'm torn." He looked at Bobby. "I know you're doing your job and trying to broker a settlement here, Bobby. I appreciate that, too." He looked at his watch. "I've got to run to a meeting now and I don't want to rush into a decision. I'd really like to think about it a little more and then check back later today, if that's OK."

"I understand," Bobby said. "I'll let Jenny know we've spoken and that we'll be talking again later in the day."

***

Jenny walked back into the funeral home at 2:00. Bobby pulled Ricky away from his work in the back room to join them. After describing his shock at learning the identity of her adopted brother, Bobby explained to Jenny that Michael had agreed to give the matter further thought but that he still seemed inclined to push for cremation because that was what Mrs. Sanchez had wanted.

Jenny apologized for being secretive about her adopted brother, mumbling something about it not being her secret to tell. Then her face contorted with rage. "How would he know what she wanted?" Jenny demanded, her voice raised and tears of frustration welling up in her eyes. "He hasn't been around in years! We barely saw him after he went off to college. He was never really part of our family! Does he really have the ability to step in here now—after being separated from the family for years—and take control like this?"

"Like I said earlier, if he's now your adopted brother, then he does have a say in this, and we can't proceed over his objections."

Jenny abruptly got up, walked to the door, opened it and peered both ways down the hallway. She shut the door and leaned back against it. Her eyes blazed. "That's just it. He's *not* our brother! He was *never* adopted. Ricky doesn't remember because he was only two years old, but Mother didn't have much choice in the matter. You remember the name *El Cazador*? We used to talk about him when we were kids like he was some kind of scary monster lurking in the shadows. Well, he's not just a phantom. He is very real. He sent this spooky-looking guy with two fingers missing to ask Mother to take custody of Sal—let's call him by his real name! He paid her handsomely so that she would never have to work again. He paid for Sal's schooling, and mine too, for that matter. It was a deal with the devil but Mother had no choice. I was listening from the next room when this creep told her that El Cazador would see to it that Ricky and I would end up just like Miguel if she didn't cooperate or if we ever told anyone. So we never even told Ricky. Every so often, this thug would show up to remind us of our bargain and make sure we were upholding our end. Mother was never the same—she's been an emotional wreck ever since."

Jenny looked at her younger brother. His eyes were wide and his mouth agape. "I'm sorry you had to find out this way, Ricky, but it's time you know—especially with what's going on now with the election. Michael is *not* our brother. He's not even a citizen! Can you imagine what would happen if the rest of the world found that out?"

Ricky blinked hard several times. "Holy shit! I can't believe this! Are you sure about all this?"

"Of course I'm sure. I've lived with it my entire life!" She turned to Bobby. "So where does that leave us—with the funeral arrangements, I mean."

Bobby looked as shocked as Ricky. He cleared his throat and looked from one to the other. "If he was never formally adopted, then he has no standing to be involved in the arrangements. But based on what you just told us, there are some significant ramifications to all this. You need to think carefully about whether you want to play that card and force him to back down."

"He definitely was never adopted," Jenny insisted. "That would have been inconsistent with their plan of just having him assume Miguel's identity. In any case, I don't want my mother's funeral to become a circus.

And Ricky, you need to understand that what I just shared cannot leave this room—under any circumstances! There are some dangerous people involved in all this, so don't breathe a word of this to anyone!"

"I won't, don't worry." Ricky said. "Not sure anyone would believe me anyway. I'm not even sure I believe it!"

"What should I do, Bobby?" Jenny asked, sounding meek and helpless.

Bobby leaned back in his chair, folded his hands and brought them to his lips. He gazed down at the table for a long moment. "Here's an idea," he said. "Since Sal is the one pushing the adoption angle, I can tell him that it's standard operating procedure for the funeral home to obtain copies of the adoption paperwork for confirmation purposes. If no such paperwork exists, then he'll know that he's not in any position to force this issue and perhaps that will get him to rethink his position. He has more at stake than you do when it comes to avoiding a circus here."

***

Just before 4:00, Michael's car pulled into the funeral home parking lot, one secret service car just ahead of his and one trailing behind. Ricky was standing outside the building's side entrance, smoking a cigarette and waiting. "Hey, Mike! Over here!" He waved and beckoned.

"Hey, little brother!" the candidate called out, casually walking in Ricky's direction. "What's up?"

"Can you spare a few minutes for a private chat?" Ricky asked, eyeing the Secret Service agents nervously.

"You bet. Anything for my favorite brother."

Ricky led the way as they walked around to the open garage on the back side of the building. On the right side of the garage were two rows of funeral cars—a limousine and a hearse in each row, parked nose-in. On the left was a wide passageway leading to the entryway to the back room of the funeral home, which was the site of the embalming and preparation room as well as the funeral home's refrigeration unit. The garage was obscured from prying eyes by a large wooden fence separating the funeral home property from the residences behind it. Ricky and Michael stepped inside the garage as the Secret Service agents remained outside, taking up positions on either side of the garage, but out of earshot.

Ricky lit another cigarette. His eyes darted from one agent to the other. "So Mike, first, I wanted to tell you how proud I am of everything you've accomplished. It's just amazing, man! I feel honored to be your brother." He took a drag off the cigarette and let out a long stream of smoke out of the side of his mouth, away from Michael. "Second, it's really great to see you again. And I hope—now that we've reconnected—that we can be part of each other's lives. I know you're a busy guy, but hey—we're family."

"I'd like that, too, Rick. I know I'll be busy, but I definitely want to stay connected. You can count on that."

"So, what I was hoping was that we could help each other out. You're doing something important and I'd love to be part of it. Maybe there's some job on the campaign I could handle for you. And once you get elected—and I know you will—then maybe there's some job I could do for you in Washington."

"Hmmm… That's an interesting offer, Rick. I'll give it some thought. What kind of work do you think you're suited for?"

"Shit, just about anything. I've got a steady gig here but working at a funeral home isn't exactly my dream job. And, I'm worth a lot more than they pay me. I think I've got talents that ought to be put to better use. I'm good with people, Mike. I've got real leadership skills. I'd be a good boss. You could put me in charge of something important and I'd do a great job for you. What do you think?"

Mike glanced at his watch. "I appreciate the offer, Rick. I'll give it some thought. Our campaign team is mostly volunteers and all the paid positions are currently filled, but you never know when something could open up. I'll keep it in mind."

Ricky tossed his cigarette to the floor and crushed it with his shoe. "You're not just blowing smoke up my ass, are you, Mike? I'm serious. I'd like to be part of your team. And I'd like to get away from this shithole." He nodded in the direction of the funeral home.

Michael looked at his watch again. "I'm late for my meeting with Bobby. I better run. Like I said, I'll give it some thought."

The candidate moved toward the open garage door when Ricky put a hand on his shoulder, stopping him. "You'd really be helping me out, Mike. And—it would be in your best interest, too." The ingratiating smile on Ricky's face had vanished, replaced by a malevolent glare.

Michael stared at the hand on his shoulder and his dark eyes shot an unspoken command that caused the hand to be pulled back. "Exactly what do you mean by that?" he demanded.

"Just what I said. Brothers should take care of each other, right? Unless of course you're not my brother." Ricky paused and let the words linger. "Then I wouldn't expect you to do anything for me and you shouldn't expect me to do anything for you."

Michael took a step closer and squared up to his full height, which was half a head taller than Ricky. He brought his face to within inches of the smaller man. He was about to speak when he glanced at the Secret Service agent out of the corner of his eye. The agent was watching them. He abruptly turned and stormed out of the garage. "Nice seeing you, little brother," he called out over his shoulder as he walked briskly around to the front of the funeral home.

"You look distracted. Is everything OK?" Bobby asked when they were alone again in the arrangement room.

"You were always good at reading me, Bobby," Michael responded. "I guess this is just tearing me up. I feel like I'm in a no-win situation. Either I ignore my mother's wishes or I get my sister upset with me."

Bobby fidgeted, unconsciously picking up a paperclip and silently tapping it on the papers in front of him. "Look, Sal. We used to be best friends. I always shot straight with you and I've got to do that now. So, here's the thing. Jenny just told me that you were never formally adopted—her family took you in and treated you as part of the family, but it was never formalized. If that's true, then I'm afraid you wouldn't have any say in the funeral arrangements. It would be entirely up to Jenny and Ricky."

"Really? That's what she's saying? Come on, she's obviously just out of her mind with grief and saying whatever she thinks she needs to in order to take control here."

"Well, that should be simple enough to sort out. In situations like this, the funeral home's policy is to ask for copies of the adoption documents. If you can just provide me with that paperwork, it'll eliminate any doubt on that issue. Then your right to be involved with the funeral arrangements will be beyond dispute."

Michael leaned forward and slammed his fist on the table. "Goddammit, Bobby! That bitch is trying to take advantage of me. She knows I can't have a long delay and I can't let word get out that there's a family argument over funeral arrangements. The press would go crazy!"

"And you're still adamant about cremation?"

"You're goddamn right I am! And you heard Ricky. He said he'd be OK with it, too. Doesn't she realize that if we wind up in court, the judge will see that's it's two against one and rule against her?"

"But you just said yourself that you don't want a delay or a public spectacle. And it's only two-against-one if you were legally adopted."

"Shit!" The candidate drummed his fingers on the glass covered table and fumed in silence. Bobby let him ruminate. After a long silence, Michael spoke up. "I want to talk to Ricky one more time," he said. "Is he still here?"

"I think he's in the back room. I'll go get him."

A few minutes later, Bobby led Ricky back into the arrangement room. "Sounds like our sister's got you by the balls," Ricky said with a smirk.

Michael shot him an irritated look. "We'll see about that," he grumbled. Then he looked at Bobby. "Give us some privacy, will you?" Bobby excused himself. Michael leaned back in his chair and folded his arms. "So Rick, about that job…"

Fifteen minutes later, Ricky poked his head into Bobby's office. "He's ready for you, boss," he said, looking bright-eyed and chipper.

Bobby returned to the arrangement room, where he found Michael looking out the window, his back to the door. "You can tell Jenny I surrender," he said without turning around. "I feel like I've done what I could to honor my mother's wishes, but I've decided not to fight Jenny about this. Let's just get on with it."

Chapter 46

THE WAKE FOR Anita Sanchez was scheduled for Friday from 3:00 to 9:00, to be followed by the funeral Saturday morning. Guests were invited to arrive at the funeral home at 9:00 Saturday morning to gather for the 10:00 procession to San Fernando Cathedral for the funeral mass. Following the funeral, there would be a procession to Sacred Heart Cemetery for the interment.

Bobby spent all day Wednesday and Thursday in preparation mode. He had nonstop conversations with representatives of the church, the cemetery, and his staff to ensure that everyone knew exactly what was expected of them and that the service went off flawlessly. He impressed upon his staff the need for perfection in every aspect of the service. The eyes of the nation would be on the service and scores of politicians and other dignitaries would be on hand to pay their respects to the vice-presidential nominee. Bobby had multiple conversations with the family members to ensure that all their wishes were clearly communicated and all their concerns addressed. The Secret Service would be there in force as would the private security company Bobby hired for the occasion. Many hours were spent coordinating that aspect of the service. Striking the right balance between having a conspicuous security presence without being intrusive was tricky but Bobby and his staff were committed to getting that—and every other detail of the service—exactly right.

On Friday morning, Bobby was awakened out of a sound sleep at 5:30. It was Javier, one of his prep room employees. The panic in his voice was unmistakable. "Mr. Bobby, you need to get here right away. We've got a problem—a big problem. It's Mrs. Sanchez."

Bobby threw on his sweats and raced to the mortuary. In a trembling voice, Javier began describing every funeral director's worst nightmare—a body had been cremated by mistake. In this instance, it was Anita Sanchez. Javier had arrived at work early to prepare Mrs. Sanchez for the open-casket viewing. That meant doing her hair and makeup, dressing her, placing her in her casket and then moving her into the visitation room. When he opened the refrigeration unit to retrieve her remains, she wasn't there. Her paperwork was there, attached to a white sheet encasing a body, but the body was that of a young Caucasian male by the name of Thomas Meyer. In retracing the chain of events, the only possible explanation was that, sometime after Ricky had brought Mr. Meyer's remains into the funeral home, the paperwork had gotten switched. Mr. Meyer was scheduled to be cremated. The crematory operator must have taken the body with the Meyer paperwork attached out of the cooler and then proceeded with the cremation. The body that was cremated had to have been Mrs. Sanchez, since she was the only other body in the funeral home's custody at that time.

"Who was working last night?" Bobby asked.

"Ricky," Javier replied. "I was scheduled to do the night shift, but Ricky asked to switch. The visitation room set-up had been completed late yesterday, and Ricky said he really wanted to spend some time here with his mother before all the craziness started today. When I got in at 5:00 this morning, I noticed that the cremation case had already been completed. I couldn't believe it! I had shown Ricky how to work the cremation retort and explained our procedures, but I made it perfectly clear that he had to be trained and certified before he could actually perform any cremations. Anyway, all the paperwork indicated that it was Mr. Meyer who had been cremated. The remains were in the urn and all the paperwork checked out indicating that was Mr. Meyer. It wasn't until I brought the other body out of the cooler to dress her for the visitation that I realized there must have been a mix-up."

"Our procedures are supposed to be foolproof! I've heard of cases like this, but in all my years it's never happened on my watch!" Bobby looked and sounded despondent as the gravity of the mistake and the far-reaching ramifications set in. He'd have to tell Jenny immediately, and Michael and Ricky too, but he first wanted to understand exactly what had gone wrong.

"I'm so sorry, Mr. Bobby," said Javier, his voice shaking and tears filling his wide eyes. "I shouldn't have switched shifts with Ricky. I don't know why he would decide to handle a cremation—he must have been in a daze because it's his mother and all. He must have assumed that the paperwork was attached to the right bodies. It probably never occurred to him to unwrap the sheets to make sure. I just don't know how the paperwork could have gotten mixed up in the first place."

Bobby was shaking all over. He couldn't think straight. With trembling hands, he dialed Jenny's number, then Michael's and then Ricky's. All three calls went directly to voicemail. He had to get in front of the family as soon as he possibly could to disclose the unexpected development and to determine how to proceed. An open casket visitation was now impossible and little time was left to formulate a Plan B.

Bobby instructed Javier to keep trying to reach the Sanchez children by phone, while he jumped into his car and set out to go knocking on their doors to deliver the news in person. Jenny answered the door in her bathrobe, obviously just awoken by the pounding on her door. She gasped and covered her mouth in horror as Bobby delivered the news. She looked like she would faint, as Bobby took her by the arm and walked her to the living room sofa.

"I can't believe this! How could this happen?" she stammered when she finally found her voice. She began weeping.

Bobby put an arm around her shoulder. "Jenny, I am so sorry. I'm just beside myself that such a horrible accident could happen. I'm—"

"This wasn't an accident!" she shrieked.

Two hours later, the entire family gathered together in Bobby's office, Jenny and Michael sitting in the two chairs opposite Bobby's desk and Ricky standing with his back against the door. Javier had reached both Michael and Ricky and told them that there had been an urgent development and that they were needed at the funeral home immediately. Bobby had spoken with Ricky privately before the group gathered together, as part of his effort to investigate the cause of this disaster. Ricky's reaction was one of defensiveness more than shock or contrition. He claimed that he was just trying to be helpful so that Javier wouldn't be rushed by the cremation and could focus on getting his mother ready. He insisted that he had followed procedure to the letter, checking the paperwork meticulously before putting the body in the retort. When confronted with the fact that the refrigeration log indicated that no one other than Ricky had accessed the cooler in the past 48 hours, and that he was the one that brought Mr. Meyer into the funeral home yesterday and completed the paperwork, he could offer no explanation for how the paperwork could have gotten switched.

Michael took charge upon hearing the news. After alluding to the significant legal exposure that the funeral home was facing, he said that it was not his desire to go there. He expressed the belief that it would be in no one's interest to make a public spectacle out of this. He stated that they should be thinking about Mrs. Sanchez and preparing to honor her life and that it would be a disservice to her to be diverting attention from that goal. Jenny looked sullenly out the window as Michael spoke. After asking for Bobby's counsel, they decided to proceed with a closed casket at the visitation and at the church. They would place a large portrait of Mrs. Sanchez just to the right of the casket, so that people could see her smiling face and remember her that way. They would keep the mishap to themselves and the outside world would not suspect anything was amiss.

"Since we're all together, I'd like to take this opportunity to discuss something else of great importance to this family," said Michael, looking serious.

"I'll leave if you want," Bobby offered.

"I'd like you to stay, Bobby. What I have to say involves you, too." Michael glanced at each of them. Jenny looked away an instant after their eyes met. "I'd like to ask a favor," Michael began in his most earnest voice. "I know you don't owe me anything, but I hope I can count on you anyway. As you know, I have before me an opportunity that very few people will ever experience. I fully expect to be in the White House as vice president of the United States in just a few months. That's certainly exciting for me but it should be exciting for you, too. In the eyes of the world, we're family. Like it or not, you will be treated very differently as a result—almost like royalty. So will I, but that's not what this is about. What matters is that I will have a big responsibility and a tremendous opportunity to make life better for our people. I am committed to living up to that responsibility. I can make a real difference. But in order to accomplish that, I must have your support. Can I count on that?"

"Hell yes! You can count on me, Mike" said Ricky. "Whatever you need, I'm all in."

Jenny continued looking out the window, in sullen silence. Michael looked her way. "Jenny?"

She turned toward Michael and glared. "What are you trying to say? Have the courtesy to speak plainly."

Michael leaned forward in his chair and looked down for a long moment. "Fair enough," he said, then he looked up at Jenny. "You and I know how we came to be family. Whether you like it or not, it is what it is. What I'm saying is that history cannot leave this room—anytime, under any circumstances. Is that clear enough?"

"Or else what? Are you threatening us?" Jenny asked, her voice dripping with hostility.

Michael shot Jenny a menacing look for the briefest instant, then his countenance quickly transformed to one of concern. "Look, Jenny. I'm not trying to be threatening. That's not my intention—not by a longshot. I'm trying to be protective of you—of all of you," he said, looking at the others. "There are powerful forces at work here. You have at least some idea of what I'm talking about, Jenny. If anything about the true nature of our relationship should come to light, people would be in danger. Not from me, I assure you, but in danger nonetheless. So I need all of you to assure me that you will keep our secret no matter what. Not only for your own safety, but for the good of the country and our people."

"Like I said before, I'm all in, bro. You have my word," said Ricky.

"Thanks, pal," Michael said, then he turned his gaze toward Jenny, who glowered at him with her arms folded tightly across her chest. "Jenny?"

"I don't like being pushed around," she said defiantly. "But you live your life and I'll live mine. I've lived with this unseemly situation my entire life. I've never said a word about it before, and I won't now, much as I'd like to."

"How about you, Seventy-Seven?" Michael asked.

Bobby rubbed the back of his neck and cleared his throat. "I've never had any interest in politics and I've spent a good part of my life trying to stay off the radar screen and avoid trouble. I'm not going to go looking for it now." He stood up. "With that said, I better get back to work and make sure everything is ready for the visitation. Think about what you'd like us to do with the cremated remains. We can bury them in her grave at Sacred Heart, or you can scatter them or take them home. We can divide them up into three parts if you'd each like to have some. We can figure that out after the service. There's no need to finalize that decision now."

The group dispersed. As he stepped outside the front door of the funeral home, Michael fingered the tiny transmitter in his shirt pocket. "I trust you heard all that, Vargas. Satisfied?"

Chapter 47

THE SECRET SERVICE sent an advance team to the funeral home just after noon. They thoroughly inspected the building and the grounds as well as neighboring properties. A sizable army of reinforcements arrived with the vice-presidential candidate precisely at 2:30. Although nothing they saw caused any alarm, the situation itself was a security nightmare: trying to provide adequate protection without screening every guest or otherwise altering the very essence of a wake was a virtual impossibility. But the candidate himself insisted on being there to greet any and all who came to offer their condolences.

The visitation commenced at 3:00 and within an hour, the spacious facility was packed with people. Colleagues of Jenny's from the university as well as high school and college friends were interspersed with the masses of political types who came to be seen or to make a favorable impression on Michael Sanchez, whom they believed would be a heavy hitter in political circles for some time to come. Ricky's friends were few, but easily recognizable. They looked like ne'er-do-wells, underdressed and poorly groomed, with lots of tattoos and piercings, which drew close scrutiny from the wary Secret Service agents.

The visitation room was set up with Mrs. Sanchez's casket and portrait placed at the front, surrounded by dozens of floral arrangements, a small card tastefully attached to each, expressing sympathy on behalf of the sender. Rows of folding chairs were lined up neatly from the front to the back of the long rectangular room, with ample space at the back and along the sides for visitors to mingle. Pictures of Mrs. Sanchez were scattered about the room and a large-screen television near the back played a video tribute, showing images from her life. At the far end of the building was a reception area that had the look of a high-end kitchen, with granite counters covered with trays of food, coffee machines, and a refrigerator full of soft drinks and water. Tables and chairs were scattered about the room for those wishing to get off their feet while they snacked.

Bobby and two other funeral directors floated about quietly, trying to anticipate the needs of the family and respond to inquiries and requests from the guests and the security team. Bobby kept a watchful eye on Jenny, noticing that her ex-husband, Phil, was hovering by her side and constantly putting his hands on her, acting as if they were very much still married.

By early evening, the crowd had swelled considerably and flowed into the lobby area, the hallways and the kitchen. Bobby watched from across the room as Jenny stood to the side of the casket greeting visitors who filed by. Phil had his arm around her shoulders. A staff member approached and handed her a cup of tea. She smiled and thanked him, her eyes momentarily scanning the room as she put the tea to her lips. Bobby saw her face freeze as she dropped her cup of hot tea. He hurried to her side as she wiped her dress and bent over to pick up the empty Styrofoam cup, obviously flustered. As Bobby handed her the handkerchief from his jacket pocket, she pulled him aside and whispered under her breath, "That man over there—the tall man in black with the dark hair. Do you see him?"

Bobby followed her gaze and spotted a stylishly dressed man with a dark complexion watching the video tribute with several other guests.

"I see him. Who is he? Is there a problem?"

Jenny covered her mouth with a clenched fist and whispered. "He shouldn't be here!"

"Would you like me to ask him to leave?" Bobby asked.

"No! Don't do that! He might get angry. I don't want to cause a scene."

With that, Francisco Vargas turned away from the video and eyed Jenny from across the room. He nodded slightly as their eyes met, then casually sauntered out of the visitation room.

"Jenny, what is it? You look like you've seen a ghost."

Jenny shuddered as she stared at the spot where Vargas had just vanished from view. "That was El Cazador's man. I haven't seen him in years but I'll never forget that face." She slowly made her way back toward the casket, where Michael, Ricky and Phil stood in a receiving line that had formed in front of them. She took her place in the line, looking shaken and distracted.

Due to the size of the crowd, the visitation extended well past the scheduled 9:00 ending time. It was approaching 10:30 before the final visitors left and the family was alone in the quiet funeral home. While the four Secret Service agents waited in the lobby, Bobby met with the family at the back of the visitation room to remind them of the schedule for the next morning. Jenny and Ricky looked completely drained. Michael looked energized.

"I need a drink," said Ricky. "Care to join me, Mike?"

"Sorry, I've gotta run. I'll see you tomorrow, Rick." Michael breezed out of the building with the agents at his heels.

Jenny and Phil trudged toward the parking lot, hand-in-hand.

***

"How did it go?" Teresa asked as Bobby entered the apartment and tossed his jacket over the sofa.

"It was a rough day, from start to finish," Bobby said with a heavy sigh. "I think I'll change and take the dog out. Care to join me?"

Teresa had just finished a rough day herself, having lost two patients in the last 24 hours. "Nah, I'm beat. I think I'll just put on my PJs and read for a while before bed." She glanced across the room. Bobby had sat down on the sofa and was staring at the television, even though it was turned off. "Oh, what the heck, why not?" she said. "Perhaps a little evening stroll would do us both good."

Bobby unloaded on her as soon as they were out the door. He told Teresa about the disastrous start to the day involving the mistaken cremation. He told her about the strained family relationships and the disagreements about the funeral arrangements. And then he told her about Jenny's husband. "He had his hands all over her—all day long!" Bobby exploded. "He acted like they were still married."

"Did Jenny seem uncomfortable with it?"

"No, she seemed fine with it. She was acting like they were still married, too."

He walked along in morose silence for several minutes, head down, while the little dog pranced ahead, pulling at his leash.

"Sounds like a rough day, Bobby. I'm sure the cremation mistake hit you harder than it would have hit most funeral directors because you're such a perfectionist about your work. But you did everything you could have, and I'm sure no one who attended the visitation had any clue that there was a glitch."

"I suppose that's true, but we let the family down and I still feel terrible."

"I know you do, but right now you need to focus on getting the family through tomorrow rather than obsessing over the mistake. And as for Jenny, I know you have feelings for her, but I wouldn't read too much into the fact that her ex was there and that he was acting very affectionate. He was probably just trying to be supportive and comforting. She just lost her mother and she must be an emotional wreck. I know I was when I lost my mother. You need to give her some time and some space right now. After a while, you may be able to pick up where you left off. And if not, that's her problem. You'd be a great catch for any girl and if Jenny can't see that, then either she's a fool or it just wasn't meant to be. You'll end up with the right person, Bobby. I just know it. Maybe it's Jenny or maybe it's someone else. If it's not her, I'm sure that the perfect girl is out there waiting for you right now. You just have to have your eyes open."

"Thanks, T. Whatever happens, I'm sure lucky to have you around. Thanks for being such a great friend."

Chapter 48

MICHAEL SANCHEZ JOGGED briskly along the trail in Brackenridge Park just after daylight. The sprawling park was located in the heart of the city, just north of downtown, but was mostly deserted at this early morning hour except for the occasional jogger determined to get in his or her run before heading into work or taking on whatever else the day had in store.

Michael slowed as he approached one of the park's old stone restrooms and entered. As he stepped up to the urinal, he glanced at the floor of the lone toilet stall, whose door was closed. There were two shiny black dress shoes, just as he expected.

"That you, Vargas?" Michael asked in a low voice.

"Uh-huh," came the reply.

"We've only got a couple of minutes. What's up?"

"Just checking in on the family situation," came the voice from within the stall. "Here's how I see it. We caught a lucky break with the old lady dying when she did. And with the cremation, no one can ever use DNA to prove you're not really her son. That plan worked beautifully. I'm not too concerned about Jenny. She's lived with our secret all these years and I gave her a subtle reminder at the wake that I'm still around. I think we'll be OK there."

"I agree. She won't be a problem. Don't concern yourself with her for now."

"I won't, but I am concerned about your brother. He came through for us during the funeral, but he still worries me. He's a lowlife, he drinks, he does drugs. That makes him unpredictable and that makes him a risk."

"Agreed. We need to manage that risk. Give him the payoff we discussed, and then we'll just have to keep him close by promising him steady work with generous pay."

"I'm meeting with him later today to give him the money. The problem is, even if you keep him employed, he could turn on you at any time, or just get careless. I'm going to keep close tabs on him."

"Understood."

"That leaves the funeral director. He makes me nervous, too. He's not family but he knows everything."

"He's OK. I've known him since we were kids. He considers me one of his best friends. He's as loyal as they come, and he's an absolute chickenshit—always has been. He runs from trouble as fast as he can. Just doesn't want to get involved. He's not a risk. Leave him alone."

"Anyone who knows is a risk."

"I'm telling you, this guy's not. Leave him alone, Vargas. I mean it!"

"OK, I won't mess with him, but remember, if you can't control him, I will. So, I'm still going to keep an eye on him. We can't take any chances."

"Fine. But focus on Ricky for now. He's the immediate problem."

***

Francisco Vargas watched from a booth in the back of the dimly-lit tavern as Ricky Sanchez ordered a round of drinks for everyone seated at the bar with him.

"Ricky Sanchez buying drinks? It must be a cold day in hell!" said one of the patrons, an overweight young man in a baseball cap, sitting a few bar stools away. "Did you win the lottery, Ricky, or what?"

"As a matter of fact, I kind of did, Spike," Ricky responded in a booming voice. "My brother is about to become vice president of the United States. I've got a big job with his campaign and pretty soon I'll be moving to Washington to take a big bucks job there."

"What kind of crazy-ass bullshit is that?" said a slightly built man with a shaved head and bloodshot eyes on the other side of Ricky. "Who the hell is your brother?"

"Miguel Sanchez," Ricky replied. "*The* Miguel Sanchez—was running for president until a few weeks ago, and now he's running for VP. Gonna win, too. If your dumb ass ever followed the news, you'd know all about him."

"I do know all about Miguel Sanchez, douchebag. Just never heard that he was your brother before. How come you never mentioned that if he's really your brother?"

"Why would I?" Ricky asked. "There wasn't any reason to. He never ran for nuthin' until now."

"My name's Washington," said a lanky black man who had been keeping to himself at the far end of the bar. "I'm sure I'm related to George goddamn Washington. Ha!" he laughed boisterously. "Sounds farfetched to me, but if the brother keeps buying me drinks, he can be whoever he damn well pleases. Cheers, my man!" He hoisted his glass toward Ricky.

The bartender had been listening with a bemused smile on his face as he served up drinks. "So Ricky, what kind of high-powered job is your brother getting you in Washington?" he asked.

"Yeah, and why the hell would he hire a lowlife like you?" asked the man in the baseball hat. "You ain't never had a decent job in your life."

Ricky threw back a shot of *Maker's Mark* bourbon. "Because we're brothers, man. He knows my talents."

A tattoo-covered waitress with stringy blond hair tapped Ricky on the shoulder and leaned in to whisper in his ear. "There's a gentleman in the back booth who'd like a word with you. Said he works with your brother and that you're expecting him."

"Another round for my friends," Ricky called out to the bartender. "Be back in a few minutes, guys."

Vargas had his back to the bar, so that his face was not visible to the patrons gathered there. He wore a cowboy hat and a long wig with gray braids hanging down his back, Willie Nelson style. "You looking for me, mister?" Ricky asked in a loud voice as he staggered up to the booth.

Vargas put a finger to his lips. "Have a seat. I'm here on behalf of your brother. We have some business to discuss." There was an open bottle of *Maker's Mark* on the table. Vargas poured them each a glass. "Here's to a prosperous relationship." He raised the glass and chugged the amber liquid. Ricky did the same, then belched and wiped his mouth with his sleeve.

"First, your brother is most appreciative for your help with the cremation. I have a token of his appreciation here in this envelope." He pulled a fat white envelope out of his jacket and placed it on the table. "There's ten grand here. We just need to finish one final step before I turn this over to you."

Ricky swayed back and forth and blinked hard several times. "What final step?"

"We don't want a full-scale investigation of the cremation mistake—by the funeral home or the regulators or anyone else. We don't need your sister digging into this either. We can avoid all that if you simply write a short letter to the family saying it was your mistake and you sincerely apologize."

"And then you'll give me the money? Sure, I can do that."

"Let's take care of that right now," said Vargas, handing Ricky a piece of paper and a pen. "You write, I'll tell you what to say."

Ricky grabbed the pen and said, "OK, fire away."

Vargas spoke slowly and paused frequently to let Ricky catch up. *"Dear Family: I am devastated by Mom's death. It's hard to imagine life without her. And then I made a terrible mistake to make it even worse for you when I mixed up the paperwork and cremated her by mistake. I just can't live with that mistake. I am so sorry to put you through this. There is no way I can make this right. So I will just say one last time, I am so sorry. Ricky."*

"Kind of a weird letter," Ricky mumbled, struggling hard to focus as he read it to himself. "What should I do with it?"

Vargas glanced at the letter without touching it. He pushed the bulging envelope across the table to Ricky and filled their glasses again. They both drank up. "Just hang onto it for now. I want to check with Michael about how it should be delivered. I want to talk to you about your new job, too, but it looks like you're a little buzzed right now, so let's talk about that later in the week. I'll track you down. I think you'll be really excited."

"Sounds awesome!" Ricky said, hiccupping between words.

"It is awesome, and I think we should celebrate!" Vargas looked around to make sure they weren't being watched, then he pulled a small plastic bag filled with white powder from his jacket and dangled it in front of Ricky's face. "Some of the best blow around," he said, with a devilish grin. "Interested?"

"Cocaine? Cool!"

"Just for you, though. I don't want you sharing it with your pals or even telling them about it. So you can go first. Take this and do it in the men's room. After you get back, it'll be my turn. I'll keep an eye on this until you get back," he said, reaching across the table and putting his hand on the envelope.

Ricky folded the letter and stuffed it into his shirt pocket, then he grabbed the small bag and stumbled off to the men's room. Vargas picked up the envelope and quietly slipped out the back door.

Chapter 49

JENNY LOOKED AROUND her once tidy living room. It was cluttered with boxes containing all her mother's worldly possessions other than her clothing and furniture. She flipped through the contents of one of the boxes she had brought home from the hospice, smiling sadly as she picked up the letters and drawings Bobby had delivered twenty years after their creation. Her musings were interrupted by the harsh ringing of her cell phone.

"Hello, this is Jenny Sanchez."

"Ms. Sanchez, this is Officer Helton with the San Antonio PD. Are you the sister of Enrique Sanchez?"

"Yes. Why do you ask?"

"I'm so sorry to have to tell you this ma'am, but I'm afraid your brother has passed away. He was found dead in the men's room at a local tavern. We won't know for sure until the coroner completes the autopsy, but it looks like a drug overdose. I'll need you to come identify the body."

"Are you sure it's him?" Jenny asked in a quavering voice.

"Pretty sure, ma'am. He had his driver's license on him and there were people at the bar drinking with him. They knew him. They're the ones who found him. But we'll need you to make a positive ID so we can be certain. And ma'am—there's one more thing. We found a note on him. Looks like a suicide note."

***

Bobby draped his giant arm around Jenny's slender shoulders as they walked into the county morgue. They had barely spoken on the ride across town to the drab concrete building now housing what was almost certainly her brother's dead body. The building seemed eerily deserted, the desk in the stark reception area unoccupied. It bore a sign stating *Ring bell for attendant*. They did as instructed, and within a few seconds a burly young man lumbered through the door leading from the back room and greeted them. Blue hospital scrubs covered most of his body but could not conceal the spiderweb tattoos on his neck and hands. He gave his visitors a somber and knowing look as they explained their business.

The attendant guided them through the door leading into the rest of the facility. The floors were shiny, covered with a gray impermeable resin, which Bobby knew was to facilitate easy clean-up of spilt body fluids. The walls were bare except for the posters warning about the presence of hazardous chemicals. They were led into a stark white room with bright fluorescent lights and no furniture.

The attendant disappeared through swinging double doors and returned several minutes later, wheeling a gurney that carried a body wrapped in a white sheet. Jenny stepped back and her hand shot up to cover her mouth as the young man positioned the gurney in the center of the room, under the bright ceiling lights. "Are you ready, miss?" he asked.

She nodded her head and moved a step closer as the attendant slowly and carefully pulled down the sheet to shoulder level. "It's him," she said, in a faraway voice, quickly averting her eyes.

"Are you sure about that, ma'am?"

She nodded. "I'm sure."

The attendant handed her a clipboard and asked her to sign a document confirming that she had positively identified the remains as those of Enrique Sanchez.

They left the building and walked to Bobby's car in silence. Once they were in the car, Bobby turned and faced Jenny from the driver's seat. "Jenny, I can only imagine how hard this is for you, and I am so sorry."

"This wasn't an accident!" Jenny snapped, her countenance turning from shock to rage in an instant.

"I understand that. The police said there was a note and it looked like Ricky may have taken his own life."

"That's not what I mean! It wasn't an accident and it wasn't suicide. Sal is behind this. I'm sure of it!"

"That just doesn't make any sense, Jenny. Ricky had three times the legal limit of alcohol in his system, plus cocaine. Sal wasn't even there."

"You don't know him like I do. You haven't been around him in twenty years. He's evil, I'm telling you!"

Bobby touched her forearm gently. "It's tragic, no matter how it happened. I'll take you home."

Jenny removed her glasses and wiped her eyes with the back of her hand, her rage transforming into quiet weeping. They drove the thirty minutes across town in silence. Bobby parked the car in front of her house and looked at her. She seemed calm, but drained. "Let me know whenever you'd like to talk about funeral arrangements," he said.

"I don't care what we do, Bobby. I can't handle another funeral. He didn't have many friends, not real ones anyway. I don't need a mob of people coming to console me. I just went through that. I can't handle it again—not now. Maybe we should just skip the funeral and have him buried in the cemetery next to Mother without any ceremony. Can we do that?"

"Of course we can. That's known as a direct burial. We can do whatever you want. One of us should probably contact Sal, though, just to make sure he isn't going to raise any objections."

Jenny gritted her teeth and stared straight ahead, "Then you call him. I don't want anything to do with him right now. And frankly, if he wants to get involved, he can do whatever he wants. I just don't care."

"OK. I'll deal with him and keep you posted."

"Thanks, Bobby." She gave him a sad smile and squeezed his hand. Then she turned away, climbed out of the car and hurried up the walkway.

***

The press was delicate in their coverage, describing Ricky's death as the story of a trouble-prone young man who was unable to cope with the loss of his beloved mother. It was portrayed as a true family tragedy for the vice-presidential candidate, losing both his mother and his brother so close together. There was no mention of funeral arrangements other than the fact that it would be a private service for family only.

Sal had informed Bobby that he wanted to have his brother cremated and have his ashes buried next to their mother. Jenny told Bobby that she would rather not have him cremated but just didn't care to get involved and would defer to Sal, provided he assumed financial responsibility for the arrangements. Sal had been in Washington and on the campaign trail since Mrs. Sanchez's funeral, so it was two full weeks before he was able to make it back to San Antonio to meet with Bobby to finalize the arrangements.

The two of them sat together in the now familiar confines of Bobby's office in the funeral home. "Such a shame about Ricky," Bobby said. "Sounds like he was sort of a lost soul who never really found his way. I'll always remember him as the sweet and innocent little guy we knew back in San Mateo."

"Life was good then, wasn't it?" Sal mused, smiling as a wave of nostalgia washed over him. "At least for a little while—until it all blew up!" He laughed and they both reflected silently for a long moment.

"That was sure a special time for me," Bobby said, breaking the silence. "I've been thinking about it a lot lately, since you and the Sanchez family suddenly came back into my life. You know, it's funny, I had such a hard time letting go of all of you. I wrote letters to Jenny and her mom after they left. I never wrote to you because I figured you were long gone and wouldn't have left any forwarding address. But I did write to Mrs. Sanchez to tell her I was praying for Miguel and looking after his grave. I even sent her a few pictures of it. I also sent letters to Jenny because I had a crazy crush on her. Anyway, all those letters came back undelivered. I'm not sure why, but I hung onto them all these years, so it was really a kick when I was able to finally deliver them to Mrs. Sanchez when she was in hospice. I had pictures from the old days that I had drawn—pictures of Miguel and you and me. I gave those to her too. She lit up like a Christmas tree!"

"Thanks for being so good to my family, Bobby. I know Jenny

probably still hates me. She never quite got over losing Miguel and I suppose I was a constant reminder of him. I'm sorry you had to get into the middle of our family issues, but I want you to know I appreciate it."

"Don't mention it," said Bobby. "So speaking of family issues, I want to be sure that we're clear with one another about funeral arrangements. They have to be authorized by the next-of-kin. If you were legally Ricky's brother—either by birth or adoption—then there's no issue. But since you've told me you were never legally adopted, technically you had no standing to make Mrs. Sanchez's funeral arrangements, and you have no standing to make Ricky's."

Sal looked peeved. "So what are you saying? Is Jenny going to go crazy again and pick a fight with me?"

Bobby took a long look at his old friend. "No, Jenny has told me she doesn't want to get involved with these arrangements, but I'm sticking my neck out here if I knowingly allow someone other than a relative to authorize cremation. My funeral license may be at risk, so I'd like to understand exactly what I'm dealing with."

"I'm not sure what you mean. I've always shot straight with you, Bobby. I was upfront with you last time we went through this. I told you that my family relationship is informal and that I was never legally adopted. That doesn't mean that we didn't consider it a real adoption in our minds. I'm not sure what else I can tell you. I've told you everything there is to tell."

"Have you? Are you sure there isn't more I should know?"

"What are you getting at? Spit it out!"

Bobby sat back in his chair and sighed deeply. "I was told that you're not even a citizen and that you lied to me about that."

"That bitch! Did Jenny tell you that?"

"No, it wasn't Jenny. Mrs. Sanchez told me that before she died. She said she kept your secret but wanted someone to know. So, is that true?"

Sal looked around the room, shaking his head, his fists clenched. "So what if it is true? Are you threatening me, Bobby? Can you imagine how the media and this whole campaign would explode if that got out? Listen pal, there are some powerful people involved behind the scenes. Politics is a nasty business. It would not be in your best interest to go public with this."

"Who's threatening who?" Bobby asked, looking hurt. "I'm not interested in politics. I couldn't care less about it. I wish I'd never been told what I was told. I just want to know what I'm dealing with—and what Jenny's dealing with, for that matter."

"Look, Bobby, hear me out. I don't want any harm to come to you or Jenny. Quite to the contrary. I'm involved in this mission—at considerable personal risk—to make things better for our people. I'm as American as you! A piece of paper shouldn't matter! I'd be perfectly legal if Congress could get off its ass and deal with this issue. Everyone agrees that people like me—kids who were brought here at a young age by their parents—shouldn't have to live in the shadows. We should be considered Americans with all the rights that go along with that. It should have happened by now but chickenshit politicians get in the way.

"I have a chance to change all that," Sal continued, his voice earnest and his eyes gleaming with passion and conviction. "This government doesn't work anymore! It doesn't serve the interests of the people, so we're going to change that—from the inside out. We're going to legalize the immigrants who are already here. We're going to open the floodgates to allow many more immigrants to get here, and they'll get the right to vote. We'll be taking over this country through the ballot box!"

Bobby grinned. "This reminds me of your rants back in The Brush when we were kids. I don't know much about politics, but I know that change is hard. Do you really think you can pull that off?"

"Look, Seventy-Seven, people are stupid! They don't think for themselves. Their knowledge doesn't go beyond sound bites, and the sound bites are just propaganda that the media and the politicians spew at the voters incessantly. They hear it often enough that they believe what they're told—that's human nature. Think about it—most people form their beliefs at a young age based on what was pounded into their heads. Most people embrace their parents' political beliefs for that reason. The same is true for religion. You're Catholic because your parents were Catholic. But what if you were born in Egypt or India? You'd be Muslim or Hindu. Brainwashing is a harsh-sounding word, but that's essentially what it is—people are impressionable, and they're conditioned by what's drilled into their heads."

"So what's your point?"

"The point is that I *can* bring about change because I know human nature and I know how to get into their heads. I know our people and I know what resonates with them and what motivates them. I'm telling them I can help them move out of the shadows and bring them into the sunlight—where their futures are bright and they will be warmed by our compassionate hearts. It's all about opportunity and that's what I'm offering. The details don't matter because people don't think at that level. They're eating up the slogans and the sound bites! Millions of our people are out there already and I will bring in legions of new voters who will think our way. We're going to take this country and make it ours!"

"You're scaring me, Sal. Who is this *we* that you're talking about? And what do you mean by *our people*? I've heard you say that before. Aren't we all Americans? Doesn't this country provide wonderful opportunities for everyone, including immigrants? Look at you—Ivy League education, wealthy and successful attorney, and now getting into politics at the highest level. If that isn't opportunity, I don't know what is! I've made a great life here, too, as a first-generation American. So has Jenny—she's a Ph.D. from Stanford and a professor at a prestigious university. My roommate Teresa came here from Panama as a child and she's as American as we are. She applied for citizenship the old-fashioned way and now she's thriving and successful and making a real contribution to our community. People like us are making a difference. We're motivated. We work hard. We're not complacent and we don't have an entitlement mentality. We're making a real impact on the American workplace, and that same impact is carrying over to politics, culture and every other aspect of our society. You've been going on these rants against our country and our government since we were kids but it seems to me that we've got it pretty good here—the system is working beautifully for us. Are you sure you're not the one with blinders on?"

"That's easy for you to say. The American government didn't wage an unjust war against your homeland and it didn't kill your father."

"C'mon, Sal. Your father was killed by a bad guy who just happened to work for the Border Patrol. There was no government plot there. And I don't know much about what happened in El Salvador, but that was a long time ago, and the people involved are no longer in power. Why dwell on the past when things are going so well for you right here and now?"

Sal brooded in silence for several moments, tapping a clenched fist against his chin. "I tend to get carried away when I speak about the Cause. You've seen me do that before. My apologies. You make some fair points, but regardless of the fact that some people are fortunate enough to capitalize on the opportunities here, many are not, and even for those of us who are, it's never like we've really assimilated. There's still a wall between us and everyone else that hasn't lived through what we've lived through."

"You're touching a nerve here, pal," said Bobby, sitting bolt upright and placing his palms on his desk. "Personally, I think that wall is only in your mind and you can break it down if you choose to. Lots of us do. Some people create their own wall by not assimilating and not learning the language. And maybe it is partly created by others—it's human nature to resent newcomers and people who are different. But people like us scale that wall every day. We cherish the opportunities here and we take nothing for granted. We put aside the persecution complex and we work hard and make an effort to fit in. We're the future. We're the lifeblood of America in the next generation. Look at all the brown faces everywhere you go. That's the face of America, right here and now! Your wall isn't holding us back—at least not most of us, not those of us who truly want to fit in. I think this country is the greatest place on Earth. We're the envy of the world because of the opportunities we have. I truly wish you the best in your political career, but I hope you'll be careful. Don't try to change things too much. There's a lot that's good about this place. I'd hate to see it get all screwed up because of some battle against an invisible wall that's mostly just in the minds of people looking to make excuses."

Sal smiled and chuckled softly. "Words of wisdom from a voter. I will take them to heart and do my best not to screw things up too badly! But back to the more mundane—what are we going to do about Ricky? Did you just tell me that you're not comfortable with me making the arrangements—under the circumstances?"

Bobby thought for a moment. "I think there's a way we can all get comfortable. Since Jenny is the next-of-kin, she has the right to control arrangements. She told me she doesn't want to be involved. Her being uninvolved doesn't necessarily give you any rights, but if she says instead that her instructions are for the funeral home to take direction from you, then we would be following her wishes. I think that works. Let me call her and make sure that's what she wants to do."

"You're a wise man and a good friend, Seventy-Seven. Maybe I can persuade you to serve in my Cabinet someday!"

"Thanks, but no thanks, Rocket. I know my place in the world and it's right here, serving one family at a time."

Chapter 50

DR. JENNY SANCHEZ stared out the window of her Southwest flight returning from San Diego. She had spent a delightful four-day weekend with girlfriends from college, catching up and having fun. She had been in a dark place since losing her mother and her brother, and her friends had insisted that some girls' time in a beautiful place would help her move past the grief and depression.

It was precisely what she needed. They hiked along coastal trails offering stunning vistas of the vast blue Pacific. They rode bikes along the crowded boardwalk at Pacific Beach, mingling with the surfers, runners, skateboarders and tourists. At night, they partied at the local bars as if they were still college kids. By the time her friends departed four days later, she felt invigorated.

She had stayed on for two additional days for some quiet reflection time before boarding her flight home. The flight path took her due west over the Pacific Ocean before the plane banked into a wide semicircle taking them south and then east, back over land, hugging the US/Mexican border. The border crossing between San Diego and Tijuana was clearly visible, not that one needed a wall to appreciate the difference between life on the north side versus life south of the border. The gleaming high-rise condominiums and office buildings of downtown San Diego stood just 17 miles north of the border, like sentries marking the entrance to life in the north with its opulence and prosperity. She could see the border wall, just off to the right as they jetted eastward. The border was made obvious by the urban sprawl that came to an abrupt halt at the northern boundary, replaced by an expanse of uninhabited desert and mountains.

As the mountains passed by below, giving way to endless miles of barren desert, Jenny resumed the reflection that had begun during her two days alone in San Diego. She had spent most of that time leisurely walking the beaches, enjoying the cool air and abundant California sunshine. It was a striking contrast to the oppressive summertime heat in South Texas and the gritty surroundings of big city life back home in San Antonio. The trip had lifted her spirits and cleared her head. She needed that clarity to sort through the swirling emotions that had been overwhelming her.

She had taken major steps toward coming to grips with some issues, yet others still felt unresolved. She was at peace with her mother's passing. At 55 years old, her mother had left this world too early, but they had always been close. She would miss her desperately, but there was nothing she regretted about their relationship—no unresolved issues or things she never got to say. Ricky's death was tragic, yet not unexpected. He had lived hard and wild, and the constant drinking and drug usage had always troubled her. She mourned him, and the bleak life he had lived, but he would be at peace now, and she would no longer have to worry about him. Some part of her still believed that his death was not a random accident, coming as it did just days after her revelations about Sal. She could envision Ricky trying to capitalize on that information in some way. But, that was pure speculation on her part, and she had no evidence whatsoever to back it up, so she pushed those thoughts from her mind.

The desert below changed seamlessly from California to Arizona to New Mexico and then to Texas. Jenny had vowed to herself that, before landing in San Antonio, she would come to a resolution on the one issue that was foremost on her mind. Phil had been lobbying hard for a reconciliation. There had been nothing ugly about their divorce, and they remained friendly afterwards. They had just drifted apart as they focused on their careers, and mutually agreed that if the passion had disappeared from their marriage, they should move on. He had been there for her when her mother took ill. He had been thoughtful and kind to both her and her mother during those final days in hospice. He had been attentive and comforting throughout those days surrounding the funeral. They were so compatible in so many ways. They were both academics. Like her, he was a Ph.D. and a professor. Their personalities meshed well. He was easy to be with and to talk to. On paper, they were a perfect match. And her life had seemed more fulfilling when he was in it than after he left.

But then Bobby Rivera had unexpectedly reentered her life. On paper, they were no match at all. Bobby was no scholar—he hadn't even gone to college—but he had a certain wisdom about him. He was not smooth or sophisticated, but he had a way with people. He was friendly and cheerful, outgoing in a low-key way. He was kind and thoughtful and compassionate—with everyone, no matter what the circumstances. He loved people and people loved him. Did she love him in the same way everyone else did, or was it something more? The scholar in her knew that the nostalgia of a first childhood romance could be coloring her thinking. The arguments against pursuing a relationship with Bobby were commonsensical and compelling, but she found herself eager to set all those arguments aside. That in itself told her something. Why not give it a try? What did she have to lose? As the flight attendant instructed the passengers to prepare for landing, a sensation of clarity and excitement settled over her, coupled with a sense of resolve. She would just have to tell Phil that she was involved with somebody else now.

Jenny got out of the taxi feeling lighthearted and energized. She hurried up her walkway and inserted the key into the lock and attempted to turn it to the left. It was already in the unlocked position. That struck her as strange. She tentatively opened the door and looked inside. She saw no one and nothing seemed amiss. The three boxes she had brought from the hospice were still there in the middle of the living room, one on the coffee table and the other two stacked next to that table, but something was different about them. She remembered putting the top back on the box that was on the table and that there had been a picture of her and her mother right on top. Now, the box was open and the picture was not there.

She opened the other boxes and found the picture at the bottom of one of those boxes, underneath several paperbacks. She began rummaging through all three boxes. Everything appeared to be there, but somehow the contents looked like they had been rearranged. Then with a start, she rifled through the box on the table, looking furiously for something she could not find—the letters and pictures that Bobby had given her mother. She distinctly remembered them being in that box, just beneath the picture of her mother and her. She had read those letters again just before she had left for San Diego. They were gone. With trembling hands, she dialed Bobby's number.

Chapter 51

TERESA GLANCED AT the wall clock above the kitchen table. It read 8:10. Bobby had told her that he would be home by 7:45 so that they could take a run in the park before dark. She paced the floor in their apartment, stopping periodically to do some pre-running stretches. She heard her cell phone vibrating on the kitchen counter as she was stretching and hurried over to read the text message. It was from Bobby: *Sorry, running late. Had to run over to Jenny's. Should be home by 8:30. Still wanna run?*

"Dammit, Bobby," she grumbled to herself. She stomped across the room and out the front door. She returned a little past 9:00, glistening with perspiration from her five-mile run. Bobby was rummaging through the refrigerator as she walked in and slammed the door behind her. She poured a glass of water from the kitchen sink and gulped it down.

"I decided not to wait. Didn't know when you'd be home and I didn't want to lose the daylight."

"I'm really sorry, Teresa. Something came up and I just couldn't get home any quicker."

"That's OK. I know Jenny's an important person in your life and when she calls, you need to come running. I understand priorities." Teresa avoided eye contact and walked past Bobby into the laundry room where she grabbed a towel and wiped her sweaty face.

"Look, T, I'm really sorry I stood you up again. I feel terrible about it. I feel like I've been a lousy friend and a lousy roommate, but there's something going on that's really bothering me. I'd like to tell you about it if you'll let me. I sure could use your advice."

The pained look on his face was obvious and sincere. "OK, just let me shower first. I'm gross and stinky." She returned ten minutes later in a tee shirt and shorts, toweling her hair dry and running a brush through it as she faced the mirror hanging on the dining room wall. "I'm listening," she said. "What is it you want to talk about?"

Bobby unloaded. "It all starts with the stories of two friends of mine from high school, Sal and Miguel. He told her about Sal's story of crossing the border from Mexico with his father and taking up residence in San Mateo. He told her about the murder of Sal's father by a crooked Border Patrol agent, which left Sal on his own in this country at the age of 15, without legal permission to be here. He told her of Miguel's tragic drowning and he told her about how both the Sanchez family and Sal disappeared from San Mateo around the same time without a trace.

"That was over 20 years ago, right? So what does that have to do with anything happening today?"

Bobby let out a deep breath and took a long look at Teresa from his seat at the kitchen table. "It has everything to do with today, but I really need you to keep what I'm about to tell you absolutely confidential, at least for now, until I figure out what to do. I probably shouldn't even be telling you these things and if you don't want to hear them, I'll just shut up."

"I have no idea what you're talking about. Tell me more."

"OK. It gets pretty crazy. First, the reason I told you about Sal and Miguel is that Sal *became* Miguel. The Sanchez family moved away from San Mateo after Miguel's death and started a new life, and Sal went with them. He assumed Miguel's identity. So as far as schools and anyone else were concerned, Sal is Miguel Sanchez, son of the recently departed Anita Sanchez, born in this country. Only he's not."

Teresa turned away from the mirror and stared at him, wide-eyed and speechless. "So here's where that past meets the present," Bobby continued. "Sal Rios—using the name Miguel Sanchez—is the person running for vice president." He told Teresa about his deathbed conversation with Mrs. Sanchez and her comments about Miguel, which he later realized were comments about Sal. He told her about the dying woman's request that Bobby watch over her children and that if anything bad happened to any of them, he could be sure that Sal was behind it. He told her about the funeral arrangements and Sal's insistence on cremation, and the fact that cremation ultimately did occur, but it was supposedly by accident. He mentioned that Ricky caused the accident, but that Ricky was now gone, so no one could be sure why or how the accident occurred. He told her of Jenny's assertion that Ricky's death was not an accident. He told of Jenny's revelation that Sal was never legally adopted and was not even a citizen. He told her that Sal admitted that to him. Then he told her about his trip to Jenny's home that evening after Jenny had discovered that her house had been burglarized. As it turned out, the only things missing were the letters and pictures that Bobby had given to Mrs. Sanchez at the hospice. He and Jenny had decided not to contact the police, because they would likely conclude that nothing of value was missing and that the old pictures and letters were just misplaced. More importantly, they did not want to invite scrutiny of the bigger picture.

Teresa sat down opposite Bobby, looking shell-shocked. "This sounds crazy! What does it all mean?"

"Here's what Jenny thinks. Behind all of this is the undeniable fact that our vice-presidential candidate is not who he says he is. He's not even an American citizen, so he's unqualified to hold that office. That's a secret he's determined to keep at any cost. That's why her mother was cremated by Ricky, who conveniently is no longer here. There won't be any DNA to prove that Sal is not really her son. Ricky learned the secret and Sal and his people couldn't run the risk of him spilling the beans, so he was killed and it was made to look like suicide. He was cremated, too. Now these pictures and letters are stolen. I just told Sal about them a few days ago, and suddenly there's a burglary and those are the only items that disappeared."

"But why would he be concerned about those letters and pictures?"

"Because those letters specifically mention Miguel's death. There's even a photo of Miguel's grave. And the pictures show me, Sal and Miguel, with our names on them. Sal is clearly recognizable as the one called Sal in the pictures, and the current VP candidate looks just like him and nothing like the picture of Miguel."

"This is just outrageous! It sounds like the kind of thing that could have happened in some third-world banana republic years ago, but not here. Not in this country. Not now!"

"I agree. But it *is* happening, and I may be the only person who knows. What do I do?"

"Oh my God, Bobby! If Jenny's scenario is even close to the truth, then we're dealing with some dangerous people. You can't get involved with that! Hopefully the truth will come out from some other source. This is unreal!" She sat down at the kitchen table and put her head in her hands as if trying to keep it from exploding. "Are they going to get away with this? I mean, is there any way at all to prove the truth of what you just told me?"

"Absolutely," Bobby said. "First, there's the real Miguel's body in the graveyard back in San Mateo. People there will remember the story about his death. And, his DNA would match up with Jenny's and Sal's wouldn't. Also, they didn't get all the letters and pictures. I still have some of those. A few of the letters were from me to Jenny and they just seemed a little mushy. I was embarrassed to let her or her mother read those, so I still have them. Those letters refer to Miguel's death and a couple of them mention Sal's disappearance at the same time the Sanchez family disappeared."

"I can't think straight," Teresa said. "This guy can't be allowed to get away with this. There must be some way to stop it. But Sanchez knows you're onto all this, right? He knows you're a threat to him. You could be in danger, Bobby! We have to put your safety above everything else. You can't be the one to go public with this."

Bobby smiled wryly. "Aren't you the one who lectured me about speaking up when something's wrong and not being afraid to get involved?"

Teresa sat down next to Bobby and leaned toward him, gripping his hands tightly. "This is different—your safety comes first. Promise me you won't forget that."

"Well, I'll try to keep that in mind, but—"

"Promise me!"

"OK. I promise. I won't be stupid, T. You have my word."

She flung her arms around him. He returned the embrace and held her tightly for a long time, rocking gently back and forth. He didn't want to let go. It felt so good holding her close like that. "I don't ever want to lose you, Bobby," she whispered in his ear.

***

Bobby slept fitfully that night, dozing lightly off and on, but mostly feeling wide awake as he repeatedly checked the clock on his nightstand. His cell phone vibrated shortly after 5:00 a.m. and he immediately read the text message from Sheriff Reid back in San Mateo. *Please call me when you can.*

Bobby promptly called from his bed. "What are you doing up at this ungodly hour, Sheriff?" he asked in a hushed voice.

"Hey, Bobby. Sorry about texting you this early. I figured you'd just call me later in the day. I should have known that a funeral director always sleeps with his phone by his side."

"Ain't that the truth," Bobby chuckled. "I'm sure you do too. Anyway, what's up?"

"I was dragged out of bed about 3:30 this morning by a call from my deputy. He was driving past the cemetery and saw some flashlights, so he went to investigate. Turns out, someone was trying to dig up a grave. They took off when they saw him coming. They just about had the casket uncovered but that's as far as they got before Benny interrupted them."

"Hmmm… That's pretty strange. You don't hear much about grave robberies anymore. So why are you calling me?"

"Because I need to contact the next-of-kin to make them aware of this. They may have some leads about who would do this, or they may want to move the body somewhere else. I think you know the person they were trying to dig up. His name is Miguel Sanchez. Benny remembers that you were pals with this kid and that he died in some kind of drowning accident. I think his family's long gone, but Benny thought you might have some idea how to reach them."

Bobby paused as his mind raced. "I definitely remember Miguel, Sheriff. Let me make a few calls to see if I can track down his family."

"I sure would appreciate that, Bobby. In the meantime, we'll just have the cemetery refill the grave and keep a close eye on it."

"Sheriff, it's not my cemetery, but I'd recommend a different plan. Those grave-robbers may come back and you can't watch that place around the clock. I'd suggest moving the burial to an unmarked grave. Or better yet, see if you can store the remains with the Medical Examiner for a few weeks. That way, he's easy to retrieve if the family decides they want him moved. And he'll be out of the reach of the bad guys."

"Good idea. I'll tell Manny we talked. I'm sure he'll be OK with that. Let me know if you're able to find the family."

Chapter 52

BOBBY DROVE TO the funeral home feeling distracted and overcome with a sense of dread. Partly it was because of his knowledge about Sal's secret and the battle raging within his conscience about remaining loyal to his friend versus doing something about the imminent miscarriage of justice that seemed certain to occur. He was also heavy-hearted about the funeral he would be presiding over at 11:00 that morning. A seven-year-old little girl by the name of Abbie Ramirez had been struck and killed by a drunk driver while riding her bicycle. Mostly, however, he was concerned about Teresa. He had told her everything he knew about the Sanchez situation. He'd had some reservations about doing so, but he had felt desperate to talk to someone about it and there was no one whose counsel he respected more than Teresa's. In the light of the new day, it seemed like a bad decision—he had unwittingly exposed her to real danger. It was possible that the disturbance of Miguel's grave was just a coincidence, but it had occurred just hours after he had told Teresa about Miguel's burial and how that might be problematic for Sal. That, and everything else Teresa now knew, made her a threat to the campaign and that was entirely his fault.

Upon entering the quiet funeral home, Bobby attempted to turn his focus to little Abbie's funeral service. Despite the tragic circumstances, the family had insisted on making the service a celebration of her short life rather than a mournful farewell. Based on that request, the visitation room had been emptied of its furniture and now resembled a gymnasium. Abbie loved to paint, so there were pictures of her artwork displayed everywhere, and easels were scattered around the room to allow the visiting children to create their own farewell tributes. She was also a soccer player, having recently been infatuated by the United States Women's National Soccer Team. Pictures of her soccer heroes were on display throughout the room, along with her own small soccer uniform and several autographed soccer balls. At one end of the room, two small goals were set up, along with miniature soccer balls. At the other end of the room was a large trampoline, enclosed with sturdy netting to prevent any of the young tumblers from falling to the floor. There would be plenty of kid-food: hot dogs, pretzels and cotton candy. A brief formal service would be held in the funeral home's chapel, to be followed by a reception in the makeshift playground area.

Bobby busied himself making sure all those preparations had been completed and that everything was ready for the service. He inspected the casket in the back room to check on Abbie. She looked good, at least to the eyes of a funeral director, angelic and peaceful in her brightly colored soccer uniform. The sight of the little girl caused his eyes to become misty and he smiled sadly at her. Sharp focus returned instantly. At times like these, he had always been able to shut out whatever might be going on in his personal life and focus on the family he was serving. He knew that for them, their funeral service was a once-in-a-lifetime event, and they deserved his very best. They deserved perfection and he was committed to delivering it. All distractions vanished as he turned his energy and focus to the task in front of him.

Shortly before the family was to arrive, Bobby felt his cell phone vibrate. The text message lifted his spirits: *How about lunch tomorrow? I'd love to talk. Jenny.*

He hurriedly tapped out a response: *Sounds great! I'm tied up all day with a service. Will call you tonight regarding time and place.*

The service went off beautifully. It was strange but heartwarming to see hordes of small children running around the funeral home, laughing and yelling to each other as if it were a playground. At 3:00, the crowd gathered for the procession to the cemetery, where Abbie was laid to rest beside her grandparents. After taking his leave from the family at the cemetery, Bobby sat alone in his car, relishing the silence. The other staff funeral directors had offered to return to the funeral home to handle the clean-up and the disassembly of the indoor playground, and he happily agreed to let them do that. Exhaustion from the long day and sleepless night had overtaken him, but he drove home feeling some sense of satisfaction. He had made a difference for a grieving family and had successfully orchestrated a meaningful and touching tribute to their precious little girl.

He trudged up the stairs to his apartment. The concerns and distractions of the previous night and morning had been successfully banished from his mind by the day's events. They came flooding back as he opened the door.

It looked like a tornado had blown through. The cushions from the couch and living room chairs were on the floor or askew. Cabinets and drawers in the kitchen were wide open, pots and pans and dishware—much of it shattered—were scattered about the counters and floor. Bobby walked toward his bedroom. It was even worse. Dresser drawers were open and clothes were strewn across the floor and the bed. He quickly moved to Teresa's room—it had received the same treatment. The little Cairn Terrier barked incessantly from the bathroom and scratched furiously at the door. He ran wildly about the apartment when Bobby opened the door to release him, continuing his frantic barking.

Bobby roamed around the apartment in a daze. He didn't know where to start or who to call. He decided to begin a hasty clean-up effort, starting from the front of the apartment and working backwards, hoping to minimize the shock for Teresa when she walked in. He had barely finished putting the living room cushions back in place when he heard a key turning the front door lock. Teresa started at the wild-eyed look of her roommate and then stared past him. Her jaw dropped. "What the—"

Bobby put a finger to his lips and shot an urgent look her way. He quietly approached her, then leaned down and whispered in her ear, "Don't make a sound!"

He guided her through the apartment, as she stared in open-mouthed disbelief. Bobby grabbed the dog leash, attached it to CT's collar, and nodded toward the front door. They walked down the stairs in silence. Upon reaching the parking lot, Teresa exploded. "What's going on? Is anything missing? Why are we leaving the apartment? Have you called the police?"

Bobby stopped and turned to face her. He dropped the leash and stepped on it, then put his hands on her shoulders. He could feel her entire body trembling. "Somebody ransacked our apartment. I just got home half an hour ago and found it like this. I don't think they took anything, but I think our place must be bugged."

"You mean someone is eavesdropping on us?"

Bobby looked grim. He nodded. "Think about it. Last night I told you all about Miguel Sanchez—and now this happens."

She looked at him blankly.

"Let's keep walking," he said. "I want to get away from here. Someone might be watching us." He looked around nervously, picked up the leash and they began walking in the direction of Kennedy Park, their usual dog-walking destination. "Remember last night I told you that there was still information out there that could prove Sal's real identity? Remember I mentioned that I had letters and pictures? I think that's what they were after. Good thing they weren't here."

"It could just be a coincidence, couldn't it?" She looked at him hopefully.

Bobby shook his head. "I don't think so. Remember I also mentioned that the real Miguel is buried in San Mateo? I got a call early this morning from the local sheriff. Someone tried to dig up his grave last night, just hours after I mentioned that to you."

"This is really scary, Bobby! What should we do?"

They walked in silence for several minutes, the question hanging in the air. The little dog stopped to do his business. Bobby leaned over and picked up the poop in a plastic bag and tossed it into a trash can. "I think you need to move out. You don't need to be part of all this."

"I'm not moving out," Teresa said. "We shouldn't let them terrorize us. That's what they're trying to do. I'm not—"

"You need to move out!" Bobby said, raising his voice and glaring at her. "The sooner the better."

"But—"

"Look, it's not open for discussion. I'm going through a lot right now and I need to be on my own. I'm tired of this shitty little dog. I'm tired of listening to your endless stories about all the people dying at the hospice! I can't take all that depression. Hell, for all I know this could be your fault. Are you sure you didn't leave the door unlocked this morning? It doesn't matter. You need to leave."

Teresa stared at Bobby, dumbfounded. Her bottom lip began quivering and she looked away to hide the tears rolling down her face. She grabbed the leash from him and began running back toward the apartment, the little dog sprinting ahead, tugging at the leash.

Bobby sat down on a park bench, looking glumly at the ground, feeling wretched. The uneasiness he had awoken with that morning had increased exponentially. He wandered slowly back to the apartment, trying to think, but the tempest in his mind and the heaviness in his heart precluded clarity of thought. He closed the door softly and made his way across the ravaged apartment to Teresa's bedroom. She was picking clothing up off the floor and throwing it into a suitcase that was spread open upon her bed.

"I'm sorry I snapped at you," Bobby said softly. "But it's really better if you move out. I'm heading out for a bite and then I'm going back to the funeral home for a while. I'll be back in a couple of hours. Don't worry about the mess. I'll clean it up as soon as I get back."

She didn't turn around, nor did she respond.

Chapter 53

BOBBY WALKED AROUND the quiet funeral home, inspecting the clean-up work. The place was immaculate. The staff must have worked diligently so that no one would have to work tomorrow, which was Sunday. There were no services scheduled so the funeral home would be empty until Monday morning.

Bobby relished the quiet and the solitude. He enjoyed being at the funeral home after hours like this. Some people might have considered it uncomfortable or even creepy, but for Bobby, it was his sanctuary. It was the place where he made his mark in the world, performing his ministry and helping people through the most difficult times they would ever experience. He felt at home there, connected to the very building itself. After the rough day he had had, there was no better place to find refuge and solace, particularly since his apartment would be filled with tension because of the way he had just treated Teresa.

He sat in his quiet office perusing the e-mails that had come in over the course of the day, the room lit only by the soft glow of his computer screen. Thirty minutes into his e-mail reading, the stillness was broken by a shrill beeping sound coming from the back room. Bobby recognized it immediately as the alarm on the funeral home's refrigeration unit, which was programmed to sound whenever the temperature rose above 39 degrees. He made his way into the back room and saw that the cooler's door was slightly ajar. He glanced at the thermometer on the outside of the cooler. It read 42 degrees, which meant that the door had not been open long. Nevertheless, he felt compelled to have a look inside and check the remains that were stored there.

He stepped into the walk-in cooler, shivering slightly as he did so. There were two bodies wrapped in white sheets resting on the shelf to his left and one on the shelf to his right. There was a clipboard with a stack of papers resting near each body, containing identification information as well as various instructions and authorization forms. One of the bodies must have come in that afternoon, as there had been only two in the cooler when he arrived at the funeral home that morning. He picked up one of the clipboards to see who the new case was. Before he could begin reading it, there was a sudden *whoosh*, followed by the sound of the door slamming as the lights were automatically extinguished. Bobby whirled in the direction of the door. He was immersed in total darkness. He stepped hesitantly toward the door with his arms outstretched like a blind man. His hand touched the cold stainless steel and he began pounding on it with his fist. "Hey! Anybody there? Open the door!"

There was no response. He listened carefully but heard nothing. He didn't know whether that meant nobody was there or whether the thick stainless steel door acted as a soundproof barrier. He groped to the right side of the door, where he knew there was an emergency release button. He couldn't locate it. In a panic, he reached for his belt, his panic diminishing just a tad as his hand grasped his cell phone. He turned on the flashlight feature and shone it on the cooler door and the wall just to the right of it. There was a gaping hole where the emergency release button had been. He shone the flashlight on the floor, revealing broken shards of red plastic, apparently the remnants of the shattered release button.

Bobby looked at the face of his cellphone. *No service.* He tried dialing anyway. Silence. He set his phone down on the shelf and looked around the tight quarters for anything that might enable him to pry the door open. He found a small stack of stainless steel trays designed to hold bodies. He lifted one and carried it to the door. It was far too thick to act as a wedge. The door was sealed tight, leaving only an impossibly thin seam. He smashed a clipboard with his foot and pried the metal clip off. Even that strip of steel was too thick to slide into the seam. He slammed his body into the door, shoulder first—it didn't budge. He repeated the maneuver over and over, hoping the force of his considerable bulk would wear out the locking mechanism. His shoulder began throbbing but the heavy steel door did not yield. He tried lying on his back and kicking the door with all the power his legs could muster, continuing the effort until the searing pain in his knees forced him to stop.

He realized he was shaking all over, partly out of fear and partly because of the cold. The normal operating temperature of the cooler was 37 degrees. He hadn't noticed the smell of the corpses when he had entered the cooler. Like most funeral directors, he had grown accustomed to it and developed a tolerance. Now it seemed heavy in the air and suffocatingly putrid. He fought off a wave of nausea.

He tried his cell phone again, in vain. He tried moving around the cramped cooler to see if some corner of it might have reception. The *No Service* message taunted him no matter where he positioned the phone. He resumed pounding on the door and yelling until he became hoarse. The clock on his cell phone read 10:15. It was still Saturday night. There would be no one coming into the funeral home until Monday morning, unless a new death call came in and one of the drivers delivered it to the funeral home sometime before Monday morning. It was late summer, the slowest time of the year in the funeral business, so the likelihood of a new case coming in over the next 35 hours was low.

His cell phone showed only 10% battery life remaining. He would need to turn off his phone to conserve power and keep trying periodically to see whether reception might come through at a different time. He turned off the flashlight and sat on the cold floor, his back propped up against the stainless steel door. He continued banging and knocking on it intermittently.

He was shivering uncontrollably now. He wrapped his arms across his chest, but it made little difference. All of his exposed skin was stinging with pain. After several hours of this, he stood up. He was stiff, and his mind was feeling sluggish. He turned on his cell phone and activated the flashlight feature, then set the phone on one of the empty shelves. He pulled one of the body trays forward on the rack, and with numb fingers, he began peeling the sheet off the remains. "I'm sorry," he whispered as he pushed the tray with the naked corpse back onto the rack and did the same with the other two bodies. He wrapped himself in the sheets and sat back down on the floor. He checked his cell phone again—still no service. The light began flickering, then it faded and then it vanished completely, plunging the small room into total darkness again. He pounded on the door for several more minutes, then he sprawled out along the length of the narrow walkway between the shelves on either side of the cooler. He tried to remain motionless, thinking his body would conserve energy if he could sleep. Physical agony and fear were winning out over sleep. He had no sense of time as the hours passed. He felt his mind becoming as numb as his body. The shivering seemed to subside as he drifted into unconsciousness.

Chapter 54

TERESA WAS HAPPY to see daylight. She had spent a long, sleepless night angry and afraid. Staying alone in her apartment after it had just been burglarized seemed foolish, but Bobby had told her that he wouldn't be gone long and then it got too late to make arrangements to go elsewhere. He hadn't returned. With the sunrise, her fear for her safety had diminished, but her anger with Bobby had escalated. It was bad enough that he'd been abrupt and mean with her, but staying out all night and leaving her alone was inexcusable under the circumstances.

She set about cleaning up the kitchen, thinking about what she wanted to say to him. She first put away all the pots, pans, dishes, cutlery and other items that were strewn around the kitchen but intact. Then she carefully picked up the larger shards of glass and broken ceramic before sweeping the floors and wiping off the counters with wet towels to pick up all the tiny slivers. She took a break around mid-morning to take a run in the park. She ran hard, still trying to clear her head and sort through her emotions.

Bobby had never stayed out all night. He had told her he would return. She knew that the funeral home was closed on Sundays. She thought about everything he had told her and about the break-in. Her anger with him was transforming into concern for his safety. As she approached her apartment building, she could see that Bobby's car was still gone. She climbed the stairs and saw a well-dressed woman standing outside her door, pressing the doorbell.

"Can I help you?" she called out. The woman turned to face her. It was Jenny Sanchez.

"Oh, hi Teresa. I'm looking for Bobby. Is he around?"

Teresa shook her head. "He's not here. I don't know where he is. Is something wrong?"

"We're supposed to have lunch today. He was going to call me last night so we could arrange the time and place, but he never did. I've been trying to reach him this morning but he's not answering his phone. I was in the neighborhood—at church—so I thought I'd stop by."

"We should talk. Let's go inside," Teresa said, easing past Jenny and opening the door. They sat on the living room sofa facing each other. Teresa couldn't help but notice that Jenny looked fabulous in her bright blue sundress, and she immediately felt self-conscious sitting there in running shorts and a sweat-soaked tee shirt. Jenny was out of her league in every way. No wonder Bobby was smitten. She pushed those thoughts out of her mind. "I'm worried, Jenny. Bobby went out around 7:00 last night and never came home. We—" She put her fist up to her mouth and abruptly stopped talking. She stood up and motioned toward the door and opened it. Jenny looked puzzled but quietly followed her outside.

"We can't talk in there," Teresa said. "I'll explain." They walked silently down the stairs and stopped in the parking lot. "Our house was burglarized yesterday. Bobby thinks it might be bugged, so we shouldn't talk in there. Anyway, as I was saying, Bobby didn't come home last night. We had a fight—he got really mean and told me to move out. Then he calmed down a bit and apologized and said he was going out for an hour or two, but he hasn't come back. I'm worried, Jenny. He told me everything—about your family, about Sal and Miguel, about all the strange things that have been happening. It's scary!"

"He told you all that?" Jenny looked incredulous. "I wish he hadn't—for your sake. So you said he was mean to you? I don't mean to pry but do you mind telling me what that was all about?"

Teresa recounted the previous evening's events and their conversation in as much detail as she could recall. "He's never even said a cross word to me before," Teresa said, her voice quiet, a pained look on her face. "And then he just went off on me last night. He was like a different person."

"That's strange. That doesn't sound like him."

"I think I'll take a drive by the funeral home," said Teresa. "Maybe he decided to sleep there or maybe some new cases came in and he got busy." She sounded unconvinced by her own words. "Care to join me?"

"Sure. I can drive. That's my car right there."

Fifteen minutes later they pulled into the funeral home parking lot. It was empty and the building appeared deserted. "Pull around back," Teresa said.

Jenny did as instructed. "There's his car!" she said as the black Buick came into view just outside the rear entrance.

They rang the bell and pounded on the door. No one answered. They pulled on the door handle, but it was locked. "I don't suppose you know the code?" Jenny asked as they stared at the keypad on the metal door.

"No. Let's try the front door." Teresa dialed Bobby's cell phone again. It went straight to voicemail. They rang the doorbell and knocked loudly on the front door, which was also locked. Again, there was no answer. Jenny noticed the sign underneath the doorbell, which provided a phone number to call for after-hours service. She dialed and got an answering service. She instructed the answering service that she needed to speak to a funeral director right away.

Within five minutes her phone rang. "This is Arturo Cepeda. I'm a funeral director with Norwood and Gonzalez Funeral Home. I just received your message from our answering service. How may I help you?" His voice was calm and sincere and utterly professional.

"Arturo, this is Jenny Sanchez. You may remember me—you helped with the service when my mom passed away recently."

"Yes, I remember, Ms. Sanchez. You're Miguel's sister. How may I help you?"

"It's Bobby. I think something may have happened to him. He didn't make it home last night. I'm at the funeral home right now with his roommate, Teresa, and his car's here but no one's answering the door. He's got to be in there and I'm afraid something's wrong. Can you get over here and let us inside? Please?"

"I just stepped out of church to take your call. I'm less than ten minutes away. I'll be right there."

Bobby had been lying on the floor for what seemed like an eternity. He had stopped shivering. His limbs were numb and stiff and he had a searing headache. He had been in a semi-conscious state for some time and he willed himself to sit up and try to remain awake. He feared that if he allowed himself to sleep he would never awaken. He intermittently banged the metal body tray against the stainless steel door, gripping it gingerly with his bruised hands. His brain felt dull, but he knew he needed to concentrate and focus on something to keep himself alert, so he thought about her. He thought about what a precious soul she was and how fortunate he was to have her in his life. He had thought so from the first time they met. He chastised himself for not being assertive and not pursuing her like he should have. He imagined a life together with her. There was nothing he wanted more. It felt good just to think about her and the possibilities.

Time passed—how much, he had no idea. He kept thinking about her. It felt good. It was comforting. It gave him a reason to keep fighting. He drifted in and out of consciousness, but he kept her in his thoughts. If he had to die here, at least she would be with him in his mind and heart.

***

Another black Buick careened into the parking lot and pulled up to the front door. The panic on the faces of the two young ladies was obvious. He turned the key and the three of them burst into the quiet building. "Hey Bobby! You in here?" Arturo called out in a loud voice. They made a beeline to Bobby's office, the young funeral director leading the way. A radio on the credenza was playing soft music. He moved the mouse next to Bobby's computer and the monitor lit up. The computer was still powered on.

"I'll check the men's room," Arturo said, hurrying off in that direction. Teresa and Jenny fanned out in opposite directions, toward the visitation rooms and the reception area. "He's not in there," Arturo called out, emerging from the restroom and following Jenny. Jenny stepped into the large, kitchen-like reception area and flipped on the lights. She turned around, shaking her head at Arturo. "Let's try the back room," he said leading the way past a row of offices and arrangement rooms and punching a code into a keypad on the door leading to the back room.

"Hey, Bobby! You in here?" he called out again as they hurried through the embalming room, the area around the cremation retort, and the garage, where the caskets and vehicles were stored. Arturo opened the door to each of the four vehicles and looked inside as Teresa and Jenny watched helplessly from just outside the large, stainless steel cooler. Arturo returned shaking his head, his hands outstretched, palms up, looking perplexed.

"We've searched every inch of this place," said Arturo. "He's not here."

"What now?" Teresa asked in a despondent voice.

"Maybe he spent the night with someone," Arturo suggested.

"I don't think so," said Teresa. "He's never done that as long as I've known him, and he just wasn't in the state of mind for that. Something's wrong. I just know it."

"Shhh! What's that?" Jenny asked in an urgent whisper.

They instantly became silent, straining to hear. At first there was no sound but the quiet hum of the refrigerator. Then they heard it. A faint metallic-sounding *tap, tap, tap*. Then it stopped.

They stood perfectly still, listening intently, eyes darting around the room trying to locate the source of the sound. *Tap, tap, tap*.

"Holy shit, someone's in there!" Arturo cried out, lunging toward the cooler. He punched in a number on a keypad and yanked the door handle. Bobby's body tumbled backwards out of the cooler as the door opened. He was wrapped in white sheets and looked nearly as gray as the corpses that normally occupied that space.

Teresa bent down and put a hand on his neck. "He's got a pulse! He's still breathing but he's ice cold. Call 911!"

Chapter 55

"YOU'RE LOOKING MUCH better today. Sounds like they'll be releasing you tomorrow or the next day. It's a good thing you're as big as you are. The doctor said having that much body mass really helped protect your organs."

Bobby smiled at Jenny from his bed. It had been four days since he was rushed to the hospital suffering from acute hypothermia. The first couple of days were touch and go, as the doctors fought to stabilize him. Jenny had been there every day but he had been in no position to speak with her. Now he was feeling alert and well on his way to being fully recovered. "I feel like I'm in a funeral home," he said, his eyes taking in the flower arrangements scattered around the hospital room. "I'm glad I'll be going back there soon—and not as a customer!"

"Me too!" she laughed. "You gave us quite a scare." She pulled up a chair, so that they could converse face-to-face. "Are you well enough to have a serious chat? I wanted to do this on our lunch date but you stood me up!"

"Sorry about that, but I'm a lot better today. I'm feeling up to just about anything."

Jenny looked at the ceiling, trying to compose her thoughts. "I'll come right to the point, Bobby. When you came back into my life, I was really happy. I had always remembered you fondly, and always hoped that our paths would cross again someday, but didn't really think it would ever happen. So when it did, I was thrilled. And when you asked if we could try again and pick up where we left off, part of me was even more thrilled. But I was going through a difficult time, with Mother's illness and then her death. On top of all that, Phil was pushing hard for a reconciliation. So when I told you that the timing was just bad, I was being completely truthful."

She paused and stared up at the ceiling again, looking more like a nervous teenager than a poised and accomplished college professor. "But I never stopped thinking about you and about whether it made sense to be something more than friends. I suppose all the recent upheaval in my life really got me thinking about what matters and what my priorities should be and what might be my best path to real happiness.

"So that's what I was planning to say to you on our lunch date, and I'm saying it to you now. If you're still open to it, I'd like to give it a shot. On paper, we're probably a lousy match, but what matters more is what our hearts say, and I'd never forgive myself if I didn't give this a chance." She stood up and squeezed his hand. "I know this may not be the best place to confront you with all this, especially on the heels of what you just went through, but I wanted to put it out there. Take your time and think it over, and we can talk more whenever you're ready."

She leaned over and kissed him tenderly on the lips. It lasted just a second, but Bobby's heart leapt. He was tempted to throw his arms around her and kiss her back, long and hard. He held her gaze, their eyes just inches apart. He had been captivated by those turquoise eyes long ago, and he once again felt mesmerized.

He caressed her hand. "Jenny, I don't need more time to think about this. My entire life, I've been hoping and praying that this day would come." He closed his eyes for a long moment, then looked at the face that had first enchanted him over twenty years ago. "But... now that the opportunity is here... I just can't do it. It wouldn't be right. I have strong feelings for you, Jenny. I always have and I probably always will. But the truth is, there's someone else in my life. I didn't even realize it until a few days ago. When I was in that cooler, thinking my time might be up, all I could think about was her. She's my best friend. She's the kindest, most thoughtful person I've ever known. I can talk to her about anything, like I'm talking to my soulmate. I've taken her for granted, but when I was faced with leaving this earth, the person I felt most connected to and most sorry to leave was her. And the crazy thing is, I don't even know if she'll have me! I've hurt her and may have driven her away. But I've got to find out. I'm sorry, Jenny, I really am. Under any other circumstances, this would have been a dream come true for me."

Jenny looked down and blinked rapidly. She wiped a tear from her eye with her forefinger. "There's no need to be sorry, Bobby. I'm the one who told you it wouldn't work, so I have no right to expect that you wouldn't find somebody else. You will always hold a special place in my heart, no matter what the future brings. And who knows what might happen down the road." She kissed him on the cheek and walked toward the door. She stopped in the entryway and turned around. "It's Teresa, isn't it?"

Bobby looked surprised. "How did you know?"

Jenny smiled. "For a smart guy, you can be oblivious to some things, Bobby. She lights up whenever she's with you and you do the same whenever you're around her. I think the whole world probably sees it—except you, apparently."

"I was so rotten to her the last time we spoke. I was just trying to protect her. I needed her to get away from me and all this craziness we're dealing with, for her own good, so I said some nasty things just to make her leave. I hope I haven't blown it."

"Bye, Bobby."

Chapter 56

TERESA HAD SPENT the past four nights with a college friend in New Braunfels, about 30 miles northeast of San Antonio. She didn't relish the long commute to and from work on Interstate 35 but staying alone in her apartment after the burglary was out of the question.

She had visited Bobby in the hospital every day and did her best to act as if things were normal between them. Bobby had apologized multiple times for the way he had treated her following the break-in and wanted to talk about it, but she had just smiled and told him not to worry—they could have that conversation once he was released from the hospital. She just wasn't ready for it yet. There was much to discuss, but Bobby was still recovering and medicated, so it didn't feel right to confront him with a host of serious issues while he was in that state in a hospital bed. Also, what they needed to discuss required the utmost privacy, and a hospital room was not conducive to that. Bobby was going to be released Thursday morning and she planned to meet him for lunch. They would talk then.

Early Thursday morning, Teresa climbed into her Volkswagen to make the long drive to work. Although the drive was barely 30 miles, it had been taking her close to an hour due to the rush hour traffic on I-35. She drove slowly through the neighborhood between her friend's home and the freeway, since there were two school zones in that one-mile stretch of road. Traffic was heavy as she approached the entrance ramp to the freeway. She had always hated this merge, because the ramp led directly into a lane of traffic traveling at full speed, with virtually no space for gradual merging.

She accelerated once she hit the ramp, and immediately sensed that something was wrong with her car. Her eyes darted to the dashboard. No warning indicators were illuminated. She continued accelerating, using her rear and side-view mirrors and glancing over her left shoulder to gauge the distance between her vehicle and the cars in the right lane rushing toward her. Her little Volkswagen started pulling hard to the left. It felt wobbly. There were vehicles behind her moving at the same rate of speed and she was already committed to entering the freeway and hitting the narrow gap that had formed between the entrance ramp and the cars speeding toward her in the right line. *Must be a flat tire*, she thought. She'd have to pull off to the shoulder as soon as she could, but there was no shoulder here, just two fast-moving lanes of traffic converging over a very short distance.

She punched the accelerator harder as she made it to the freeway. The car lurched violently and pulled her to the left, into the next lane of traffic. Then the car pitched downward and further to the left. She heard the sound of metal scraping against asphalt for just an instant before she felt the impact and heard a sickening crunch as another vehicle rammed her from behind. The freeway became a blur as her car spun around. Her airbag exploded, striking her hard in the face. Horns blared and brakes screeched. She heard another crunching sound of metal hitting metal, and then another.

Then everything was still. She felt herself shaking uncontrollably. With trembling hands, she pulled the airbag away from her face. She felt blood oozing from a gash above her eye where the airbag had smashed into her sunglasses. She flexed her arms and then felt for her legs. Everything seemed to be intact. A young man pounded on her window and she saw others running toward her. "Are you OK?" he was yelling. She didn't answer. She looked around at the scene in a daze. Cars were stopped. Some were smashed. Some were facing sideways or completely turned around. Her car seemed to be facing the right direction, but straddled two lanes, the front left corner of the vehicle drooping downward.

"Hey miss! Can you open the door?" the young man yelled. She pulled the handle. Strong but gentle hands helped her exit the vehicle. Her legs buckled but he grabbed her forearm and then put an arm around her shoulder, guiding her as she walked slowly and unsteadily away from the wreck. The scene was utter chaos. The three right lanes were completely stopped and resembled a massive parking lot, with multiple wrecks forming roadblocks. The far-left lane was moving at a snail's pace but was inching by. Sirens wailed, and she could see the flashing lights of the approaching emergency vehicles.

"What happened?" she stammered as she stared at the mess that she had apparently caused. "Was anybody hurt?"

"I think everyone's OK—just wrecked cars," said the young man. "You're lucky. Your front tire came flying off and bounced all the way across the freeway. Someone hit you from behind and your car did a complete 360. It's a miracle you didn't get hurt."

***

After being released from the hospital, Bobby headed straight to the funeral home. He had assured the doctors that he would rest for another day or two before returning to work, but he wanted to stop in briefly to say hello to his team and make sure that they had adequate staffing lined up for any services that might have come in while he was out. He also needed to catch up with all the text messages and voicemails people had left him. At the doctor's urging, he had kept his phone turned off. After that, he would meet Teresa for lunch and then head home to rest.

"Hi, Cheri! I'm back!" He flashed a big smile at the elderly receptionist as he walked in the front door.

"Thank goodness you're OK, Mr. Bobby. I've been praying for you." Her usually smiling face looked troubled. "Teresa's called a couple of times this morning. She's been in an accident. She'd like you to call her right away."

His stomach did a somersault. "An accident? What happened? Is she OK?"

"It was a traffic accident on the freeway. She sounds pretty shook up and she was calling from a hospital."

Bobby raced into his office and slammed the door, a host of scary possibilities swirling through his mind as he punched the speed dial on his cell phone. "T? Are you OK? What's going on?"

"I'm OK—just really shaken up. It was so scary, Bobby!"

He could hear her weeping softly and felt tears welling up in his own eyes at the sound of her voice. "What happened?"

"My tire came off just as I was getting on the freeway. I couldn't control my car and someone slammed into me and spun me around. It all happened so fast. I thought for sure I was about to be killed. I'm lucky to be alive."

"I'm on my way, T! Where are you?'

"I'm in Santa Rosa Hospital, in New Braunfels. I probably didn't need to come here but the police insisted that I get checked out. My face is cut up and bruised from the airbag, but otherwise I'm OK. I really want to get back to San Antonio today, but my car's totaled. If you could give me a lift, I'd really appreciate it."

"Like I said, I'm on my way. I'll be there in less than an hour. And T—" He bit his lip to keep his voice from breaking. "I'm so glad you're OK."

He pushed the end call button and gasped for breath. His heart was pounding and he was shaking all over as he contemplated the fact that he had almost lost her. Shock transformed into rage as he thought about the possible cause.

Chapter 57

BOBBY SCROLLED THROUGH the contacts on his cell phone as he hurried to his car. He found the name *Michael Sanchez* and looked at the array of numbers Sal had provided when they were discussing funeral arrangements for Mrs. Sanchez. He dialed the first number, which was designated *Michael Sanchez—Mobile*. There was no answer other than a message telling him the voice mailbox was full. He sat in his car and typed a text message to that number. *Hi Rocket. It's Bobby. Please call me right away. It's urgent!*

He put the car in gear and punched in the next number as he drove out of the funeral home's parking lot. "Campaign Office—this is Cindy," came the cheerful voice manning the phone in the San Antonio office that had once served as campaign headquarters for presidential candidate Miguel Sanchez. It was now a local campaign office for the Connett/Sanchez ticket. "How may I help you?"

"Hi Cindy, this is Bobby Rivera. I'm a friend of Mr. Sanchez and I need to reach him right away. It's urgent."

"I'm sorry, but Mr. Sanchez isn't here right now. I'm not exactly sure when he's going to make it this way again. He's on the road campaigning."

"I realize that, but can you get a message to him?"

"I'll do my best, but he can be hard to reach when he's on the campaign trail."

He thanked her and then dialed Sal's law office and the national campaign headquarters in Washington, with similar results. He put his phone down and turned his attention to the mission ahead of him.

An hour later, he walked into the emergency room at Santa Rosa Hospital. A nurse led him back into an area where a dozen patient "rooms" were formed by curtain partitions. She pulled back one of the partitions and led him into the small compartment where Teresa was sitting up in a hospital bed holding an icepack to her face. Teresa removed the icepack when she saw him. The area under her left eye was red and swollen and a white bandage covered the gash just above her eyebrow.

"Guess I must look like a boxer," she said.

Bobby stood there with his mouth agape. He had spent most of the drive thinking about exactly what he wanted to say to her, but words escaped him. "I've seen worse," he said, smiling weakly. He stood glued to the floor staring mutely at her face. It was a face that had always been so naturally pretty and radiant, exuding good health and a cheerful confidence. Now it was bruised and battered, the liveliness normally present in her dark eyes replaced by a look of fear and uncertainty.

He sucked in a deep breath, making an audible shuddering sound as tears filled his eyes and cascaded down his cheeks. "I am so sorry, T," he stammered. "When I think about what could have happened…"

She hoisted herself off the bed and threw herself into his arms. Bobby wrapped her in a tight embrace, squeezing her banged up body as hard as he dared, both of them weeping quietly. "It's all my fault," Bobby whispered in her ear, his tears trickling down the side of her neck. "I treated you so badly… I didn't want to… it just tore me up… I just wanted you to be safe and I thought you needed to be away from me. I didn't want to see you get hurt… and now this… The thought of losing you… I just can't bear it. I don't ever want to lose you… I'm so sorry…"

"It's OK, Bobby… I'm OK," she whispered hoarsely as they gently swayed back and forth.

***

Bobby surveyed the crowd outside The Wells Fargo Arena on the Arizona State campus. Two days had passed and Sal had not returned any of his many phone calls. He was unwilling to wait any longer, so he had caught a Southwest flight to Phoenix, determined to catch up with his old friend on the campaign trail.

Security was tight, as legions of young people had flocked to see the dynamic young vice-presidential candidate give another one of his rousing speeches. It had become obvious that Hugh Connett had made an ideal choice for a running mate, as Miguel Sanchez had proven to be brilliant at drawing crowds and inspiring a level of passion and enthusiasm rarely seen in recent memory. As classes resumed for the fall semester, college campuses were now an ideal setting for his campaign rallies, since younger voters were among his most enthusiastic constituents, but his support had been rapidly spreading among all age groups and across the racial, ethnic and religious spectrums. His rallies were media events and the crowds were standing-room-only, requiring him to search for ever larger venues.

Bobby had arrived at the arena nearly two hours before the scheduled speech, hoping to snag a good seat and perhaps get lucky enough to catch the candidate before he took the stage. Even at that early hour, there were long lines at every entrance. It took him over an hour to pass through security and make his way into the arena. There were rows of folding chairs covering the main floor that normally served as a basketball court. Those seats were nearly full, and the mezzanine and balcony levels were filling quickly as well.

Bobby made his way toward the front and found one of the last empty seats in the fifth row. He noticed several young volunteers walking up and down the aisles handing out campaign fliers. He asked the girl next to him to save his seat and he approached one of the volunteers, a preppy-looking young man wearing an Arizona State golf shirt adorned with a big Connett/Sanchez button. "Hi there!" he called out. "I was hoping you could do me a favor."

"I'll try," the young man responded cheerfully.

"I'm an old friend of Miguel Sanchez. Came all the way here from Texas for this event. Can you get a message to him for me?"

"Sorry, I don't think I have the clout. I'm just passing out these fliers. I'm not sure I'm even going to get to meet him. Why don't you ask one of those guys?" He nodded to a couple of Secret Service agents standing in front of the stage.

Bobby looked in the direction of the agents. They looked grim and serious. "Good idea, maybe I'll try that," he said, returning to his seat. He looked at his watch. The start of the rally was still thirty minutes off. He scanned the room, trying to assess his options. He might have to wait until the speech was over. The candidate usually worked the ropes, shaking hands with his supporters after his speeches. As Bobby surveyed the room trying to figure out where a rope line might be set up, he noticed a third Secret Service agent approach the stage and strike up a conversation with the two agents who were already positioned there. He recognized the face. It was Tony, the lead agent assigned to the candidate and the agent he had worked closely with when they were coordinating Mrs. Sanchez's funeral.

Bobby approached the stage. Tony had his back to him and the other two agents gave him a hard look. "Excuse me," Bobby said speaking loudly over the crowd noise. "Tony?"

The agent turned and stared at him. Recognition set in quickly and his faced brightened. "Hello, Bobby," he said as if they were old friends. "You're a long way from home. What are you doing here?" They shook hands.

"Bobby glanced at the other two agents and then back at Tony. "Can we talk for a minute?" he asked.

"Sure. What's up?" They walked away from the other agents, turning at the corner of the stage, putting them in an area that was off limits to visitors.

"I need to speak with Mr. Sanchez about a family matter. It's really important."

"I'll get word to him."

"Great. I really appreciate it, Tony. Will I be able to catch him after the speech? I just need a few minutes."

"To be candid, Bobby, I don't know. He's got a very tight schedule today. We're heading to Tucson from here and then to San Diego tonight. But I'll be sure he knows you're here and that you'd like to see him."

Bobby watched the speech, mesmerized like just about everyone else in attendance. He was struck by the stage presence and the masterful oratory coming from his old high school friend. The VP candidate worked the crowd into a frenzy and left the stage when the frenzy was at its height. He bounded down the stairs as the crowd surged toward the rope, hoping to shake the hand of the rising political star who had just inspired them. Bobby elbowed his way to the front, apologizing as he bulldozed his way through the crowd. He positioned himself right in the center of the rope line and watched as the candidate worked his way through the line, pressing flesh and exchanging greetings. He gripped Bobby's big hand before he looked at his face. Bobby held his hand firmly. "Great speech, Rocket!"

For an instant, the candidate looked startled then he quickly composed himself and flashed a bright smile. "Bobby! Great to see you! What are you doing here?"

"I came to see you," Bobby said. "We need to talk—in private. Can you spare a few minutes after you finish up here?"

"I've got a plane to catch, pal, and I'm already running late. I'll be back in San Antonio in a couple of weeks. Let's talk then." He attempted to loosen his grip and started leaning toward the next outstretched hand.

Bobby tightened his grip. "It's urgent! I wouldn't be here if it wasn't. We really need to talk now!"

Sal looked irritated, then he glanced over his shoulder at the Secret Service agent standing just a few feet behind him. "Tony! Take Bobby backstage. I'll be there as soon as I finish up here."

Tony nodded at another agent who took his place behind the candidate, and then led Bobby around the back of the stage to an office underneath the stands that was used by visiting basketball coaches. Bobby sat behind the desk and Tony kept him company until the candidate bustled in twenty minutes later. "Give us a few minutes, Tony," Sal instructed.

Tony closed the door behind him and Sal took a seat in front of the desk, opposite Bobby. "You caught me off guard out there," he said. "I take it this isn't just a social visit."

"It's not," said Bobby leaning forward and staring intently at his old friend. "There's some bad stuff going on, and if you don't know about it, you should."

Sal looked both confused and annoyed. "What are you talking about?"

"Someone tried to kill me. Someone tried to kill my roommate. My apartment has been bugged. And I think your campaign is behind this!"

"That's crazy, Bobby! What makes you think—"

"Listen—here's the story. First, Ricky dies suddenly. Maybe that's an accident, but maybe not. In any event, it's convenient for you. That leaves only me and Jenny knowing your secret. Then right after I told you about the letters and pictures that I gave to Mrs. Sanchez, Jenny's house is burglarized. And guess what? Nothing was taken except those letters and pictures. Then I made the mistake of telling my roommate the whole story—and I haven't told anyone else, by the way. I told her that I kept some of those letters and pictures—and then my house is ransacked the very next day. During that same conversation with Teresa, I mentioned that if someone was onto you, they could simply dig up Miguel's body and prove that he's him and you're you. That very night someone tries to dig up his body. Someone must have been eavesdropping on Teresa and me. And it gets worse—"

Sal put a finger to his lips and opened the door a crack. Tony was standing across the hall, about eight feet away. "We'll just be a few more minutes, Tony." He closed the door. "Keep your voice down, OK?" Sal asked in a hushed voice. "Go on. What else?" He was frowning and looking like he might be sick.

"Then someone tried to kill me—at the funeral home. Locked me in the freezer. It almost worked! And then a few days ago, my roommate winds up in the hospital after a car wreck. The front tire came flying off her car at 60 miles an hour on I-35. The police said her lug nuts must have come loose. Lug nuts don't just come loose by themselves!"

"Have you contacted the police about any of this?"

"No—not yet anyway. But I'm not going to let this continue. I told you I have no interest in politics. I was disturbed when I found out what you were doing, but I had no intention of getting involved, partly out of loyalty to you as an old friend, and partly because I just didn't want to invite trouble. But I'm not going to stand around and do nothing if it means that Jenny's life is in danger, or Teresa's, or mine!"

Sal leaned forward and rubbed his forehead. "Shit!" he hissed through clenched teeth. "Sonofabitch! Listen to me, Bobby. I don't know anything about any of this. I swear to God, I'm not involved. I've told you before that I've never forgotten the kindness you showed to me when we were kids and that I've always considered you to be a special person in my life. I meant that. I would never do anything to harm you or anyone close to you. I've also told you that there are some dangerous and powerful people behind the scenes. Politics is a dirty business. I know that, and I've made peace with that, but this kind of shit—it's not OK! I will get to the bottom of this, I promise you."

Sal stood up and walked to the front of the desk, placing both fists on it as he leaned in toward Bobby. "I know you have no reason to trust me, but I'm telling you, I had nothing to do with this! I don't know anything about it. But you have my word—I will look into it immediately. I hope to God that no one on my team was involved in any way. Whether they were or weren't, I will make sure that no one associated with my team will ever lift a finger against you or Jenny or Teresa. I will stake my life on that!"

Chapter 58

MICHAEL SANCHEZ WALKED across the bustling campus, a Secret Service agent at his side and another trailing about 20 yards behind. Normally, visits to Yale stirred up feelings of nostalgia as well as excitement about the future because they typically involved visits with Professor Vega. Today, all he could feel was raw, simmering anger. That had been a constant state of mind since his meeting with Bobby Rivera at Arizona State.

He had completely altered his campaign travel schedule to make this trip, which required considerable explaining to the campaign team. He justified it as a series of rallies at some of the Ivy League schools to further amp up the student get-out-the-vote efforts. There would likely be greater media coverage at the Ivies than at most other schools and he could hit several of them on the same short trip because of their close proximity to one another. Also, it would underscore his Yale pedigree.

One agent stationed himself at the entryway to the faculty office building while another followed him inside, positioning himself at the end of the corridor, giving himself a clear view of Professor Vega's office without seeming intrusive. The door was shut. Michael knocked firmly. It opened, and a familiar face greeted him, only it was not the face he expected.

He stepped inside without a word and waited for Francisco Vargas to close the door behind him. "What the hell are you doing here, Vargas? I don't recall inviting you!"

Vargas sat down in the Professor's chair behind the old mahogany desk, motioning for Michael to take a seat opposite him. Michael remained standing, legs planted wide, his arms folded, staring coldly. Vargas casually lit a cigarette. "You were pretty agitated when you contacted me after the visit from your funeral director friend. In fact, you were downright rude to me, but that didn't concern me. It was your request that concerned me."

"You haven't answered my question. I didn't ask to meet with you, or the Professor, for that matter. I asked to meet with *him*."

"I'd say it was more of a demand than a request. I'm here to assess the situation and decide whether facilitating such a meeting makes sense."

"Listen, Vargas, I don't have time to be playing games. I'm about to be vice president of the goddamn United States of America, one of the most visible and powerful positions on the planet. I'd say I've earned the right to meet him. There are some very serious issues to discuss. Issues that could derail everything. So, have you arranged a meeting or not?"

Vargas took a long drag from his cigarette and slowly blew the smoke in Michael's direction. "Maybe. But first I need to understand where you're coming from. You were pretty hostile when we last spoke—threatening even. I'm trying to determine where your head is."

Michael bit his lip and fumed quietly. It was becoming apparent that Vargas was the gateway between him and the man he wanted to meet and that it would be counterproductive to antagonize him. "Look, I'm sorry I blew up at you, Vargas," he said in a voice that was steady, and bordering on contrite. "I was angry—I've told you some of the reasons, without going into detail—but mostly I was concerned, and I still am. I'm afraid this thing could explode in our faces if we're not careful. This is so important that I really feel like I need to see him face-to-face to be sure he understands the risks that are out there. I'm the one in the best position to make sure he understands those risks."

"And I'm assessing the risks, too—one of which is having you go off the reservation and forget how you got here."

"I will never forget," Michael said in his most sincere voice. "Everything I am I owe to him. I can't imagine where I'd be if it weren't for him—probably back in Central America, living in some shithole. I would do anything he asks. Even if he told me to withdraw from this race tomorrow, I'd do it in a heartbeat. I might want to debate him about it first," he said with a grin, "but I would do it. I will be eternally grateful for everything he's done for me. Please tell him that, Vargas."

"Why don't you tell him yourself," Vargas said.

The door to the private restroom opened and Professor Vega stepped out. "Hello, Michael. I'm sorry about the little cat and mouse game here, but Francisco was under strict orders to get a reading on your loyalty before introducing you to your benefactor. You passed with flying colors!"

Michael looked bewildered. "It's nice to see you, Professor, as always. When Vargas suggested we meet here because it would be unlikely to arouse suspicions, I thought that made perfect sense. I figured you might be here, but I was really hoping that our mutual friend might be here with you."

Vargas and the Professor glanced at each other in silence.

Michael looked from one to the other. "Look, I'm happy to share with both of you the information I want to share with our leader, but I was really hoping to visit directly with him rather than communicate through intermediaries. No offense, Professor, but as you probably heard me telling Vargas, I'm concerned that we're at a potential crisis point, and I don't want anything getting lost in translation. There are some things going on that I think are best communicated directly by me."

The Professor looked at Vargas with just a trace of a smile around the corners of his lips and nodded almost imperceptibly at Vargas. "Michael, I'd like to introduce you to your godfather," Vargas said.

Michael started, then looked from one to the other, expectantly. "Where is he? Is he hiding out in there, too?" He looked at the closed restroom door.

Professor Vega stepped forward. "Michael, I am Juan Carlos Vega Calderon. Your father was my closest friend. I miss him greatly, but it has been a pleasure watching you grow up. You are so much like him. I was honored when he asked me to be your godfather. Many have asked that of me, but I have always declined. You are the only one. You have made me very proud and I know your father would be proud."

Michael stared in open-mouthed disbelief. "I don't understand. So *you* were El Jefe? The leader and special friend my father talked about? He mentioned that you were a scholar. That fits. But then who is the soldier and the revolutionary? Who is *Señor* Calderon, the businessman? Who is El Cazador? Does he even exist?"

The Professor slowly poured tobacco into his pipe from the old leather pouch and struck a stick match against the desk. The flame ducked and danced in and out of his pipe as he sucked in puffs of air. He blew a smoke ring and watched it rise. "Some have called me El Cazador in the past. I have been that person when it suited me, mostly long ago. In another time and place, strong-arm techniques were a very effective means of cultivating influence and power. That provided the capital I needed to develop my business enterprises. Everyone now knows of Calderon Enterprises, my family business. I stay out of the limelight and allow my brother Diego to be the face of the company, but it's really all me. In that realm, I am known as Carlos Calderon, the reclusive scion of a vast business empire that includes agriculture, manufacturing, publishing, energy, utilities and a host of other very profitable enterprises. In today's world—in this country and south of the border—I find that being a billionaire gives me tremendous influence. Whether it's financing political campaigns or causes, providing jobs and business opportunities, controlling the media, or countless other avenues of influence, having real wealth translates into power on a grand scale. But deep down, I'm still a scholar at heart, and most comfortable in academia. In that world, I go by Juan Carlos Vega. My mother was named Susanna Calderon and my father was Vincente Vega. I use both names. The naming conventions in our culture can be convenient, don't you think?"

Michael continued staring, eyes wide, a look of incredulity on his face. "I never imagined... Did my father know this?"

"Of course he did, but other than Francisco here—and now you—very few people know my story. Your father taught me a valuable lesson long ago and it has served me well: Information can be a source of vast power or great vulnerability. When you have information about someone that is not commonly known, you have power over them. If others have information about you, you are vulnerable because that information can be exploited. Make it a point to know everything you can about others you must deal with, whether they be friends, enemies, business associates or even family, but always keep at least some secrets from even those closest to you."

"I guess my entire life is a testament to that, isn't it?" said Michael.

"So it is," Vega replied. "And because of that secret, you will always be vulnerable."

"That's why I am here. I *am* vulnerable, and things have been happening that I fear are increasing that vulnerability rather than controlling it."

"Tell me more."

Michael shot a look at Vargas. "That's OK," said Vega. "He can stay. He needs to hear this, too."

Michael looked from one to the other, then fixed his eyes on the Professor. "So here's what I came here to say. There have been some disturbing developments involving people who are close to me. As you know, my adoptive mother died a few months ago, which was a stroke of good luck. We don't have to worry about her sharing things she shouldn't. But since then, there have been other things…"

The Professor blew another smoke ring and watched it float toward the ceiling. "Such as?"

"First, Ricky Sanchez dies just a few days after he finds out he's not really my brother. He was a lowlife and it was considered an overdose, so nobody really questioned it. But then right on the heels of that, someone breaks in to Jenny's house and steals some letters and pictures that could tie me back to San Mateo."

"And there's a problem with that?" Vargas asked. "Seems to me that if there is troublesome evidence out there and it disappears, that's a good thing."

"Not if she gets so terrorized that she decides to start talking to the police or the media or somebody else!" Michael shot back, an edge in his voice. "And it gets worse. The funeral director—Bobby Rivera—he mentions the break-in to the young lady he's living with. Tells her that he has more letters and pictures and mentions that it would be easy to dig up the real Miguel in San Mateo, and the next thing anyone knows, his place is ransacked, and someone tries to dig up Miguel's grave. His place has clearly been bugged and he knows it. Then someone locks Bobby in a freezer and almost kills him. Then his roommate is involved in a car wreck. Someone loosened the lug nuts on her tire and she gets on the freeway and almost gets killed. This is getting out of hand!" He glared at Vargas. "I told you to lay off the funeral director—he's harmless and he's my friend. Going after him is not OK!"

"Take the emotion out of this and look at it logically, Michael," Vega said calmly, tapping his pipe on an ashtray. "We just talked about the fact that information creates vulnerability. The only people who know your secret are the funeral director, his roommate and Jenny. The reality is that as long as they're out there, you're at risk. Our entire cause is at risk. We are on the cusp of changing the course of history, of effectuating massive change in the very fabric of American government, with repercussions for millions of our people, in this country and throughout Latin America. There is far too much at stake to be taking chances."

"But we are taking chances—that's my point! We're *increasing* our risk level. If these people feel threatened, don't you think they're more likely to cause problems? Besides, I care about these people, and it's not OK that no one consulted me about this."

"The less you know about this kind of thing, the better," said Vargas, his eyes narrowing and a hard edge in his voice.

"I'm not talking to you, Vargas," Michael shot back. "Professor, like I said, I've got a real problem with this! And taking the emotion out of it, as you suggest, I think this is very unwise. Messing with these people just increases our risk. If they're scared, they're more likely to cause trouble. And if there are any more tragedies involving my family or people close to my family, it's going to start looking suspicious. The two biggest problems are out of the picture and no one is asking questions. Let's not invite closer scrutiny."

"Michael, this is a simple matter of risk management and cost-benefit analysis," said Vega. "The benefits of achieving our goal are incalculable. We are closer than any of us ever thought we would be. It doesn't make sense to take foolish chances. We must do what we must to manage this risk," he said in a tone of icy finality.

Michael's eyes blazed. "And I must do what I must—I'm the candidate! I'm in the driver's seat. You certainly helped along the way, and I was sincere when I said that I will always be grateful, but I made this happen! I will be calling the shots when I get to Washington. I think I deserve some respect and deference. And I'm telling you to back off—leave these people alone!"

Vega stared hard at his protégé. "Don't forget the Cause, my friend," he said, his voice thick with menace. "It would be easy for someone to let ego and power go to his head when he has achieved what you have, particularly at such a young age. But remember where you came from. Remember the Cause. We've been committed to that mission for a long time. That's what matters."

"I've been hearing about the goddamn Cause my entire life—first from my father and then you two drilling it into my head over the years. I embraced it and obsessed over it, but now I'm starting to think I've been brainwashed. I'm not going to be anybody's tool. I will make a difference, but I will be my own man. I'm just a few months away from the vice presidency. I will wield a level of power never before known to that office. I will utilize our friends in Congress and our friends in the lobbying world and all the other allies you have recruited, and I will really make things happen. The way things are playing out, the presidency will be a virtual certainty. So don't be treating me like I'm still your student. My mind is my own and my decisions will be my own. And if your cause tells you that people close to me need to be sacrificed, then that's not my cause, so back the fuck off!"

He stormed out of the office, slamming the door behind him. "C'mon, Tony. Let's get out of here," he snarled as he breezed past the agent standing just inside the building's ancient wooden doors.

"Everything OK, sir?" the agent asked, observing the unmistakable scowl on the candidate's face.

"Yeah, everything's fine. These ivory tower types drive me nuts. I just had some professor with his head up his ass trying to tell me how to run the country, that's all."

***

"That was most unsettling, Francisco." Vega tapped his pipe against the desk, his eyes fixed on the door that had just slammed shut.

"Yes it was. What do you want me to do?"

"He's not thinking straight. We need to act quickly and decisively whether he's onboard with it or not. Tie up the loose ends and do it fast."

"Consider it done. Anything else?"

"I'm afraid we are at risk of losing control of our most valuable asset. We need to watch him very closely. I truly hope it doesn't come to this, but we may have to cut him loose. Be prepared for that possibility."

"We may have already lost him."

"You may be right, Francisco, and that would be a monumental tragedy. I saw his talent from an early age and always thought he could play a valuable role in our efforts, but never in my wildest dreams did I imagine he would rise to these heights, and at such a young age. We have a golden opportunity with him. We may never get another one this good, but if he's not fully on board, then he becomes dangerous. He becomes a liability. We can't put the Cause at risk. The mission will just have to continue on a longer timetable. We have plenty of other assets in the right places who can assist us. For now, let's monitor this closely. Maybe he was just blowing off steam. But if it looks like we've lost control of him, you know what to do."

Vargas rubbed the stubs of his missing fingers. "If it comes to that, I will do what I must."

Chapter 59

"HERE YOU GO, Sal. These are Ricky's ashes." Bobby slid a black rectangular plastic box across his desk toward Sal. "This is just a temporary container. You can buy an urn if you'd like something nicer looking."

Sal looked like he had been handed a box of snakes. "What am I supposed to do with this?"

"Whatever you want. You can scatter them, you can keep them, you can put them in a cemetery. It's your call. The funeral contract and the cremation authorization paperwork provide that Ricky's remains are to be returned to you. Now you have them."

Sal pushed them back across the desk. "I don't want them. I only made this appointment so I could come here and we could have a place to talk that wouldn't look suspicious. Keep them a while longer, OK? I'll tell the agents in the car that I decided to have them buried alongside his mother and that you're making arrangements."

"That's fine," said Bobby. "Now tell me what you came to tell me. Then I've got something I want to show you."

"I took care of things. You don't have anything to worry about now, neither does Jenny or Teresa."

"What do you mean 'you took care of things?'"

"Like I've told you before, there are some powerful people who are very interested in seeing my campaign succeed—and they are very interested in seeing that the past stays in the past. I explained to them what's been happening around here. They admitted nothing, but I read them the riot act. I told them that those kinds of things have no place in my campaign—that I would cut all ties with them if any of you were harmed or subjected to even the slightest harassment. I really came on strong and they know I mean business. They gave me their word. I'm quite confident that none of you will have any further problems."

Bobby looked unconvinced. "That doesn't really put my mind at ease. The word of some shady, nameless characters who admit nothing doesn't exactly sound reassuring. So I want you to tell them something for me, Sal. I want you to tell them about this." He opened his desk drawer and pulled out a bulky manila envelope, which he handed across the desk to Sal. "Have a look."

Sal pulled out a stack of papers about half an inch thick. "What's this?" he asked.

"That's an insurance policy. Take a close look at it. You can keep those. They're just photocopies. I still have the originals."

Sal flipped through the pages slowly, reading every word, his countenance turning increasingly grim. There were three letters addressed to Jenny Sanchez, dated approximately 20 years earlier. The letters expressed condolences over the recent death of her brother, Miguel Sanchez. The letters referenced the sudden and unexplained departure of the Sanchez family from San Mateo and two of them also mentioned the disappearance of Sal Rios at the same time the Sanchez family had vanished.

There was a copy of a photograph of Miguel's gravestone, bearing his name and date of death. At the bottom of that page was a handwritten note that read: *These remains have been moved for safekeeping. The sender of this letter knows their current location.*

Finally, there was a copy of a picture that Sal recognized immediately. Three teenaged boys in football uniforms. A handwritten note was scrawled across the bottom of the picture: *Number 22 above is Sal Rios, 77 is Bobby Rivera and number 30 is Miguel Sanchez. Each one of them signed his name in his own blood on the back of this picture. Compare the picture to the team photo in the school yearbook. Check the DNA from the blood sample to verify identities.*

Sal looked nauseous. "You can have those," Bobby said. "I kept the originals and I gave them to someone I trust with strict instructions that the originals should be sent to the FBI and copies sent to every major newspaper in the country if anything unfortunate should happen to me or Jenny or Teresa. I want you to share that information with these powerful people behind your campaign you keep telling me about."

"What are you doing, Seventy-Seven? I thought we were friends. Are you trying to ruin me? I'm so close to fulfilling a dream for our people. I'm so close to being able to bring about real change in this country. Why are you turning on me?"

"I'm trying to protect my friends, since their connection with you seems to have dangerous consequences. And I'm trying to stay alive."

"So this only sees the light of day if something happens to you or the girls?"

"It will definitely be front page news if that happens. Beyond that, I haven't decided what to do. I may decide to release it anyway."

"Why? What good would come of that? Whose interest would be served?"

"I'm an American, Sal, and I am proud of it. This is a great country. It's provided wonderful opportunities for millions of people like you and me. Maybe I owe it to my country to stand up for what's right here."

Sal slammed the papers on the desk as he moved to the edge of his seat and leaned in. "Listen, Bobby. You can't do that! It would be my death warrant—and yours! If I drop out of the race because of this, I am no longer of any use to these people. I become much more of a liability than an asset. And you'll be a dead man, too. So will your friends. I know how these people operate. They're big on sending messages. They will want the whole world to see that anyone who crosses them will pay for it. As long as you're alive, you won't ever be safe. They'll find you and it won't take long."

"You're glaring at me like I'm betraying you. I haven't done any such thing, at least not yet. I'm the one who was almost killed, and so was Teresa. So cut the crap and stop trying to act like you're the victim here!"

"Sorry, that wasn't my intention. But just look at this in terms of self-preservation. If I'm elected, then these people have every incentive to leave me alone because I'll be serving their cause. And you and the girls will be safe because of this." He pounded an index finger on the stack of papers Bobby had given him. "Everybody's safe."

"But are we, really? For how long? Because as long as Jenny and Teresa and I are out there, your people know that we pose a threat."

"A threat that you've neutralized with this. And Jenny's safe regardless. There's no surer way to shine a spotlight on all this than for something to happen to her. It would be front page news, especially after Ricky and her mom. And besides, she's already demonstrated that she's able to keep a secret—she's done it for 20 years! Now think about the other scenario. If I'm not in office, then I'm a huge threat to them because of what I know. There are Congressmen, judges, lobbyists and plenty of other powerbrokers and political types that are in our camp. I've gotten to know who they are, at least some of them. You'd be stunned. The whole world would be stunned. If I'm not in office, I'm no longer of any use to them and I'm a huge risk. I'm a dead man and so are you."

"So you think the best thing for you and me and our country is to have you elected? So you can push some hidden agenda and serve the interest of some zealots? The 'Cause,' as you used to call it?"

"Look, Bobby, my thinking on that has evolved. Like we talked about before, if you hear a certain creed your whole life from people you respect, you tend not to question it. And you were right—my thinking was undoubtedly impacted by certain people over the course of many years. But I've learned to challenge my own assumptions. Don't get me wrong—many of my beliefs about the need for immigration reform are as strong as ever. But I intend to be my own person. I want to bring about change for the good of the country, but through the right channels. I will not be beholden to anyone if I'm elected."

"It's good to hear you say that, but based on what you've told me about your supporters, aren't you concerned about how they're going to act if they feel like they're not in control?"

"It won't matter. Once I'm VP, I'm in control. I'll have the power! They will realize that this is just a stepping stone to the presidency. I just have to get elected. That's the best answer here. Once I have the power, everything else will take care of itself."

Bobby's cell phone vibrated. From where he stood, Sal could see the caller ID: *Jenny*. Bobby answered the phone. Sal immediately heard the distress in Jenny's voice and noticed the troubled look on Bobby's face.

For the most part, Sal couldn't hear what Jenny was saying, but he heard one word very distinctly. It was a name, and it told him everything he needed to know.

"I've got to run, Sal. Be sure to share that with your people," Bobby said, pointing to the stack of papers. He hurried out, leaving the vice-presidential candidate sitting alone in his office, staring after him.

Bobby climbed into his Buick and slammed the door. He gripped the steering wheel tightly but did not hit the ignition button. Both knees bounced up and down furiously. He stared straight ahead and took several deep breaths, then he reached for his cell phone and punched in a number. "I want you to go ahead and send the package," he said in a firm voice. "FBI, *The New York Times* and everyone else on the list."

"You sure about that?" came the reply. "Once it gets out there, they have no reason to lay off of you."

"Doesn't matter. This is way bigger than me."

Chapter 60

PROFESSOR JENNY SANCHEZ was consistently voted one of the best-liked instructors at the University. Her lectures were known to be funny, interesting and engaging, and her classes were always full. She was a gifted speaker, moving about the front of the classroom, speaking effortlessly, without notes, engaging the students in spirited dialogue. Her students were understandably surprised when she suddenly became flustered and cut her class short just ten minutes into it, claiming that she was not feeling well.

The sight of Francisco Vargas sitting in the back row of the lecture hall had unnerved her. Many years had passed without a visit from the spooky thug until he had shown up at her mother's wake. That was unsettling. She associated him with troubling times and bad people. Out of nowhere, he had suddenly appeared again in her four o'clock American History class. She had no idea what his presence meant, but a feeling of dread and fear overcame her when she saw his expressionless face watching her intently. It threw her, and she became distracted to the point that she knew she could not go on with her lecture, so she had mumbled something to the class about suddenly feeling ill. She had hurried to her office and called Bobby.

Bobby would be there within the hour, but the building housing her office seemed eerily quiet and deserted. She decided she would feel safer outdoors, so she quickly changed into her running clothes and drove across campus to the track. She ran hard, hoping the exertion would calm her nerves. At least half a dozen other runners were using the track and another handful of students were warming up, exercising nearby, or just milling about. As she rounded the bend approaching the end of her second mile, her eyes drifted to the aluminum bleachers on the right side of the straightaway. They were empty except for a lone figure dressed in black street clothes sitting in the top row: Vargas.

She avoided eye contact and continued running, doing her best to appear unaware and unconcerned. As she approached the bleachers on the next lap, he was gone. She headed straight to her car and drove back across campus to her office.

She waited in the parking lot until she saw Bobby's black Buick pull in ten minutes later. In a state of great agitation, she told Bobby about the Vargas sightings. Bobby had caught a glimpse of the man during Mrs. Sanchez's funeral and remembered how his presence there had rattled Jenny. His meeting with Sal had given him at least some sense of control and confidence about their safety, but this development immediately caused him to question those feelings. Sal would not have had an opportunity to share his information yet.

Jenny expressed concern about returning alone to her empty house, so Bobby suggested that she follow him to his apartment, where they could try to sort things out. "Mind if I use your shower?" Jenny asked upon entering Bobby's apartment. "I'm still sweaty and sticky from my run."

"Help yourself. You can use the one in Teresa's room. She moved out. She left some of her things in the laundry room so feel free to borrow some shorts and a clean shirt."

Jenny emerged from the shower, feeling refreshed but still shaken. As she toweled herself off, she heard a knock on the front door. "Hey, Jenny!" Bobby yelled from his room. "I'm in here changing. Can you see who that is? Check the peephole first."

Jenny wrapped a towel around her and cautiously approached the front door, opening it after peering through the peephole.

Teresa was startled to see the door opened by a half-naked woman. "Uh... hi Jenny. Is Bobby here?"

"Hi Teresa. Yeah, he's getting dressed. Come on in."

Teresa hesitated. "Looks like I came at a bad time. I can come back later."

"It's not a bad time at all, really. Come on in." She stopped as she noticed the stunned look on Teresa's face. "Oh, this," she smiled sheepishly, gesturing at the towel wrapped around her. "Don't worry, it's not what it looks like. I just came over—"

Teresa turned and left abruptly without uttering another word.

"Who was that?" Bobby asked, entering the living room, having exchanged his charcoal gray funeral director's suit for blue jeans and a white golf shirt.

"It was Teresa. When she saw me here, she said she'd come back later. She seemed a little miffed."

"Damn! I'll have to call her later. We need to figure out what to do."

They left the apartment and talked while they meandered through the neighborhood. Bobby told Jenny about his meeting with Sal and his reasons for believing that they now had some basis for feeling safer, assuming that it was people connected with Sal who had been the source of their trouble. He made a point of mentioning that Sal had assured him in the strongest possible terms that his people had a very strong interest in leaving Jenny alone. "Tell you what," Bobby said. "I'll follow you home and check out the house and make sure it's OK. I'll spend the night if you want. In fact, I insist on it. At least until we're all feeling a bit more secure, you don't need to be spending the night there alone. But I'm sure you're not in danger. This Vargas guy probably just wants you to know that they're out there watching so you won't do anything to interfere with their plans. If he wanted to cause you any harm, he could have done that, and he sure wouldn't be showing up in these public places."

They returned to the apartment and Bobby tossed a few things into a gym bag. He dialed Teresa as they walked down the stairs toward the parking lot. His call went directly to her voicemail. "Hi T, it's Bobby. Sorry I missed you. I'd really like to catch up. It's early Thursday evening. I'm with Jenny. We're going to grab some dinner and then head over to her place. I may be spending the night there, but you can reach me on my cell phone anytime."

Chapter 61

IT WAS DARK as Bobby pulled up in front of Jenny's home in a quiet neighborhood near the University. "You wait here. I'll go inside and check it out." Jenny handed him the key.

She could see the lights go on in each room as Bobby made the rounds on the first floor. Then she saw the lights go on in each of the three upstairs bedrooms. Every room in the house was lit up. She waited.

After coming downstairs, Bobby made another pass through the kitchen to make sure he had checked the closets. He stopped in his tracks as he saw the back door wide open. "That you, Jenny?" he called out. No one answered. He peered out the door into the darkness. There was no one in sight. He turned to reenter the kitchen and found himself face-to-face with Francisco Vargas. They were eyeball-to-eyeball. Vargas was big—as tall as Bobby but not as broad. He was lean and muscular, his scarred face and the coal-black eyes completing a look of pure menace and danger. Bobby's stomach turned and his heart pounded in his chest.

"I didn't expect to run into you here tonight, but this works out nicely," Vargas said with a sneer, reaching inside his windbreaker. Bobby's eyes shifted and looked past the sinister face. Jenny appeared at the other end of the kitchen, her face frozen in horror. Vargas wheeled around to stare at her. As soon as his head turned, Bobby exploded off the floor like he was back on a football field. He threw his arms around the intruder's torso, lifting him off his feet as he lowered his head and drove with his legs until they smashed into the pantry door on the opposite wall. Wood splintered and dishware rattled in the cabinets as Bobby hurled his

stunned adversary to the travertine floor with the force of all his considerable bulk landing on top of him. He could hear the dull thud of skull
hitting stone and felt the body go limp.

Bobby rose and stared at the motionless figure at his feet, just as Sal
burst in through the back door. "What the hell?" He stared at the prone
figure of Vargas in astonishment, then looked from Bobby to Jenny. "Are
you two OK?"

Bobby could feel himself trembling all over. "Friend of yours?" he
shouted, shooting an accusatory look at Sal.

"I know him," Sal said. "I overheard Jenny mention his name when
she called you this afternoon and I've been trying to track him down
ever since."

Like a boxer who had been knocked out in the ring, Vargas came to
with a start, raising himself to a sitting position as his eyes struggled to
focus. Sal squatted in front of him and violently grabbed his collar. "What
the fuck are you doing here, Vargas? I told you to leave my people alone!"

Vargas's eyes came into sharp focus as he grabbed both of Sal's wrists
and violently shoved him away. Sal fell backwards out of his squat and
Vargas raised himself to a standing position, sliding his back up the splintered door behind him for support.

Sal sprang to his feet, eyes blazing and fists clenched and took a step
toward Vargas. He stopped cold as he saw the shiny pistol emerge from
Vargas's jacket and point directly at his chest.

"Don't make another move," Vargas hissed. "I wasn't going to hurt
your sister. She's been good at keeping secrets for 20 years, so we're
really not concerned about her. I was just stopping by to remind her of
the importance of remaining discreet. Besides, too many casualties in
one family would attract unwanted scrutiny. But this guy here..." He
turned the gun on Bobby. "He's a dead man walking. So is his pretty
little roommate."

Sal took a step closer and Vargas turned the gun back from Bobby
toward Sal. "Don't even think about it, Vargas," Sal said. "That would be
the dumbest thing you could do. They have information that could be
very damaging. I just saw it this afternoon. If—"

"We all know that! That's why they're toast."

"You're not listening to me Vargas. You *don't* know what they've got. If anything happens to them—"

"It's too late. The wheels are already in motion. I wasn't going to touch your funeral director pal until he made it so convenient by showing up here, but I've arranged for someone else to take care of him."

"Call it off, Vargas!"

"I couldn't even if I wanted to. You know how this works. I called a guy who called a guy. So you just need to butt out and focus on politics. You know who's calling the shots, so you better step in line—fast."

"That's over! I'm in charge. I'm going to be vice president of this country and then I'm going to be the goddamn president of the United States! I let myself be brainwashed by your bullshit for way too long, but I'm done with all that! I'm done with you and I'm done with your boss. I'm in control now."

"Afraid not, Mike," said Vargas coolly. A shot rang out and Sal sprawled backwards. Another shot knocked him to the floor. As Vargas took aim again, Bobby launched into another vicious tackle, reaching for the outstretched gun hand as he did. He heard the gun explode in his ear. He put one hand around Vargas's neck as he hurled him to the ground in a ferocious body-slam, making sure that his massive hand pounded the skull into the hard tile as the full weight of his body drove Vargas into the unforgiving stone floor. He felt the body go limp beneath him once again.

He stood up as Jenny handed him the gun. He felt dizzy and wobbly. There was a searing pain in his right ear and a ringing that muffled all other sounds. He saw Sal lying a few feet away bleeding profusely and hurried to his side. He knelt down and felt for a pulse. "Jenny, grab some towels! We need to stop the bleeding!" She ran into the powder room and returned with several white hand towels. Bobby placed one on the chest wound and the other against Sal's thigh which was spewing blood rapidly. "It must have hit an artery! Jenny, call 911! Tell them we need an ambulance fast. Get the police here too!" He pulled off his belt and wrapped it tightly around Sal's thigh, above the wound.

Sal's eyes fluttered, then opened weakly. "I'm sorry I put you two in the middle of all this... I'm so sorry..."

"Don't try to talk, pal," Bobby said. "Help is on the way."

"Tell them I was here to discuss family business... then this... intruder burst in. They'll think it was some whack job trying to assassinate me." He winced in pain and took several quick breaths. "Reach into my pocket."

Bobby gently reached into the pocket of Sal's jeans and pulled out a small brown envelope. He opened the envelope and poured out the contents—a small, silver thumb drive.

Sal grimaced as he looked up at Bobby. "That's *my* insurance," he said. "It's a list of people who are connected with these guys. Some big wheels—Congressmen, governors, judges, business leaders, billionaires. It's not everyone, but it's a start. If someone puts the squeeze on these guys, it may lead to others. It'll connect them to their leader, and once this all gets out, he'll be toxic. But you need to get out of here, Bobby! Teresa too. You heard him—they're after you. Go far away and go now! It's your only chance."

Bobby could hear the sirens blaring. He glanced nervously at Vargas. He hadn't stirred. Sal groaned loudly and held out a blood-covered hand. Bobby clasped it. Sal's grip tightened. "The man who's after you is El Cazador—the one I told you about when we were kids." His voice was weak, a strained whisper. He gasped and struggled for breath. "He prides himself on being a hunter. As long as you're alive, he'll be trying to hunt you down... I'm sorry Seventy-Seven..." Then all strength left the grip and his eyes closed.

"You need to go," Jenny urged. "I can handle this."

"I'm not leaving you with him," Bobby said watching Vargas for any sign of movement.

The screaming sirens reached the front of the house. Bobby stood by the back door and stared at Vargas's prone figure and saw him starting to stir. Then he heard the front door open and the sound of boots across the hardwood floor and voices of police and EMTs calling out. He gave Jenny a long look, then raced out the door.

Chapter 62

THE NEWSPAPER WAS several days old but had just made its way from San Antonio to the office of Sheriff Ray Reid in San Mateo. He glanced at the headline through watery eyes as he sipped his morning coffee:

ASSASSINATION ATTEMPT

VP Candidate Sanchez Fights for His Life

Vice presidential candidate Miguel Sanchez was gunned down at the home of his sister at approximately 10:00 pm. last night in a quiet residential neighborhood near UT San Antonio. Sanchez suffered bullet wounds to the chest and thigh and is in critical condition in Memorial Hospital under tight security. An unidentified suspect is in custody, who is also in critical condition with a fractured skull. A third man, a local funeral director by the name of Roberto Rivera, fled the scene before police arrived and is being sought for questioning.

"Shit!" the Sheriff muttered as he pushed the paper aside and gulped down the last swallow of stale coffee. This was going to be a rough day—for him and for the entire town of San Mateo. After the Sanchez shooting and the events that followed, the media had swarmed the tiny town, trying to pry from the local residents whatever information they could get about Bobby Rivera. The funeral was today and Reid had no reason to expect any sensitivity from the press. To the contrary, it would make a dramatic backdrop for their stories and they would play it up for everything they could.

He arrived at Our Lady of Guadalupe Church at 9:00 a.m., thirty minutes before the funeral mass was to begin. Reporters with their microphones and television cameras were everywhere, and he did his best to shoo them away and ask them to set up at a respectful distance across the street. Reid had attended many funerals over the years, but he had never seen the church this full, except perhaps when Bobby's parents were killed in a plane crash years earlier. He spotted his old friends, Manny Quintana, the Medical Examiner, and Alex Zamora, Bobby's old boss, near the hearse parked in front of the church.

"Quite a tribute, isn't it," Quintana said, as he watched the crowd pouring into the old church.

"He was a fixture here," Zamora said. "Part of the fabric of this town. He knew everyone, and they all knew him. Everyone loved Bobby. I can't believe we're never going to see him again." The elderly funeral director sniffled and dabbed his eyes with a handkerchief.

Reid looked away and drew a shaky breath, tears flowing freely down his rugged face. "He touched a lot of lives, mine included," he said, his voice breaking. He pulled on the pall-bearer gloves. "I owe Bobby Rivera more than I could possibly repay."

Quintana stared at the white gloves Zamora had just handed him. "I'm glad we're able to help him out one last time."

***

One hundred and sixty miles north, another funeral service was about to commence at Norwood & Gonzalez Funeral Home. Jenny Sanchez sat in the parking lot, bracing herself for what she knew would be a heart-wrenching experience. Her eyes wandered over the article published three days earlier in the local newspaper. She had read it repeatedly, as if reading it one more time would cause her to wake up and realize it was all a bad dream.

PERSON OF INTEREST IN SANCHEZ
SHOOTING KILLED

Local Funeral Director Dies in Fiery Crash

Roberto Rivera and a companion perished outside of San Mateo when his vehicle veered off of Highway 281, overturned and burst into flames. The local Medical Examiner conclusively identified the remains as those of Roberto Rivera, 35, and Teresa Cruz, 28, both of San Antonio. Rivera was being sought for questioning by law enforcement authorities in connection with the attempted assassination of vice presidential candidate Miguel Sanchez. The local Sheriff's Office and the FBI are investigating. At this point, no evidence of foul play has surfaced, but it has not been ruled out.

Entering the funeral home where Bobby had worked was another stark reminder that he was gone. Bobby's young protégé, Arturo, met her at the door and extended his condolences, then guided her to the small visitation room. About twenty people were standing around, speaking in hushed tones, shock and grief projecting from their somber faces. Jenny recognized some of them from the hospice where Teresa had worked. She walked to the front of the room, where a large portrait of Teresa was on display, surrounded by floral arrangements. The picture showed Teresa exactly as Jenny remembered her—full of life, her eyes shining above the infectious smile that naturally lifted the spirits of anyone she encountered. The thought of that vibrant young spirit coming to an abrupt and violent end ripped through her, and she backed away from the portrait as her emotions rushed to the surface.

She covered her tear-filled eyes with her hand and looked downward. She felt a stranger put an arm around her shoulder, and Jenny turned toward the stranger and embraced her, burying her head in the young woman's shoulder as her entire body shook with quiet sobs. She felt the stranger tenderly patting her back and she stood back to look at her, wiping her eyes and smiling sheepishly and sadly. The compassionate stranger looked to be about Teresa's age. She had shoulder-length strawberry blond hair, a pale complexion and bright blue eyes, rimmed with redness. "I'm sorry," Jenny said. "This is so hard. She was such a sweet soul."

"Were you close friends?" the woman asked.

"I got to know her a few months ago when she took care of my mother at the hospice. Our paths crossed from time-to-time since then."

"I'm Patty," the young woman said. "Teresa and I were roommates in college. I got busy with medical school and starting my practice, so I hadn't seen much of her lately, but she was a special friend." Patty wiped her nose with a tissue. "This is such a tragedy and I'm absolutely heartsick, but we should be grateful that we knew her. Even though she's gone, she touched our lives." Her voiced cracked and she let out a deep breath, struggling hard to control her emotions. "She had such a zest for life and so much compassion for other people—we can learn from her example. Life is precious and we shouldn't waste a single day." She squeezed Jenny's hand and walked away, wiping her eyes.

Chapter 63
Two Weeks Later

THE BIG MAN with the straw hat and the dark tan stepped back from his easel on the beach. He observed his work and nodded, a look of satisfaction crossing his face. It was a vibrant replica of the panorama stretched out in front of him: a deserted beach on a Panamanian island, colorful fishing boats dotting the horizon, and a tiny village off in the distance.

"Hey there, Picasso! How about an ice-cold lemonade?" The shapely girl in the red bikini and floppy sun hat emerged from the lushly landscaped path holding a tall glass in each hand and a stack of newspapers under her right arm.

"You're the best!" he replied, setting down his paintbrush and wrapping a big arm around her waist, roughly pulling her forward and kissing her on the lips.

She giggled as the newspapers slid out from under her arm and cold liquid splashed onto her hands. She handed him a glass. "Cheers!" she said. They clinked glasses then she stooped over to pick up the newspapers. They sat side-by-side on a pair of rustic-looking chaise lounges. "News from home. Check it out." She handed him the newspapers.

The paper on top was *The New York Times*, one week old. The headline screamed off the page:

SANCHEZ CITIZENSHIP SCANDAL!

Republican Ticket Reeling from Allegations

Last week, it looked as if Miguel Sanchez was the lucki-est man alive. It appeared that he had miraculously turned the corner and was on a path to full recovery from his wounds. Now, his world is in turmoil once again. Explosive allegations have surfaced that are certain to rock the polit-ical world. Sources say that Sanchez, long an advocate for immigrant rights, may himself be an illegal immigrant, throwing the Connett/Sanchez ticket into chaos just weeks before the election.

The article laid out a three-page exposé based on letters, pictures and testimony provided by an alleged childhood friend, along with DNA evidence, the results of which had not yet been released. There were quotes from numerous residents of San Mateo, Texas, who knew both Miguel Sanchez and Sal Rios, supporting the theory that Rios had assumed the identity of Sanchez after Sanchez died in a drowning accident over 20 years ago. The article identified the primary source of the information as Roberto "Bobby" Rivera, a funeral director based in San Antonio who recently died in a mysterious car accident. The article also alleged that Sanchez was beholden to corrupt foreign influences, including myste-rious Mexican billionaire Carlos Calderon, and that Calderon's long tentacles had extended deep into the halls of power in Washington DC and around the country. Ominously, there was a promise of a follow-up article that would release names of those implicated.

The next paper was the *USA Today*, dated two days later. The lead article announced that Sanchez had denied the allegations but had with-drawn from the ticket to spare his party the distraction resulting from the media onslaught as well as the various investigations that were underway. The Republican ticket had plunged almost twenty points in the latest polling, virtually ensuring victory for Democratic presidential candidate Thomas Nelson.

The final papers were editions of the *San Antonio Express-News*, nearly two weeks old. The first mentioned the deaths of Bobby Rivera and Teresa Cruz in a car accident and the second contained their obituaries.

"Sure wish I could've played Tom Sawyer and hidden up in the balcony to watch my own funeral," Bobby said, grinning and sipping his lemonade.

"Me too. Seems that a girl ought to attend her sweetheart's funeral. Forgive me?" Teresa smiled at him.

"Absolutely! Hey, I didn't attend yours either! I still feel bad about pulling a fast one on everyone, but if they knew what we were up against, I'm sure they'd understand."

Teresa's face took on a serious look. "That article mentions that the FBI is investigating our accident. Should we be worried?"

"Not at all," said Bobby. "My pals really came through. Sheriff Reid wrote up the accident report. They made sure my car actually veered off the highway and rolled over into the ravine. Manny wrote up the autopsy report and authorized the funeral home to proceed with cremation. He's the M.E. and it's his jurisdiction, since there was no family for either of us. Sheriff Reid signed the funeral home's ID paperwork based on his personal acquaintance with me. He fibbed a bit and indicated he knew you personally as well. Anyway, that gave Mr. Zamora everything he needed to proceed with cremation. All that paperwork—the accident report, the Coroner's report, the funeral home documentation—it's absolutely perfect and airtight. It should convince anyone investigating this that you and I perished in that car crash and then were cremated after all the normal identification processes were completed. There's no reason for the FBI or anyone else to question that. Zamora even pulled some old unclaimed cremated remains out of his storage closet and put them in urns with our names on them. There's no way to prove that's not us. The FBI might be upset that they weren't contacted before the cremation, but our guys just played dumb and said they had no reason to know the FBI was looking for me. It's small town South Texas, and they're pretty isolated from the rest of the world."

"Your friends really stuck their necks out for us. Every one of them said they owed you big time."

"I guess I helped them all through some pretty tough times, but that's what friends do, right? I never thought they owed me anything, but I'm sure glad they came through."

"I'm still worried about Jenny. Do you really think she's OK?"

"Yes, particularly now that Sal's secret is out there. If she was in danger before, it was because she could blow the whistle on all that. But now that it's out in the open, they have no reason to consider her a threat. And both Sal and Vargas said they would never go after her because it would arouse suspicion. That's more true now than ever, so I think she'll be fine."

"And what about Sal? What do you think will happen to him?"

"I suppose he'll be deported. He's the highest profile illegal immigrant in the country right now, but the government sure isn't going to cut him any slack after he perpetrated such an elaborate fraud."

Teresa stared at the boats out on the horizon. "Seems ironic, but his case may actually help the cause of the immigrants who were brought here by their parents as kids and now have no legal status. Sal was one of them and look what he accomplished. He became educated, he worked as a successful lawyer and built a thriving legal practice. He even took a case to the Supreme Court that resulted in changes to federal law. He became a passionate advocate for immigration reform and inspired millions of people. He accomplished a lot but it all blew up because he lacked a piece of paper—the one granting him citizenship. Should that piece of paper really matter? There's sure to be a big outcry that people like that should be legalized."

"You're right, and I hope they are. But there will also be some that say we need to be careful not to let a criminal element into our country—and they'll use Sal as an example, too."

"And what about his behind-the-scenes friends—Calderon and that bunch? Will they go after him?"

Bobby's face darkened. "He's not much use to them now. He's strictly a liability, and they're dangerous people." He paused and stared at his lemonade, swirling the ice cubes around the glass. "I hope he's OK. He's made mistakes, but I think that deep down, there's some good in him. He was conditioned from an early age to believe that America was bad and needed to be changed. He was subjected to some powerful influences.

But in the end he gave me that thumb drive with the list of names. I like to think he did that because he'd made up his mind to cut his ties with that group."

"Maybe he did it just because he thought he was dying and had nothing to lose. Maybe he just wanted vengeance."

"Maybe. We'll never know, I guess. Either way, with enemies like that, I'm afraid his future looks pretty bleak."

"And what about us? Do you think we're still in danger?"

Bobby reached across the sand between their chairs and took her hand. "We'll be fine, T. Sal's cohorts—whoever they are—will probably be running for cover and trying to keep a low profile. But I think we do have to take what Sal told us at face value, at least for now. These are bad people. Sal said they're very good at hunting down anyone who's crossed them, so they can send a message. He said they could find us anywhere on earth as long as we're alive. That's why it was so important for them and everyone else to believe we're dead. We'll be safe here. We're just not Bobby Rivera and Teresa Cruz anymore, and we're not from Texas."

"You did the right thing, Bobby, and I'm really proud of you." She kissed his hand. "But does it make you sad? We fled from the country we loved. It was our home. Our parents made great sacrifices so that we could live our lives as Americans. We were living the American Dream. We fit in and were making a real contribution—and we were happy! Now that life is out of reach."

"You know, T, I agonized over whether to send that package to the FBI and the newspapers, because I knew it would mean leaving our home and going into hiding. But I felt I needed to do that, even if it meant making that sacrifice. I'm so glad you felt the same way. America did right by us—look at the life it provided to you and me and countless others. The freedom and the opportunity there are limitless—and price-less—and I will never take that for granted. And yes, America has plenty of problems—the toxic politics and self-interested politicians, the irre-sponsible news media, the laziness and materialism and celebrity-worship that seem so prevalent. But the good far outweighs the bad. I'm proud to be an American and I will always love my country. America may be a mess but it's a beautiful, wonderful, glorious mess!"

Teresa sat upright in her chair, swinging her knees around to face Bobby. She removed her sunglasses and looked at him, her eyes bright with hope. "Maybe in a few years, this El Cazador character and his allies will be dead or in jail or disbanded. Maybe then we can go back home— right through the front door. We are American citizens after all. They may think we're dead, but we're not. It's still our home and we have every right to live there. In the meantime, we get to live in this island paradise. We'll make our way here. We've got talents, we're willing to work hard, and we connect with people. If you're wired like that, you can make it anywhere!"

Bobby sat up and swung around to face his beautiful companion. Their knees touched, and he grasped her hands. "Teresa, I know our lives have taken an unexpected turn. This isn't what our parents had in mind for us, but plans change, countries change, politics change and sometimes that causes homes to change. I may have lost my homeland, but I gained something even more important. I have you, and that matters more than anything. Countries can create borders and fences and walls and maybe we're on the wrong side right now, but that doesn't matter. As long as we're together, then wherever we are will be our home, and it will be a good home."

She leaned over and kissed him, slowly and tenderly. "I love you, Bobby Rivera. And what's not to like about our new home? We have the prettiest swimming pool I've ever seen," she said, nodding toward the aquamarine waters lapping up against the shore. "Let's go for a swim."

DISCUSSION QUESTIONS

1. Bobby, Sal, Jenny and Teresa came to America from other countries or have parents who did. They worked hard, fit in, and made real contributions to society. Do you see similar examples around you? Where, and how common is it?

2. Has the complexion of America changed during your lifetime—in general and where you live? To what extent? How will it change in the future?

3. Sal tells Bobby that most people are "conditioned" to believe certain things as a result of their upbringing or the people they are surrounded by. According to Sal, this conditioning is so prevalent and powerful that most people don't break out of it and don't truly analyze the world around them thoughtfully and objectively. Do you believe that? Do people generally see the world through their own filters and instinctively resist ideas that don't fit their world-view? Was Sal himself an example of that phenomenon?

4. Sal states that most people are persuaded by the sound bites hurled at them incessantly by candidates and the media and that they don't engage in deep thinking or independent analysis when they take a position on political issues? Do you agree?

5. Sal tells Bobby that no matter how hard an immigrant or an immigrant's child—particularly a person of color from Latin

America—tries to fit into American society, there is an invisible wall that prevents true assimilation. Bobby disagrees, and suggests that wall is only in one's mind and can be broken down by hard work, determination and making a real effort to fit in. Who is right?

6. Bobby and Sal clearly believe that children brought into this country illegally by their parents should be granted legal status. They believe that this should be an easy decision and that most Americans are in agreement. Do you agree? Why or why not? Should they be provided a path to citizenship in addition to legal status and protection from deportation? If most Americans are in agreement, why haven't the politicians gotten this done?

7. Does America need a stronger and more complete wall along its southern border? Consider this: Both Sal and his father turned out to be killers. Will a border wall help keep dangerous people out of our country?

8. Professor Vega states that Washington politicians are motivated by power and self-interest and that getting elected and staying in power is their highest priority rather than the interests of their constituents and the nation. Do you agree? If so, how can that be changed?

9. Vega saw the connection between money and power. He was able to develop influence in this country by accumulating great wealth. Do you believe that money in the hands of wealthy individuals or companies influences policy and politics in this country to an unhealthy extent? If so, what should be done about that?

10. Sal runs for president as a third-party candidate. Despite his charisma and the timeliness and relevance of the issues he represents, he ultimately is not competitive and withdraws. Is there any chance that a third party (or an independent) could prevail

in a national election in America? Would that be a good thing? What are the obstacles?

11. Sal starts out as an idealist—he wants to make major changes to immigration policy and achieve that change from the inside, through the ballot box. Does he lose focus on that and buy into Vega's position that his primary goal should be assuming power? Do you think Vega started out more idealistic and changed over time? Do you think it is common for American politicians to follow that course, i.e., starting out as a public servant with good intentions but then evolving into a more self-interested, power-hungry politician? If so, why does that happen?

12. Sal, his father, and Professor Vega frequently state "we do what we must" to justify actions that are taken in the interest of furthering their cause. Is this type of mindset acceptable if the cause is a just one? Are there people who live their lives in accordance with that creed?

13. Bobby's upbringing trained him to fear the government and deportation and to avoid attention from authorities at almost any cost. Do you believe that many immigrants share this fear? Does it continue even after they have obtained legal status (temporary or permanent)? Does Bobby overcome those fears?

14. Sal illegally enters this country, assumes a false identity, and then goes on to lead a successful and prosperous life here. His story is an extreme and perhaps unrealistic example, but does that scenario really happen, where someone without legal status assumes a false identity and proceeds to live a normal life in this country as if they had legal status? If so, do they generally keep a low profile? Could people doing that ascend to positions of power and influence while keeping their true identity secret? In the business world? Politics? Government? Education?

15. Are Sal and his father heartless, cold-blooded killers? Does their passionate belief in their cause make their actions more acceptable?

16. Does Sal change by the end of the story? How? What do you make of the fact that he created a thumb drive holding incriminating information regarding his backers and then gave Bobby a copy?

17. How did Bobby's priorities and behavior change from the start of the story through the final scene?

18. Bobby says, "America may be a mess but it's a beautiful, wonderful, glorious mess." What is your reaction to that statement?

ABOUT THE AUTHOR

Joseph Hayes is a native of Chicago and grew up on the city's South Side. After obtaining his law degree from Berkeley, he practiced law in Chicago, San Diego and Houston. He also served for many years as the chief ethics officer for a large, publicly-held company.

OTHER BOOKS BY JOSEPH HAYES

When No One Is Watching

On the eve of announcing his run for Congress, a charismatic Chicago politician causes a deadly accident. Panicked, he frames his best friend, a good-hearted alcoholic, and flees the scene. As one man tries to pick up the pieces of his shattered life, the other embarks on a meteoric rise to political stardom. But when a dogged detective digs deeper into the case, the political superstar must decide just how far he is willing to go to keep his dark secret. Hayes combines page-turning suspense with a poignant tale of inspiration and redemption as he asks, is "the greater good" just a lie we tell ourselves to justify the sins we commit when no one is watching?

Consequential Damages

Rick Black and Jake McShane are former law school classmates with very different approaches to life and the law. Rick is a brilliant, ultracompetitive trial lawyer who believes winning is everything. He openly mocks the legal system, claiming that a lawyer who is a great storyteller can fool a jury every time. He is determined to exploit that weakness in our system, regardless of the havoc that wreaks on innocent lives.

When an upstanding pillar of the community is victimized by Rick's unscrupulous tactics, Jake is determined to bring his former classmate to justice—if he can do so without sacrificing his own integrity. Their approaches, skills and convictions are put to the test when they clash as opposing counsel in a high-stakes class action lawsuit. Dirty tricks, intimidation, intrigue—even homicide—become part of the backdrop as the litigation unfolds.

Consequential Damages is a compelling legal drama full of twists, turns and suspense. And, it will make you think!

CPSIA information can be obtained
at www.ICGtesting.com
Printed in the USA
FSHW010840161218
54513FS

9 780692 147931